Sylvia, Rachel, Meredith, Anna

# Sylvia, Rachel, Meredith, Anna

*a novel*

## Robert Slentz-Kesler

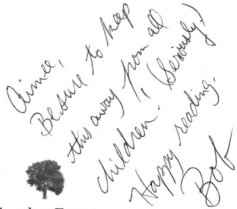

Aimee,
Be sure to keep
this away from all
children. (Seriously)
Happy reading,
Bob

Thatcher Forest
Durham, NC

Publisher's Cataloging-In-Publication Data

Slentz-Kesler, Robert Shaw Caspar, 1968—
Sylvia, Rachel, Meredith, Anna: a novel / Robert Slentz-Kesler

1. Recovered memory—Fiction.   2. Grief—Fiction.   3. Cello—Fiction.
4. Men/women relations—Fiction.   5. Extramarital relations—Fiction.
6. Basic training (Military education)—Fiction.   7. Race relations—Fiction.
8. Military recruiting and enlistment—Fiction.   9. Antwerp, Belgium—Fiction.
10. Family—Belgium—Fiction.   11. Diamond industry and trade—Fiction.
12. Gangs—Fiction.   I. Title

PS3569.L4 S9 2007
813.6—dc22                    2007901402
ISBN 978-0-9670504-8-5

Thatcher Forest Publishing
Durham, NC
*ThatcherForest.com*

8   6   7   5   3   0   9

Printed and bound in the United States

# Acknowledgments

*Diamant Verbiest, Inc.*
*Durham, North Carolina*

*Andrew Hand Kesler*

# One

Gerard Kelderman crashed out the front door of the St. Philip fraternity house and marched to the sidewalk. The gallon of water he'd guzzled sloshed in his stomach but did nothing to dull the hangover tapping at the bridge of his nose. He turned toward campus and walked, determined to face only forward and to ignore the joggers and dog-walkers and other students with backpacks and couples who had the nerve to hold hands and laugh and smile at each other.

Even after becoming Gerard's fiancée, Sylvia had played around with someone else during their entire junior year. He wanted to forget the scenes of sex between Sylvia and her secret lover that played over and over in his brain—not imagined scenes but detailed sequences of acts he'd foolishly read in the seventeen love letters tucked away in Sylvia's dresser.

Gerard stopped in front of the Rotunda steps. He pressed his palms against his pulsing temples and squinted up through the high oak branches at the blue sky. He looked at his watch. 9:30 a.m. He walked up the steps of the Rotunda and then back down again. Then up again. Then down again. He gasped and wheezed. He needed to lose weight. His breath was heavy. He walked along the cobblestone path next to the Lawn—a vast, sunlit green scattered with squirrels and thick maple trees. Exams were to end tomorrow and most students had gone home for the summer. Gerard and Sylvia would graduate from Monroe Hill College in five days with the class of 2002 and would process down the center of this lawn, bringing four years of undergraduate study to an end.

And Gerard's relationship with Sylvia would end. It had to, didn't it? How could he marry someone who'd been unfaithful? Maybe she wasn't right for him anyway, with her continual criticism of Gerard, especially about his clothing, his rumpled brown hair, and his weight. She was right about the weight. Gerard's 6'4" frame lugged around all 250 pounds of him, draped usually in baggy khakis and loose flannel shirts. He clashed with Sylvia, just 5'5", whose silky blond hair bounced when she walked. She wore white Capri pants and pink tank-tops that hugged her tan skin, contrasting her elegance and Gerard's awkwardness and feeding his fear that she would leave him for someone else. He knew it. He'd always known it, and now the letters from her lover confirmed it.

Still, he was determined not to let her go without a fight. He would woo her again with his cello playing, the way he had in the early days of their relationship. Sylvia Landon had fallen for Gerard because of the cello. When his bow pulled across the strings of his cello, she melted; Gerard was her pied piper. He would play the Shostakovich *Cello Concerto No. 1* or the cello solo from Beethoven's "The Ghost" piano trio, and Sylvia's eyes would sparkle. Even when she was uptight and rude and cranky, Gerard could play any of the four cello parts of *Calm Sea (Op. 3 No. 2)* by Schubert, and Sylvia's tense shoulders would soften and her body would unravel so that she struggled even to say "Oh, Gerard" through tears and long breaths. In those rare moments, *he* was in control.

Gerard stopped in front of the student center café where people sat with steaming cups of coffee, reading books at tables on the outdoor patio that was cooled by the wide morning shade of a high hedge. A young woman wearing a long summer skirt crossed her legs and sipped from a ceramic mug. The woman and the stone floor of the patio and the iron legs of the tables made Gerard think of his baby sister, Anna, and how she'd died fifteen years earlier, when he was just seven. That was odd—he was realizing in this moment that her death had had something to do with a patio and café tables. During the past few weeks many of his childhood memories had begun to thaw, and he was sure now that the story of Anna having been struck on the sidewalk by a swerving car wasn't true; his parents had been lying to him and to everyone else in their lives. Gerard was there when she'd died, but he'd long ago forgotten exactly what had happened. Since age seven he'd relied on his parents' story and protected himself with the tricks he'd learned to keep his brain from remembering the details of the accident.

The woman at the café table tucked her black hair behind one ear and smiled at Gerard. He realized only then that he'd been staring at her. He turned away and headed along the cobblestone path toward the Waterford Road dorms.

Gerard stared down at the smooth cobblestones as he walked. He and Sylvia had held hands many times on this very path, even during their senior year *after* her infidelity. How could she do that? How did Sylvia's conscience allow her to hold Gerard's hand, after her own hand had stroked her other lover to climax just a year earlier? How could she come back to Gerard and kiss him after having taken another man into her mouth? Gerard felt sick to his stomach. He had to stop thinking about it.

He walked to the front of Shepard Hall—the music building—and stood looking up at its freshly painted white columns. In this building tomorrow morning he would perform his final cello recital of the year. He thought of his mother, who had always wanted him to play the cello and who had forced him to take lessons as a child. She wanted him to be a professional. And Gerard's Belgian father was just as sure in *his* knowledge that his son's diamond-cutting skills would earn him a comfortable living.

"Gerard should be spending at least two hours a day with his cello," his mother would say. "I don't want him distracted by anything else."

"Yes, yes, that's fine," his father would answer. "He's been polishing at the diamond wheel almost as often, anyway."

Each of Gerard's parents had a specific idea about his career. Sylvia didn't care which path Gerard chose, just that he choose *something*, that he set some goals for himself. For most of the spring semester of their senior year she'd been criticizing Gerard for avoiding decisions that would affect his future, for not caring what lay beyond graduation. Gerard's hard-charging classmates were off to law school and business school and graduate school, but he had no plans, and he shrugged when anyone asked. It made Sylvia furious.

Now as Gerard stood in front of Shepard Hall he felt a surge of confidence about tomorrow's recital. He had memorized Britten's *Sonata in C-Major, Opus 65* four months earlier and had spent so much of the winter rehearsing it in the basement practice modules that his dreams cascaded with pages from the score, and even while eating or reading, the fingers of his left hand busily scurried over imaginary strings on the cello neck. He turned away from the music building and walked toward the amphitheater. It was possible, though, that Gerard's obsession with the love letters would derail his focus during the recital; he hadn't considered that. Or maybe it would work the other way, and the cello would rescue him from his nattering thoughts.

Sylvia, Sylvia, Sylvia.

He walked down the steps between the amphitheater seats and plopped down on the bottom row. The early morning shadow of Shepard Hall darkened the stage and the seating. Gerard felt the cool of the rough concrete bench through his khakis. He leaned back and spread his arms on the next row up. His heart pounded and his armpits sweated. He stared up at the stage, where a squirrel stood hunched over, spinning a walnut between its paws while nibbling and gnawing the shell off. Sylvia. She still didn't know that he had read her love letters. Three days had passed since he'd found the letters; he'd discovered them Saturday night in her bedroom.

On that Saturday night Gerard had been lounging on Sylvia's bed while she showered. They were planning to eat out but hadn't yet decided where. Sylvia would be in the shower for at least ten minutes and Gerard had nothing to do. He rolled off the bed and lolled on the floor on his back. He puffed his cheeks and blew air through his loose lips. He held his arms straight up, toward the ceiling, and affected a pompous, operatic voice while singing the baritone line of the Poulenc *Salve Regina*. He turned onto his side and sang to the spare shoes and crumbs of dust under the bed. On top of an old coat hanger there were sheets of paper. He pulled them out. It was a letter from someone in Oxford, where Sylvia had spent her junior year studying English literature. If the letter had been open on the dresser or on her desk, Gerard probably wouldn't have been interested in reading it; he'd never snooped around in Sylvia's belongings before. But this was under the bed. The mystery was irresistible.

Right around the middle of the first page, Gerard felt dizzy. Oxford, rowing, kisses, aggressive sex, cognac, James Joyce novels, the taste of Sylvia, he misses her. Oh my God. Sylvia had had a lover in Oxford, even as she and Gerard were engaged to be married. How could— What did— How long had this gone on? And who was this, this Gilberto, who wrote with such passion to Sylvia—*Gerard's* Sylvia?

Gerard jumped up from the floor and marched toward the bathroom door where steam seeped through the bottom. Wait. No. He couldn't. He had to know more first. Surely there were more letters. He dropped back to the floor and squeezed his head under the bed. Nothing. He got up and lurched across the room, tripping on the corner of the bed and smacking his forehead on the bottom drawer of her dresser. Gerard rubbed his head and stood back up. He lunged at Sylvia's desk and groped and shuffled the papers there. Her laptop—surely it had clues. But there was no time to boot it up and search for files; Sylvia would be out of the shower soon. Gerard pulled back the bed pillows, opened desk drawers, looked in her file cabinet. Come on, come on, come on, if I were secret love letters, where would I hide? He opened dresser drawers and fumbled through shirts and socks and sweaters and bras and panties. Aha. What was this? Paper. Stacks of paper. His quivering hands pulled them out and sifted through the pages. He glanced at the top of each one. 17 June 2001—Dear Sylvia. 9 July 2001—Dear Sylvia. My God. 24 July, 2 August, 30 September. Some of them were four and five pages long. Gerard leafed through the sheets.

Seventeen. Seventeen letters. Seventeen love letters from a Rhodes Scholar named Gilberto Cardenas.

Okay. So this was it. Sylvia had a secret lover. Okay. He sat on the corner of her bed and carefully folded the seventeen letters. Okay. He straightened up the desk and the bedspread. He tucked the letters under his arm and walked to the bathroom door.

"I'm going back to the house," said Gerard through the hot steam.

"I thought we were going to have dinner," said Sylvia.

"Yeah, I'm not up for it. Let's do it tomorrow."

"Um, okay," said Sylvia.

Gerard sprinted out of her room. If he'd stayed a second longer he would have screamed at her. Why would she want to have dinner with him anyway? Wouldn't she rather be with Gilberto? He took the seventeen letters back to the library at St. Philip Fraternity. He smoothed them out, neatly stacked them, carried them from room to room, sorted them by length and then by chronology. The date on Letter One was 17 June 2001. (Was this the English way of writing dates? Was Gilberto—a Brazilian—trying so very hard to be *English*?) Letter Seventeen was dated 1 May 2002. The letters spanned almost one year. Seventeen letters in eleven months; that was roughly one and a half letters per month. All told, the seventeen letters comprised eighty pages of notebook paper, so the average page length of each letter was four and three-quarters. They were written in the same blue ink, single-spaced, with very tidy handwriting; Gerard guessed the slant of the letters to be about sixty degrees to the right. No smudging on the pages suggested Gilberto wrote with his right hand. None of the letters had a single mistake—no spelling errors, no strike-outs, no corrections. And another thing, on the second and third pages of each letter Gerard could see no imprint of the pen from the previous page; Gilberto must have placed each page on a separate cushion sheet before writing. Was this attention to the detail of language and writing attractive to Sylvia?

Gerard closely read each letter four times until he could nearly recite them from memory. In Letter Three, Gilberto Cardenas had quoted Homer. Referring to the early days of their courtship, Gilberto had written that the small rock of Sylvia's mild resistance to him was holding back the great wave of his passion for her. The overwrought prose in the letters made Gerard want to vomit— Gilberto had even annotated his own reference to *The Iliad*. Maybe Sylvia, as an English major, appreciated this sort of thing; maybe Gerard hadn't been scholarly enough for her. Not that every part of the letters was scholarly. Gilberto had a bawdy side too, which he showcased in his explicit reviews of their sexual adventures at Oxford; they read like the play-by-play of an athletic event. It was as if Gilberto was worried Sylvia would forget about him and everything they'd done together—so graphic were the sex scenes in these letters; Gerard was equally nauseated by the realization that there had probably been much more activity than Gilberto had chronicled. Gerard survived five quiet hours that night in the St. Philip library with the help of a bottle of vintage tawny port.

Gerard imagined that Gilberto Cardenas was tawny—broad-shouldered, muscular, and tawny—tightly clutching his oars and pulling his crew along the 4¼ mile course on the Thames (in Letter Six, Gilberto had smugly reminded Sylvia he was 6'5"). Gerard knew about rowing; didn't that count with Sylvia? When he was in high school at Belden Academy in Vermont, his roommate woke at 5:30 each morning to row on the Abenaki River and had taught Gerard all the jargon—how the oarlocks were mounted on riggers, how the boats were called shells, and the difference between sweep rowing and sculling. But none of that mattered to Sylvia. What mattered to Sylvia was sneaking after-hours into the training boathouse at Wallingford (Letter Eleven) and having Gilberto— solid, tawny Gilberto—grip her slender hips with his strong hands and thrust into her. That was what mattered to her; that was what she wanted. And still she called herself Gerard's fiancée. She had been away from Gilberto and Oxford for eleven months now, and she carried on with Gerard as if nothing had ever happened, as if nothing were different! Maybe Sylvia needed more than one man to be satisfied, or maybe Gerard wasn't enough of a man for her. She'd long been disappointed with his physique ("If you'd just lose a few pounds, Gerard"), but Gerard had always assumed she would tolerate him the way he was. Was he not manly enough for her? Were people from Brazil manlier?

The squirrel on the amphitheater stage rooted through the shell shards for any last bits of nut meat. Gerard imagined the squirrel as an actor, perhaps just finishing up a monologue. It looked up from its work into the audience and then stood up straight, its short arms hanging down over its white belly. The squirrel glanced at Gerard and then at the empty seating, as if suddenly saddened to realize the audience had quietly gone home during the performance. It hopped away and leaped from the edge of the stage onto the trunk of a walnut tree.

Gerard sighed and hefted himself up from the concrete bench. He jogged up the stairs to the back of the amphitheater and stepped again onto the cobblestone path in front of Shepard Hall. He walked with long strides, and with each step he thought the word *Sylvia, Sylvia, Sylvia.* Why hadn't Sylvia dumped him? Did she ever intend to tell Gerard about her infidelity? And then as he walked and huffed and clenched his fists, the word changed to *Rachel, Rachel,* and he thought about how he had nearly taken revenge on Sylvia by sleeping with Rachel.

Last night there had been a party at St. Philip fraternity. Rachel Sheehan got Gerard drunk and then high. He was relaxed but still alert enough to be angry about Sylvia's cheating, so that when Rachel pulled up her short denim skirt and straddled Gerard on the upstairs lounge sofa, he decided instantly he wouldn't resist. And just as Gerard succumbed to the clutch of her thighs around his hips and the clamp of her moist mouth onto his, the Lambeth police raided the house in search of drugs. Charles, one of the St. Philip brothers, deftly flushed their joints down the toilet, and the police left after twenty minutes of hunting and yelling. Gerard went to sleep that night groggy with alcohol, with a headache from the marijuana, and sexually unfulfilled because the police had interrupted Rachel. Gerard had lost his first chance to catch up with Sylvia and Gilberto. He had a lot of work to do!

Gerard strode under the colonnades along the Lawn and then turned a sharp right into the corridor of serpentine brick walls between the pavilion gardens. The torment of the scenes presented by Gilberto Cardenas in the seventeen letters was wearing him down—sex in kitchens, on sofas, in cars, on park benches. Gerard worked hard to force the images out of his head by turning his thoughts to the previous night's party at the fraternity house—loud music, cool keg beer, dark rooms, high ceilings, dirty floors, open windows, warm breezes, frayed window curtains, blue plastic cups, spilled drinks, dancing, smoking, yelling, smiles, sweat, laughs, high-fives, short skirts, Rachel, marijuana, Rachel's strong legs, the couch, Rachel on top of him, Rachel's warm breath on his neck, Rachel's hair dangling in his eyes.

Gerard crossed Waterford Road, passed the stadium, and headed downtown. Part of him wanted to walk away and never come back; the other part wanted to go find Rachel right now and finish what they'd started last night at the party. Gerard marched along the sidewalk. He passed Neil's Deli, the thrift store, the Fun Time arcade, Jin-Lee's China Café, the army recruiting office.

He turned back and looked through the window of the recruiting office at the posters lining the walls. The men in the posters wore uniforms with shiny badges and ribbons and had sharp haircuts. In one poster a soldier stooped over a log in a dense jungle, face-painted with camouflage, cradling a black machine gun. These men were strong and fit and confident and knew what they wanted. The pictures wove in to the dreamlike mix with other scenes in Gerard's mind—Sylvia and Gilberto, marijuana, the black machine gun, his final cello recital tomorrow morning, Rachel moaning, the silver bayonet, Sylvia screaming, camouflage, Gilberto rowing his boat away down the river, Sylvia and Gerard at the altar with Gerard in an army uniform.

It was quarter of ten. The recruiting office didn't open until ten, but a sergeant was inside getting ready for the day and saw Gerard's gawking face through the window. He rushed to the door with his keys.

"It's a little early, but come on in," said the recruiter. "I'm Staff Sergeant O'Ryan." He held out his hand.

"Gerard Kelderman," said Gerard.

"Have a seat." The recruiter pulled out a chair for Gerard and then sat down behind his desk.

Gerard plunked into the chair and clenched his eyes closed and then open again. The hangover still throbbed through his skull, squeezing his tender brain like a sponge. He looked around the office at the vivid colors in the posters on the wall and the little plastic stands with brochures and the American flag in the corner with a silver eagle at the top of the pole. One poster had a diagram of rifles, machine guns, grenades, missiles, and other glinting weapons.

"I want to get into the army," said Gerard.

Sergeant O'Ryan's hands were on the desk with his fingers interlocked. He pointed his thumbs upward. "There's a lot of different jobs, depending on what you're interested—"

"I want something rigorous," said Gerard.

"Shouldn't be a problem," said the sergeant. "There's a lot of choices."

Gerard stared at the poster on the wall behind the recruiter with its row of uniformed men wearing white gloves and resting rifles on their shoulders. The man in the middle had one of those strong faces Gerard yearned for, with skin that sloped inward below the cheekbones down to his sturdy chin. And those eyes—they sparkled with confidence. Gerard imagined himself dressed that way, looking fit, maybe fifty pounds lighter, and the effect he would have on Sylvia. This was it. This was what he needed to become. Sylvia had probably cheated on Gerard because he was overweight with a round face and eyes that were kind. She had told him that— that his eyes were kind and loving, and when Gerard studied the faces of the men in these posters, he felt embarrassed about his own soft and weak eyes. Maybe Sylvia had spent a year sleeping with Gilberto Cardenas because she needed someone strong.

"What's that?" Gerard pointed above the recruiter's head at one of the soldiers in the poster. "That blue thing on his shoulder."

The recruiter answered Gerard without turning around. "That's the infantry cord."

"And that," said Gerard. "That little silver wing badge."

"Airborne jump wings," said the recruiter.

"I want both those," said Gerard. "How do I get those?"

"You enlist in the infantry and go to jump school," said the recruiter. He slapped a slick, colorful booklet down on the desk and flipped it open. "Take a look."

Gerard leaned over the colorful two-page spread of rank insignia, badges, and ribbons.

"You're kind of a big fellow," said the recruiter. "How tall are you?"

"Six-four," said Gerard.

"How much do you weigh?"

"Something like two-fifty," said Gerard.

"You'll need to slim down. How fast can you run two miles?"

"I don't know." Gerard hated running.

"You gotta be able to do at least thirteen push-ups before you start basic," said the recruiter.

"Okay." Gerard couldn't remember ever doing a single push-up, but surely he could manage thirteen.

Gerard looked back down at the brochure and scanned the splash of colors: gold stripes, silver leaves and stars, crossed rifles, green ribbons, berets, patches.

"You can take that with you," said the recruiter.

"No, no, I want to do this now. I want to sign up. I mean, I'm graduating from Monroe Hill in a week, but I want to leave as soon after that as I can."

"Shouldn't be a problem," said the recruiter. "I'll need some documents to start the paperwork: your birth certificate, social security card, and a transcript of your college credits so far."

"I'll go get them right now." Gerard jumped up and flew out the door of the recruiting office.

He jogged along the sidewalk of downtown Lambeth back toward the Monroe Hill campus. The recruiter had mentioned a two-mile run, so maybe this was a good time to start getting in shape.

He shuffled past the county courthouse and the public library. He was already exhausted, sweating and gasping. The last time he'd weighed himself the scale read 250 pounds, which even at 6'4" was too heavy. And if he ever forgot, Sylvia was there to remind him.

"I'm just suggesting you could do with more exercise, Gerard," she would say. "No, I'm not criticizing, but I'm allowed to have opinions, aren't I?"

He slowed to a walk under the shade of oak trees along the sidewalk and put his hands on his hips. His lungs sputtered and his heart pounded, but this was good. The sweat and heavy breathing would slim him down. He was excited by the thought of what he would become. It was perfect, this sudden change in the direction of his life. Gerard blew out a mouthful of air and started jogging again, keeping his eyes down to avoid tripping over the cracks and bumps in the sidewalk made by tree roots. He would never have thought to initiate such a drastic shift on his own, especially in the intoxicating stupor of spring and the ending of his undergraduate career. Gerard and Sylvia were both to graduate in a week, and he was going to spend a leisurely summer at home in Evans Glen, Virginia, before moving with Sylvia to Denver where she would start a Ph.D. program in English. They were planning to get married in May of 2003, after Sylvia finished her first year of graduate school.

Gerard stopped in front of the St. Philip fraternity house. His shirt was soaked and heavy. He was sure he had a copy of his birth certificate somewhere in his room. He galloped in through the front door and up the stairs. Birth certificate, transcripts, and what was the third thing the recruiter had mentioned? Social Security card. The windows in the house were open and the window curtains puffed into the parlor with the May breeze, carrying through the upstairs hallway the warm scent of lavender from the garden and stale beer from last night's party. Many of the brothers had gone home for the summer. Gerard's roommate, Mike Nesmith, was in their room cleaning out old textbooks and notes, throwing papers into a large trash can in the hallway to the thumping tune of Fog Hat's *Slow Ride.*

"Dude, you're all sweaty," yelled Mike.

"Yeah," said Gerard. He walked to his side of the room and opened his desk drawers. Four minutes later he was back out the door.

"Where you going?" said Mike.

"To enlist in the army."

"What?" said Mike. "You're kidding."

"Nope," said Gerard.

"Dude, that's crazy. Oh, Sylvia called."

Gerard stopped in the hall and looked back. "What did she say?"

"Just to call her," said Mike. "She's wondering why you haven't called. Hey, we're eatin' at Neil's tonight. You wanna come?"

"No, I'm taking Sylvia to the Tangled Oak," said Gerard.

"You're kidding about the army, right?" said Mike.

"Nope."

Gerard hopped down the stairs and bounced out to the sidewalk, where he settled into a slow trot back to the recruiting office. The jogging seemed easier now that he was warmed up. Eventually physical fitness would be a snap. He'd call Sylvia later, after signing the army contracts. Man, he couldn't wait to tell her about this. She'd been criticizing him for months about not making a career decision. Until now he hadn't cared what would happen after graduation; he was sure something would present itself. But now—now he had a sudden purpose. He was sure. He was confident. With one decisive move he would eliminate Sylvia's concerns about his weight and about his career.

Gerard crashed through the door of the recruiting office, panting and sweating.

"Here," said Gerard. He dumped the documents onto the desk. His social security card was wet.

"Okay," said the recruiter, lifting the limp card with his finger and thumb. He placed it gently on the table and pulled out a white form. "Let's get started. Fill in each box I've marked with an X."

Gerard clicked the black pen and started scribbling onto "DD Form 1966/5: Record of Military Processing—Armed Forces of the United States." This would be a breeze.

*Current address*: The St. Philip Fraternity house on Cricket Road.

*Home of Record Address*: 330 West Dixon Road, Evans Glen, Virginia.

*Citizenship*: U.S. He'd had dual U.S. and Belgian citizenship until age eighteen.

*Religious preference*: None. Gerard had studied enough religion to appreciate the folly of actually following one.

*Proficient in foreign language*: Flemish and Afrikaans. His father had groomed him for a career in diamonds.

Gilberto Cardenas was a language expert too. Maybe that was what had attracted Sylvia to Gilberto, that he had a master's degree in Historical and Comparative Philology and Linguistics. Pembroke College at Oxford called it an MPhil. Was Sylvia tired of Gerard and his cello? Did she need to be involved with someone who was studying to earn a DPhil? Did that excite her?

*Relatives, including citizenship*: Mom—U.S. Dad—Belgian.

*Have you ever traveled to a foreign country?* Yes, Belgium and South Africa, many times with his father.

*Are you the only living child of your parents?* What was this? Why did they care about that? Gerard had a sudden, silly feeling that the government was monitoring his thoughts; why else would such a question spring out from an army questionnaire? Gerard pictured the inscription on his baby sister's grave marker in Unity Cemetery in Evans Glen: *Anna Kelderman. Our Sweet Baby. We Will Never Hold You Again. June 5, 1985 - July 19, 1987.* Anna had been dead for fifteen years now, but Gerard had indefinitely postponed his grief so he could spend the rest of his childhood comforting his father and mother; their rage and sorrow so debilitated them that they were unable to imagine that young Gerard might be in pain too. How could anyone possibly understand what it was like, at age seven, to stand in front of the tiny oak casket of your own two-year-old sister, who only days before had been sitting in her high chair in the kitchen, singing and stuffing her face with chocolate chip cookies and washing them down with milk from her favorite plastic Pooh-bear cup? He swallowed hard, forcing down the lump in his throat.

"What?" said Gerard. The recruiter had said something.

"I asked how long you want to enlist for?"

"What are the choices?"

"For infantry, you could do two or four years."

Four years didn't sound like a long time. Gerard was now at the end of four years of undergraduate study at Monroe Hill College. In six days he would graduate with a B.A. in music performance and a minor in religious studies. So he'd be twenty-six when his enlistment ended.

Gilberto Cardenas was twenty-six now. Another thing Gilberto would do was speak to Sylvia in Portuguese while they were making love. It turned her on and made her more vocal during sex, this game they played; Gilberto knew so many languages that he would let (let!) Sylvia choose a different one each time—Portuguese in the boathouse at Wallingford, French in the sports center on Iffley Road. It seemed from the letters that Sylvia's favorite place for having sex was the sports center. Maybe she was excited by the smell of sweat and the steam on the windows, or by the thought of eight men working their muscles in the indoor rowing tank—lusty, strong, manly men.

But now Gerard would be manly—an infantryman. He was going to learn all about being a soldier and parachuting from airplanes in the dark and using fancy night-vision eyewear and shooting machine guns and returning from maneuvers to Sylvia, his wife. Gerard suddenly wished he hadn't found Gilberto's letters. But no, if he'd remained ignorant of Sylvia's cheating then he wouldn't have known that something drastic was needed to salvage his relationship with his fiancée; he wouldn't have known anything was wrong.

"So are you thinking four years?" said the recruiter.

"What?" said Gerard. He hadn't been paying attention. It reminded him of being in Latin class at Belden Academy, where spry Dr. Douglas delighted in embarrassing Gerard for letting his mind wander out the window and across the Belden River. *"Observa! Sequere animo!"* he'd say. "Pay attention!"

"Your enlistment," said the recruiter. "Four years?"

"Yes, four," said Gerard. His four years at Monroe Hill had glided by with the quickness of one breath. Four years was nothing.

"Okay, four-year option, airborne infantry." The recruiter was scrawling on another form.

Gerard looked down at his own form to see that he was now on page 5, Box 41, "Data Verification by Recruiter."

"Do I fill out this part too?" said Gerard.

"No," said the recruiter. "I'll take that." He snapped up DD Form 1966/5 and flipped through the pages. "Okay, looks good."

"So do I get to choose my army base?" said Gerard. Sylvia would start her graduate studies in Denver in the fall. If Gerard was stationed nearby, they could still get married and live together.

"You can list your preferences by priority, but there's no guarantee," said the recruiter.

"My fiancée is moving to Denver in August," said Gerard.

"Shouldn't be a problem," said the recruiter. "You could try for the Fourth Infantry Division at Fort Carson. That's half an hour from Denver."

Perfect. Sylvia was going to love this.

"Okay, you're all set," said the recruiter. He was staring at his computer monitor. "I've got you in the system for the computerized ASVAB in Richmond on Monday, May 20th, you'll process in at the MEPS on Tuesday, May 21st and ship out to Benning Tuesday night. Exactly one week from today."

"What's the ASVAB?" said Gerard.

"Armed Services Vocational Aptitude Battery," said the recruiter. "Shouldn't be a problem."

"What's MEPS?"

"Military Entrance Processing Station," said the recruiter. "Vision test, hearing test, medical exam (don't volunteer anything they don't ask for), fingerprinting, criminal check, pre-enlistment interview, oath of enlistment. Shouldn't be a problem."

♦　　　♦　　　♦

Gerard bounced home from the recruiting office with a handful of brochures and booklets; the recruiter had even given him a gray T-shirt that said ARMY in black letters on the front. He felt appropriately armed for breaking the news to Sylvia. The idea of telling her exhilarated him (he wanted her to be proud), even as a small part of him worried she might not be too happy with the news. He was hoping that the possibility of being stationed at Fort Carson would soften the blow.

Later that afternoon Gerard sneaked the letters back in to Sylvia's bedroom while she was out having her nails done. He carefully placed the first sixteen letters under those turquoise panties in the bottom drawer and then shoved Letter Seventeen, unfolded, under the bed exactly where he'd found it. Had Sylvia noticed they were gone? His first reaction was to reassure himself that she'd been acting normally these past few days, so she probably hadn't missed the letters. Of course, her demeanor during their whole senior year had been "normal" too, hadn't it? Gerard hadn't known she was such a skillful actor.

As he sat sipping wine that night with Sylvia in the warm candlelight of the Tangled Oak restaurant, Gerard schemed to roll out his new information gradually over dessert and port wine. Sylvia would be relaxed by then. She looked so beautiful in this light, with the edges of her blond hair brushing the smooth, bronzed skin of her shoulders. But after drinking two glasses of Syrah and staring into Sylvia's eyes—those sparkling blue diamonds—Gerard let it burst out.

"I know this seems sudden, but I've made a decision about a job after graduation," said Gerard.

"Really?" said Sylvia. She stopped buttering her bread and smiled at Gerard.

"Yes," said Gerard. "I've enlisted in the army, in the infantry. It's going to be great. I'll get in shape and I get to serve my country and I'll probably lose a lot of weight and the recruiter told me I might be able to get stationed at Fort Carson in Colorado, which is only half an hour from Denver, so I'll be right near you while you're in graduate school, and we'll still be able to get married next spring, just like we planned."

"Wait, wait, wait," said Sylvia. "What? You're thinking of joining the military?"

"No, I've already done it. I'm in!"

"You're *in*?" said Sylvia.

"Mm hm." Gerard sipped his wine.

"For how long?"

Gerard swallowed. "Four years."

"*Four years*?" said Sylvia. "What about us? What about me?" She gripped the sides of the table and leaned toward him. Her thin neck veins bulged as she whispered. "Why didn't you didn't talk to me about this first?" Her lips trembled.

"I wanted to surprise you."

"Well, I'm surprised." Tears dribbled down Sylvia's cheeks. She sat back in her chair. "You got what you wanted. I'm surprised." Her breath quivered. "How could you betray me like this? How could you go and do something in secret like that?"

"I didn't betray you." Gerard wanted to cry too. He started to feel angry. He wanted to say, "not the way you betrayed me with Gilberto," but he didn't. He sighed.

Sylvia sat up straight. She neatly folded her napkin on the table and slid her chair back. She blew her nose into a tissue. She stood up. She clicked her purse closed. "You did surprise me, Gerard." And she walked away from the table. "You did surprise me."

Gerard looked around the restaurant. Other diners glanced down at their plates as Gerard scanned the room. They'd probably heard all of it. He looked at his own table with its two full plates of angel hair pasta and two bowls of salad and warm bread with butter. He picked up his fork and started scooping and chomping. One of the reasons Gerard was so sure Sylvia would be proud of him for enlisting (or at least accept his decision) was his belief that her criticism of him couldn't possibly get any worse. Obviously she appreciated Gerard's cello playing, but she often questioned the usefulness of a music degree with a minor in religious studies. Gerard couldn't counter with any comments about her B.A. in English because she was on her way to a Ph.D. She had made plans and was pursuing goals and missed no chance to remind Gerard he was doing neither. Gerard set aside his empty plate and reached across the table for Sylvia's pasta.

So much for Sylvia being proud of him. Over the next few days they discussed the matter again and again, and each time Gerard felt Sylvia was growing into the idea, but then she'd fly loose again and cry and throw her purse at him. She grilled him about what would happen after his training, about the supposed certainty that he'd be stationed at Fort Carson. Gerard told her what the recruiter had told him—that there was no guarantee, but that he would be allowed to prioritize his choices. A couple of times he suggested to Sylvia that they get married before he shipped out. The recruiter had told Gerard that married people are more likely to be assigned a post of their choosing. But each time, Sylvia answered that she couldn't think about marriage at a time like this. This was all too much.

That was how Wednesday through Friday went, just before graduation weekend. Arguing with Sylvia was good practice for facing his parents. Gerard had no idea how he would present his story to them, but he hoped they would be more understanding than Sylvia had been. Gerard knew his mother would want to raise the subject of his career plans as soon as she saw him, so starting Saturday morning when his parents checked into the Lambeth Hilton, Gerard spent the entire day keeping them occupied with small talk. It was hard work—not allowing even a three-second pause in any conversation.

"You're awfully full of energy, aren't you?" his father said to Gerard while they walked along the sidewalk in front of the university art museum.

"Well sure, I guess I'm excited, I mean it's the end of four years," said Gerard. "I still can't believe it. What I'm really excited about right now, though, is that we're having dinner tonight at the Neighbors' Tavern. They have great selections of Riesling, Mom.

And the Belgian beers there, Dad—you'll love them. Have I taken you there before?"

And so on, for hours and hours. Gerard was a verbal athlete, swiftly dancing and dodging with the stamina of an Olympic competitor. He sighed and relaxed his shoulders when the sun went down and he dropped off his mom and dad at the hotel to freshen up for dinner.

An hour later, Gerard and Sylvia met his parents at the Neighbors' Tavern on the Corner. (Sylvia's parents wouldn't arrive from Atlanta until later that night.) When he and Sylvia walked into the restaurant, his mother and punctuality-obsessed father had already arrived and were drinking at the bar. Gerard's parents. They were a family of three; he had been an only child for fifteen years now. He did remember his baby sister, but he couldn't remember what it was like to be a big brother—what it felt like. No, for most of his childhood, it was just him and his two parents, Rebecca Ward and Willem Kelderman.

Gerard had grown up having to explain to everyone that yes, his dad and mom really were married; his mother had kept her own surname because she'd launched a successful singing career as Rebecca Ward long before her marriage to Willem. And when Willem got up from the bar in his wrinkled suit to give Gerard a hug, Gerard noticed he had scrubbed the hands which were usually lead-gray at the fingertips from diamond cutting and polishing. Willem Kelderman had made his money in diamond sales and trade, but he still did the cutting and polishing himself. "The only way to get it done right," he would say. He was a graduate of the Githo school in Nijlen, outside Antwerp, and a master diamond-cutter, even with one finger missing. During Gerard's childhood, Willem's finger had been severed while he was adjusting a motor belt underneath the diamond-polishing wheel. Rebecca Ward, in her cruel moments of drink and depression, would deride Willem and accuse him of secretly delighting in not having to wear his wedding band because of the accident. It was the perfect symbol, Rebecca claimed—a sacrifice brought on by the devotion and attention Willem poured into his diamond work.

Gerard turned to his mom and hugged her, careful not to squeeze her lean and wiry frame too tightly. He was surprised she had come to Lambeth for his graduation. Because she was a professional singer and often traveled on weekends, his earliest childhood recollections of Rebecca Ward were weekday-memories. As Gerard held her now, he wished he could have spent more Saturdays and Sundays with his mom when he was a kid; maybe that would have made her a more cheerful person.

She wasn't quite cheerful now, but she did seem happy. She greeted Gerard and Sylvia with genuine contentment, smiling through jaw muscles that were forever clenched and tightened; the lower part of her face was toned from years of teeth grinding, but her eyes and forehead sagged with exhaustion and grief. The debilitating depression she'd suffered after baby Anna's funeral had done its work over the next decade and beyond, her face and body and disposition twined together in a wilting droop that gave the impression maybe she'd lost her daughter only yesterday. When Rebecca wasn't rehearsing in the music parlor at home, she was sitting silently on the floor of Anna's bedroom with the lights off and two candles lit—one for each of Anna's birthdays. To this day she spent more time in that room than when Anna had been alive.

After the greeting and the hugs when they all sat down at a table, Willem's smiling face relaxed back to its default position, long and gloomy (what a dismal couple his parents made!), and Gerard felt a familiar sting of guilt, as if he were personally responsible for the years of Willem's unending anguish. The feeling wasn't logical to Gerard, and he always had to remind himself that the seven-year-old inside him had taken on oceans of guilt when his sister had been killed. It's what kids do, he'd recently been telling himself.

Gerard ordered two glasses of Six Grapes port, one for him and one for Sylvia. She was so tense, he suspected, because she knew this was when Gerard would tell his parents of his big career decision—not that he was just thinking about it, but that it was a done deal, that he would be stepping onto a plane for Fort Benning in just three days. Three days! And while they were all sipping and laughing and having a good time (everyone but Sylvia, anyway), Gerard was thinking through how he would say what he wanted to say; he was waiting for that pause—that space that wouldn't be just a space but would be swollen with a silent sign to him, like a voice whispering *Now. Now is the time. Say it.* But that voice never came. Instead, impatient Sylvia got things rolling.

"This is unbearable, Gerard," Sylvia blurted. "Get it over with and tell them."

And two sets of eyes—his parents eyes—widened and turned to him. No doubt they expected him to announce that he and Sylvia would be having a baby or that they had been married this morning at the courthouse downtown.

So Gerard shared his big news the same way he had told Sylvia four nights earlier at the Tangled Oak: all at once in a compact, full-force exposition that stunned his listeners and might as well have blown their hair back.

A long silence followed, with Sylvia staring at her glass on the table, swinging her leg over her knee, her arms clasped across her chest. Willem slowly sipped his beer as he looked at Rebecca. Clearly everyone at the table understood that Gerard's mother had the next line. Her own father had been a navy captain and had dragged the family around the globe for twenty-five years, leaving Rebecca with a sharp disgust for the military, so her reaction was predictable.

"You mean, just like that?" said Rebecca. "That's it?" Her eyes were getting wider.

She was about to take off. Gerard tried to slow her down. "Mom, it's—"

"Holy fuck," she said.

"Rebecca," said Willem.

"Shut up, Willem," said Rebecca.

And Sylvia just stared at the stem of her wine glass, shaking her head.

"What the *hell*, Gerard," said Rebecca. "I don't know what to say. So you'll just get on a bus and we won't see you for four years?"

"I'll have time off, M—"

"Four fucking years?" said Rebecca.

"Rebecca," said Willem.

Tears popped from Rebecca's eyes. "I'm losing my only other child."

"You're not losing me, Mom."

"Do I have to lose *all* the people I love?" Rebecca pounded her palm on the table. "*Dammit. Dammit. Dammit.* God!"

Willem put his hand on Rebecca's shoulder.

Rebecca hid her face in her hands. She breathed in, then out. She picked up her wine and guzzled it down. "Waiter!"

Gerard sighed. "It's not like you won't see me, Mom."

"And the cello," Rebecca said. "What's going to happen to your cello playing after four years? You didn't think about that, did you?"

"I'm sure I'll find time to practice, Mom."

"Oh, is this before or *after* you're learning to kill people?" said Rebecca. "You think you're going to get rehearsal breaks in the army? Is *that* what you think?"

"Calm down, Rebecca," said Willem. "It's going to be fine."

For Willem Kelderman everything was always going to be fine. Like every other male citizen of Belgium, he had endured two years of required military service when he was eighteen.

"It's not so much of a big deal," said Willem. "When Gerard is done, he can pick up his life where it left off."

Sylvia looked up. "Oh, do *I* just wait, then? What about me?"

"Sure, we'll all wait," said Rebecca. "No big deal, Willem? Are you fucked in the head?"

"What about it, Gerard?" said Sylvia. "Will you just 'pick me up' where we left off after you're done 'being all you can be'?"

"But we'll see each other," said Gerard.

"Oh, will we?" said Sylvia. "You sound so sure."

"They'll let you bring a cello into the army, Gerard, is that what you're saying?" said Rebecca.

"Mom, it's like a normal job," said Gerard.

Sylvia hugged her torso tighter. "And even for normal jobs, people consult the ones they love before making decisions."

"Does this mean you don't love us, Gerard?" said Rebecca.

"Mom."

"Rebecca," said Willem.

"It's a funny way to show love, Gerard," said Sylvia.

Rebecca jumped up and stormed into the restaurant bathroom. Gerard, Sylvia, and Willem stared silently at the table.

The force of his mother's reaction was no shock to Gerard, but Sylvia surprised him: he was hopeful *her* hysteria had peaked the other night at the Tangled Oak. But with the impetus of Rebecca's energy, Sylvia propelled herself to new heights of drama and frenzy. It took her a long time to cool off that night after Gerard's parents returned to their hotel and she had a couple of hours away from alcohol. When Gerard and Sylvia went to sleep that night in her bedroom, they were both too exhausted to talk about it any more.

Sunday was the graduation ceremony; Sylvia was actually cheery that sunny, clear morning. She held Gerard's hand during the procession on the Lawn. After dinner with their parents that evening, Gerard and Sylvia spent a long night on the Rotunda steps hashing through the direction of their future. Gerard would leave for Richmond the next day. There was crying and hugging and yelling and sighing and silence and in the end, Sylvia told Gerard that of course she was still his fiancée and wanted to get married and would wait while he was away. After all, she reminded him, didn't they hold it together for an entire year when she was off studying at Oxford?

Why Gerard was such a coward, even now, he wasn't sure. At first he considered that his fear was rooted in the shame he felt for reading her letters, but he ultimately realized that what he most feared was losing Sylvia. He was afraid that if she knew he had found out about her relationship with Gilberto Cardenas, she would dump Gerard and move ahead in her life without him. Tonight, on the Rotunda steps, Sylvia reaffirmed her commitment to Gerard, and that was enough for him. It was a mandate; he would hold on to Sylvia. He resolved to put the Gilberto business behind him, to forget about it, to silently forgive Sylvia and go forward without looking back.

# Two

"You got about three seconds to get off that truck!" The drill sergeant grabbed Gerard's duffel bag off the cattle truck and threw it across the pavement. "And get your bag too."

"Move it, Kelderman." The other recruits behind Gerard shoved him out the back door of the cattle car and onto the white sidewalk.

"Get in line right here. You, next to him. And you, here. Drop your bag on your left side. Now!"

Gerard shuffled back, lugging his fifty-pound duffel bag.

"Where have you been, soldier?" said the drill sergeant.

"I was retrieving my bag."

"You were what? Hey Drill Sergeant Hammer, come here and listen to this." The drill sergeant peered down at the name tape on Gerard's chest. "Kelderman. Okay, Private Kelderman, tell Drill Sergeant Hammer where you were."

"I was retrieving my bag."

"Did you hear that, Drill Sergeant Hammer? He was retrieving his bag!"

Drill Sergeant Hammer stood like a sculpted, black granite statue with his fists on his hips. "Good for you, dipshit."

"What kind of name is 'Kelderman,' Private?" said the drill sergeant.

"It's Belgian, Drill Sergeant."

"Belgian? What country is Belgium in?"

"It's not *in* any count—"

"Shut up, Kelderman. Get back in formation."

Gerard stumbled into line. "What have I done?" he mumbled to himself.

"I heard a voice, goddammit." Drill Sergeant Hammer bent over and peered into the faces of the soldiers in the front row.

Robert Romberg stood to Gerard's right and spoke from one side of his mouth. "You signed on the dotted line, man."

Romberg was short and bulging with muscles. At the reception station, he had told Gerard he'd been lifting weights since he was sixteen and had worked as a lifeguard before enlisting. Romberg had also bored Gerard and the others with descriptions of the small-arms weapons systems of foreign armies: Israeli, German, and especially the old Soviet Union. On his right forearm, which looked to Gerard like one of Popeye's, he had a long tattoo of a silver sword that extended from his elbow down to his wrist. "Excalibur!" Romberg would yell with such triumph and excitement that the other soldiers would step backwards.

"We all signed on the dotted line," said Romberg.

"I heard another voice," said Drill Sergeant Hammer. "I'm hearin' voices, and I don't like it."

In seconds, these two drill sergeants—one white and one black—had arranged Gerard and his fifty-five cohorts into a formation of four even rows. The thin, white drill sergeant stood before them with his wide-rimmed hat tipped forward.

"Welcome to Bravo Company, 1st Battalion, 47th Infantry Regiment," the drill sergeant said. "My name is Drill Sergeant Womack. Drill Sergeant Hammer and I are in charge of this platoon. You tick-turds are now part of Third Platoon. Do you understand that?"

A few recruits yelled "Yes, Drill Sergeant."

"Everybody get the fuck down!" screamed Hammer from behind the formation. The soldiers of Third Platoon tried to drop to the push-up position, but there was no room! They'd been crammed into such tight rows that there was no way they could all get into push-up position at the same time. Gerard bent over, but his rear end poked up into the air, and the black combat boots of the soldier in front of him were crushing his fingers.

"Ouch, my hand."

"Shit."

"Get the fuck out of my way, Berkowicz."

"Fuck you, man, there's no fuckin' room."

"Get up!" said Womack. "Everybody get back up at the position of attention."

The recruits scuffled and shifted and stood up.

"When I ask you a question, Third Platoon, you sound off," Womack said. "Is that understood?"

"*YES, DRILL SERGEANT!*" thundered Third Platoon.

"That's better," said Womack.

A lanky, black soldier in the second row whispered, "Hey, Romberg, that drill sergeant kinda looks like you. Is that your dad?"

"Fuck you, Fuller."

"No, wait," said Fuller. "He looks like your mom."

Romberg turned around.

"Who's that turning around in formation?" Womack stood in front of Romberg. Romberg faced front.

"Not me, sir."

"My name is Drill Sergeant Womack, bonehead. Repeat it!"

"Drill Sergeant Womack bonehead."

Snorts and giggles arose from the formation.

Drill Sergeant Hammer paced behind the back row. "What's so goddamn funny? Who's laughin'?"

"Very funny, Private Romberg," said Womack. "Get out here."

Romberg ran forward and stood in front of Womack.

Drill Sergeant Womack was long and wiry. The right side of his face was scarred, from his chin all the way up to his ear. Gerard was facing front, but he couldn't keep his eyes from fixing on the lumpy, shiny mass tucked under the left side of Womack's drill sergeant hat. Was that his *ear*? Womack towered over Romberg.

"Get down, funny man," said Womack. "Twenty push-ups."

Romberg dropped to the smooth concrete. His triceps swelled out against the rolled-up sleeve of his camouflage shirt.

Womack watched with his gristly arms folded.

Gerard sneezed.

"Front and center, Private Kelderman," Womack said.

Edward Parker, a hulking, black-skinned man, leaned toward him from behind. "That means get out there, asshole."

On his first morning at the reception station, Gerard had tried to open the wrong wall locker. He was sure it was his, but the padlocks all looked the same. Parker had appeared in a bath towel and rammed Gerard across the aisle into Steven Cooper, who'd been sitting on his bunk lacing up his boots. Gerard would have cracked his skull open on the metal railing of the bunk if Cooper hadn't broken his fall. "Off my shit, motherfucker," Parker had said.

Now Parker shoved Gerard out of the formation, toward the drill sergeant.

Hammer faced the platoon from the side of the formation. "I want to know what's so goddamn funny in there."

Gerard stumbled forward and stood in front of Drill Sergeant Womack.

"Get down there with him for twenty, Belgium Boy. We don't sneeze in formation in the U.S. Army," said Womack. "Count out loud when you're doing your push-ups, Private Romberg."

"One, two, three."

A ripping sound erupted from the second row.

Drill Sergeant Hammer ran around to the front. "Who farted in my formation?"

"Private Romberg, you say 'drill sergeant' after each push-up," said Womack.

"Five drill sergeants, six drill sergeants, seven drill sergeants."

"It's not a Kindergarten counting game!" Womack looked up and scanned the faces of Third Platoon. "You." He pointed at Parker. "Come here. What's your name?"

"Private Parker, Drill Sergeant Womack."

Gerard started his push-ups. "One Drill Sergeant, two Drill Sergeant—"

"Sound off, Private Kelderman!" said Womack.

"Who passed gas?" Drill Sergeant Hammer circled the formation with long strides. "I want a name, goddammit."

"Private Parker, you only say 'Drill Sergeant,' not 'Womack'."

"Yes, Drill Sergeant."

"No one admittin' they farted?" Hammer said. "Alright, everybody put your duffel bag on the ground between your legs."

Gerard's face was red. "Five Drill Sergeant, six Drill Sergeant."

"Private Parker, get down and do ten push-ups, and show Private Romberg how to do them."

Parker dropped to the ground. "One Drill Sergeant, two Drill Sergeant."

Hammer faced the formation. "Now, when I say sit, you sit on your goddamn duffel bag. Got it?"

"*YES, DRILL SERGEANT!*" yelled the platoon.

Womack pointed at Parker. "Look at him, Private Romberg. You see how he's doing push-ups? His backside is not poking up into the air like the Washington Monument, and he's sounding off. Now get going."

Romberg lowered his rear end. "Eighteen Drill Sergeant, nineteen Drill Sergeant."

"Sixteen Drill Sergeant, seventeen Drill Sergeant," Gerard groaned.

"Private Kelderman, you're slowing down," said Womack. "Are you overweight, Private Kelderman?"

"Yes, Drill Sergeant."

"How much do you weigh, Kelderman?"

"Two hundred fifty pounds, Drill Sergeant."

"How tall are you?"

"Six-four, Drill Sergeant."

"You're off the chart, Kelderman," said Womack. "Did you know that?"

"Yes, Drill Sergeant."

"At your height, this army says you need to weigh two hundred seventeen pounds," said Womack.

"Yes, Drill Sergeant," said Gerard.

"We're going to take care of that," said Womack. "I have another guess. You've got some college, don't you?"

"Yes, Drill Sergeant." But Gerard didn't volunteer that he'd *finished* college. The people at the MEPS in Richmond had screwed up his processing and given Gerard the rank of E-3—Private First Class—when he should have been given an E-4 Specialist rank because he had a college degree. Gerard knew better than to bring that up now.

"I knew it," said Womack. "You look like a smarty. Do you think your education is going to help you in the U.S. Army infantry?"

No. 'No' was definitely the right answer. "No, Drill Sergeant."

"Have you ever seen a real weapon, Kelderman?" Womack said.

"No, Drill Sergeant."

"We're going to change that," Womack said. "We're going to train you to kill people, Private Kelderman."

"Twenty, Drill Sergeant," Romberg yelled.

"Get back into formation, Kelderman," said Womack.

Gerard stood with a groan and jogged to where his duffel bag lay slumped on the floor in the middle of the third row of soldiers.

Drill Sergeant Hammer shook his head. "Fifty-six yard-birds and that's all the sound you got? You better sound off."

*"YES, DRILL SERGEANT!"*

"Sit!" yelled Drill Sergeant Hammer.

Everyone sat down.

"Get back up," said Hammer. "Stand up, goddammit."

"Private Parker, Private Romberg, fall in," Womack said.

Parker sprinted into formation. Romberg jumped up and ran a full circle around the platoon formation, flapping his outstretched arms, before getting back in line.

"Private Romberg!" said Womack.

"Yes, Drill Sergeant?" Romberg said.

Drill Sergeant Hammer continued. "When I say 'sit,' I should hear fifty-six asses hittin' the bags at one goddamn time."

Womack shook his head like a wet dog. "I want to know what that was, Private Romberg."

Romberg stared straight ahead. "Nothing, Drill Sergeant."

"Nothing?" Womack walked in front of Romberg. "Private Romberg, I don't believe you."

Gerard glanced over at Romberg, who was pursing his lips.

Womack edged closer. "Private Romberg, don't you ever lie to me, do you understand? I want to know what that was."

"I was scaring away the ravens, Drill Sergeant."

Womack looked up at the sky. "Ravens?"

"I see them sometimes, Drill Sergeant," said Romberg. "I imagine they're attacking me. I can't help it."

"Sit!" said Hammer.

Fifty-six recruits dropped to the sitting position.

"I mean *one* simultaneous thumping sound when your asses hit that bag, Third Platoon. Now stand back up," said Hammer. "Sit!"

Gerard threw his knees forward and squatted on his duffel bag.

"Stand up!" said Hammer.

"Private Romberg, did you volunteer for this army?" said Drill Sergeant Womack.

"Sit!" said Hammer.

"Yes, Drill Sergeant," said Romberg.

"Do you still want to be here, Private Romberg?" said Womack. He leaned down each time Romberg sat.

"Stand up!" said Hammer.

"Yes, Drill Sergeant," Romberg said.

"Then we shouldn't be hearing about any more ravens, should we?" said Womack.

"No, Drill Sergeant," said Romberg.

"Fuck!" said Drill Sergeant Hammer. "I said everybody stand back up. You want to be soldiers and you can't even sit your undisciplined asses down at the same damn time. Shit."

Romberg sat down. Parker grabbed his camouflage shirt collar and pulled him back up.

"He said 'shit,' not 'sit'," said Parker.

Drill Sergeant Hammer hung his head. "Oh man."

Womack turned to Parker. "Did Drill Sergeant Hammer ask for your comments, Private Parker?"

"No, Drill Sergeant!"

"Did a drill sergeant tell you to help Private Romberg?" said Womack.

"No, Drill Sergeant," said Parker.

"Then get it straight—you don't do anything until you're told," said Womack. "Do you understand?"

"Yes, Drill Sergeant."

"That goes for the rest of you, Third Platoon. Did you hear me?" Womack said.

"*YES, DRILL SERGEANT!*"

"Where are you from, Private Parker?" said Womack.

"Detroit, Drill Sergeant."

"What?" said Drill Sergeant Hammer from behind the formation. "*I'm* from Detroit." He walked around front to face Parker. "You better *not* be from Detroit, Private."

There was a long silence. Gerard wanted to turn sideways to watch Hammer and Parker; he wanted to watch Parker trying to decide what response the drill sergeant wanted. Gerard took a breath. He was hot. Beads of sweat were piling up on the top of his shaved head, but they couldn't evaporate under his camouflage baseball cap. He reached up and lifted it slightly. A gentle breeze puffed across his shining orb.

"Private Kelderman!" said Womack.

Crap. "Yes, Drill Sergeant."

"Why are you lifting your headgear?"

"I—"

"Did I issue a command to the platoon to lift headgear?"

"No, Drill Sergeant," said Gerard.

"Did I issue a personal command to you to lift headgear?" said Womack.

"No, Drill Sergeant."

"No I didn't," said Womack.

"Answer me, Private," Hammer said to Parker. "Are you from Detroit?"

"Yes, Drill Sergeant," said Parker.

"Bullshit!" said Hammer. "Get your ass down and gimme ten push-ups."

"Private Kelderman, you're soft in the middle, aren't you?" Womack said.

Gerard decided the question was rhetorical. He stayed silent.

"Parker, *my* ass is from Detroit," said Drill Sergeant Hammer. "There ain't no *way* two of us can be from Detroit, you understand?"

"Yes, Dri—"

"So any time I ask you where you from, you best come up with something else."

"Yes, Drill Sergeant," Parker said.

"Private Kelderman, answer me," said Womack.

"Yes, Drill Sergeant," said Gerard.

"Yes what?" said Womack.

"Yes, I'm soft in the middle," said Gerard.

"Get up," said Drill Sergeant Hammer.

Parker snapped to his feet.

"Private Kelderman, have you ever had a day of hard work in your life?" said Womack.

"Yes, Drill Sergeant," Gerard said.

"No you haven't," said Womack. "Have you ever done anything hard at all?"

Gerard glanced into Womack's eyes, but he couldn't help his gaze from drifting to the scar along Womack's cheek. And that ear! It looked like a knot of silly putty. Gerard couldn't look away.

"Face front, Private Kelderman!" said Womack

Gerard looked forward.

Womack inched closer to Gerard and spoke softly into his face. "Private Kelderman, have you ever done anything hard at all?"

Gerard clenched his teeth. Did cleaning out and throwing away your dead baby sister's toys count? Gerard's dad had wanted to keep everything of Anna's intact and to leave her bedroom untouched. After a nasty fight Rebecca had convinced Willem that they needed to move on and that all the baby things had to go, with the exception of a handful of items Rebecca would use to create the shrine in Anna's room. And while they argued, Gerard had boxed up Anna's toys and clothes and dragged them out to the curbside of West Dixon Road for the trash collectors.

Gerard sighed and stared straight ahead at the brick wall of the battalion building.

"Private Kelderman, this isn't going to be easy for you," said Womack. "I've seen your type before. You might not even make it. How does that sound?"

At the moment, it sounded fine. Gerard hadn't even considered stopping. He was hot, thirsty, hungry, and his arms hurt. When he'd been standing in front of the recruiting office window back in Lambeth, he hadn't imagined it would be like this.

"Don't get any ideas, Private Kelderman," said Womack. "Romberg's already got a few of his own."

"Yes, Drill Sergeant," Gerard said.

"Shut up, Private Kelderman," said Womack. "I didn't tell you to say anything."

The air was so humid and hot that sweat trickled down Gerard's back and soaked onto his black belt and camouflage trousers.

"You know what I do for a living, Kelderman?" Womack said. "I train soldiers. And since you swore to protect and defend the Constitution of the United States, it's my job to prepare you to do that. Do you understand, Private Kelderman?"

"Yes, Drill Sergeant."

"You forget about whatever you left behind, and you focus on what's going on here," Womack said. "If you lose your focus, you're gonna get burned. Don't forget that."

"You, what's your name?" said Drill Sergeant Hammer.

"Private Eddie, Drill Sergeant."

"Eddie?" Hammer said. "That your last name?"

"Yes, Drill Sergeant."

"That's fucked-up, Private Eddie," Drill Sergeant Hammer said, shaking his head. "That is one fucked-up last name."

"Yes, Drill Sergeant," Eddie shouted, staring straight ahead.

"Where you from, Private Eddie?"

"From Ohio, Drill Sergeant."

Hammer stretched his head high and shouted into the formation. "Parker, where you from?"

"Canada, Drill Sergeant," yelled Parker.

"Fucking Canada!" Hammer said. "Outstanding."

"Private Libby, why are you wearing white socks?" said Drill Sergeant Womack.

"What?" said Hammer as he strode to the front of the formation. "Someone's wearin' white socks?"

"Answer me, Private Libby," said Womack.

"I don't know, Drill Sergeant," said Libby. He reached up with his right hand and scratched his cheek.

"Get your hand down, Private," said Hammer. "You're at the position of attention."

"Yes, Drill S—"

"Libby, you didn't answer my question," said Womack. "You're in violation of army dress protocol. Why is that?"

"I don't kn—"

"Gimme that bag, Private." Hammer grabbed Libby's duffel bag and hurled it into a set of empty metal bleachers. "You better get your bag and find some regulation green fuckin' wool socks."

"Yes, Drill Sergeant," said Libby. He dove forward, tripped, and rolled onto the floor before stumbling into the bleachers and fiddling with the clasp on his bag.

"Shit," said Hammer. "Always gotta have at least one. Probably gonna get somebody hurt."

"Okay men, listen up," said Drill Sergeant Womack. "When I tell you to, I want you to pick up your duffel bag with your left hand. Do it."

Gerard reached down and picked up his duffel bag, a fat pack of green canvas stuffed with all his uniforms and his second pair of combat boots. The small Asian women at the reception station had issued him clothing that was one size too large. He got two sets of BDUs (Battle Dress Uniform—the camouflage outfit), brown underwear, two pairs of heavy combat boots, a winter BDU coat, black leather gloves, caps, a cold-weather hat, two summer physical training—PT—outfits, one winter PT outfit, two pairs of green dress slacks, black dress shoes, two short-sleeved dress shirts, black socks, green socks, and a long black overcoat—the type you'd expect to see on a downtown flasher. There was also a lengthy list of items the army required its soldiers to have but which it didn't issue. Soldiers were given an advance on their first paychecks and allowed to spend it in the company store on brown towels, washcloths, flashlights, shoe polish, shave cream, razors, soap, laundry detergent, and deodorant. By standing inside his duffel bag and jumping up and down, Gerard had crammed everything in and made it fit.

"Too slow," said Womack. "Drop 'em."

Gerard hoped the powdered laundry detergent in his bag wasn't leaking.

"Private Kelderman!" said Womack.

Gerard snapped out of his daydream. "Yes, Drill Sergeant."

Womack walked over to Gerard. "One of these things is not like the other, Private Kelderman."

Gerard looked to his right at the other soldiers.

"Drop it," Cooper said. "Let go."

"Shut up, Private Cooper," said Womack. "I'm having a chat with Private Kelderman."

"Why are you doing things different?" said Womack. "Are you special?"

"Drop your bag, asshole," said Parker, from behind.

Gerard dropped his bag on the concrete.

"You were off in your own little world, weren't you Private Kelderman?" said Womack.

"Yes, Drill Sergeant."

"Get down and gimme ten," said Womack.

Gerard stepped forward and stooped down again onto the floor.

Womack bent down. "Private Kelderman, in this army, we pay attention."

"One Drill Sergeant, two Drill Sergeant." Gerard slowly pumped.

"When we don't pay attention, bad things happen," said Womack. He stood up and strode to the far end of the formation.

Gerard finished his push-ups and stepped back into line.

"Dude got his head up his ass," said Parker, quietly.

Gerard couldn't figure out if Parker treated everyone this way, or if he had singled Gerard out. Gerard turned around, though he wasn't sure why. Gerard was taller and bigger than Parker, but Parker was harder; Gerard would have been no match for Parker's massive biceps.

"Man, turn your *sorry* ass back around," said Parker. "You want me to make you cry?"

"Is that Parker I hear?" said Drill Sergeant Hammer. "Parker, you talking in formation again?"

"No, Drill Sergeant," said Parker.

"Good," Hammer said. "Where you from, Parker?"

"Delaware, Drill Sergeant!"

◆          ◆          ◆

Gerard rubbed his eyes and looked at his Casio digital wristwatch. 1 a.m.—Zero One Hundred. Third Platoon stood in formation. The company area was dimly lit like an empty parking garage and staggered with brick pillars holding the low ceiling above them where each platoon had a bay of fifty-six single-level bunks. Everyone had learned to call them bunks by hearing Libby screw up and call them beds. Drill Sergeant Womack had punished Libby by forcing him to yell, for ten full minutes, "I sleep in a bunk. I sleep in a bunk." Second and Fourth platoons were upstairs in their bays being harassed—the army term was 'smoked'—by their drill sergeants. Gerard heard occasional muffled roars of "Yes, Drill Sergeant" and "No, Drill Sergeant" from above. First platoon had been marched to the sawdust pit in the center of the quarter-mile running track and was rolling around and doing push-ups. But Third Platoon, for the moment, stood in four quiet rows of fourteen men each. The drill sergeants had told them to wait and then had disappeared. Gerard couldn't remember seeing where they'd gone. He was fighting not to fall asleep on his feet.

To fight the heaviness of his eyelids Gerard thought back over the last week and a half. Ten days ago he'd left home and completed his enlistment in Richmond. The army had flown him to Fort Benning and dropped him into a place called the Reception Station where he'd waited for nine days. At 2:30 p.m. today, over ten hours ago, 224 recruits had loaded the cattle trucks at the reception station and been trucked here, where they were unloaded and divided into four groups of fifty-six each. Only now, with time to reflect on those first minutes, did Gerard appreciate how efficient the process had been. Eight drill sergeants had organized four platoons of fifty-six soldiers each by last name and then assigned roster numbers. Gerard was in Third Platoon, roster number 29—Bravo Company roster number 329. In the rigid grid of green uniforms and gleaming, shaved heads, Gerard could take solace in having a unique roster number.

After an hour or two (it could have been three; Gerard didn't really know) of free-form yelling, Drill Sergeants Womack and Hammer had initiated a shakedown of Third Platoon in which each soldier dumped the contents of his duffel bag onto the concrete floor, in formation. Gerard's stuff mixed with Libby's and Libby's mixed with Mueller's and so on. Gerard imagined it was part of the standard harassment, or that the drill sergeants were doing it for fun, but Womack claimed it was necessary to find contraband. Private Berkowicz had a canister of aspirin in one of his pockets; it cost him twenty push-ups, and he had to throw the aspirin into the trash. The video they'd been forced to watch at the reception station stated that such an infraction should have led to a court marshal or Berkowicz's immediate removal from the army. After watching the video the recruits had been paraded, one by one, through an amnesty room and given an opportunity to get rid of any banned objects or substances with no questions asked and no consequences. Romberg later told Gerard he'd discarded two bottles of prescription medication, though he didn't say what they were. Gerard was sure it was a mental illness prescription—one that might have prevented the raven incident earlier that day. According to Private Fuller, soldiers can be thrown into the stockade for hiding medicine and for having withheld information during the physical exam at the MEPS—the Military Entrance Processing Station. "Yeah, but not if my recruiter told me to hide stuff from the doctors," Romberg had said. It was one of the scores of discussions that kept Gerard and his fellow recruits entertained during the endlessly boring days at the reception station.

The reception station at Fort Benning had been Gerard's introduction to the army. One of the pamphlets given to him by the recruiter back in Lambeth had described what would happen "during your brief three-day stay at the reception station" as a first stop when arriving at an army post for basic training. But the place was so crammed full of eager recruits that there weren't enough training companies starting their cycles to accommodate them all. So for the first three days they followed the reception station routine—the army's term was 'inprocessing'—clothing issue, haircuts, immunizations, dental exams, ID card issue, dog tag issue, commander's briefing, chaplain's briefing, education briefing, personnel affairs briefing.

"Mother fuck, man. Are they gonna give us a briefing on how to take a shit, too?" Romberg had said while they waited in a classroom for a finance briefing.

It was in the space of all the waiting that Gerard had gotten to know his fellow soldiers. Private Fuller was a fourth-generation soldier who knew everything about the U.S. Army, past and present. He had been raised to love the army. His father was still on active duty as a first sergeant, his grandfather had been an artillery colonel, and his great-grandfather had been a sergeant during World War I. Fuller's eyes sparkled when he talked about his great-grandfather, whose shoulder had been torn apart in the trenches by a spray of bullets from a German MG08 machine gun.

Romberg had jumped eagerly into the discussion with the comment that the caliber of the MG08 was 7.92 mm. Of course Romberg had made a name for himself with his Excalibur tattoo, but he was also a self-professed Special Forces expert. "I'm goin' for the fuckin' green beret, man," he'd announced during lunch through a mouthful of chili mac. "I can't wait."

And right alongside these two gung-ho recruits was Cooper, who at nineteen years old had left Ohio to spend four years studying meditation and yoga in India and then five years in a monastic community at Taizé, France, where he had lived an intentionally simple life, renouncing all ownership and passing hours each day in deep prayer. Akron, India, France, then Fort Benning. Gerard would never have met someone like this in the cloister of Monroe Hill College.

The story Gerard shared about himself was that he'd become bored with school and wanted to do something more interesting. "Fuck, yeah!" Romberg had said to that. Gerard wasn't yet sure how much of himself to reveal; he did mention that he'd been to college (which wasn't atypical of army recruits; many had started college and then ended up in the service after failing out or getting their girlfriends pregnant), but he wasn't ready to say he had a degree in music and religion. Nor did he yet feel safe telling the truth about his motivation to enlist: that he suspected his fiancée needed more of a man than he was. He was prepared to provide a more detailed explanation about his reason for enlisting, but no one ever asked. Every answer to the question "Why'd you sign up?" was accepted unconditionally. Fuller always wanted to be a Ranger, Libby wanted to jump out of airplanes and get paid for it, Berkowicz was after the Army College Fund, Griffin had finished college and needed to pay off his loans, Hopson wanted to avoid working for his father as a carpenter, Cooper shrugged and said he just wanted to gain experience, and Mueller had enlisted in a rage after being dumped by his girlfriend.

Thank God Sylvia hadn't dumped Gerard for Gilberto! Gerard missed her. He closed his eyes and remembered their last hug just two weeks ago. She said she forgave him and that she'd wait for him in Denver, but Gerard couldn't shake the feeling that he was going to lose her, especially now that he'd be away for four months. The last time they'd been away from each other for a long time, she had found comfort with someone else. Gerard looked to his left and right and saw only rows of men in camouflage outfits and boots; there'd be no such comfort for him. Thinking of Sylvia made him breathe deeply and feel a pull at the center of his chest, as if he couldn't quite catch up to his own breath. At the reception station he'd written letters to Sylvia and his mother, but no one could write him back until he was assigned to a training unit with a mailing address. Now he was in a training unit but didn't have time to write letters.

"We'll be able to write letters in a few days, I'm sure," Cooper said to Gerard.

"Shut up!" said Parker. "Drill sergeant said to stay quiet."

Gerard turned to Cooper. "What made you say that?"

"Shut up!" Parker said.

"Hey, chill out, Parker," Romberg said. "I don't see any drill sergeants around here."

"We've been standing here for like twenty minutes," said Private Berkowicz.

"Just shut the fuck up," Parker said.

"I don't know," said Cooper to Gerard. "I just had a thought."

He just had a thought? It was a strange coincidence. Maybe Gerard had been mumbling out loud, which wouldn't have been the first time. Sylvia had often told Gerard he talked in his sleep. That sort of habit wouldn't go over well in an infantry basic training unit, if they ever did get to sleep.

"Where's the drill sergeant?" said Romberg. "What are we supposed to do?"

"We're supposed to wait, dumb-ass, like Womack said."

"Fuck you, Snodgrass," said Romberg.

"Phillips flipped out worse than you, Romberg," said Snodgrass.

"Nine hours into basic and the fool slit his wrists," said Parker.

"You mean tried to," said Private Wiley from the third row. "I saw him. He cut 'em the wrong way. Fucking communist."

"He's just trying to get out," said Romberg.

The company office door banged open and Drill Sergeant Hammer walked toward Third Platoon.

"Shut up, here he comes," said Parker.

"I hear talking," said Drill Sergeant Hammer. His round-rimmed hat was tilted forward. Gerard wondered if it made drill sergeants feel more menacing to tip their hats forward.

"Who was that?" said Hammer. "Parker, that you?"

"Yes, Drill Sergeant."

"I thought so. You think you're hot shit, dontcha?"

"No, Drill Sergeant."

"Yeah you do. Can't even keep your mouth shut in formation. Step out and gimme ten."

Parker dropped to floor and pumped out his push-ups.

"Alright Third Platoon," said Drill Sergeant Hammer. "You got five minutes to get upstairs, change out of those nasty green BDUs, and get into your PT uniforms. Parker, you're in charge. If this platoon ain't back in formation in five minutes, dressed for PT, guess who's gettin' it?"

"Yes, Drill Sergeant. Me, Drill Sergeant."

"Fall out."

The four rows burst apart, and the sea of green soldiers swept up the stairs. Inside the bay, wall lockers slammed open and black boots kicked off.

"Where's my fucking socks?"

"Shit, I broke a shoelace."

"My padlock is on backwards."

"They had a drug-sniffing dog up here while we were out," said Fuller. "They probably opened your locker."

"How do you know all this shit?"

"Out of my way, Snodgrass."

"Move it, bitch-fuck."

Gerard unfastened the olive buttons of his shirt and wiggled out of his fatigues. He sat down and started pulling on his white socks.

"Kelderman, get off my bunk," said Private Libby. "You're wrinkling the blanket."

"Sorry." Wrong bunk. Gerard hopped onto his own bed and yanked on his running shoes.

On went the gray t-shirts, shorts, white socks, and running shoes.

"Come on, let's go," yelled Parker.

"What's the rush, Parker?" said Cooper, smiling.

"Move it, asshole." Parker pushed Cooper out the door.

One by one, in their gray PT uniforms, the soldiers ran out the bay door, down the stairs, and into formation in the company area. Parker stood at the front.

"How many more?" said Parker.

"Seven," said Gerard. "No, eight."

"Shit, shit, shit," said Parker.

More stragglers ran down the stairs.

"Fix your socks, Berkowicz," said Parker. "And tie your shoes. How many more up there?"

"Just Libby," said Berkowicz.

"Shit," Parker said. "He's been fuckin' up all night."

The two drill sergeants came out of the company office in their PT uniforms and running shoes. They looked funny without their hats; the shiny knob of Womack's cauliflower ear jutted out sideways from his thin head. Hammer looked at his watch. Womack looked at the Third Platoon formation and then turned to look at the stairwell.

Libby dashed down the stairs with his shirt hanging out, holding his shoes, and jumped into formation.

"Five minutes and forty-two seconds. Not even close, Hot Shit," said Hammer. "What happened?"

"Libby fucked up, Drill Sergeant."

"Bullshit!" yelled Hammer. "You fucked up. I put you in charge. You fucked up. Repeat after me, 'I fucked up'."

"I fucked up, Drill Sergeant."

"Front leaning rest position—move!"

Parker snapped down into push-up position. Hammer got down into push-up position with him.

"Alright, Hot Shit," said Hammer. "We're doin' push-ups, you and me. Let's go."

They pushed in rhythm like synchronized swimmers.

"Okay, Third Platoon," said Womack. "The rest of you are coming with me for physical training."

Drill Sergeant Womack marched the platoon out to the sawdust field inside the quarter-mile track, which was lit like a baseball field with bright floodlights glaring down from the dark night sky through swirling clouds of moths and insects. A few minutes later Parker and Drill Sergeant Hammer emerged from the company area and jogged across the sawdust to join the platoon.

"Fall in, Parker," said Womack.

"I smoked you, didn't I Parker?" said Hammer.

Parker's PT uniform was wet with sweat. Water dribbled down his black cheeks and steam rose from his shaved head. "Yes, Drill Sergeant."

"You ready for more, Parker?" said Hammer.

Parker was silent.

"Did you hear me, Parker? Are you ready for more?"

"Yes, Drill Sergeant!"

"Good."

Womack surveyed the faces in the formation. "What's wrong, haven't you been smoked enough tonight? It's only 0120 hours. The night is young, gentlemen."

Hammer stood with his arms folded. Gerard could see his shoulder and bicep muscles rippling underneath his gray PT shirt. "They don't look too excited now, do they, Drill Sergeant Womack? Not like they did gettin' off that truck."

"No, I'd say they don't look too happy. Except this one. Private Cooper! Have we been smoking you enough?"

"Yes, Drill Sergeant," said Cooper.

"Why do you look so content standing there in formation?" said Womack.

Cooper's round face lit up with a smile. "I'm always content, Drill Sergeant."

"What? You think you're gonna go through basic like that?" said Hammer.

"Yes, Drill Sergeant."

"Private Cooper, come here!" Womack said.

Cooper jogged out from the back of the formation. At age twenty eight, he was one of the older members of Third Platoon. He was short and wide and had a round face that was, so far, always smiling and joyful. He bounced along and then stopped at attention in front of Womack.

"Cooper, I've heard you're a strange individual," said Womack.

"Yes, Drill Sergeant."

"Let me finish, Cooper."

"Yes, Drill Sergeant."

"I heard that you meditated each day at the reception station. Is that true, Cooper?"

"Yes, Drill Sergeant."

"You're into meditation?" said Womack.

"Yes, Drill Sergeant."

"What are you, Cooper, some kind of new age fruitcake?"

"No, Drill Sergeant."

"Private Cooper, do you listen to Yanni?"

"No, Drill Sergeant."

"Well maybe you should start, because that's what I'm going to call you."

Cooper smiled.

"What's so funny, Yanni?" said Womack. "Why don't you give us a concert to make us feel better about ourselves? Can you do that for us, Yanni?"

"No, Dri—"

"Shut up, Yanni. I will not have anyone coming through Bravo Company 1/47th with a happy look on their face. Do you understand me?"

"Yes, Drill Sergeant."

"Get back in formation, Yanni."

Cooper ran back to the fourth row.

"Okay, Third Platoon, listen up," said Womack. "This is physical training, also known as PT. You are wearing your official PT uniform, and you will wear it whenever we have PT. Kelderman, what does PT stand for?"

Gerard was so tired he felt dizzy. "It stands for physical training, Drill Sergeant."

"Very good. Your daddy paid a lot of money for you to be so smart, didn't he?"

"I suppose so, Drill Sergeant."

"Private Kelderman, get up here."

Gerard jogged up to the front.

"Kelderman, you need motivation. You're going to be my special helper during PT today. Okay, Third Platoon, listen up. My helper is standing at the position of attention. When I call out an exercise, he will repeat after me. The push-up!"

Gerard's eyes were closing.

"Kelderman, wake up."

"The push-up!" yelled Gerard.

"Louder, Kelderman."

"The push-up!"

"Better," said Womack. "Try again. The push-up!"

"The push-up!"

"Start position, move," Womack said. "Now, you assume the position."

Gerard bent down slowly into the push-up position.

In the back row of the formation, Parker slowly shook his head.

"Whatsa matter, Parker?" yelled Drill Sergeant Hammer. "You think you can do better?"

"Yes, Drill Sergeant."

"Then *get* your ass out here."

Parker ran to the front.

"Piss poor, Kelderman," said Womack. "Stand up."

Gerard stood up.

"Too slow, Kelderman. Get down."

Gerard got back down into the push-up position.

"Too slow, get up."

"The push-up!" Hammer yelled.

"The push-up!" Parker answered.

"Start position, move."

Parker snapped down into push-up position.

"Too slow, Kelderman," said Womack. "Get down."

Gerard got back down.

"Give me ten push-ups, Kelderman."

"One Drill Sergeant, two Drill Sergeant."

Hammer leaned over Parker and snarled. "I'm gonna be watchin' you, Hot Shit."

"Yes, Drill Sergeant."

"Position of attention, move," said Hammer.

Parker jumped up to attention.

"Get back in formation, Hot Shit."

Parker dashed back into line.

"Nine Drill Sergeant, ten Drill Sergeant." Gerard was sweating.

"Get up, Kelderman."

Gerard stood up. His legs buckled, and he fell back onto the sawdust. Cooper rushed out of the formation and lifted him up.

"Private Yanni, did I ask for your help?"

Gerard held on to Cooper and brushed himself off.

"Get back in formation, Yanni," said Womack.

Cooper trotted back into formation.

Drill Sergeant Hammer walked up to Cooper. "Did anyone tell you to move, Cooper?"

"No, Drill Sergeant."

"Then don't move," said Hammer.

"Yes, Drill Sergeant."

"Ten push-ups is too much for you at zero one thirty, isn't it?" said Womack.

Sweat dripped down Gerard's face. His legs and arms felt like jelly.

"Remember this the next time you address a drill sergeant," said Womack.

Gerard groaned.

Womack walked close to Gerard.

"Kelderman, do you want another motivation exercise?"

Gerard stood up straight, arms at his side. "No, Drill Sergeant!"

"Fall in."

Gerard sprinted back into formation.

"Sorry ass," said Parker.

"Who, me?" said Gerard.

"Yeah, asshole," said Parker.

"Up yours," said Gerard. What was he thinking?

"Kick his ass!" yelled Romberg.

"Private Romberg, shut up," said Womack.

"Kick his ass, man," Romberg said. "Rock and roll!"

Parker faked a lunge at Gerard. Cooper jumped between them. Gerard jumped backward, and Parker laughed.

"The fuck's going on in there?" said Hammer.

"You four tick-turds get out here," yelled Womack.

Gerard, Parker, Cooper, and Romberg ran forward and stood in front, facing the formation.

"You have just volunteered for remedial, basic skills PT. While I do PT with the rest of the platoon, Drill Sergeant Hammer will take you four individuals for a special PT session."

Hammer marched the four privates to the far end of the saw-dust field.

♦         ♦         ♦

An hour later Third Platoon stood back in the company area—the parking garage—damp with sweat. Steam swirled up from their shoulders and heads. Parker, Cooper, Romberg, and Gerard had sawdust and black dirt stuck to their faces and arms. The others had fresh, wet mud caked on their shoes and socks.

Drill Sergeant Womack stood in front of the formation. "You will have exactly four minutes to change your smelly selves into army-issue brown underwear and get ready for lights out," said Womack. "When I come up to that bay, I want every one of you tick-turds standing at attention at the end of your bunks. Fall out!"

The formation broke and the soldiers ran. Parker was the first one up the stairs. He opened the bay door and stopped. On the floor inside the door was a large, white towel. He jumped over the towel.

"Look out," said Parker.

Soldiers crashed through the door and jumped over the clean towel.

"What the fuck?"

"Watch out."

"Drill sergeant must've put it here," said Parker. "It's probably a trick. Look out."

One by one, the recruits jumped through the door over the towel. The last one through the door was Romberg.

"Jump over, Romberg."

Romberg stopped in the door and looked down. He looked up at Parker and smiled. He put one leg through the doorway and held his shoe over the towel.

"Don't do it," said Parker.

"Come on, man," said Romberg. "Where's your fuckin' sense of adventure?" He stepped onto the white towel and rubbed his shoes into it. Brown dirt from the sawdust pit ground into the fibers of the towel, and he twisted around, sliding across the shiny linoleum floor.

"Rock and roll!" he screamed. "I'm Chubby fucking Checker." He twisted his body back and forth as Parker watched with his mouth hanging open.

"You crazy, man," said Parker. "You tryin' to get thrown out."

Romberg finished wiping his shoes on the towel and casually walked into the bay.

Parker ran to his wall locker and began yanking his clothes off. "Oh man, oh man. I can't believe he did that."

"What?" said Berkowicz.

"Romberg wiped his dirty-ass shoes on that towel. Drill Sergeant gonna smoke us all for that."

"At ease!"

The bay door slammed open and Drill Sergeant Womack stood at the end of the aisle. Everyone dashed to the edge of their bunks and stood at attention.

"I want to know one thing," said Womack.

"Oh shit, oh shit," said Parker.

"I want to know who wiped their shoes on my clean white towel."

Gerard glanced at Romberg, who had a smirk on his face. He was jutting his head forward and backward, the way chickens do when they walk.

Romberg stepped forward. "I did, Drill Sergeant."

"Come here, Romberg."

Romberg walked down the aisle and stood in front of Womack.

"Stand over there, Romberg."

Romberg moved over next to Womack.

"Third platoon, I put that white towel on the floor inside the door, and one man wiped his nasty, dirty shoes on it." Womack looked down the long aisle. No one moved.

"Only one private wiped his shoes," Womack said. "I went to all the trouble to put that towel down for you to clean off your shoes, and only one man was courteous enough to accept my hospitality."

Romberg grinned.

"Gentlemen, my feelings are hurt," Womack said. "The push-up!"

"*THE PUSH-UP!*"

"The push-up!" yelled Womack.

"*THE PUSH-UP!*"

"Start position, move."

Fifty-six bodies dropped to the cool, linoleum floor.

"Not you, Romberg. Get up."

Romberg stood back up at attention.

"Ready, begin. One, two, three—"

"*ONE!*"

"One, two, three—"

"*TWO!*"

Gerard pumped. He sweated. After Drill Sergeant Hammer's special PT session, he could no longer feel his arms. The last time he remembered losing sensation in an arm was when he had spent four straight hours practicing cello. The cello—what a distant memory. Everything was a distant memory: his parents, his fraternity brothers, Sylvia, the seventeen letters. Maybe Gerard could write Sylvia seventeen letters and close the last one with "So am I tied with Gilberto now?"

"Kelderman, sound off," said Parker from across the aisle.

"*NINE!*"

"One, two, three—"

"*TEN!*"

"On your feet," said Womack.

The soldiers snapped up and stood straight.

Womack turned to Romberg, who was still standing at attention. "Romberg, how many men in a Spetsnaz unit?"

"Eight to ten, Drill Sergeant."

"What's the per-soldier standard issue of ammunition?"

"400 rounds, Drill Sergeant."

"What's the per-soldier load, in pounds?" said Womack.

"88, Drill Sergeant," said Romberg.

"In kilos."

"40, Drill Sergeant."

"You really want to be a soldier, don't you Romberg?"

Romberg's spine straightened. "Yes, Drill Sergeant."

At the position of attention, Gerard normally stared straight forward at Parker across the aisle, but he was now glancing to the side every few seconds to try to watch Womack and Romberg. Womack was standing with his hands on his hips, facing Romberg and clicking his teeth, as if trying to figure something out. Gerard had never heard of Spetsnaz, and Womack was clearly perplexed that Romberg not only knew what it was but was able to spout arcane facts about it.

Womack walked to the exit door of the bay and flipped the light switch without looking at it. "Lights out, men." He walked out and the door closed behind him.

"Thank fucking God."

"Damn."

Gerard sat down and pulled off his running shoes and sweaty socks.

"Romberg, you jerk," said Private Carroll.

"Oldest trick in the book!" said Romberg. "I knew it. I knew that one! Spetsnaz, man. Russian special forces. Oldest trick in the book."

"Fuckin' nut case," said Wiley as he yanked off his shoes. "Why do you know about Spetsnaz? You a communist?"

"Fuck you, Wiley," Romberg said. "It's called reading, you fucking redneck."

Gerard climbed into bed and stared at the ceiling. Was this the part of basic training where the entire platoon turned on one man and beat him while he slept? Was that going to happen to Romberg? Gerard suspected not, mainly because of Romberg's manic energy and his abnormally enthusiastic attitude about being in the army. How anyone could be so energetic after such extreme sleep deprivation was beyond Gerard. His eyelids clanged shut.

# Three

It was now the sixth day of basic training. To Gerard, six days felt like a month. In that short time Bravo Company had been propelled through first aid training, Drill and Ceremony instruction, equipment issue, two five-mile road marches, six wall locker inspections, fourteen equipment shakedowns in the company area (Fuller was keeping track), three four-mile formation runs, Nuclear Biological Chemical warfare training, and more muscle-tearing PT sessions than Gerard could count. Romberg laughed wild-eyed after PT every morning and claimed he wasn't getting enough. Cooper maintained his look of calm contentment at every moment, even after Drill Sergeant Hammer had forced Third Platoon to do sit-ups for an hour in mud and three inches of standing water. "Man, I've probably got some kind of water parasites up my ass now," Private Wiley had proclaimed soon afterwards, as he stood in formation with his hand down the back of his shorts. And Parker was forever trying to impress the drill sergeants with his efficiency and physical prowess; he raced to be the first one to make his bunk or to be the first one in formation or to sound off more loudly than any other soldier. Gerard wondered if Drill Sergeant Hammer's nickname for Parker—Hot Shit—fulfilled Parker's need for attention and validation.

A nickname bestowed by a Drill Sergeant was a mark of acceptance, in the army's own way. Cooper smiled whenever Womack called him Private Yanni. Hammer yelling 'Hot Shit' only made Parker's chest puff out farther. Womack hadn't yet repeated 'Belgium Boy' to Gerard, a hint that Gerard hadn't yet proved himself worthy of a permanent nickname.

But while personal nicknames were conferred with the jocular spirit of fraternity hazing, there was no mistaking some of the more general phrases as downright demeaning. Two Third-Platoon soldiers had stopped training because of injury. Becker had run into a fire hydrant and crushed his kneecap. Cortes had fallen down the stairs and shredded the ligaments connecting his foot to his ankle. While most of the soldiers of Bravo Company trained, these two spent their days answering the office phones and being referred to as "limp dicks." The phrase was effective, especially during morning formation when the drill sergeants wanted to find out if any soldiers needed to go on sick call.

"Any limp dicks today?" Hammer would say.

What aspiring infantryman, even in sickness, would answer yes to a question like that? And when Gerard had fleeting thoughts about faking an injury to get thrown out of the army, his inner infantryman would remember peer pressure and guide him back to the realization that he needed to have a strapping, sturdy erection if he was going to move through this and come out on the other side. If he completed basic training and became an infantryman, Sylvia would consider him more manly than Gilberto Cardenas.

"What time is it?" Libby said.

"0630," said Parker.

Third Platoon was assembled in the company area waiting—forever waiting—for their drill sergeants. Yards away the drill sergeants for First, Second, and Fourth Platoons were harassing their recruits. The company area echoed with the sounds of screaming and hoo-ah-ing and counting and groaning. Bravo Company was waiting to move into the classroom for instruction on the Uniform Code of Military Justice; like all blocks of instruction in the classroom, it was an exercise in staying awake. None of the army commercials Gerard had seen on T.V. and none of the posters in the recruiting office had shown recruits sitting in classrooms.

"Eighty-six days and a wake-up," said Carroll.

"We've only been here a week?" said Phillips.

"Yeah, Phillips, it's only been six days since you tried to off yourself," said Romberg.

"Shut the fuck up, Romberg," Phillips said.

"Admit it, man—you suck with a knife," Romberg said. "Let me do it next time."

Parker laughed.

"Fuckwad," Phillips said.

Six days. Six down and eighty-seven to go. Three nights earlier the drill sergeants had allowed them to write letters. Cooper had been right! Gerard had scribbled two brief letters: one to his parents at 330 West Dixon Road in Evans Glen, Virginia, and one to Sylvia at her parents' house in Atlanta. Mainly he wanted to give them his mailing address and beg them for letters. He was confident his mother would write, but what about Sylvia? Was she writing Gilberto letters, even now? Maybe she was seeing him. Maybe now that Gerard was safely out of the way, Gilberto would come to the U.S. to be with her. As Gerard had scrawled his letter to Sylvia, he found himself digging the pen into the paper as he thought about her time in Oxford. He'd considered adding a brief line at the end of his letter: "P.S. I know about Gilberto," but he decided that would be the best way to have Sylvia *not* write him at Fort Benning, and what he badly wanted right now was mail. In the middle of this Fort Benning summer heat and dust and heavy army fatigues and screaming drill sergeants, Gerard wanted something from Sylvia that would let him know everything was going to be fine. Everything would be as it was, and Sylvia would forget about Gilberto. It was a temporary fit of insanity she'd undergone, Gerard figured. During the year she'd spent at Oxford, she had needed to get it out of her system.

Gerard missed home. He missed his parents and his room and his yard and Hrothgar the cat—a mound of an animal who relished eating fresh steak or ground beef and would hover next to the barbecue grill while Willem Kelderman cooked hamburgers. Gerard missed playing his cello. Not since age seven had he gone a week without playing the cello, and it depressed him. He longed for the feel of the bow in his right hand and to be in the music parlor at 330 West Dixon Road, where he would spend hours practicing until his mother would remind him he needed to eat. He remembered sitting in the practice modules in the basement of Shepard Hall at Monroe Hill College and bowing the cello until his arms and fingers pulsed with pain.

Gerard craved the feeling of lying on the Lawn at Monroe Hill at dusk with his head in Sylvia's lap. They would sit there sometimes for hours after dinner outside Sylvia's room—she was one of the few senior students with a room right on the Lawn, in the original brick section of the college built in 1825. They'd lounge under the trees as Sylvia read poetry to him. In the early weeks of their relationship—during their sophomore year—Gerard had confessed to Sylvia how much he hated poetry. He tried hard to avoid classes that involved reading and writing, but Monroe Hill College required a remedial writing class as well as something called the second writing requirement, for which Gerard enrolled in a 200-level literature survey course crammed full of silly and irrelevant "classical" literature. Sylvia took very seriously her studies in the English department and adopted Gerard as her special case.

"You need to be awakened, Gerard, to see how beautiful literature can be," she'd said to him as they lounged on the Lawn.

And she'd done it. She'd made poetry interesting. It was beyond Gerard how anyone could have patience for Keats, but it filled him with joy to think of lazing on the thick green grass in front of the Rotunda, listening to Sylvia read Keats's "To Autumn." So as he stood in formation with these sweaty, bald men, he closed his eyes and imagined the orange and yellow leaves swirling across the Lawn and the words streaming through his head:

> *Season of mists and mellow fruitfulness,*
> *Close bosom-friend of the maturing sun;*
> *Conspiring with him how to load and bless*
> *With fruit the vines that round the thatch-eaves run;*
> *To bend with apples the moss'd cottage-trees,*
> *And fill all fruit with ripeness to the core;*
> *To swell the gourd, and plump the hazel shells—*

"Who left shit in the goddamn shitter?" Drill Sergeant Hammer was pacing toward the formation.

Libby's eyes widened. "Uh, I did, Drill Sergeant."

"Well get on up there and flush it."

Libby broke formation and ran up the stairs.

Drill Sergeant Womack emerged from the company office and strode toward Third Platoon. "We've got ten minutes until we move into the classroom, men. Drill Sergeant Hammer, let's assign battle buddies."

"Roger that," said Hammer.

"Any of you tick-turds know what a battle buddy is?" said Drill Sergeant Womack.

Romberg raised his hand. "Your buddy in battle, Drill Sergeant?"

"Brilliant, Romberg," Womack said. "After you are assigned a battle buddy, it will be your job to know everything about your battle buddy: where he's from, his birthday, even what his favorite color is. For tasks requiring more than one person, you will partner with your battle buddy."

"I don't need a fuckin' battle buddy," whispered Parker.

"What's that, Hot Shit?" Hammer said.

"Nothing, Drill Sergeant."

"The person who bunks across the aisle from you in the bay is your battle buddy for the entire training cycle."

Gerard pictured the bay and the bunk across from his. Parker was his battle buddy. Gerard looked down the squad row and saw from Parker's face that he had figured out Gerard was his battle buddy. Parker glanced quickly at Gerard and faced front again.

"Drill Sergeant!"

"What is it, Parker?" said Womack.

"Request reassignment of battle buddy, Drill Sergeant."

"Bullshit, Parker," said Drill Sergeant Hammer. "This ain't fuckin' Burger King. What you get is what you get."

Murmurs trickled through the platoon. Libby ran back down the stairs and jumped into formation.

"Shut up. Everybody shut up," yelled Womack. "You will also receive your rotating duties this week. Rotating duties include platoon guide, squad leaders, mess hall motivator, fire guard, and charge of quarters."

Libby raised his hand. "Drill Sergeant, what's fire—"

"Shut up, Libby. You'll get a briefing later."

"Yeah, Libby, shut up," said Romberg.

"Romberg, shut up," yelled Hammer.

"Yes, Drill Sergeant."

"Each squad will have a squad leader," said Womack. "The squad leader marches at the front of the squad line and is responsible for everyone in the squad. Berkowicz!"

"Yes, Drill Sergeant."

"You're the squad leader for First Squad. Move to the front of the squad."

Berkowicz ran to the right side of the formation and his squad mates shifted left.

"Libby, you're the squad leader for Second Squad."

Libby ran to the end of the squad line and tripped over Hopson's boot. He flailed his arms and steadied himself on Hopson's shoulders before straightening himself and pushing his shoulders back.

"Second Squad, you should be proud," said Womack.

Romberg chuckled.

"Shut up, Romberg," said Hammer.

"Yes, Drill Sergeant."

"Third Squad, Wiley. Fourth Squad, Kelderman."

"Lovely," said Gerard.

Cooper smiled at Gerard. "Way to go. You'll do great."

"Get over there, Squad Leader," said Parker.

Gerard ran to the right end of the squad and stood behind Wiley. He had no idea what he was supposed to do.

"And now for platoon guide," said Womack. "The platoon guide stands in front of the platoon during formation and receives instructions from me and from Drill Sergeant Hammer."

Parker stood straight and puffed his chest out.

"Snodgrass!" said Womack.

"Yes, Drill Sergeant."

"Get out here. You're the platoon guide."

Snodgrass ran to the front.

"Shit," said Parker.

"Parker!" Drill Sergeant Hammer was right behind him.

"Yes, Drill Sergeant."

"You think we can't hear you because Fourth Squad's on the back row. You forgot I was back here, didn't you?"

"Yes, Drill Sergeant."

"Well shut the fuck up, Hot Shit," said Hammer.

"Yes, Drill Sergeant."

"Stand up straight and face the platoon, Snodgrass," said Womack. "Third Platoon, Snodgrass is your platoon guide. If he tells you to do something, you do it, understand?"

*"YES, DRILL SERGEANT!"*

"And Snodgrass, if the platoon screws up, guess whose fault it is?"

Snodgrass tucked in his chin and widened his eyes.

"That's right, dippy." Womack looked at Snodgrass. "You."

Snodgrass gulped.

"Okay men," Womack said. "Let's move out for chow."

◆          ◆          ◆

Third Platoon shuffled silently through the front door of the dining facility—the D-FAC. The small, square lobby could accommodate about eighty soldiers because of a series of metal railings that resembled the line for an amusement park ride. Drill Sergeant Womack went ahead of them into the serving area and came back out seconds later.

"They're not ready for us yet," Womack said. "We'll have to wait. Platoon Guide, keep 'em quiet."

"Yes, Drill Sergeant," said Snodgrass.

Womack walked back around the corner toward the company area, leaving Third Platoon alone.

"What time is it?" said Berkowicz.

"It's 6:30," said Snodgrass. "And be quiet. You're not supposed to be talking."

"That's 'zero six-thirty'," said Private Fuller.

"Can you believe it?" said Romberg. "6:30 and we're waitin' for breakfast. I wouldn't even be *up* at 6:30 back home."

Home. During the past six days, everyone in Third Platoon had talked about missing home. Gerard had heard many variations on "I can't believe I've gotten myself into this shit," and "What the hell was I thinking?" during this first week of training. For six days the pace of their lives had been so frantic that Gerard had only been able to think in small pockets about his former life (as Berkowicz called it). It all seemed like years ago: Monroe Hill College, Sylvia, his home in Evans Glen, Virginia. In this moment, as he waited silently in line, Gerard yearned for home. He wanted to be in his own house with his mother and father, to feel summer morning breezes glide through the screen door of the kitchen, to drink in the warm scent of honeysuckle at dusk.

Willem and Rebecca, in deciding where to settle to raise a family, had been instantly smitten with Evans Glen: its horses, thick trees, and rolling hills reminded Rebecca of her own home in Knoxville, Tennessee. Willem liked Evans Glen because of its proximity to Washington, D.C. and Dulles airport—both important to his diamond business.

Gerard never imagined he would miss Evans Glen. To a child and then an adolescent, it was a boring place one hoped some day to leave. The town sits about thirty miles northwest of Washington, D.C., on Route Seven, below the foothills of the Blue Ridge mountains. Drill Sergeant Cifuentes of Second Platoon had taken a turn harassing Third Platoon two days ago in the company area and had referred to Gerard as "mountain man." Cifuentes associated Virginia with mountains, though he said he'd never been to Virginia.

Evans Glen was founded in 1758—as George Town—but was renamed after the civil war for Fort Evans, a stronghold built on the heights outside the east end of town in the winter of 1861. Because the town was so close to Balls Bluff National Cemetery, it attracted all manner of Civil War freaks: battle scene re-enactors, weapons collectors, and retired people who spent most of their waking hours culling the fields with metal detectors. Mr. Meerschaum, one of Gerard's neighbors, had been arrested twice by the Evans Glen police for using his metal detector directly on the confederate graves at Balls Bluff.

Gerard had grown up believing military service was only for right-wing, warmongering idiots—probably because of the flag-waving hysteria (U.S. and Confederate) that gripped the citizens of Evans Glen—and when he was eighteen he'd spent many hours trying to talk Donald Meerschaum, Mr. Meerschaum's son, out of enrolling in naval ROTC at the College of William and Mary. Mr. Meerschaum's chest billowed five-fold the day Donald received his acceptance letter; finally his class clown of a son was going to amount to something.

So what was Gerard thinking now? Here he was standing in a line outside the D-FAC—a silent and orderly line of spit-shined leather boots and baggy camouflage pants. The last time Gerard remembered standing in a straight line was in the Cauthen Elementary School cafeteria waiting for his partitioned, plastic tray and hoping for more than the usual six tater tots. Here at the 1/47th D-FAC, the perennial hope was that you'd get more than just two pieces of bread with your meal—a silly hope, because portion sizes were tightly regulated. Everything was regulated—how to march, how to make your bed, how to fold your clothes, how to hang your dress shirts, how to salute, how to sit when eating, how to tuck your chin when standing at attention. Sometimes Gerard couldn't believe he was here, that he had held up his right hand and sworn to protect and defend the constitution of the United States.

Had the confederate soldiers of Evans Glen sworn to protect and defend the confederacy? Thanks to the fanaticism of Mr. Meerschaum, Gerard had been subjected to Evans Glen history lessons throughout his childhood. It was in May of 1861 that the citizens of Evans Glen had voted to support the Virginia Secession

Ordinance. Had they been fully aware, Gerard wondered, that their town was a mere 51 miles from the Mason-Dixon line, and how difficult that would make it for them? Did the citizens make a hasty, hot-headed decision, the way Gerard had only two weeks before? Gerard had recently been doubting the wisdom of his decision to enlist, and he wondered now how much real thought the citizens of Evans Glen had given to their decision to secede.

Evans Glen fared well in the early months of the Civil War. The excitement of the Confederate victory at Balls Bluff in October of 1861 infected even the ordinary civilians of Evans Glen, who made a social event of strolling downtown to gawk at the Union prisoners being held on the courthouse lawn. But over the next four years the town was ravaged by armies on both sides of the conflict. Union troops seized the town (but not before the citizens of Evans Glen strategically burned their own mills and bridges) when the Confederates were pushed as far south as Richmond. The 2nd Virginia Cavalry reclaimed Evans Glen in time for Lee to tromp his entire army, with all its equipment, through the town on his way to Antietam. The Union returned in 1863, crossing through Evans Glen three times in one year. 100,000 Union troops crossed Edwards Ferry in June 1863 alone. For four years the town was shelled, trampled, and bombed by the Maryland Cavalry, Federal artillery, the Cornwall Guard, White's Commanches, the Potomac Greys, Mosby's Rangers, and countless other companies and battalions of artillery, cavalry, and the rugged, ground-pounding backbone of any army: the infantry.

But in spite of all that pressure for so many years, Evans Glen was now a vibrant town. Gerard had never been fond of the town while he was growing up, but he missed it now. He shouldn't have enlisted. He should have stayed home. If he'd gone home to Evans Glen after graduation, his mind would have cleared and he could have thought the problem through more exhaustively with the support of his parents and the solace of the downstairs music parlor. When he was home in his own house, he could handle anything.

The house of Gerard's childhood sat on a hill at 330 West Dixon Road in downtown Evans Glen. Built around 1890, the house had high ceilings, brown brick masonry, and six spacious bedrooms. There had long been a nickname associated with the property, like Hillview or Pine Meadow or some other retirement-home-sounding name. But from the time of Gerard's childhood, the house was called the Kasteel.

Rebecca's father, George Randolph Ward, had been sixty-seven years old at the time and was visiting from his home in Knoxville.

"You got people down the street who can't afford health insurance, and you just bought a damn castle. Willem! What's the Dutch word for 'castle'?"

"*Kasteel*," Willem had said. "And it's Flemish."

"Huh?" Grandpa Ward had said.

"It's not Dutch, it's Flemish."

"It's a damn castle, is what it is."

Eventually Willem must have agreed that Kasteel was a fine name for a house, because he always called it that. Rebecca resisted using the word, probably because it had been suggested by her tyrannical father.

But who cares what it was called? What Gerard missed about his home went beyond the name: the basement, the attic, the five flights of stairs, and the carriage house at the back of the property. Since the original owner of the house had owned horses and a carriage, all successive owners of the property had referred to that structure as the carriage house.

"Stop calling it a shed, Willem," Rebecca Ward would have to keep telling her husband. But it did look like a shed, decaying and crumbling with rusted holes in its tin roof. When Willem and Rebecca bought the Kasteel they'd had to spend a good bit of money cleaning up. The previous owner was a distracted World War II veteran named Jarmaroni who had almost lost the sale of the property by convincing Willem that the Kasteel was haunted. He had put no money or effort into maintaining the house. Gerard's parents had told him that, when they moved in, there had been vines growing up the sides of the brick walls and into the bedroom windows. It looked like the Addams Family's house.

"It was unbelievable," Rebecca had told Gerard as she sipped Riesling in the living room. "Almost as unbelievable as what we found after our first night in the house."

During the final walk-through with the real estate agent, Willem and Rebecca had noticed so much crap around the Kasteel property—stacks of rotten firewood, old tires, rusty tools—that they didn't give a second thought to all the additional crap in the basement. Just to the right of the antique coal furnace there were clothes, a cot, and a small refrigerator. After spending the first night in their new house, Rebecca and Willem descended the grand staircase the next morning. As they reached the bottom step, the basement door swung open, and out stepped a thin, weathered, elderly man wearing a flannel shirt and dirty jeans.

"Who are you?" Rebecca said.

"I'm Nelson. Who the hell are you?"

"We're the owners," said Willem.

"Oh, new owners," Nelson said, leaning on the banister. "That explains it. Well, I live in the basement—take care of all the chimneys. Been doin' it for thirty-some-odd years."

"You *live* in the basement?" Rebecca said.

"Yup." Nelson picked his teeth.

And after recovering from his initial shock, Willem worked out an agreement with Nelson that would let him continue to live in the basement and take care of all the chimneys.

"Christ, Willem," Rebecca had said later. "He's got to do more than take care of the chimneys if he's going to live here." The idea of a hired man was new to both of them.

Rebecca Ward didn't trust Nelson; she never fully recovered from Nelson's emergence that cool October morning through the basement door. Willem, on the other hand, thought it was a grand bonus that they got Nelson along with the house; he trusted Nelson completely, even with all his diamond equipment and Belgian beer in the basement (it wasn't hard—the diamonds were always locked in the safe, and Nelson had said many times he'd hated the nasty, bitter swill Willem was always offering him).

So Nelson stayed on, doing light work around the house as well as caring for the chimneys. As it turned out, having Nelson care for the five chimneys and all the fireplaces saved the family a lot on heating oil. Nearly every room at the Kasteel had its own fireplace, and Nelson kept them blazing all winter with pea-coal trucked in from West Virginia. Nelson often reminded Rebecca that he also used to maintain the antique coal furnace in the basement, before the installation of an oil heater. Nelson needed to show Rebecca that he *was* useful at the Kasteel, that he made a difference—that he wasn't simply a lingering charity case of Willem's compassion.

Inside the front door at the Kasteel, just off to the left, was a wide room clearly intended as a library. Both Willem and Rebecca knew, even before that final inspection, that this would be the family's music rehearsal room; it was Rebecca who had first called it the music parlor. God, the hours his parents would spend there together—singing duets, or with Rebecca singing and Willem playing piano (he washed his hands thoroughly; his fingers were never as free of gray diamond dust as when he was playing Chopin or Rachmaninoff or any of the other composers whose works he'd committed to memory).

Spanning an entire wall of the music parlor was a grid of shelves that stretched from the floor to the ceiling. Gerard's parents had divided the wall in half. To the right of the fireplace, Willem had crammed all his piano sheet music, loosely arranged by composer. On the other side of the fireplace, Rebecca's music was meticulously arranged chronologically, according to her singing career; consequently she was the only one who could find anything there. The organization of the music was as scattered as her singing career: one weekend it was Verdi's *Requiem*, the next it was Schubert's *La Pastorella*.

"I'm fuckin' starved," said Wiley.

"Open the mess hall!" Romberg yelled.

"Romberg, shut up," Snodgrass said.

"It's the D-FAC, Romberg," said Fuller.

Private Fuller had let Third Platoon know—in case they hadn't heard him the first six times at the reception station—that he was a fourth-generation soldier and loved the military. He was current on all the latest army terms and trends, both those in the trenches and those imposed on enlisted people by the top brass. "Mess hall" was out, dining facility—D-FAC—was in. Fuller even claimed there was an official army policy that drill sergeants weren't supposed to use foul language.

"Yeah, like that one's really sticking," Wiley said.

"That's crap, man," Romberg said. "I enlisted to be cussed at. The drill sergeants know that."

"Everybody shut up," said Snodgrass. "You're gonna get us all in trouble."

"Oh, waa, waa," said Wiley.

"Hey, I didn't exactly volunteer for this job," Snodgrass said.

Gerard nodded at that. He hadn't volunteered to be squad leader either. Gerard had never been the leader of anything, unless you counted being first-chair cello in the Monroe Hill College Orchestra. He had worked for that—he had set his sights on it and then earned it. Dr. Anthony Logan, Gerard's faculty advisor and sponsor in the orchestra, had told him that some of the other professors grumbled that a student had arrived so quickly at the first chair position. Gerard had pressed Mr. Logan for names, but Mr. Logan would only give him vague comments about whiny violinists.

But this—Gerard did not want this. He had no desire to be a squad leader, especially with Parker as a member of the squad. Gerard was stuck with the job because Womack had pushed him into it.

Gerard remembered that as a child he hadn't always been interested in playing cello; he'd been pushed into that as well, by his mother. Since the age of four he'd taken piano lessons, but when he was seven—right after his baby sister Anna had died—he had begun a dizzying regimen of intense cello lessons. From the moment of Anna's death Gerard had started a new life—one he hadn't chosen and had no control in directing. His mother had been the

force behind his cello lessons. He'd known all along that Rebecca
had made the arrangements for his lessons, but Gerard was now
aware of how forceful she'd been. Rebecca Ward drove Gerard to
play the cello.

"I don't care if it interferes with his piano playing," Gerard remembered Rebecca saying to Willem, through crying eyes and a
soggy face. "His piano playing's fine. It's just fine. Playing cello
might even make him better, don't you think?"

"Of course it will," Willem had said, pulling Rebecca close and
wrapping his arms around her.

That same afternoon Rebecca had put Gerard into the Mercedes
200 Diesel and driven out of Evans Glen on Route Seven to Washington D.C. "And it isn't going to be any kiddie cello, either," Rebecca had said, cramming the gear shift into third as they merged
onto the beltway.

"What if I don't want to play the cello, Mom?" Gerard had said.
"Isn't piano enough?"

"You'll love it, Gerard," she'd answered. "Just wait and see."

They'd pulled down the off-ramp (Gerard just now remembered
the exit number was 57B), and after spending two hours in the
Brobst Violin Shop, Rebecca and Gerard had returned to Evans
Glen with a 1909 Alberto Blanchi cello and a J.P. Bernard, silver-
mounted cello bow. Gerard wouldn't find out until years later how
many tens of thousands of dollars his mother had spent that day.

"You learned to play on this cello, on an Alberto Blanchi cello?"
Mr. Logan would say years later when Gerard was a sophomore at
Monroe Hill College. "Are you aware that such a cello can cost as
much as $100,000?"

But Willem Kelderman had made no complaints about the
price. His only protest was that the bow had been produced at
Maison Bernard—the problem being that Maison Bernard is in
*French*-speaking Brussels. Rebecca was sitting on the couch in the
parlor and had let down her black hair; its fine, soft waves eased
gently down her back past her waist and swirled on the red leather
upholstery. She'd stared at Willem for a good five seconds before

asking him if he'd prefer she drive back to D.C. to find a Flemish cello bow-maker.

"I'm joking, Rebecca," Willem had said, sitting down at the piano. He played Debussy's "La Fille Aux Cheveux De Lin" while Rebecca leaned back on the couch and Gerard clicked open his new cello case.

One week later the lessons began. It was all very sudden, this whole cello business, and Gerard now wondered if Rebecca had needed him to take up something that was her idea. For a brief moment Rebecca had shed the somber cloak of her depression by focusing on the task of Gerard's schooling in the arts. Piano wasn't enough; diamond-cutting and piano-playing were both introduced to Gerard by Willem. Rebecca needed Gerard to take up something *she* had presented, and maybe the ferocity with which she pressured Gerard grew from feeling behind; if you counted diamonds and the piano against the cello, the score was Willem two, Rebecca one. Gerard now understood why Rebecca had fought so hard when Willem later suggested Gerard learn to speak Flemish. So much pressure she'd created for herself! Was all this why she'd developed such a fondness for Riesling? She'd always liked to drink wine with dinner, as far back as Gerard could remember, but in those days—in the late summer of 1987—she'd have sipped half a bottle by the time Dr. Beale arrived for Gerard's cello lesson at four o'clock two days a week.

"Come in, Kenneth," Rebecca would say to Dr. Beale as he stepped through the grand front door. By then Gerard would already have spent fifteen minutes in the parlor with his cello warming up his fingers. This had been Rebecca's insistence—she didn't want any of Dr. Kenneth Beale's expensive time wasted. By four o'clock Gerard was to be warmed up and ready to go. The ritual continued for many years: Gerard would begin warming up at 3:45 p.m. on Tuesdays and Thursdays, Dr. Beale would walk through the front door at 4:00 p.m., and for an hour and a half Gerard would play cello scales and exercises with Dr. Beale hovering over him.

"The *edge* of the chair, dammit, the *edge*," Dr. Beale would say, shoving Gerard from behind. "You're slipping toward the back again." Gerard loved Dr. Beale for saying 'dammit' so freely in front of a child. "*Hug* the cello, dammit, *hug* it."

Twice a week Gerard and Dr. Beale would sit in the music parlor beneath the looming wall of scores. Over the years Gerard became so proficient on the cello that Dr. Beale could reach to the music wall, pull off a score, and Gerard would rip through it without a single mistake. Dr. Beale made a game of it. He'd reach for the wall without even looking and pull down whatever his fingers found. And most of the music on the wall was not scored for cello, but Dr. Beale and Gerard followed the rules of the game to the letter: if Dr. Beale pulled it down, Gerard had to play it. Sometimes it would be a standard like the oboe line of the Bach "Concerto in A." Other times Gerard would have to concentrate on the notes while Dr. Beale roared with laughter—like the time he'd played the entire vocal score from *Oklahoma*. It would have been easy enough, but if Dr. Beale pulled down something he thought wouldn't challenge Gerard, he'd add conditions.

"*Oklahoma*," Dr. Beale had said, pulling the music out. "Okay. Ha! Here, do it. Oh, and play double-stops to add harmony," he'd said, waving his hand around. "Make it up as you go along."

In the long run Gerard came to love playing the cello—probably because Dr. Beale had been so consistently cheerful and energetic—but in the early days he despised it. It was so difficult in the beginning, and the feeling was so foreign to him that he couldn't imagine why anyone would be drawn playing an instrument. And as with any uninteresting task that demanded attention, his mind glided to more appealing places. He spent much of the early rehearsals lamenting the fact that he wasn't downstairs in the basement with his father, cutting and polishing diamonds.

Gerard worked in the cool basement with Willem so often—especially when Rebecca was away on singing trips—that he knew every cut of diamond: the pear, the marquise, the baguette. He loved the feel of the saw and the whir of the iron polishing wheel. Willem's instruction was demanding and precise. Gerard could not recall a time when he didn't know anything about diamonds. What he did remember is that he started learning how to use the machinery at age six. Did Rebecca know what was going on down there all that time? In later years Gerard spent so much time in the basement with diamonds that Rebecca would look scared, then upset, then crazed.

"Gerard, have you practiced your cello today?" she would say as she glowered at Willem.

"Two and a half hours, Mom," Gerard would answer.

"He's going to be a real Yo Yo Ma!" Willem would say, smiling and sipping dark ale from a glass chalice.

Rebecca would sigh. "He needs to practice more."

And then her face would slide downward. Gerard came to recognize the pattern instantly—the hints that signaled Rebecca's imminent descent into her own dark fog. Nothing Willem or Gerard could say or do would pull her out or stop the long, gloomy spiral accentuated by long sighs.

"You need to practice more if you want to be really good," Rebecca would say quietly, mounting the stairs to go sit in Anna's dark room.

Gerard remembered wanting to become a better musician, but looking back on it now he realized his motivation in the early days was his mother. How she beamed when he played Bach's "Prelude to Cello Suite #1," and what a rush that gave him. She cried so often, there in the living room with pictures of Anna, that it gave Gerard a huge flood of happiness and warmth to see her pleased with him. His love for diamonds had come naturally, from the start, but the cello—he had learned to love the cello. For years he'd worked at it to please his mother, and then—probably around age ten, it was hard to remember—something inside him changed and he became as possessed as his mother had been.

Now as Gerard stood in line outside the D-FAC, towering over Private Jameson and staring at the bald top of his head while they waited for chow, he had a realization: in those early years he must have believed that if he played enough cello Rebecca would have become so pleased her depression would be cured. It was up to him to rescue her from the grip of her illness. The poor little guy, Gerard thought! He'd really believed that, though he could never have articulated it then. Only now did this idea present itself to Gerard; it had taken the expanse of silence and inactivity given to him by the United States Army to cause this thought to arise. After all, when was the last time he had spent twenty minutes doing nothing? It had simply never happened. In his everyday life there were always distractions available to him: the cello, diamonds, his Monroe Hill College studies, seeing Sylvia, watching television. But what did he have now? He knew what he had now: he had the top and back of Private Jameson's scaly head, so it made sense that his mind looked for other places to wander.

Gerard remembered thinking as a boy that his mother faked her depression to make him feel guilty, to make him feel responsible. Such silly logic was perfectly normal for a young child, but Gerard knew better now. Whenever Rebecca Ward chose to blame anyone for anything, it was Willem. It was always Willem. If by 10:30 at night the dogs hadn't had their dinner, she blamed Willem. If Rebecca came home and Gerard was watching television instead of practicing cello, she blamed Willem.

"If you came out of that cellar for even fifteen minutes you'd see that Gerard is not practicing," she would say, with a slam of the basement door. "Gerard, turn off that idiot-box and get into the parlor."

And when Willem and seven-year-old Gerard had stepped off the airplane at Dulles Airport, from Antwerp, escorting the body of two-year-old Anna Kelderman in a padlocked carton, Rebecca didn't even have to say it. To her it was simple cause and effect: when Rebecca had left her daughter with Willem, Anna had been alive, and when he returned with her, she was dead.

It *was* in Belgium that Anna had died, and Gerard had been there. Why hadn't his parents told him that? They knew he'd forgotten almost everything, and they were always evasive when Gerard asked questions about the accident. He'd never persisted with his questions, though, because he could see the pain he caused by asking. "Why was that car driving on the sidewalk?" little Gerard would ask, and Rebecca would stroke his hair as her eyes filled with tears. He would have a faint memory, like a flash of a café somewhere in the Belgian countryside, he'd ask his mom or dad about it, and then he'd stop. It was the expressions on their faces. In Willem it was dejection and the slump of a deflated spinal column. With Rebecca it was incessant weeping or silent gloom or violent anger, though she never inflicted her anger on Gerard; Willem was the lightning rod for her rage. By the time Gerard reached his early teens he so feared these reactions that he'd stopped asking about Anna.

It was also the time he'd stopped going into her room. Rebecca wanted the room maintained as a shrine, and no one except her was ever allowed in. There was a pea-coal fireplace in that room, but even Nelson was ordered to stay out. Years later when Nelson died, Rebecca hired a maid who was allowed to enter Anna's bedroom once a week only to clean it. Rebecca gave her meticulous instructions—how the things on the shrine at the far end of the room were to be dusted or laundered and then placed back in exactly the same spot. The three significant items at the center of the small table, between the two lavender candles, were a pair of pink gingham shorts that Anna had worn the day before leaving for Antwerp, a blue pacifier that had fallen behind the crib during Anna's last night sleeping at the Kasteel, and the book *Hop On Pop*—the last bed-time story that was read to her. On Sunday afternoons Rebecca would open the doors and windows for exactly two hours to air out the room. Hrothgar, Rebecca's beef-eating cat, had one day grabbed the brown stuffed teddy bear from the edge of the altar. Rebecca had cornered Hrothgar in an upstairs hallway closet, wrestled the bear away from him, and wiped off the sticky cat spit before returning it to Anna's room.

But even with all these icons as reminders Gerard couldn't remember the details of the accident. He remembered Anna, his only sister—sweet little baby Anna, with her stuffed "hippomuspottamus" and her insistence, right at age two, of doing everything "by myself." These faint memories of his baby sister stirred up a sadness in Gerard that he had learned to control from an early age.

At first he'd learned to use the cello to quiet his grief. If he couldn't hide in the cool underground of the diamond workshop, he always had his cello. He would think of Anna—the way she liked to strip off her diaper and run squealing through the upstairs hall—and the sadness would churn gently at the bottom of his belly. As it moved up toward his throat, he would run to his cello and play. It was a race. The sadness would begin its slow, swirling dance in his stomach and writhe upward. Slowly up his esophagus it would sway, inching up his neck toward his throat. But Gerard would always win; he kept his grief in check by racing to the cello. He always reached his cello in time.

As soon as his bow stroked the moaning C string the sorrow would slide back down, and when that happened Gerard would play and play to keep forcing the sadness downward. He'd reach to the music parlor wall and pull out whatever his hand touched—the way Dr. Beale always did. Even when he was alone Gerard would honor the rules of the game; it comforted him. He had to give the same attention to the trite "Celeste Aida" as to pieces he loved, like Ralph Vaughan Williams's *Fantasia on a Theme of Thomas Tallis*. When Gerard felt sad, familiar routines pulled him through. There was solace in the structure of Dr. Beale's game; within the confines of the structured ritual, Gerard found something outside himself— something hopeful and good.

And once he hit that place, he couldn't stop. Private Cooper, who had apprenticed himself to gurus in India, had described deep meditation the same way—that you often start by focusing and quieting the chattering mind, but eventually you reach a place of deep peace where you're locked in. Gerard was sure that in those moments he could have played the cello for days without stopping if he hadn't been limited by his body. He would play until his left forearm hurt so badly he could no longer move it; the tendons would tingle and buzz, and then his arm would stop. Gerard would collapse on the red leather couch under the bay window of the music parlor and sleep, and when he finally woke up—usually as Rebecca was covering him with a blanket and telling him dinner was nearly ready—he'd have forgotten all about Anna.

"Ten more minutes, men." Drill Sergeant Womack was coming out the front door of the D-FAC.

"What are they doin' in there?" Hammer said to Womack. "We got training to get to."

"Yeah, I know," Womack said. "Hurry up and wait." Womack adjusted his hat. "Platoon Guide!"

"Yes, Drill Sergeant," said Snodgrass.

"You keep this platoon quiet," said Womack.

"Yes, Drill Sergeant."

Both drill sergeants disappeared back toward the company area.

And while Gerard's parents competed with each other to see which craft—diamonds or the cello—Gerard would master more fully, there was an unspoken rule of tolerance for each other and for their agendas. Not so with learning Flemish. For reasons Gerard would understand only later, Rebecca forbade Willem to teach Gerard and Anna how to speak Flemish.

"What's the point, Willem?" she would ask her husband. "How the hell is learning *Flemish* going to help them at all, ever?"

Rebecca always leaned into the word *Flemish* that way whenever she used it; it was her way of sneering. Dutch would have been useless enough, Rebecca always said, but teaching Gerard "a dialect of Dutch" would have been an even bigger waste of time.

"Dialect?" Willem would say, slamming his palm on the kitchen table. "Dutch?" If anything got Willem Kelderman's blood boiling, it was the mention of anything Dutch. Like most citizens of Flanders Willem hated the Dutch more than he hated French-speaking Belgians.

"Belgium's the size of Maryland, Willem," Rebecca would say. "And the Flemish-speaking side is half that. What's the point?"

But for Willem it wasn't about points. Gerard knew that Willem had always felt guilty about emigrating from Belgium to the United States, and that teaching his children Flemish would have let him hang on to at least one of the many parts of his culture he'd left behind: Flemish food, Flemish social customs, and everyone in his family. It was Willem's family—the Kelderman-De Boek clan in Brasschaat, outside Antwerp—that incessantly hammered Willem with feelings of guilt. His older brother Robin was especially vicious, accusing Willem of abandoning their mother and leaving Robin to take of her in her old age. To this day Robin would call Willem in Evans Glen—as he had on every Sunday evening for the past twenty-five years—and rip Willem apart for leaving Belgium, for not caring about their mother. And each time it was the same: Willem would spend fifteen minutes on the phone with Robin, the exchange would turn nasty and then end, and Willem would descend to the basement to work with his diamonds for an hour.

And when the teach-the-kids-Flemish argument came around between Willem and Rebecca, Rebecca always won with her forcefulness. Willem did manage to teach Gerard small phrases every now and then, some *Goeindag* (Hello) or *Tot ziens* (See you later), but nothing of consequence. Then came the accident that killed baby Anna, and Willem underwent his own bout of fanaticism. To hell with Rebecca, Gerard was going to learn Flemish. Perhaps Willem was alarmed by losing fully one-half of his offspring: now his only hope of keeping Flemish alive in the family was Gerard. From the time Gerard was seven Willem would speak Flemish to him in the basement at the Kasteel while they worked on diamonds. He returned from one of his trips to Antwerp with cassette tapes to help Gerard learn. Thankfully these were not boring language-instruction tapes; they were albums from one of north Belgium's most crass stand-up comedians: Grote Van Kloten.

Willem had to know what was in those Grote Van Kloten albums; he had to know that he was exposing Gerard to some of the most vulgar swear words in the Flemish language. And Gerard loved them. He would close the doors of his room upstairs and listen to the tapes, memorizing complete monologues from stand-up routines and full albums of songs, even before he completely understood what all the words meant. Sometimes when Rebecca heard Gerard cackling in his room, she would demand that Willem tell her why Gerard was laughing.

"Jesus Christ, Willem, you're exposing our son to this?" she had said, after Willem had translated a line in a song about Grote's younger sister having a sexual relationship with her Uncle Hector. "Get down into the parlor and pick up your cello, Gerard."

One cold December afternoon, Willem had some Flemish friends over for beer at the Kasteel. Gerard remembered that Joske Vermeulen, a fellow master diamond-cutter, was there. Who else had been sitting in the living room that day? Tall and curvy Margareta Van Leuven was there, an Antwerp contact of Willem's who was in charge of his overseas diamond sales. They were all sipping beer around the coffee table when Willem summoned Gerard downstairs.

"*Luister, hé? Hij kan al in 't Vlaams zingen,*" Willem said to his friends, boasting about Gerard's Flemish singing skills. "Gerard, sing to us from Grote!"

So Gerard let them have it. Rebecca was there too, but she didn't understand any of the words. For this performance Gerard chose one of Grote's finest compositions: *Ik Loop Achterover en de Geiten Geven Over*, a slow blues ballad about walking backwards into goat vomit. He was convinced only Grote Van Kloten could make such a silly song work, but Gerard didn't even make it through the first chorus before Willem, Joske, and Margareta were howling and sloshing beer all over the furniture. Rebecca's jaws clenched and her face flushed red. She stood up and rushed out of the living room, but not before telling Willem to "clean up this goddamn mess."

♦ ♦ ♦

Gerard was tired of memorizing the contours on Private Jameson's head. At last the chow line started moving. Breakfast! Gerard had been hungry for a week and would wake each morning fantasizing about pancakes with strawberries and real maple syrup. He wanted strong coffee swirled with milk and cream, or fresh-squeezed orange juice with all that lovely pulp. And because of the abuse his muscles had suffered during the past week (would his pectoral and bicep muscles ever stop aching from all the push-ups?), he craved the protein of plump breakfast sausage and salty ham and thick bacon. Only meat would repair the tearing and shredding of muscles that came with push-ups and pull-ups.

Pull-ups were actually easy, so far, since soldiers were required to do only one pull-up before each meal. On the way into the D-FAC this morning each man had stopped at the bar to do one pull-up. Gerard had never really done pull-ups before, but he had managed to heave his stout trunk upward far enough to stretch his chin above the bar. Before every meal during this first week of training they had to do one pull-up. Next week it would be two pull-ups. The theory was that by the end of thirteen weeks every soldier in the platoon would be able to do thirteen pull-ups.

Poor Private Carroll. He weighed 250 pounds, just like Gerard, but his height was only six feet, and his mass was proportioned in thick blobs around his waist and neck. Carroll had arrived at Fort Benning a month earlier than the other recruits—weighing a solid 270 pounds—but since he was unable to do the minimum thirteen push-ups at the reception station, he'd had to endure a month in the Fitness Training Unit ("with all the other fat boys," Fuller had said) until he could do the push-ups. Fuller informed Third Platoon that between five and eight percent of all new recruits now ended up in the FTU.

But even though he was now stronger and had lost some weight, Carroll still could not manage even one pull-up. Yesterday he hung from the bar, sweating and grunting as everyone else waited for the drill sergeants to yell or ridicule or make fat jokes. Instead there was silence; they left him hanging there. Finally Cooper broke formation and wrapped his arms as far as they would go a-round Carroll's waist. Cooper heaved and grunted, but Carroll was too heavy for him. Only when Private Cory emerged from Second Squad did Carroll do his pull-up. Cory was tall and lean with a thin waist and wide shoulders; he had been an Olympic diver before entering the army. Cooper stepped out of the way, and Cory wedged his hands under Carroll's armpits. When Cory lifted, Carroll shot straight up and bumped his nose and chin on the bar. Cory lowered him back down and the three of them returned to the formation.

And there'd been no yelling from the drill sergeants! They were standing right there watching—both Drill Sergeant Hammer and Drill Sergeant Womack. Why didn't they say anything? It was frustrating. Gerard was sure he had figured out their main rule: don't do anything until you're told. But here Cooper and Cory had made a decision on their own, and the drill sergeants said nothing. Did this mean they approved? Did it mean they were tired and didn't care? Gerard didn't think it was apathy; he'd closely watched Womack, whose eyes stayed riveted on Carroll, as if he were studying.

The day before, upstairs in the bay, Drill Sergeant Womack had calmly explained that if his billets weren't spotless within ten minutes he was going to initiate a full-gear inspection (Gerard hadn't yet heard the word "billets"—apparently it was another outdated army term). Third Platoon would later learn about full-gear inspections: dragging every single piece of issued equipment from the wall lockers down the stairs and spreading it all out in rigid order on the floor of the company area. As soon as Womack was done speaking, Private Libby had dashed from the end of his bunk and started straightening the blanket on his bed.

"Libby!"

"Yes, Drill Sergeant."

"Why did you move?" Womack had said.

"Because I thought—"

"You're not being paid to think! Get back at attention until I dismiss you."

So there they had it; very simple. Not thinking was easy—simply wait to be told what to do. It was like being a kid again. But now Cooper had upset the formula by deciding on his own to help Carroll, and the drill sergeants hadn't ripped his head off. Gerard couldn't figure out the pattern or the logic. Maybe that was the point.

"Squeeze in tight, men," said Drill Sergeant Hammer. "Make your buddy smile."

The drill sergeants walked through the glass door from the lobby into the D-FAC. Gerard watched as Womack's cauliflower ear disappeared around the corner.

Man, if one of the recruits had had an ear like that, they'd never have heard the end of it. Two human characteristics were irresistible to drill sergeants: funny names and physical deformities. First Platoon had a Private Butts, the poor guy. The platoon guide for Fourth Platoon had a huge, brown birthmark from his left cheek bone down to his chin. If the drill sergeants were feeling compassionate, he was Private Patch; otherwise, it was Shitface.

Gerard thought of his dad's deformity. People didn't really notice Willem Kelderman's missing ring finger unless they were paying close attention. And when someone did see it, there were varieties of reactions. Some ignored it. Some couldn't stop staring at it. Every once in a while someone would ask what happened, prompting one of Willem's three versions of the answer. The first was simply to say there'd been an accident. The second was slightly more detailed—that he'd been making repairs to his diamond wheel and had gotten his finger caught in the machinery. Then if there was time, and if Willem liked the person who was asking, he'd give the full story.

It had been December 1987, when Gerard was seven years old. Willem was bent down under the scaife—the diamond polishing wheel—trying to adjust the motor and belt. Nelson was in the basement of the Kasteel that day too, tanked up on Captain Morgan's Rum, and was poking around in front of the machine, fingering the parts and asking questions. "What's this do?" he said as he pressed the green power button, right as Willem had his hand wrapped around the motor belt. The machine kicked on, and the 3,000 r.p.m. motor yanked Willem's ring finger between the belt and the metal pulley, crushing the bone and severing his finger.

Unfortunately there was someone else in the basement that day as well: Hrothgar the meat-eating cat. Willem remembered later that he'd seen Hrothgar perched on the floor near the old furnace, probably stalking a mouse. When Willem screamed and the spinning belt flung his finger onto the dusty basement floor, Hrothgar pounced and snatched it up. Rebecca found the bone—actually three bones, attached by dried ligaments—a week later on the pantry floor. She had thought it was an old toy of some sort, but then she'd seen the wedding ring next to it. She saved the bones and locked them in a jewelry box on her dresser.

"Squad leader Kelderman. Kick ass!" said Romberg, from the back of the chow line.

Gerard shook his head. Squad leader. Why was he put in charge of anything?

"You'll do fine," said Cooper, who was standing in line behind Gerard.

"I'm not cut out for this," Gerard said.

"Embrace it," Cooper said. "What do you have to lose?"

"Well, let's see: sleep, my dignity, my life."

Cooper smiled. "When it's all over you'll be glad you did it."

"Shut up in line over there," said Snodgrass, settling in to his new role as platoon guide.

"Man, fuck you, Snodgrass," said Parker.

Romberg laughed.

"Drill sergeant put me in charge," said Snodgrass, adjusting his glasses.

"In charge of what?" Parker said.

"The platoon."

"That include me, asshole?" Parker said.

Snodgrass frowned and sighed.

"I didn't think so," said Parker. "This is bullshit, man."

"What's bullshit, Parker?" Romberg said. "You think you should be in charge?"

"Hell yeah," Parker said.

"Mutiny, man! Rock and roll," said Romberg. "Let's overthrow the government—what do you say?"

"Whack, man." Parker shook his head and pursed his lips. He was trying to stay serious, but it wasn't working. He chuckled. "You ain't right."

The platoon lurched like a slow assembly line through the glass doors and into the dining hall. One by one each soldier grabbed a tray and a large spoon before side-stepping along the triple-railed metal ledge in front of the serving area. The drill sergeants materialized and broke the silence.

"Move it, men," said Hammer. "We ain't got all day. Grab a plate and move."

"You better side-step, Libby," yelled Womack. "And keep that head looking straight forward."

Libby straightened his spine and tucked his chin.

"I thought you were a squad leader, Libby," said Womack. "You should be leading by example."

"Yes, Dill Sergeant." Libby's tray flipped up off the rail and his spoon flew across the room.

"Airborne!" yelled Romberg.

"Romberg, shut up," said Hammer. "Drop and give me ten."

"No push-ups in the D-FAC, Drill Sergeant Hammer," said Womack.

"You gettin' smoked outside, Romberg," Hammer said.

"Private Libby, how did that happen?" Womack said.

"My hand slipped, Drill Sergeant," said Libby.

"You're uncoordinated, aren't you, Libby?" said Womack.

"No, I mean, yes, Drill Sergeant."

"What's your favorite fruit juice, Libby?" said Womack.

"I don't know, Drill Sergeant."

"It doesn't matter anyway, because you won't be getting any today."

"No, Drill Sergeant."

"Grab that plate and move out."

Libby snatched the plate of eggs, potatoes, and bacon from the ledge above the serving line and side-stepped along toward the toast and fruit bins.

Gerard studied the plates on the ledge.

"Grab one and go, Private Kelderman," yelled Womack. "This isn't a four-star restaurant."

Gerard took a plate with a lump of biscuit smothered by gray sauce. He moved through the line and sat at a long table in the mess hall.

"Sit on the edge of your chair, and sit up straight," yelled Hammer.

Gerard thought of Dr. Beale and the cello. *The edge of the chair, dammit, the edge.*

"Eat up, ladies, we have training to get to," Womack said.

"What the fuck is *this*?" Hammer said.

Each man put his spoon down and looked at Drill Sergeant Hammer.

"Keep eating!" screamed Womack. "He didn't tell you to stop."

"Private Parker, what's that on your plate?" Hammer said.

Parker sat up straight. "Breakfast, Drill Sergeant."

"Is that bread, Parker?"

"Yes, Drill Sergeant."

"How many pieces, Parker?" said Hammer.

"Three, Drill Sergeant."

"What? *Three*?" Hammer said. "Drill Sergeant Womack, this private has three pieces of bread."

"Parker, you must be special," Womack said.

"You tell me why everybody else only gets two pieces of bread, Parker," said Hammer.

"Who's your squad leader?" said Drill Sergeant Womack.

"Private Kelderman, Drill Sergeant."

"Kelderman!" said Womack.

Gerard choked down a dry knot of biscuit. "Yes, Drill Sergeant."

"Why does Private Parker have three pieces of bread?"

"I don't know, Drill Sergeant."

"You said you'd been to college, Kelderman. I thought you were smart," Womack said. "Private Parker is in your squad. It's your duty to inform him of the rules here."

"Yes, Drill Sergeant."

"So inform him."

Gerard looked across the table at Parker. "Private Parker, you're only allowed two pieces of bread."

"You mean you didn't know that, Parker?" said Hammer.

"Yes, Drill Sergeant, I did know," Parker said.

"Then you fucked up, didn't you, Parker?" said Hammer.

"You screwed up, didn't you, Kelderman?" Womack said.

"Yes, Drill Sergeant!" chimed Parker and Gerard.

"What are you going to do now, Private Kelderman?" said Womack.

"I—I don't know, Drill Sergeant."

"Tell you what," said Womack. "When Drill Sergeant Hammer and I come back here in thirty seconds, this problem had better be fixed."

"Yes, Drill Sergeant," said Gerard.

The drill sergeants walked away from the table.

"Get rid of it, Parker," said Gerard.

"Fuck you, man."

"Eat it," said Berkowicz. "Quick."

"Don't do it, man," Snodgrass said. "They'll know."

"You're some fucking platoon guide," said Berkowicz.

"Fuck off," said Snodgrass.

"Get rid of it, Parker," Gerard said.

Romberg reached across the table and grabbed the bread. Parker lunged at Romberg's hand, but Romberg stuffed the bread into his mouth.

Parker sat back down. "I'll kill you, asshole."

Romberg chewed.

"Problem solved," said Snodgrass.

Gerard looked at Parker. "You got me in trouble."

Parker snarled. "Tough shit."

"I'm the squad leader, and you're supposed to do what I say," said Gerard.

Parker threw a fist across the table and punched Gerard in the jaw. Gerard's chair tilted back and he fell on the floor with a crash.

"Yes!" yelled Romberg. "The knockout punch." Romberg sprang up from the table, unbuttoned his BDU shirt, pulled off his undershirt, and ran circles around the mess hall tables.

The drill sergeants rushed over. Once again every soldier in the mess hall stopped eating to watch.

"Romberg, sit your ass down." Drill Sergeant Hammer ran after him.

Womack stood over Gerard. "Private Kelderman, why are you lying on the floor?"

Gerard stood up and groaned. He held his hand against his jaw. He glanced at Parker. Parker looked down at his tray and started shoveling his face with scrambled eggs.

"I fell, Drill Sergeant," Gerard said.

Womack looked at Gerard's jaw, then at Parker, then back at Gerard.

"Well get back up." Womack pointed at Parker's tray. "I see our little bread problem is solved."

"Yes, Drill Sergeant," said Gerard.

"Knockout punch!" Romberg sprinted among the tables. "Rock and roll!"

"But there's another problem, Kelderman."

"What, Drill Sergeant?"

"Pull your head out, Kelderman," Womack said. "Isn't Romberg in your squad?"

"Yes, Drill Sergeant."

"Did you tell him to throw off his shirt and run around the mess hall like a Victory Drive stripper?" Womack said.

Romberg jumped up onto a table and tiptoed among the trays.

"No, Drill Sergeant."

"He's doing a table dance, Kelderman, and you're his squad leader," Womack said. "How do you explain this?"

"I can't control him, Drill Sergeant."

"Why not, Kelderman?" said Womack. "Aren't you the leader?"

"I'm not a leader, Drill Sergeant."

"Yes you are."

"I didn't ask to be a leader," said Gerard.

"Doesn't matter," Womack said. "You're in charge. You're responsible for every swinging Richard in your squad."

Romberg jumped down from the table and raised his stocky arms with clenched fists. "Yes!"

Hammer picked up Romberg's shirt and threw it at him. "Put on your shirt, Private. You're comin' with me."

"Eat your chow, Kelderman," said Womack. "I'll deal with you later. Private Carroll, why are you just sitting there?"

"I'm done, Drill Sergeant."

"Good God, Carroll. We've only been in the D-FAC for two seconds, and you're finished eating."

"Yes, Drill Sergeant."

"You're a human vacuum cleaner, aren't you Carroll?"

"Yes, Drill Sergeant."

"Is that why you're such a fatty?" said Womack.

"Yes, Drill Sergeant."

"Since you're so good at eating, I think you should be the mess hall motivator," said Womack. "Do you know what that is?"

"No, Drill Sergeant," Carroll said.

"That means you get to make everybody else eat faster," said Womack. "Stand up. It's your job to motivate your platoon mates to scarf and barf. Go to it, Carroll."

Carroll looked around and then looked back at Drill Sergeant Womack.

"Let's go Carroll. Tell them to eat faster."

"Eat faster!" yelled Carroll.

"That's it," said Womack. "Now walk around and make sure they can hear you."

"Eat faster! Come on, let's move. Wiley, eat faster."

"Hey, fuck you, man."

Womack slammed his hands onto the table. "Private Wiley, you don't speak to the mess hall motivator that way. Are you volunteering for the job?"

"No, Drill Sergeant."

"Then shut up and eat," said Womack. "Carroll, Private Yanni is not eating fast enough. I want you to motivate him."

"Eat faster, Cooper!"

"Get over there close to him, Carroll," said Womack. "He can't hear you."

Carroll leaned over the table. "Eat, Cooper, eat."

Cooper ate evenly, slowly chewing his hash browns.

"Louder, Carroll."

"Faster, Cooper!"

"He can't hear you," said Womack.

"Eat faster, Cooper!"

The clicking and clatter of spoons at the table quickened, but Cooper kept his own pace.

"Yanni, sometimes I feel like we're not getting through to you," said Womack. "Are we getting through to you, Private Yanni?"

Cooper stopped eating and sat straight. "Yes, Drill Sergeant."

"Are you meditating after each bite, Yanni?"

"No, Drill Sergeant."

"Is this food healthy enough for you?"

"Yes, Drill Sergeant," Cooper said.

"Do you wish we served granola and wheat grass, Yanni?"

"No, Drill Sergeant."

"You're a soldier now, Yanni, so eat like one," Womack said.

"Yes, Drill Sergeant."

"Chow's over, Third Platoon," said Womack. "Move out!"

Chairs scraped the floor. The platoon stood up and moved toward the exit.

"Squad leaders, make sure your people put their trays on the belt," said Womack. "Push in your chair, Libby."

The soldiers shoved out the doors of the D-FAC.

"Platoon Guide, I want a formation back in the company area," said Womack.

"Yes, Drill Sergeant," said Snodgrass. "Move it, men."

A stampede of combat boots shuffled out the door and down the long breezeway to the company area.

"Form up, men," said Snodgrass. "Quick. Romberg, where have you been? You're all wet."

Romberg gasped. "Drill sergeant—smoked—me."

"Get into formation," said Snodgrass. "Squad leaders, make sure everybody's here."

Gerard's squad—Fourth Squad—was lined up in the back row. He counted fourteen, including himself.

"Put that apple away, Carroll," said Wiley. "No food outside the mess hall."

"Someone has food?" said Snodgrass.

"Carroll smuggled an apple out of the D-FAC," Wiley said.

"Gonna fuck the whole platoon," Parker said.

"Get rid of it, Carroll," said Snodgrass.

"I'm still hungry," Carroll said. "It's in my pocket."

"They'll notice." Wiley pointed. "I can see it from here."

"Idiot," said Libby.

"You take it." Carroll tossed it to Libby.

Libby lobbed it to Snodgrass. Snodgrass pitched it back to Carroll. Carroll threw it to Gerard.

Drill Sergeant Womack walked around the corner. "Kelderman!"

"Yes, Drill Sergeant."

"Get out here."

Gerard shoved the apple into the right cargo pocket of his BDU pants and ran forward.

"Get in the front-leaning rest position, Kelderman," said Womack.

Gerard got down into push-up position.

"Snodgrass, you get down too."

Snodgrass dropped to the concrete.

"Private Romberg is having a little trouble adjusting to military life," said Womack. "Kelderman, you're his squad leader. Snodgrass, you're the platoon guide. When Romberg has one of his little episodes, I'm holding you responsible. It might cure him. Let's start with push-ups."

"One Drill Sergeant, two Drill Sergeant."

Gerard's arms had no trouble with the push-ups, but the half-chewed food in his stomach felt like a clot of lead.

"Okay, stand up," said Womack. "Now run in place."

Gerard and Snodgrass ran in place, facing the platoon.

"Stop. Get down and do push-ups until I tell you to stop."

They dropped down and started pumping.

"Stop," said Womack. "Get up. Run in place."

They stood up and ran.

"Stop. Get down. Push-ups."

Gerard leaned down. The apple rolled out of his pocket. Fifty-seven silent heads watched the apple bounce across the floor before bumping into Drill Sergeant Womack's spit-shined left boot.

Womack looked down at the apple and then at Gerard. "Private Kelderman, are you still hungry?"

"No, Drill Sergeant," Gerard moaned.

"Kelderman, is this the mess hall?"

"No, Drill Sergeant."

"Then why do you have food?" said Womack.

"I—it wasn't—" Gerard looked up at the platoon. Carroll's eyes were wide.

"Snodgrass, get into formation," Womack said.

Snodgrass jumped up and ran to the back.

"Push-ups, Kelderman, move. Stop. Get up. Run in place."

Gerard ran. The fatty biscuit bounced in his gut. Sweat rolled off his bald head, down his face, and onto his shirt.

"Faster, Kelderman, move. Stop. Get down."

Gerard slowly leaned down.

"Too slow. Get up. Run in place."

Gerard ran, but only the heels of his heavy boots would lift off the floor. He felt dizzy. His head burned hot.

"Too slow. Get down."

Gerard leaned over. Saliva coated the walls of his mouth an instant before the thick, knobby sauce rushed up his esophagus and forced chunks of biscuit out onto the concrete floor. He was on his hands and knees, facing the platoon, pitching forward and heaving out his entire breakfast.

"Private Kelderman, why are you barfing in my company area?" Womack said.

Gerard wiped the goop from his lips and stood up.

"Get into the latrine and clean yourself up, Kelderman," said Womack. "Third Platoon, you have ten minutes to get up there and clean the barracks before we move out for training. Platoon Guide, get out here and make sure this puke gets cleaned up."

"Yes, Drill Sergeant."

"Fall out!"

# Four

It was now Monday morning on the eleventh day of training. Third Platoon sat silently in the mess hall, frantically shoveling breakfast. Five long days had passed since Gerard had performed his vomiting act in front of Third Platoon. Snodgrass and the squad leaders had agreed that the platoon needed to get out of bed half an hour before the normal wake-up time so they could be dressed and the barracks cleaned when the drill sergeants arrived. So each morning at 4 a.m. Third Platoon woke up and began madly preparing for the day with their flashlights on. During this time Gerard had to square away his own area and make sure his squad members were pulling their weight as well. He'd only had to be strict once when he'd discovered that Mueller had crawled underneath his bunk and gone back to sleep while everyone else cleaned.

For the past few days Bravo Company had suffered through even more classroom instruction. Gerard wouldn't have thought it possible that the army could come up with enough topics to fill days and days of classroom instruction. They'd been subjected to classes on customs, core values, leadership, and sexual harassment. The 1/47th battalion sergeant major had given a talk, as had the battalion commander—Lieutenant Colonel Pinkerton. Gerard remembered his name because soldiers were forced to memorize their chain of command, from company commander all the way up to the president. Recruits were also required to memorize pages and pages of useless information from the IET (Initial Entry Training) Soldier's handbook (also called the 'smart book'): The Non-Commissioned Officer (NCO) Support Channel, army rank insignia, the Soldier's Code, the Code of Conduct, the three General Orders, military acronyms and abbreviations, and so on. Private Fuller had arrived for basic training with the handbook memorized; he said his father, a company first sergeant at Fort Leonard Wood, had forced him to study it every day since he was a freshman in high school.

Third Platoon finished breakfast. Gerard chewed his bacon as he jogged out of the D-FAC. He shuffled back into the company area and joined Fourth Squad at the back of the platoon formation. He burped and tasted cherry Jell-O. To eat more quickly Gerard had mimicked a trick he'd seen other platoon members employ. Whenever Jell-O was available at a meal, Gerard used it as a cooling agent. Regardless of what was on his plate, he would dump on a serving of Jell-O and stir the whole mess to cool it down. The food would taste funny, but these days eating wasn't about enjoyment—it was about refueling. He'd had some interesting dishes during the past few days: chili mac with lime Jell-O, spaghetti with meat sauce with orange Jell-O, and this morning, eggs and sausage with cherry Jell-O. Perhaps after basic training Gerard could put his ideas into a cookbook, *Eating the Army Way*.

"Okay, Third Platoon," said Womack. "First and Second Platoon have already drawn weapons. It's our turn. One squad at a time. Start with First Squad. Platoon, Atten—tion!"

The boot heels clicked together and all eyes looked straight ahead.

"Right—Face. File from the left, column left—March."

First Squad peeled away, one soldier at a time, from the platoon formation and jogged toward the arms room. This was the first day Bravo Company would handle the M16 rifle—M16A2, Fuller had clarified. First Squad formed a line along the brick wall behind the arms room window, which looked like a bank teller's window with vertical iron bars and a small, rectangular space at the bottom, barely large enough for a rifle to slide through.

Three soldiers from Fourth Platoon were inside the arms room under the supervision of the armorer—a young, skinny specialist-fourth-class who tried to intimidate the recruits by yelling and stamping his feet. Specialist Sanchez squeaked when he spoke, like a hamster being squeezed, but because of his E-4 rank no recruit was allowed to laugh. An E-4 could smoke any basic training recruit, even recruits who had college degrees and had *entered* the army as E-4s. Specialist Griffin in Second Squad had a B.S. in physics and would return home to his National Guard unit in San Diego after infantry school, but aside from referring to his branch of service as "The National Girls," the drill sergeants gave Griffin no particular attention.

"You're moving too slow." Specialist Sanchez's shrill voice trickled through the bars of the window, smothered by the clangs and crashes of locks, chains, and brackets on the rifle racks. The three soldiers grabbed rifles from the racks and shoved them through the bars of the window.

Berkowicz stepped up to the window. A black M16 rifle came shooting through the opening at the bottom of the bars. Berkowicz snatched it just in time. He held the rifle and looked down at it.

"Don't stand there like an idiot, dipshit," yelled Drill Sergeant Hammer. "Move out and get back in formation."

Gerard watched as the soldiers of Third Squad filed by the window, catching rifles as they flew out through the bars.

"Yeah, baby," said Parker. "Won't be long now."

Romberg smiled. "A gun. Rock and roll."

"Kelderman," said Parker. "You ever capped anybody?"

"No," said Gerard, swallowing his last bit of bacon. Gerard was sure he'd never 'capped' anyone.

Libby was shaking his head. "This is going to be awesome."

"Man, Libby, you best not come near me when you got a rifle," said Parker. "You fuck-up."

"Fourth Squad, move out," yelled Hammer.

Gerard jogged to the brick wall and stood in line behind the last soldier in Third Squad. He stepped up to the window and looked through the bars. Someone in the arms room had dropped an M16.

"Shit, Private," squealed Specialist Sanchez. "You think we can go buy another weapon when you fuck it up? Pick the shit up off the floor."

The private grabbed the rifle from the floor and pushed it through the bars. Gerard caught it as it flew by. He stooped as he tried to steady himself and hold on to it. The rifle was heavy and metallic and warm and slippery with oil. He ran back to the formation.

Cooper stopped at the window but didn't extend his arms to catch his rifle. The long, black M16 sailed out through the bars and landed with a smack on the smooth, hard floor of the company area. It bounced and scuffed and scraped along the concrete. Drill Sergeant Hammer picked up the rifle before it could skid to a halt.

"What the fuck?" Hammer said. "Something wrong with your hands, Private?"

Womack walked up to Cooper. "What's the problem, Yanni?"

Cooper stood silent.

Hammer held out the rifle. "Here, Private. Take it."

Cooper didn't move.

"Take the weapon, Yanni," said Womack.

"No, Drill Sergeant."

"What?" Hammer said.

"Why not?" said Womack.

"I can't do it, Drill Sergeant."

Womack screamed. "Take the rifle, Yanni!"

Cooper folded his arms.

Hammer grabbed Cooper's arm. "Get out of line. You're holdin' everybody up."

Carroll and Parker drew their weapons and ran into formation.

"The fuck's wrong with you, Cooper?" said Hammer.

"It doesn't feel right," Cooper said.

Womack threw up his arms. "It doesn't feel right? Hey, Drill Sergeant Hammer, running five miles doesn't *feel* right today, so I'm going to sleep in. Sound okay?"

"Yes! I've got the power!"

Romberg was holding his rifle above his head with both arms.

"King of the world!" Romberg danced in place, turning around in circles and shaking his rifle up and down.

"Settle down, Private!" yelled Hammer. He walked toward Romberg. Romberg ran and hid behind a brick pillar. He peered around the corner of the pillar with wide eyes.

Parker stepped out of formation. "Romberg, what are you doin'?"

Romberg stuck his head out from behind the pillar. "Get out of the way, Parker."

"Man, *fuck* you, Romberg," said Parker. "*Get* your ass back in formation."

Romberg dashed from behind the pillar, holding the butt of the rifle with both hands. He charged at Parker and raised the rifle high above his head, wielding it like a club.

"Romberg!" Womack yelled.

Parker froze in place. "Slow down, man. It's cool."

Romberg charged faster. The veins in his arms poked out around his knobby biceps. "Is it cool, man? *Is* it?" he screamed.

As Gerard watched Romberg run, a movement flashed in the right corner of his eye. He turned and saw Cooper sprinting in a straight line, diagonally across the floor of the company area. In that moment everything ran through Gerard's mind in slow-motion, like the instant-replay of an Olympic gymnastics meet.

Parker stood still, erect. Romberg charged toward Parker, as if he might step into Parker's locked hands and be flipped and twisted gracefully over Parker's head to execute a perfect landing. Cooper dashed toward Parker as well; both Romberg and Cooper were converging on Parker from different corners. When Cooper was within ten feet of Romberg, he lunged into the air, arms extended, hands in front—a smooth, perfect dive. For a moment it seemed the two gymnasts would collide, but Cooper's dive was so high and Romberg was so short that Cooper glided gracefully over Romberg's head and deftly snatched the M16 rifle from his hands.

Romberg slowed to a walk, looking up at his empty hands. Cooper sailed a few more feet before tumbling to the floor, tightly gripping the rifle and holding it to his chest.

Parker lunged at Romberg. "Mother fucker. I'll kill you." He grabbed Romberg's throat and walked him backwards. "Crazy-ass bitch, got no business in this army."

"Let him go, Hot Shit," Hammer said.

"Mother fucker ain't right."

"I know, Hot Shit. Let him go."

Romberg tried to speak through Parker's choke hold. "Parker— I'm sorry man—I didn't mean—"

"*Shut* up," said Parker. "You ain't right."

"No he ain't," said Hammer. "But let him go, Parker."

Parker pushed Romberg away. Romberg gagged and coughed as Drill Sergeant Womack took him by the arm. "Let's go, raven man." They disappeared into the company office and the door slammed behind them.

"Everybody in formation, now!" barked Hammer.

Cooper stood up, still clutching Romberg's rifle. Hammer grabbed it from him and forced another one into his hands.

"This one's yours," said Hammer. "And I don't wanna hear about how it feels."

Cooper ran into formation with his rifle. Drill Sergeant Hammer walked to the arms room window with Romberg's rifle and gave it back to Specialist Sanchez. Cooper stepped into the back row next to Parker, who was still breathing heavily.

Parker looked at Cooper. "Romberg ain't right in the head."

Cooper shrugged. "He's confused. He's been through a lot." He looked down at the M16 in his hands. "I don't know if I can hold on to this. It's so heavy."

"Confused, my ass," said Parker. "He ain't the only one been through a lot."

"His demons are stronger than he is right now, but he'll make it," said Cooper.

"Demons?" said Berkowicz. "His 'demons' are gonna like get someone killed."

Cooper smiled at Berkowicz. "No they aren't."

"He's outta here, man," Wiley said. "He's so outta here."

◆     ◆     ◆

A week passed since the initial weapons issue when Romberg had gone mad and charged across the company area like a possessed troll. Private Wiley was sure Romberg would be removed from the army, though Gerard wondered if it was merely wishful thinking on Wiley's part. Third Platoon knew Romberg was unpredictable and off-balance, but Wiley was actually afraid of him. (This may have been because of Romberg's threatening to grab Wiley "by his red neck and wring his windpipe like a wet fucking towel.") Private Fuller authoritatively assured Third Platoon that Romberg had an uncle who was a three-star general.

"So?" Wiley had said.

"So he'll fucking stay in the army as long as he wants to," Fuller had answered.

"Bullcrap," Wiley had said.

"You'll see," Fuller had said. "It's the way the army works, man."

That evening before chow Romberg had returned to Third Platoon after spending the entire afternoon in the company office. He'd apologized to Parker and told him it wouldn't happen again. Parker had nodded with a squint in his eyes, and Wiley had simply shaken his head. If there'd been doubt in anyone's mind about Fuller's military expertise—even after his incessant spouting of facts and details—there was no question now. No one even thought to ask how Fuller knew out about Romberg's uncle; Gerard later learned that Romberg hadn't told anyone about his brass family ties.

Gerard was tired. His head was heavy. It was 8:30 Sunday evening. Tomorrow Bravo Company would start its third week of training. The platoon sat on the bleachers outside the company area shining boots—a banal ritual, but Gerard looked forward to it every day because the drill sergeants always disappeared. Womack or Hammer would send the platoon up to the bay to get their red ammo cans that contained boot-shining accessories, they'd reconvene in the company area, and then they'd be released to go to the bleachers and shine their boots for twenty minutes before getting ready for bed.

Bed. Gerard couldn't wait. Sometimes the tiredness sank so deeply into him that his eyelids felt as heavy as his combat boots. Twice during a class on military customs he had nodded off; his head had bobbed slowly forward and then snapped backward.

"Stand up, Kelderman!" Hammer had yelled from the back of the room.

Anyone falling asleep while seated in the classroom was forced to stand up. It was less a punishment than a measure to keep it from happening again. But now Third Platoon was shining boots, and soon Gerard would get to sleep. He couldn't remember the last time he'd been excited about going to bed, or the last time he'd gone to bed at *nine o'clock*. The platoon griped about the constant lack of sleep. Libby had remarked that if the drill sergeants would just let him sleep eight or nine hours a night, his brain might be able to retain all these tricky tasks soldiers were expected to master during training.

Food was another cause of complaining and bickering: there was never enough. The dearth of food was only the beginning; there were wildly varying theories about the processing and delivery of the food. Wiley was sure the food was rotten—that the government had to buy old food to get the best deal. Berkowicz had Third Platoon convinced that the army loaded the food with saltpeter, as evidenced by the fact that he hadn't "got a hard-on in three damn weeks." Regardless of what was in the food or where it came from, everyone agreed that they needed more.

Romberg complained most loudly about the food—even more loudly than Carroll; he was always bartering with other soldiers for more food. One day in the field he had offered Parker five dollars for a corn muffin.

"What the fuck I'm gonna do with five dollars?" Parker had asked Romberg. "Walk downtown and buy some more food?"

But Romberg was never deterred from trying to increase his caloric intake. The day before, during dinner, Second Platoon had kitchen duty—KP, though no one ever used the term 'kitchen police'—so they had to help serve the food in the D-FAC. When Romberg side-stepped in front of the bread tray, he tried to convince the bread-guy from Second Platoon that the heel of the loaf of bread wasn't a real slice and therefore didn't count toward the rationed two slices.

"Hey man, you gave me a heel," said Romberg.

"Yeah?" said the bread-guy. "So what?"

"So you're supposed to give me another one," Romberg said.

"No way—you only get two slices."

"The heel doesn't count, dude!" Romberg said. "Let loose and gimme another slice."

Romberg held up the chow line arguing with the bread-guy about how the heel didn't count—that if you got a heel, you got two normal slices of bread in addition. It nearly worked; Romberg almost got away with three slices of bread, but in the end the bread-guy stood firm. Romberg had to take a heel as one of his two pieces.

"Fucking Second Platoon piece of fucking shit," growled Romberg.

"It's two pieces," said the bread-guy, shrugging his shoulders.

"I'm gonna kick your fucking ass," said Romberg as he side-stepped away. "I'll kick your whole platoon's ass. Second Fucking Platoon."

And so began Romberg's obsession with "Second Fucking Platoon." After the bread incident, Romberg would stand in formation, thinking out loud about how to exact revenge on Second Platoon.

"When we have KP we could piss on their bacon."

"That's really gross, Romberg," said Carroll.

"The food's already gross," said Wiley. "I'm tellin' you man, it's surplus food."

"And anyway, Romberg, it wasn't the whole platoon that gave you the heel," Carroll pointed out. "It was just that one guy."

"Yeah, but I can't remember what he looks like," Romberg admitted. "Fuckers all look the same."

"Let it go, Romberg," said Private Hopson, a light-skinned black soldier in Third Squad.

Cooper nodded vigorously.

But Romberg wasn't interested in letting go. It reminded Gerard of his mother, Rebecca. Letting go was something Willem would always try to tell Rebecca to do. "Let it go, Rebecca" ran a close second to "Calm down, Rebecca." Neither ever worked.

"Let it go?" Rebecca would say. "How's Gerard going to get into the National Symphony Orchestra if he doesn't practice more? Let it go. I'll let it go when you let it go—you and your goddamn diamonds. You're wasting precious time teaching him that garbage."

"My 'goddamn diamonds' paid for this house," Willem would answer. "What exactly has your goddamn singing paid for lately?"

And that would sting her; you could never tell what would affect Rebecca Ward—it was always a surprise. One moment she was mounting an aggressive verbal assault, and seconds later she would deflate, crumpling on the couch with her face in her hands. "I know, I know. Jesus Christ. I'm sorry."

Willem would sigh and then sit down and wrap his arms around her as she wept into her hands. "Anna could have played the cello too," she would say.

"She'd have been an excellent cello player," Willem would say, gently rocking her as she cried harder.

Gerard now remembered a series of such exchanges all ending the same way—with Rebecca crying and with Willem feeling bad for letting himself get swept up in her fury. Gerard pictured his parents sitting on the couch in the living room at the Kasteel and remembered that what he most wanted in those moments was to scramble up between them and be rocked too—to cry and be rocked by his mom and dad. He should have; it would have been so easy, and surely his parents would have welcomed it. He was a kid, their son, now their only child. But he could never do it. It was too scary. In those moments he'd convinced himself that he had to be the strong one, the one to keep control. It didn't make sense to Gerard that a little guy would take on such a burden, but that's what he would do, even as he fought his own grief. He would watch

Rebecca fall apart and he'd instantly miss Anna. He would feel the deep sadness expand inside him, and then run to the music parlor and play the Elgar *Cello Concerto, Opus 85* in its slow, mournful E-minor. God, he missed his cello—the sleek contour of the neck against his left thumb, the swaying of his supple right wrist as he sent the bow gliding back and forth over the strings. Holding that instrument made him feel strong and powerful in the shoulders and arms, and graceful in the hands and fingers. Only one activity could strip that feeling of elegance from his hands, and that was the grueling regimen of diamond processing forced on him by his father in the basement of the Kasteel on West Dixon Road.

The tools and technology available to diamond cutters in the 1990s were remarkable: lasers, polishing wheels, lathes, phosphor-bronze saw blades, but Willem Kelderman forced Gerard to learn the old-fashioned way of processing diamonds, from beginning to end. Cleaving was no problem; it was like tapping a stone with a hammer and chisel to create the basic shape of the diamond. Bruting is what destroyed Gerard's hands, rendering them swollen and calloused and unable even to touch the cello for days after the work was done.

The purpose of bruting is to form the girdle—the outside rim—of the diamond by chipping away pieces to create a uniform, round shape. In the very old days, the craftsman would place the diamond into an egg-shaped cup and then strike it repeatedly with another diamond affixed to the end of a wooden dowel. Gerard was eleven when Willem taught him how to do this, and after three days of it Gerard was sure he'd never become a diamond cutter. It was too hard! Bruting is a misleading word; it's actually smacking and grinding, over and over and over. Gerard's palms and fingers would grow huge calluses, soft and white and full of fluid, but even then he'd have to keep grinding until the calluses ruptured and oozed, leaving open, tender, bright-pink sores that stung to the touch. Gerard's hands were so covered with wounds there was no-where to stick the adhesive ends of bandages. Only after Gerard's hands leaked clear liquid and then blood did Willem allow him to use a diamond-tipped cutting tool, and then, finally, the electric bruting lathe. When Gerard watched the whirring of that $12,000 piece of machinery, he wanted to cry and punch his father for putting him through all that unnecessary pain.

But even as difficult as it was learning to take a diamond through the entire process from rough to polished, and even though Gerard spent years resenting Willem for wasting time teaching him rudimentary techniques that were no longer used, Gerard missed all of it now. He thought longingly of the hours spent at the polishing wheel as his fingers turned graphite-gray and then black. A polished diamond held in the black fingers of a cutting master has a unique shine—fresh and bright and clear. And Gerard couldn't think of diamonds and polishing and cutting without thinking of Antwerp, the diamond headquarters of the world.

Looking back now, Gerard was surprised Rebecca allowed Willem to take him on trips to Antwerp. Gerard remembered thinking, after Anna's funeral, that he would probably never again get to travel to Antwerp; he imagined Rebecca wouldn't want *him* to die there too.

But it wasn't long after Anna died before Rebecca and Willem were back to their old pattern: Rebecca would fly away for a long weekend to sing (this time to play the part of Desdemona in a production of *Othello* at the Cleveland Opera), and Willem would be stuck with Gerard, even as he needed to fly overseas on diamond business. 'Stuck with' wasn't fair—Willem never used that phrase or even hinted that he didn't want Gerard along. Especially after Anna died, Willem was happy to have Gerard as a travel companion. On Gerard's first trip to Antwerp three years earlier, before Anna was born, Willem had been more preoccupied with all his business associates and their important work. But this time—even on the six-hour flight to Brussels—Gerard sensed that Willem was focused on him. For most of the flight, Willem chattered incessantly about how Gerard would get to see all the sights in Antwerp that he'd only seen in books on the coffee table in the living room at the Kasteel. He would hear the bustle of Hoveniersstraat, witness the haggling at the diamond exchanges, and tour the offices of the Hoge Raad van Diamant—the High Council for Diamonds—headquartered on Lange Herentalsestraat.

From Brussels they caught a train that took them straight to Central Station in the heart of Antwerp. Willem had their luggage delivered to the Carlton hotel on the Quinten Matsijslei before they even checked in; he couldn't wait to get started.

"First we'll head to Pelikaanstraat," said Willem. "No, no, that wouldn't do. The *Provincial Diamant* museum would be better, as an introduction."

Willem clearly imagined the whole trip as a coming-of-age ritual for eight-year-old Gerard, his debut on the diamond scene. Gerard would spend many years learning the hands-on work of diamonds in the basement at the Kasteel, and this trip to Antwerp would be part of his education, part of his field study.

They walked west from Central Station on De Keyserlei and then Leysstraat. When Gerard and Willem turned the corner onto Jezusstraat Willem changed his mind yet again.

"Oh, no, wait," said Willem. "This is even better. Yes, this is perfect!"

"What?" said Gerard.

"There's something I want to show you." Willem stopped on the sidewalk and pointed up at the building. "There. Look at that."

One story above them on the outside wall of the stone building was a bas-relief, a gray statue of a man wearing what looked like one of those freakish outfits from a Renaissance festival. He seemed to be wearing tights and a beret that drooped down the right side of his head.

"Lodewijk Van Berckem," said Willem. "Say it."

"Lodewijk Van Berckem," said Gerard, but it wasn't good enough. His father made him say it again. Willem was that way about all Flemish words—insisting that Gerard pronounce them exactly right, paying attention to every syllable, every diphthong and every rolled *r*. Without rolling the *r* one might be mistaken for a Hollander, Willem would say. Gerard braced for another tirade against the Dutch, but for the moment Willem was too intent on his pronunciation lesson.

It was unnerving the way he leaned down and peered closely into Gerard's face, forcing Gerard to study Willem's lips; Willem would repeat the habit many times over the following years as he taught Gerard Flemish. Gerard was eight at the time, but Willem's in-your-face, wide-eyed, Kindergarten-teacher way of enunciating Flemish words made Gerard feel like a four-year-old.

"Looooh-duh-waaaeeek Van Berrrrrrckuhm," said Willem again, emphasizing the *ij* diphthong—sort of an 'aa-ee' sound—and rolling the *r* in Berckem.

"Loh-duh-wike Van—"

"No, no," said Willem. "It's Loh-duh-waaeek."

"Loh-duh-waaeek," said Gerard. But now Willem wasn't happy with Gerard's *L*—it wasn't dark enough. Gerard sighed and looked around him at the hurried pedestrians on Jezusstraat. A woman brushed by him clutching a cone made from newspaper that was soaked through with grease. Gerard could smell the hot French fries.

"Pay attention," said Willem. "Llllllloh-duh-waaeek Van Berrrckuhm."

"Lodewijk Van Berckem," said Gerard, with perfect fluency.

Willem lit up with a bounce like the annoyingly chipper French teacher Gerard would have to tolerate years later in the eighth grade at Babson Middle School in Evans Glen. Now that Gerard had said the name to Willem's satisfaction, his father continued with a history lesson.

According to Willem Kelderman, diamond cutters worship Lodewijk Van Berckem. He operated out of Bruges during the fifteenth century and was the originator of modern diamond-polishing methods. Willem told Gerard that up until that time no one really knew how to polish diamonds using a wheel. Lodewijk Van Berckem figured out that if he rubbed two diamonds together for many hours, a fine dust collected below them. He then rubbed the diamond dust into an iron polishing wheel along with some olive oil and used the wheel for polishing diamonds. The process took hours, but the shine on the diamond was like nothing ever seen before.

Gerard would later learn that the story probably wasn't so simple. Two of Willem's closest Flemish friends and business associates, Joske Vermeulen and Margareta Van Leuven, had varying theories about Lodewijk Van Berckem. Joske doubted the guy even existed; he was sure Lodewijk was a myth. Margareta agreed with Willem that Lodewijk Van Berckem was a historical figure, but she thought it unlikely that he invented this polishing technique. Probably, she argued, he simply brought to light what had been known for centuries by secret guilds of diamond craftsmen.

Whatever the case, Lodewijk Van Berckem had earned a position in diamond-polishing legend and a statue in Antwerp at the corner of Jezustraat and Leysstraat. Gerard looked up at Lodewijk and made a briefly frank effort to figure out what was so interesting. In addition to Lodewijk's silly sixteenth-century outfit, a winged cherub held a halo above his head, and Lodewijk was clasping a rough diamond between the thumb and forefinger of his right hand.

As Willem stood there reverently staring at the statue (Gerard half expected Willem to cross himself, or to leave an offering at the foot of the statue), a bird fluttered down and landed on Lodewijk Van Berckem's ring finger.

"Well, take a look at that." Willem smiled. "Hello little fellow."

Gerard grinned as he imagined what might happen next—since the bird was facing to the left, its tail hovered directly above the rough diamond Lodewijk was pinching so daintily. The bird didn't disappoint. The white splotch of poop that sprayed out of its rear end splattered Lodewijk's index finger and then oozed down onto the diamond. Willem's mouth dropped open.

"My Lord." He pulled a handkerchief out of his pocket and examined the wall in front of him. "I've got to climb up and clean that off."

"Come on Dad, let's go," said Gerard. "The rain'll wash it off."

"This will only take a minute," said Willem, grunting and grabbing a stone pillar to hoist himself up.

The policeman ambling by didn't even give Willem a chance to explain himself. He took hold of Willem's coat-collar and muttered something in Flemish Gerard couldn't remember.

So their next stop wasn't the *Provincial Diamant* museum; it was the police station at Lange Nieuwstraat and Noordlaan. Gerard worried his father would be tossed into jail and he would be left alone to navigate the streets and forage for food and find his way back to the hotel, but the only suffering Willem had to tolerate was the good laugh the other police officers at the station enjoyed when he told them why he'd tried to scale the wall.

"Let me guess," the clerk at the desk said. "You're from Nijlen, right?"

"Actually, I grew up in Brasschaat," said Willem.

"Yeah, but you're acting like someone from Nijlen. Githo School?"

"Yes," said Willem.

"Usually we get you crazy diamond people in here when you've attacked someone else who's vandalizing that statue," said the clerk.

"Well, someone has to protect Lodewijk."

And they spent five minutes bickering about who was protecting the statue, with the clerk reminding Willem that the policeman had protected Lodewijk from Willem, and Willem saying again that he was trying to clean off a desecration. Willem must have finally realized he would get out of the police station more quickly if he just stayed quiet and agreeable.

For years after that Gerard would struggle with two conflicting feelings about diamonds: embarrassment at his father's fanaticism, and the draw of that same zeal in himself. Over time he developed something that fell in-between. Gerard became passionate about diamonds, but he believed he was more clear-headed than Willem; he knew how to see through some of the nonsense his father embraced.

For example, Willem refused to appreciate the skill of his Dutch colleagues. Gerard came to see this as a symptom of Willem's hatred of Dutch people in general. Gerard hadn't grown up in Flanders—he'd been raised in Evans Glen, in Northern Virginia—so he had no reason to care one way or the other about the Dutch. Willem hated and made fun of the Dutch more than he did French-speaking people from the southern region of Belgium.

A favorite story of Willem's had to do with a Dutch diamond polisher who always cut corners ("The way the Dutch always do," Willem would say) by re-using the dirty diamond dust that collected in the cup below the iron polishing wheel, instead of buying fresh diamond dust or using the clean dust that resulted from bruting. Did Willem really believe that, or did he enjoy pretending a diamond polisher could truly be that careless and stupid? Either way, to Willem it was the perfect example of Dutch incompetence. "Always looking to save money by sacrificing quality," he would say.

If Willem was drinking beer while telling this story, he would inevitably follow it with a series of bawdy and childish jokes about Dutch people. He'd remind Gerard, or anyone else who was nearby, that the Dutch bury their dead naked, face-down, with their bottoms poking out of the ground so that the living have somewhere to park their bicycles. And he would tell these jokes with the gusto and sincerity of the story teller who's forgotten that this audience has heard them before—many, many times. Gerard was that audience, and he could only sit and listen. Sometimes Gerard would remind his father that a joke, say, the one about parking bicycles, was a rerun.

"Oh. Well, it's a good one, isn't it?" Willem would say, leaning back on the couch and taking a long sip of Steenbrugge brown ale.

How Gerard longed to be polishing diamonds right now instead of combat boots. He rubbed black polish into the toe of his boot. Fuller sometimes called them LPCs—Leather Personnel Carriers.

"Technically we shouldn't be polishing boots," Private Fuller said. "When you rub polish into the leather you fill in the pores, and then your feet can't breathe."

"Yeah, no shit!" said Wiley. "And you think the enemy's going to give a rat's ass what my boots look like when I'm driving a bayonet through his fucking communist gut?"

"What is it with you and communism?" said Berkowicz.

"Commies are evil, man," said Wiley.

"You're an idiot," Berkowicz said. "You're like living in the 1950s or something."

"Hey shut up, man," Wiley said. "My dad says—"

"Then your dad's a fucking idiot too," Berkowicz said.

Wiley leaped from the top row of the bleachers and grabbed Berkowicz by the collar. They rolled down across the gravel and onto the sidewalk, swinging and punching at each other. The first time Berkowicz and Wiley brawled, on the fifth day of basic training, everyone had gotten excited and moved closer to watch. Romberg had yelled and screamed, egging them on and getting himself worked up. But by now they'd established a pattern: Berkowicz and Wiley would argue, then scream at each other, and then the fists would fly. It had become commonplace. So as they flopped around on the sidewalk grunting and slamming and pummeling each other, the other soldiers of Third Platoon sat quietly on the bleachers polishing their boots. When Wiley and Berkowicz had had enough, they clanked back onto the bleachers and resumed polishing.

Gerard dipped his cotton ball into the tray of water he had collected in the lid of his shoe polish can. He swiped the cotton into the creamy shoe polish and rubbed the toe of his boot with small circular motions. The tips of his fingers were black. He rubbed and rubbed—small circles—around and around.

"That's some shiny shit, Kelderman," said Romberg.

"Yep," said Gerard, not even looking up. He loved polishing.

In his teens Gerard had gotten so good at polishing diamonds that Willem would let him do much of the work by himself. Gerard would start with the easy jobs: cutting and cleaving, marking the diamonds with a kerf—a small notch indicating exactly where the cut would be. Then Willem would let Gerard polish the table of the diamond, and then each facet. Gerard learned that he had to hold the diamond against the polishing wheel at exactly the right angle, being mindful to push *with* the grain of the stone, or nothing would wear away from the diamond and no dust would collect in the tin cup under the wheel.

When Gerard turned sixteen Willem shocked him with a generous gift. They were having a small party in the living room at the Kasteel: Gerard, Willem, Rebecca, and Gerard's neighbor Meredith (despite the casual intimacy of a relationship that included an incalculable number of sexual liaisons, neither Gerard nor Meredith would ever use the words girlfriend and boyfriend). Gerard had blown out the candles, and everyone was happily eating cake.

"I almost forgot," said Willem. "There's one more package." He handed Gerard a small jewelry box.

Gerard lifted the lid and peered inside. The average person would not have been impressed; tucked into the burgundy tissue paper was a bumpy, gray, cloudy stone the size of a small marble. But Gerard knew instantly what he was looking at: a rough diamond, probably from Zaire.

"Whoa," said Gerard. "Is this for me?"

"Yes it is, Gerard," said Willem. "You're the second-best diamond cutter in the house. Do with it what you want."

"Okay!" Gerard wolfed down his last hunk of cake and headed for the basement door.

"Gerard, your guest," said Rebecca.

"Don't worry Ms. Ward," said Meredith. "I'm used to it."

Gerard worked on the diamond for a week in the basement of the Kasteel. He did everything himself, without asking his father even one question.

After carefully studying the structure of the diamond's crystal, Gerard drew on it a series of lines with Chinese ink. He sat down at the saw and cut through the ink lines to remove unwanted chunks of the diamond. When he was done sawing, he weighed the diamond; it was just under one carat. He had preserved 51% of the original rough stone, which was nearly perfect. Willem had taught him that 53% was the goal.

For the next step—faceting—Gerard sat down at the wheel. He loved the wheel with its 40 pounds of smooth iron, made by Rico Tools of Antwerp, where Willem bought all his equipment. The face of the wheel was flat on the table, much like a record on a turntable. Gerard tore open a small packet of fresh diamond dust and rubbed it onto the oily wheel until the dust disappeared, packing down into its tiny pores. He reached under the table and clicked the motor on. The wheel whirred and hummed its way up to 4,000 RPMs.

Gerard attached a jeweler's loupe to his right eye and picked up his new diamond. He pushed the girdle of the diamond against the polishing wheel and then squinted through the loupe to check his progress. This was the part of diamond work he loved the most, when time melted away and Gerard lost himself in the ritual and repetition. He held each facet of the diamond against the iron wheel and pushed forward with the grain of the stone for just one second. Then he'd lift the stone again to the loupe and squint to inspect it. Back to the wheel. Press, lift, inspect. Press, lift, inspect. Hours passed. Because Gerard was doing a brilliant cut—and specifically the Flanders Brilliant—the faceting phase was the most difficult and demanded the most intense focus.

But Gerard pulled it off, and it made him proud. Once he finished the faceting without making any mistakes he knew the stone was going to be perfect. And as he sat now on the bleachers in the warm Fort Benning evening, polishing the toes of his combat boots, he remembered the final phase of work he had done on that little gem. For three days he didn't leave the house or touch his cello; every so often Willem brought him snacks as he hunched over the polishing wheel in the basement, working with such intensity that his parents had to remind him to sleep. It was like hitting a runner's high: he couldn't stop. He made meticulous angle calculations, he polished the star facets with their points toward the girdle, he polished the half-facets for the pavilion; and if the stone overheated even slightly, he'd dip it in borax to cool it off.

In the early years of Gerard's apprenticing, Willem had put him through grueling book studies of diamond geology. He taught Gerard that diamonds are formed when liquid carbon deep in the earth is exposed to temperatures of 2,500 degrees Fahrenheit and pressures of one million pounds per square inch over millions of years. It was awesome to imagine the long work of earth, air, fire, and water, and to realize that a diamond isn't completely born until it's been pushed, squeezed, hammered, and had such pressure exerted on it you'd think it would crack and crush and pulverize under the stress of all that force. But it's the opposite. The pressure is exactly what creates it, and once the elements do their part, the diamond master steps in and cuts the stone. This is the most critical stage for a diamond, the stage that will unleash its power and essence—when it's cut.

When Gerard was done creating the Flanders Brilliant he marched triumphantly up the basement stairs and into the music parlor. Rebecca was sitting at the piano, softly humming a vocal line from Ivor Gurney's "In Flanders." He told Rebecca to close her eyes, and when she did, he placed the gleaming, perfect diamond on the piano ledge.

"Okay, open," said Gerard.

Rebecca opened her eyes and gasped. "Gerard—it's—oh my God."

Gerard beamed.

She picked it up and ran her fingers across the ridges. "But Gerard, this was *your* birthday present. Your father—"

"It's yours now Mom," said Gerard. "I made it for you."

Rebecca jumped up from the piano bench and grabbed Gerard. She hugged him close and held him. "It's gorgeous, Gerard." She swayed left and right. Gerard leaned against her and released himself into her rocking.

"Three minutes, Third Platoon," said Snodgrass as he dumped a black polishing brush into his red ammo can.

Gerard rubbed the last bit of polish into his boot and popped the lid back onto the can of polish. The soldiers of Third Platoon jogged across the company area, up the stairs, and into the bay to get ready for bed.

# Five

"So Cooper, you gonna bolo or what?" Carroll stuffed a spoonful of warm, sodden green beans into his mouth.

Cooper smiled and shook his head. "I don't know."

The platoon sat on parched grass and sand under pine trees. The eight drill sergeants of Bravo Company stood under the picnic shelter in a semicircle around First Sergeant McFadden. The first sergeant was doing all the talking, gesticulating in choppy jerks of one hand while holding a clipboard in the other. Third Platoon had twenty minutes to eat lunch before returning to the firing range on this last day of Basic Rifle Marksmanship—BRM. Every soldier had to pass the final test that afternoon to move ahead in training. Cooper had not done well during the morning.

"All you got to hit is twenty-three," said Snodgrass.

"I know," said Cooper. "I know."

Fuller wiped his mouth. His Adam's apple protruded like a walnut. "You gotta hit twenty-three out of forty targets. If you bolo BRM, you can't stay in the army."

"Or you can start basic training over again," said Phillips.

"Well yeah," Fuller said. "They can recycle you. But they can kick you out, too. The drill sergeants don't talk about that because they don't want anyone doing it on purpose. The infantry can't use a soldier that can't shoot. You bolo, you're out."

Parker threw an empty milk carton at Romberg. "You hear that, Romberg? You can get out easy. Don't gotta make up no more shit about ravens."

"And Phillips," said Berkowicz, "it's easier than like slicing your wrists."

Phillips stared straight ahead and chewed slowly.

"Fuck you, Parker," said Romberg. "I'm hittin' forty."

"Third Platoon, you got fifteen seconds to give me a formation over here." Drill Sergeant Hammer stood on the gravel driveway in front of the firing range.

The recruits leaped up and dumped their plastic spoons and paper plates into black trash bags. In about fourteen seconds, they formed four rows in front of Drill Sergeant Hammer.

Bravo Company was now at the end of the second week of rifle marksmanship training. Gerard calculated that he must have fired 500 rounds of ammunition. First Sergeant McFadden had put the company through bayonet training during the same two weeks (RBFT—Rifle Bayonet Fighting Training), to increase soldiers' confidence in handling the M16. Gerard's forearms were tender and sore for days after bayonet training with its hours of running with the rifle, thrusting it, jabbing it, holding it with two hands above his head, stabbing his bayonet into rubber mannequins, some of which had hats with the faint remnant of a red star.

According to Private Fuller, it wasn't long ago that the army was teaching its recruits to hate Soviet communists; this was confirmed during the past week when one of the older sergeants who taught rifle marksmanship kept slipping and referring to the targets as Ivan. It was a tidy name, a generic term for the communist enemy. Not only was the army slow to remove the red star and AK-47 rifle from its targets and mannequins, the troops were confused about what name to use, now that no one really knew whom to hate. Even after the Gulf War and the attacks on the World Trade Center, the drill sergeants couldn't really motivate basic training recruits with phrases like 'rogue nation' or 'terrorist cell.' Some of the drill sergeants tried referring to Osama Bin Laden and Saddam Hussein by name, but that was no good for the average infantry soldier, who would never personally see either of those characters. The ground-pounding troops of the infantry needed something personal, something up-close they could grab and maim and torture. So the drill sergeants and marksmanship instructors stuttered and fumbled and tried pathetic phrases like I.B. (Iraqi Bastard; it never stuck). Private Wiley, forever obsessed with communism, slid into blissful rapture when Fuller announced that the targets used to be called Ivans. On the bayonet course and on the firing range, Wiley would joyfully shriek the name with such vigor that he drowned out the drill sergeants and matched the enthusiasm even of Romberg's "Rock and Roll." At times the firing range looked like a scene from a Marx Brothers movie, with drill sergeants scurrying from foxhole to foxhole, trying to silence maniacal cries of "Rock and Roll" and "Die Ivan."

Gerard stood in formation and ran his fingers along the plastic hand guards of his M16. Holding the rifle made him feel firm and steady and grounded. His weapon was as comfortable to him as his lacrosse stick had been after three years on the lacrosse team at Belden Academy (he hadn't made the cut during his freshman year). He caressed the handle, the heavy plastic butt, the hand guards, the warm metal of the magazine release catch, the trigger,—

"Kelderman!" yelled Hammer. "Pay attention. This ain't a fuckin' porno movie and that ain't your girlfriend."

The platoon laughed.

"Listen up, men," said Hammer. "This afternoon you gotta pass BRM. We been training you all week. Some of you got it. Some of you can't shoot worth a fuck. Cooper!"

"Yes, Drill Sergeant."

"You gonna pass?"

"Yes, Drill Sergeant."

"Good."

"Romberg!"

"Yes, Drill Sergeant."

"You been seein' any more fuckin' ravens?"

"No, Drill Sergeant."

"Good," Hammer said.

"Parker!"

"Yes, Drill Sergeant."

"You ever fire a weapon before comin' in the army?"

Silence.

Drill Sergeant Hammer pushed his way between Third and Fourth Squads and stood beside Parker.

"Parker, I asked you a question," Hammer said.

Parker clenched his fists.

"Parker, you from Detroit, right?"

Parker was silent. Gerard guessed, as Parker probably had, that Hammer wasn't playing his little where-are-you-from game.

"What were you?" said Hammer.

Parker sighed through his nose.

"What were you, Parker?"

"I drove a concrete mixer for two years, Drill Sergeant."

"Bullshit, Parker. I'm from Detroit too. What were you?"

Parker looked straight ahead. Hammer stood to Parker's side, and he moved his face close to Parker. "You know what a Warlord is, Parker?"

"Yes, Drill Sergeant," Parker said softly.

"I was a Warlord, Parker. What were you? Were you a Vice Dragon, Parker?"

Parker clenched his teeth and his fists.

"Private Parker, were you a Vice Dragon?"

"Yes, Drill Sergeant!" Parker yelled.

"I thought so," said Hammer. "But that's all behind us now, ain't it, Parker?"

"Yes, Drill Sergeant."

"Parker, look at my uniform," said Hammer. "You and me wearin' the same uniform now."

"Yes, Drill Sergeant," said Parker.

Hammer walked back to the front of the formation. "Third Platoon, on my command, fall out and sit down in those bleachers behind you. Fall out."

The platoon turned around and clanked onto the metal bleachers, jostling and clattering their ammo pouches, canteens, and ponchos. Drill Sergeant Hammer walked away toward the range tower.

Gerard turned to Parker. "What was all that about?"

"Shut up," said Parker.

"You gotta tell us, man," said Carroll.

"I ain't gotta tell you nothin', fat boy."

"What's a Vice Dragon?" said Berkowicz.

"Yeah, and a Warlord," said Romberg. "Sounds killer." He stood up on the bleacher and put his arms in the air. "Warlord!"

"Sit the fuck down." Parker yanked Romberg's shirt. "It's all gang shit, man. It's fucked up."

"You're in a gang?" said Gerard.

"Used to be," said Parker. "I joined up to get away from that shit. Now I gotta watch my ass here, too." He looked toward the tower.

"Naw, not Hammer," said Romberg. "He's cool."

"You don't understand," said Parker. "You don't know what I'm tryin' to get away from—why I left Detroit."

"So tell us," said Gerard.

"No!" said Parker. He hung his head. "I was supposed to be safe here. The shit even followed me here."

"You're safe," said Cooper. "Don't worry."

"Man, shut up," said Parker. "All y'all shut up. I wanna leave it behind and forget it."

The firing range erupted in a shower of sharp cracks. Fourteen members of Second Platoon were firing at the green pop-up targets.

"I can't wait!" said Romberg.

"Hey, Cooper, you ready for this?" said Libby. "You think that little girl in you can hit at least twenty-three targets?"

"I don't know," said Cooper. He smiled. "We'll see."

Cooper often spoke openly about his belief in reincarnation. At dusk every evening during boot shining in the company area, Cooper shared memories of his previous lives. Gerard was fascinated by the details and by Cooper's sincerity. Whether the stories were true or not, Cooper really seemed to believe them. Gerard considered it a slight lack of judgment on Cooper's part when he revealed, to a group of infantry school recruits, that he specifically remembered being a young girl in one of his previous lives. Of all the tales he had recounted, that was one that would never be forgotten by the soldiers of Third Platoon, especially by Wiley. Private Wiley was a firm Southern Baptist who—empowered by Drill Sergeant Womack's calling Cooper a new-age fruitcake—had concerns about Cooper's beliefs and the way he quoted Christian scripture.

"The word of God isn't for new-age, moral relativists," Wiley had told Cooper, though when Cooper had asked what a moral relativist was, Wiley couldn't explain; it was a term he'd heard one day on AM radio. Still, Wiley's stupidity didn't stop him from continuing with a lecture about how Cooper wasn't right with God, or how the devil had got hold of him, or how he was superstitious.

The word 'superstitious' jogged Gerard's brain and made him miss his dad. Willem Kelderman had for years been tormented by his certainty that the Kasteel was haunted, providing another target for Rebecca's scorn and belittlement. One rainy Saturday Gerard and his neighbor Donald Meerschaum had figured out how to descend from the attic between the walls inside the house, and when they had reached the bottom floor they'd slowly pushed closed the sliding doors of the music parlor. Almost instantly they had heard Willem shriek from the living room and run to find Rebecca to say he told her so.

Even when Wiley directly attacked Cooper (Wiley enjoyed calling him Private Satanist), Cooper never argued back; he just smiled and nodded his head. What chance did Wiley have to rile Cooper if two U.S. Army drill sergeants had failed three weeks into basic training? And besides, Romberg had taken such a liking to Cooper that whenever Wiley began cranking the wheels of a dogmatic tirade, Romberg could be counted on to tell Wiley to "cork his backwards-ass, shit-spewing pie hole." Gerard took Romberg's side in considering Wiley a much bigger fruitcake than Cooper.

And Cooper persistently nudged Gerard to uncover his own destiny during this life. It wasn't a new concept to Gerard; at Monroe Hill College he had studied many religions that touted destiny and purpose. Maybe Cooper was a Christian after all—some sects of Christianity believed in destiny, that your fate was fixed even before your birth. But Cooper believed in reincarnation too, which didn't rule out Christianity—only Western Christianity. Cooper believed that Jesus's parable of the farmer and plow referred to reincarnation. According to Cooper Jesus was telling his disciples not to waste time delving into the memories of their past lives by looking behind them—that this life was the most important and where the real work was.

"So you're a Christian?" Gerard had asked Cooper.

"I don't know if I'd use that word," Cooper had answered.

"But you spent five years at Taizé," said Gerard. "How can you say you're not a Christian?"

"It's just a word," said Cooper.

How infuriating! Gerard had read that the brothers of Taizé were deeply rooted in Christianity. Until he'd met Cooper, Gerard had never known anyone to use phrases and speak of experiences coming straight from many of the texts Gerard had studied as a religion minor at Monroe Hill. And Gerard couldn't resist the academic urge—the need—to put a label on Cooper. What *was* he? It was inconceivable to Gerard that someone would disregard words, especially for describing oneself. But Cooper said he had let go of the limitation of labels and words while studying meditation in India.

Gerard thought back to Evans Glen and the Kasteel at 330 West Dixon Road. Willem Kelderman was Catholic, Rebecca Ward was Episcopal. His neighbor Meredith had always called herself agnostic, and Gerard chose to call himself an atheist. It was easy to sit on the outside of a religion—of all religions—and declare what one was not. But at least Gerard would go a step further and use an actual word for himself—atheist. It was direct and tidy.

"Then you're not a Christian?" Gerard had asked Cooper.

"Well, I don't know if I'd say that either."

"I give up," Gerard had said.

Gerard surmised he hadn't turned out Christian because his parents were so tepid about their own faiths. Rebecca Ward had managed on a few occasions to drag the family to St. Luke's Episcopal church on Wickham Street in Evans Glen, but the service wasn't Catholic enough for Willem. Since leaving his native country Willem had never found a church to call home; St. Luke's wasn't Catholic enough, and Belgium was too Catholic. Robin Kelderman, Willem's brother back in Brasschaat, used religion as an angle to make Willem feel guilty for emigrating to the United States from Belgium: not only had Willem abandoned Robin and their mother, he had forsaken the true church and gone to live with the heathen. But Willem often talked about how glad he was to be free of the religious nonsense his Belgian relatives still clung to with irrational fervor. Willem admitted that he loved his brother Robin but that Robin's dangerous combination of being both very stupid and very religious had caused many problems over the years.

For instance, back when Willem and Robin were teenage boys in Brasschaat, outside Antwerp, some local hoodlums had vandalized the life-sized wax nativity scene displayed every winter in the market square. The townspeople woke one morning to find that the heads of Joseph and Mary had been lopped off and placed on the back of the wax mule. Monique Kelderman-De Boek, Robin and Willem's mother, described angrily how the perpetrator should be punished—that whoever did this awful deed should be stripped naked and strapped into the manger while the townspeople nailed his exposed crotch with snowballs. Robin dutifully listened to every word his mother said and then rounded up some of his buddies. When the gang found one of the offenders, they carried out what Robin had heard as his mother's specific instructions. The snow was so cold and so hard that the poor ruptured victim spent four days in the hospital and another two weeks in a wheelchair.

Willem always talked about wanting to remind Robin of such stories from their past when Robin called on Sunday evenings to make Willem feel bad for leaving Belgium and living in the United States. After the Sunday-evening phone conversations, and after Willem had spent his hour in the basement, he would talk through everything he *wished* he had said on the phone. When stupid people were fervently religious, Willem claimed, there was always violence.

But what would Willem have made of Cooper? Cooper was fervently religious, in his own way, though he claimed he wasn't. Cooper meditated, Cooper prayed, Cooper gave speeches on the power of religious icons, Cooper whispered in his sleep: "Lord Jesus Christ have mercy on me. Lord Jesus Christ have mercy on me." Some mornings Gerard would tell Cooper what he'd been chanting during the night, and Cooper would shrug and say he didn't remember—that probably it was the Holy Spirit praying through him. And still Cooper said he wasn't religious!

Gerard watched the soldiers on the firing range. He removed the yellow foam plugs from his ears and stuffed them into the plastic container that hung on a chain from the breast pocket of his BDU shirt. He'd grown accustomed, during the past week, to the loud pop of the M16A2 rifle and to the sharp, stinging smell of the powder from expended rounds.

Destiny. Purpose. If he had met Cooper a month ago, Gerard might have explained his purpose in terms of career: playing cello, cutting diamonds. Or Sylvia—he definitely believed Sylvia was part of his destiny. He'd worked very hard to keep her, and he wasn't going to let go. After he finished basic training and advanced infantry school, he and Sylvia could work through their problems— even though she had no idea that he knew what he knew and that he felt there were problems to work through. He was still angry about Gilberto, but he couldn't let go of Sylvia, not even after having read the seventeen letters. He decided right there on the bleachers that he would never release Sylvia. He would show her that his commitment was greater and stronger than her silly, temporary transgression.

"It doesn't matter anyway," Cooper said.

"Huh?" said Gerard.

Cooper smiled. "The words are never what matter. It's what we *do* that counts."

"On your feet, Third Platoon!" Drill Sergeant Womack stood in front of the bleachers. "Platoon formation right here. First Squad, move out to the firing range. Single file. You're next. Second Squad, right behind them."

"Drill Sergeant, are we allowed to fire at the wildlife?"

"Shut up, Romberg," Womack said. "Have you forgotten our little talk last week?"

"No, Drill Sergeant."

"Twenty-three targets, Romberg," said Womack.

"More like forty," Romberg said quietly.

Third Platoon lined up at the entrance to the firing range. They waited while First Squad walked out and lowered themselves into the foxholes. They waited while the soldiers shoved their sandbags into place below their arms and the muzzles of their rifles. They waited as the familiar string instructions droned out of the range tower loudspeakers ("Rotate your selector switch from *safe* to *semi*, and watch—your lane"). They waited through the firing session while forty targets, one after the other, popped up and then flapped back down. And then they waited some more while Second Squad, and then Third Squad, jerked slowly like robots through the same sequence of rote actions.

Parker blew out a long, loud sigh through puffed cheeks.

"Man, how much longer?" Wiley said.

"Hurry up and wait," said Romberg.

"Okay, Fourth Squad. Move out," said Womack. "Libby, keep that weapon pointed down-range. You're gonna hurt someone."

Gerard trudged down the sandy firing line to his foxhole, a large concrete cylinder stuck down into a raised mound of earth. He lowered himself in and adjusted the sandbags under his rifle. He looked down his target lane. In the lane to his right was Private Phillips. On his left was Romberg.

The sergeant in the firing range control tower barked out commands, in sequence, over the loudspeakers. Gerard's hands and fingers snapped through every motion without his brain even engaging. He picked up the loaded magazine, popped it into the magazine well on his rifle, smacked it tight on the bottom, pulled back and then shoved forward the charging handle, then whacked the bolt release catch with his left palm to chamber a round. He aimed down range. He pressed his right cheek against the cool butt of the rifle, oily from the grease of his own face. He squinted his left eye closed and focused through the sight. His thumb rested on the safety switch, ready to click it off when the command came. Drill Sergeant Womack was standing behind Gerard, probably getting ready to harass him.

The loudspeaker blared: "Rotate your selector switch from *safe* to *semi*, and watch—your lane."

Gerard's thumb slipped the safety switch off, and he breathed a heavy sigh. Out on the range the first green targets flipped silently upright.

A simultaneous crack from the rifles echoed against the Georgia pines. A few single shots followed, maybe from those who were more careful with their aim, and finally one or two bangs fired from rifles of soldiers who probably just then realized their safety switches were still engaged.

"Wuh-hoo!" said Romberg.

"Romberg, shut up." Drill Sergeant Hammer walked up onto Romberg's mound and stood behind him with his arms folded.

Gerard hit the first target, the 50-meter. 50 meters was so close that the round struck the target while still on an upward path. This required aiming at the base, right near the sand; if you aimed at the center of the 50-meter target, the round would fly right over its head. He felled the second one at 150 meters. The third target was the 250-meter. Gerard fired and missed. How could he concentrate with Womack standing right behind him, ready to yell any second? During practice Gerard could never hit the 250-meter targets. The 300-meter was easier: he always aimed directly above the top of its head. 300 meters was so far that the round had enough distance to rise and then descend during its flight to strike the target in the center.

Gerard inhaled, exhaled, and gently squeezed the trigger with the center of the top section of his index finger. The 200-meter target fell.

Womack wasn't saying anything! All through BRM practice the drill sergeants had no shortage of snide comments. "You're supposed to *hit* the targets, Belgium Boy," Womack had said three days earlier. But now he was silent. Was he still back there?

Gerard yanked the trigger and missed another 250-meter target.

"Rock and Roll," yelled Romberg.

"Steady, Private. Keep on shooting." Gerard could hear Drill Sergeant Hammer softly speaking behind Romberg's mound.

"He's shooting my fucking targets." Phillips dropped his rifle and turned around.

"Phillips, pick up your weapon," yelled Drill Sergeant Hammer.

"Libby's shooting in the wrong lane," Phillips said. "He's hitting my targets."

"Pick up your weapon and get firing, Phillips." Drill Sergeant Hammer ran behind Libby's firing hole. "Libby, shoot your own damn targets."

"Yeah, Libby, shoot your own fucking targets."

"Phillips, shut up," Hammer said.

Gerard fired and missed the 200.

"Rock and fucking roll! Die motherfuckers, die!" Romberg was standing up straight, without supporting his arms.

"Romberg, lean back down in the supported position," Womack yelled.

"Drill Sergeant, make him stop," whined Phillips.

"Libby, your lane's right there." Hammer was pointing.

"Yes, Drill Sergeant!" said Libby as he knocked down the 100-meter target in Phillips's lane.

"Assfuck." Phillips picked up his rifle and fired seven consecutive shots at Libby's lane.

"Private Phillips, you're wasting ammunition!" Womack said.

"One shot, one kill," said Romberg. "One shot, one sorry-ass, dead motherfucker."

Romberg dropped back down and leaned on his sandbags. Libby continued happily shooting Phillips's targets. Phillips was done; he was out of ammo. Drill Sergeant Hammer and Drill Sergeant Womack stood quietly again behind the firing mounds as another round of targets popped up. Gerard breathed and squeezed. The 200-meter target snapped backwards. He tried not to breathe while waiting for the next target. It never came. They were done. The loudspeaker clicked on and began its drone: rotate the selector switch to safe, clear the chamber, drop the magazine. The soldiers of Fourth Squad climbed out of their foxholes and marched back to the bleachers.

"Fuckin'-A, dude, that was awesome," said Romberg. "We should do that every day."

"So how badly did you fuck up, Libby?" said Wiley.

"Shut up, man. I hit a lot of targets."

"Yeah, my targets," said Phillips. "Dickfuck."

"Fuck you, Phillips," Libby said.

"Fuck you, Libby," said Phillips. "Can't even tie your fucking shoes right."

"Yeah, I can't tie my shoes," Libby said. "And you can't slit your own fucking wrists the right way. How fucked up is that?"

Phillips raised the butt of his rifle and knocked Libby's Kevlar helmet. Libby fell forward off the bleacher bench and onto the sand, still clasping his M16. He jumped up and charged at Phillips, but Carroll grabbed Libby's rifle as he ran by and swung him to the right.

"Kick his ass!" yelled Romberg.

"Libby!" Drill Sergeant Hammer grabbed Libby's pistol belt. Libby made swinging motions at Phillips. Parker held Phillips's arm. Hammer yanked Libby back and pulled him to the ground.

"Phillips, get off that bench and come here," Hammer said.

Phillips clunked down the metal benches and stood in front of Drill Sergeant Hammer.

"Get on the ground with him," Hammer said.

Phillips lowered himself into push-up position.

"Now both of you, get up."

Their gear clattered as they stood up.

"Front leaning rest position, move!"

Libby and Phillips jumped down into push-up position.

"Private Libby, explain something to me," said Hammer. "How many times did you practice firing your M16 last week?"

"I don't remember, Drill Sergeant."

"It was a shitload, wasn't it?" Hammer said.

"Yes, Drill Sergeant," said Libby.

"Why the fuck were you shooting in Phillips' lane?"

"I don't know, Drill Sergeant."

"You don't know?" Drill Sergeant Womack stood next to Drill Sergeant Hammer.

Libby looked up at Womack. "No, Drill Sergeant."

"Stand up," Womack said.

Libby and Phillips stood up.

"Private Phillips, you fired seven shots into Libby's lane. Did you see seven targets?" said Womack.

"No, Drill Sergeant. I was mad."

"Get down."

Libby and Phillips lowered themselves to the ground.

"Too slow, get up," said Drill Sergeant Hammer.

"Too slow, get down," said Drill Sergeant Womack. "Get down!"

Womack dropped to his knees and screamed in Libby's face. "Private Libby, what if I was in battle with you. What if you were my battle buddy and you decided to shoot me instead of the enemy? Would you do that, Libby?"

"No, Drill Sergeant."

"I don't believe you, Libby." Womack stood up. "Get up, Privates. Too slow, get down. Too slow, get up."

"Private Berkowicz, would you trust Private Libby in battle?" said Womack.

"No, Drill Sergeant."

Sweat dripped through Libby's eyebrows and ran down his face. He looked up at Berkowicz.

"Neither would I," said Womack. "Phillips, what if you ran out of ammo and had to defend me in our foxhole? Answer me!"

"I—"

"Do you think this is a game?" said Womack.

"No, Drill Sergeant," yelled Libby and Phillips.

"If you idiots die in battle, whose fault is it?" said Womack.

"Ours," said Phillips.

"Mine," said Libby, his head hanging.

"Is it?" said Womack.

"Hold your head up, Libby," said Hammer.

Womack stood up. "We had a trainee here a while back, thirteen weeks with us, going through the same training you're going through. He left here and shipped out to the desert with the 82nd Airborne, right into the middle of the Gulf war. When he came to Bravo Company, he had his head in his ass just like you, Libby. We spent thirteen weeks pulling it out, and it wasn't pretty. Any idea how this story ends, Libby?"

"I—I don't know, Drill Sergeant."

Womack stood with his arms folded, staring down at Libby.

"I'll tell you what happened," Womack said. "He found a hand grenade in the sand, and what do you think he did? He picked it up. We trained him how to handle grenades and he picked it up. How does this story end, Libby?"

Libby was gulping and choking, and his eyes were wet.

"How does it end, Libby?"

"I—I—" He shook his head back and forth.

"It blew him in half, Libby, in two pieces, right at the stomach," said Womack. "What do you think his wife thought of that? Her husband came home in a bag, in two sandy pieces. Whose fault was it, Libby?"

Tears rolled down Libby's cheeks. Phillips' eyes bulged wide. In the gravel assembly area, the other platoons were gelling into a company formation in front of the first sergeant.

"Fall out, both of you, and get in those bleachers," said Womack.

Phillips and Libby shuffled to the bleachers and sat down. The drill sergeants faced the platoon.

Drill Sergeant Womack paced back and forth. "Third Platoon, there's a reason for *every*thing we tell you to do. Stay alert, stay alive. If you don't listen to every word we say, you are going to die."

"You hear that, Hot Shit?" Drill Sergeant Hammer came close to Parker.

Parker's fingers drummed the butt of his rifle. "Yes, Drill Sergeant."

"Are you alert, Hot Shit?"

"Yes, Drill Sergeant."

"Parker, why did you come here?" Hammer said.

"To be a soldier, Drill Sergeant," said Parker.

"Bullshit," Hammer said. "You gonna tell me, or am I gonna find out?"

"I want to start over, Drill Sergeant."

"You think you can do that?" said Hammer. "You think you can leave all that behind?"

"Yes, Drill Sergeant."

Drill Sergeant Hammer walked closer to Parker and spoke directly into his ear. If Gerard hadn't been standing next to Parker, he wouldn't have heard what Hammer said. He was probably the only other person who could hear. "I know about you, Parker," said Hammer. "I know what you did."

Parker turned his head toward Drill Sergeant Hammer.

"Face front, Private!" said Hammer.

Parker waited, silent. Gerard was dying to know what this was about. He worried Hammer was going to say something and he wouldn't hear. He wished he could stretch his ear without moving his head.

"We're movin' forward, right Parker?" Hammer said.

Parker didn't answer.

"Parker!"

"Yes, Drill Sergeant."

"We ain't lookin' back, are we, Parker?"

"No, Drill Sergeant."

"We're gonna forget all that mess and let it go," Hammer said.

"Yes, Drill Sergeant."

"Do you believe me, Parker?"

Parker stared straight ahead.

"Answer me, Parker."

"Yes, Drill Sergeant."

♦       ♦       ♦

At 12:30 a.m. the soldiers finally crawled into their beds in the dark Third Platoon bay. After BRM qualification that day Bravo Company had trudged two miles down the road and then suited up with Nuclear Biological Chemical—NBC—gear for more live-fire target practice. The week before that, when they had undergone NBC training that included a snot-inducing trip through a chamber filled with chemical smoke, Romberg had asked the drill sergeants when they would get to dress in peacock outfits. It had cost him twenty push-ups.

Gerard was tired but happy to have passed rifle marksmanship. He had hit thirty-one targets and earned a sharpshooter badge, which was tantamount to a B or a B-. During Gerard's years at Belden Academy Rebecca would look over his report card and sigh when she saw Bs and Cs. He always got a C in anything related to English: writing, literature, grammar. His neighbor, Donald Meerschaum, had always had the same trouble, and Mrs. Meerschaum made the excuse that her son had been a "victim of whole-language" reading instruction in elementary school.

As a freshman at Belden Academy Gerard been required to take a remedial reading and spelling class for which he'd had to study a yellow booklet titled *Systematic Spelling*. That little book with its conspicuous yellow shine was a mark of shame. With so many hundreds of bright middle school students applying to Belden each year, it seemed strange to Gerard that the academy even had a freshman class in remedial reading. Why bother with it? The school might easily have obliterated the class and admitted twenty-seven other students who *could* read on grade-level.

"Oh well," Rebecca would say, handing Gerard his report card back. "At least you're not failing out. And your cello playing's improving, isn't it? You'll always have the cello."

But in the infantry there was nothing else to fall back on if you couldn't effectively fire a rifle. Four members of Third Platoon—including Cooper—had failed rifle marksmanship by hitting fewer than twenty-three targets. Those soldiers would now have to suffer through a week of remedial marksmanship training and one last chance on the firing range. Drill Sergeant Womack had made the four of them stand in front of the platoon as he and Drill Sergeant Hammer humiliated them for shooting like sissies. Cooper had wisely trained himself to drop his usual smile, but he retained his grace and composure even to the point that the drill sergeants had given up trying to ruffle him.

"Don't you know how to shoot, Private Yanni?" Womack had yelled.

"Yes, Drill Sergeant."

"Do you need to do some more meditating, so you'll learn to shoot better?"

"Maybe, Drill Sergeant," Cooper had said.

"You do whatever you need to do to get through this, Yanni, do you understand?"

"Yes, Drill Sergeant."

Libby had failed as well, since most of the targets he had hit were not even in his own lane.

"What you need, Libby, is someone as stupid as you are, firing in the next lane, to hit *your* targets," Drill Sergeant Womack had said. "Then you'd pass."

Parker had earned an expert badge with a score of thirty-seven. Hammer had ribbed him, saying he wasn't surprised given Parker's extensive experience with firearms on the streets of Detroit. Since their exchange in the formation at the qualification range, Hammer hadn't let up—sometimes he seemed to be teasing Parker, calling him Hot Shit and asking him where he was from, and at other times he stood with his mouth in Parker's face, talking softly but intently and causing Parker to clench his fists as he stood at attention. Because Parker and Drill Sergeant Hammer had been members of rival gangs in Detroit, Parker was convinced that Hammer was out to get him. Other members of the platoon thought he was being paranoid.

"He's a drill sergeant, man," Romberg would say. "The worst he can do is make you do push-ups."

Parker would shake his head. "Hunh-*uh*, man. Gang shit is serious."

Gerard fluffed his pillow and rolled onto his side. He lifted his head up and squinted through the dark at Parker's bunk. Parker was lying on his back. Gerard had noticed that Parker always slept on his side, and this late into the night, if Parker was on his back, he was awake and probably troubled. Was he really worried about gang violence in the forests of Fort Benning? It didn't seem likely, but then what did Gerard really know about gangs? He had never met anyone who had *been* in an actual gang. He'd read about the Crips and the Bloods in the paper every now and then when he was growing up, but white people in suburban Northern Virginia were far enough from Washington D.C. never to have to bother with crime and violence and gangs.

Willem was similarly ignorant about gangs in the United States, but he was interested in their activity in South Africa. Gerard had come to recognize that Willem was conflicted about the wealth he'd accumulated in the diamond business—that like Cecil Rhodes, the founder of De Beers, he'd risen to comfort and luxury on the backs of impoverished, black South Africans. Willem subscribed to four South African daily newspapers, all of which arrived at the Kasteel anywhere from one to two weeks after they'd been published (Gerard had long ago given up trying to convince Willem to subscribe to those newspapers online; Willem wanted nothing to do with the Internet because he had convinced himself that hackers would somehow find their way into all his bank accounts if he looked at even one Web page). Willem liked to stay on top of news about De Beers and diamonds, but he'd also been so saddened by the gang violence in Cape Town that he desperately searched for somewhere to donate money to help the situation. Willem would read to Gerard and Rebecca at the breakfast table. He was particularly saddened by how effective gangs were at recruiting children to do their dirty work.

"Listen to these gang names," Willem had said one morning as he set his coffee mug down and shook the newspaper to straighten it out. "Cat Pound, Mongrels, Corner Boys, Cisko Yakkies, Boston Kids, Dixie Boys." He shook his head. "They use kids to do their dirty work because children aren't sentenced as heavily in court."

Just before Gerard had started his freshman year at Monroe Hill, his father had taken him along on a flight to Johannesburg. It was a typical trip, a harried pace of racing around offices and diamond workshops and meetings with De Beers officials. Willem admonished Gerard to pay close attention so he could learn about De Beers and its history. What Gerard carried away from these whirlwind South Africa trips was a general sense that De Beers used to control the entire diamond industry (even to the extent that it could force buyers to buy bad gems to earn the privilege of buying good ones), but as more players became active in the diamond industry (Australia, Canada, Russia) and as De Beers made major changes like moving from being a public company to a private one, it had to focus on making money in the retail market.

Gerard remembered flights to mines in other countries—Tanzania, Botswana, Lesotho—and that he and his father were never asked for their passports. Willem's answer to Gerard was, simply, that De Beers was their passport. On trips to South Africa, Willem bent his knee to De Beers and made sure Gerard knew that their livelihood sprang directly from Willem's association with that company. The magnificent Kasteel on West Dixon Road, first-class airplane tickets, Gerard's tuition at Belden Academy—without De Beers, none of it would have been possible. Then when they were safely back in Evans Glen, Willem impressed on Gerard the other side of the De Beers story: their strong-arm tactics in the worldwide diamond trade, the hoarding of diamonds to propagate the perception of scarcity and rarity, and the oppression of blacks in southern African countries.

"Goddamn I'm fucking hungry," said Romberg through the dark from his bunk. "I want hot wings."

"Oh that's uncool, man," said Snodgrass.

"With a shitload of lumpy blue cheese dressing," said Romberg. "And French fries."

"Shut *up*," said Wiley.

Gerard's stomach rumbled. Hot wings sounded great right now. He was hungry too. He wanted chicken or a grilled hamburger or salmon. In Johannesburg Willem had taken him to a restaurant where he had eaten pan-seared salmon with slices of fresh kiwi. He couldn't remember the name of the restaurant (something with 'smoke' in the title) but he could picture the space—a single, open room where diners could watch their food being prepared. Gerard remembered the smell of shrimp and onions and smoke from the steaming skillets behind the counter. Willem and Gerard were having lunch that day with a black man named Ramaal, a former De Beers employee who now worked for an organization called the People Against Gangsterism and Drugs—Pagad. Willem was considering giving money to Pagad, since the South African government and its police force were unable to control the gang problem.

"Sometimes the police are in on it," Ramaal explained. "Police officers in the Western Cape don't earn very much, so they're always easy prey for bribery. Almost every gang has an insider on the police force." Ramaal lifted his tea cup to his mouth. His nostrils flared as he took a slow slurp of the hot tea and swallowed. "Pagad was formed because we got tired of relying on the police to protect us."

"Oh, I know," Willem said. "I've been reading the papers."

"And it isn't that the police are not capable," Ramaal said. "Years ago, they were very effective and creative in cracking down on opposition to apartheid. Where is their creativity now?"

"Yes, good points," Willem said. He nibbled a sugar wafer.

Out on Frances Road, in front of the restaurant, a police wagon screamed by with its siren wailing.

Willem pursed his lips and nodded. "Well, I know Pagad has good intentions, and I want to support it, but what about all this mayhem, like Rashaad Staggie and then the Planet Hollywood bombing?"

Gerard remembered being impressed with Willem's knowledge of the history of Pagad. He had read the South African newspapers too, and he'd been worried that Willem was going to throw his support behind Pagad without asking questions about its sometimes violent tendencies. Rashaad Staggie had been the leader of the Hard Livings gang in Cape Town; he'd been shot two years earlier by an angry mob of Pagad members and then burned alive.

The Planet Hollywood restaurant bombing had happened just a few days ago.

Ramaal shook his head. "We had nothing to do with the Planet Hollywood incident. For some reason the media have decided that we must have been involved."

"But the police are sure," said Willem.

"The police are not fond of us," said Ramaal. "It's always easy to pick on Pagad. The police refer to the group responsible as a 'rogue Pagad G-force.' It gives us all a bad name."

"And Rashaad Staggie?" said Willem.

"That murder was not condoned by organizers of Pagad," said Ramaal. "Some angry members took the law into their own hands. We condemn such violence."

"Well, I've read a lot about the gang activity in Cape Town, especially involving children," Willem said.

Ramaal nodded slowly, staring Willem in the eye. "That's the worst part for me as well, my friend." Ramaal's voice turned soft and velvety. His lower eyelids bulged with tears. "The gangs now target the children of their enemies, as revenge."

And now Willem's eyes were wet too. "Like little Chantine Veldsman."

"Yes," Ramaal said. "Three years old and shot in the head at close range by a masked gunman. She was only playing with her friends. She was just being a child."

And then there was silence. Gerard chewed his salmon and looked from Ramaal to Willem and back to Ramaal.

Ramaal spoke again. "Some people can have no idea what it's like to lose a baby girl."

Willem picked up a napkin and wiped his eyes. He was shaking as he drew a deep breath. Wow, what a salesman Ramaal had been; he must have known that Willem had lost a baby girl.

"Where is the comfort in such a thing?" Ramaal said. "I have often wondered why these things happen. They make me feel helpless. I cannot understand them. The answer for me has been to remember that regardless of what may have happened in the past, the present moment can still be used well. The gift of the present moment, the amazing thing about it, is that *it* holds power over the moment after it. A mindful present moment makes for a better next moment, and so on and so on. That power lies within each of us, whether we yet understand it or not."

And then the entire scene faded out of Gerard's mind as if it had been scripted to end. He tried to remember what Willem had said after that and where they had gone after they'd left the restaurant, and what the return flight had been like, but he couldn't recall anything else. How frustrating that his memories had a life of their own. They were his memories, inside *his* brain! Why couldn't he control them? Why didn't they do his bidding?

"Good night, Gerard," Cooper said from the next bunk.

"Good night," Gerard said. How curious that Cooper called Gerard 'Gerard.' He had been a soldier for less than a month, and already Gerard's first name sounded strange to him. He couldn't bring himself to reciprocate by calling Cooper 'Steven.' It sounded wrong. So Gerard was Gerard and Cooper was Cooper. Cooper didn't mind.

Gerard wished he could control the next moment and the next moment and so on and so on. Cooper probably could. During a hurry-up-and-wait session on the NBC range, when Gerard was complaining about possible nerve damage caused by the chemical smoke they'd inhaled, Cooper had delivered a variation of the "each moment creates the next moment" speech. Had Ramaal and Cooper studied the same curriculum in mysticism? Was there a secret manual somewhere that could help rescue Gerard from the agony of being controlled by his own thoughts? According to Cooper, thoughts had form; when your brain generates thoughts, Cooper claimed, those thoughts are projected into existence and then have a life of their own—their own life and their own form. But Cooper wouldn't talk about where thoughts come from, and that was what Gerard wanted to know; he wanted to investigate the source of his own thoughts. Two facts were definite: 1) Gerard did not want to think about Sylvia's infidelity; 2) Gerard spent a lot of time thinking about the adventures of Sylvia and Gilberto.

Gerard wished he could continue the reel of the last short movie that had played through his brain—the scene in the restaurant with Ramaal and his father—but he couldn't do it. He remembered that Willem later decided to give money to Pagad. "To restore some balance," Willem admitted to Gerard. His relationship with De Beers pulled him in two directions: he wanted to maintain his comfortable living standard, but he felt guilty about the poverty and oppression of black South Africans, much of which Gerard had seen firsthand. In one of the coastal mining towns they visited, for example, married black couples were forced to live separately in run-down, single-sex hostels. Willem had learned that there were no such restrictions for white miners, and that the black diamond workers might get time with their families about three weeks a year. And this was after the end of Apartheid.

*The weak are vanquished and enslaved, and the strong hold the title deeds to the future.*

This quote from Cecil Rhodes—the founder of De Beers—pulsed in whispers through Gerard's head. Cecil would have been proud of the way his company continued to oppress the weak. But Cecil Rhodes was a philanthropist too—he was a good guy! If it hadn't been for Cecil Rhodes and the scholarship program created after his death with money made trampling the vanquished, Gilberto Cardenas would never have received a Rhodes Scholarship and Sylvia wouldn't have met him. So Willem had De Beers to thank for his comfortable life, and Gerard had Cecil Rhodes to thank for the entry of Gilberto Cardenas into Sylvia's life and into Gerard's thoughts. Because of Cecil Rhodes, Sylvia met Gilberto at Oxford and came to learn she enjoyed being rammed and pounded from behind (Letter Twelve) while leaning over Gilberto's kitchen table (in Gilberto's *flat*, as he had written).

But Gerard couldn't entirely blame De Beers for Sylvia's infidelity; after all, didn't the whole Gilberto Cardenas escapade simply reveal a tendency of hers that would have eventually come to the surface anyway? The letters exposed countless tendencies of Sylvia's that were new to Gerard. He was astonished to learn in Letter Nine that Sylvia had a fetish for pouring red wine down her front during sex. Why had she never told Gerard this? It was odd, yes, but Gerard could imagine himself happily pouring red wine on Sylvia, if that was what she really wanted. It was good that he had found out all these things now, while they had time to work on their problems, before they were married with children.

Gerard glanced at his watch. It was 1:00 a.m. Even as exhausted as his body was, his mind had been chattering for half an hour. At home when this used to happen to him, he would pad down to the kitchen for a snack, maybe an ice cream sandwich or a bowl of cereal. Gerard's stomach growled, so he flipped onto his front to try to soothe it. Wake-up time was just a few hours away.

# Six

Couldn't they take a break from PT for one day? They'd been up until 12:30 the night before, and here they were at 5:30 a.m., standing in a quiet formation in the sawdust pit waiting for instructions from Drill Sergeant Womack. Though the sky was still dark, the high floodlights splashed bright rays across the field of mud and wood chips lined with grids of soldier formations from three companies: Bravo, Alpha, and Delta. The air echoed with roars and yelling and group counting.

"The side-straddle hop!" Drill Sergeant Womack yelled as he stepped off the running track and walked toward Third Platoon.

"*THE SIDE-STRADDLE HOP!*" said the platoon.

"Start position, move."

Carroll stuck his arms out sideways. Libby jumped down into push-up position. Womack always tricked someone with that command. One of the requirements of PT was memorizing the start position for every exercise. The push-up start position was easy—drop to the push-up position. For the start position of the windmill, you had to spread your legs and hold your arms up parallel to the ground. Drill Sergeant Hammer, after making sure Womack wouldn't see, had taught Third Platoon the start position for the Titty Twister, an exercise that involved extending your arms in front of you, elbows locked, and twisting your hands at the wrists, as if vigorously tuning two large radio dials. Gerard grinned at the thought of writing home to his mother about the Titty Twister. Third Platoon had had a grand time chuckling about the Titty Twister, until their shoulders burned. Thirty seconds into the exercise the laughter slowly trickled away, and after five grueling minutes of the Titty Twister, there were only gasps and groans.

Drill Sergeant Womack's little joke was that the start position for the side-straddle hop—jumping jacks—was the position of attention; the platoon was already standing at attention and had been for ten minutes. Sometimes when Womack did his little start position gag, he would fling his arms out and lunge forward with one leg. At least two soldiers always copied him, and down they'd go for push-ups. It would be a sad day for Womack when no one fell for his trick.

"Carroll, Libby, ten push-ups, now," Womack said. "The side-straddle hop!"

"*THE SIDE STRADDLE HOP!*"

"Ready, begin. One, two, three—"

"*ONE!*"

"One, two, three—"

"*TWO!*"

Romberg broke rank and raced around the platoon, his arms flapping.

"Get down, Romberg," screamed Womack. "Get down!"

Romberg dropped to the push-up position next to second squad.

"What's wrong with you, Romberg?" said Womack.

"The ravens—"

"Shut up!" Womack said. "We're tired of the ravens. If you wanted out of the army, Romberg, why didn't you just bolo BRM? Help me understand, Romberg. You hit forty targets, a perfect score. What's going on?"

"I want to stay in the army, Drill Sergeant."

"This army isn't big enough for you and the ravens," Womack said. "One of you's got to go."

"Yes, Drill Sergeant."

Womack wiped the sweat from his forehead with the back of his hand. "Okay, Private Romberg, here's what you're going to do. Run back to the company area, draw a weapon from the arms room, and be back here in five minutes in full battle gear. Move."

Romberg hopped up and sprinted across the pit toward the battalion building.

The platoon finished jumping jacks, did a long, stomach-tearing round of butterfly kicks, and was in the middle of sit-ups when Romberg shuffled back across the sawdust, saddled with a backpack, helmet, shoulder harness, canteens, and his rifle.

Drill Sergeant Womack put his fists on his hips. "Kelderman!"

Gerard snapped upright. What had he done now? "Yes, Drill Sergeant!"

"Get up here."

"Yes, Drill Sergeant." Gerard broke rank and dashed forward.

"Private Romberg doesn't enjoy doing platoon PT. He's decided to develop his own PT program. What do you think of that, Kelderman?"

"Well, Drill Sergeant, I find it perplexing. I—"

"Perplexing? Shut up, Kelderman."

"Yes, Drill Sergeant."

"Kelderman, Private Romberg needs special attention, and I've decided that you're perfect for the job. From now on you are personally responsible for everything Romberg does, even after you get fired as squad leader. Twenty-four hours a day, Kelderman. Do you understand?"

"Yes, Drill Sergeant."

"This morning, you will provide Private Romberg with PT motivation. Private Romberg will run laps around the pit, holding his weapon above his head. That should keep the ravens away."

Romberg groaned.

"Is there a problem, Private Romberg?"

"No, Drill Sergeant," Romberg whined.

"Good." Womack wiped a drop of sweat from his nose. "While running in a motivated and spirited manner, Private Romberg will yell repeatedly, as loud as he can, 'I am a dumb-ass' until our platoon finishes PT."

Womack paused and then erupted. "Why are you still here, Romberg?"

Romberg jumped, gear clattering, and ran to the perimeter. He raised his rifle and began a slow shuffle around the quarter-mile track. "I am a dumb-ass, I am a dumb-ass."

Womack faced the platoon, "Private Parker, get out here and lead platoon PT."

"Hey, I thought *I* was the platoon guide," Snodgrass mumbled.

Parker sprinted up and stood in front of the platoon with his chin tucked and his chest thrust outward.

Womack scowled at Gerard. "Kelderman, I can't hear Private Romberg! He's not loud enough."

Gerard looked at Womack, then at Romberg. He cleared his throat. "C'mon Romberg, louder!"

"I am a dumb-ass." Romberg's voice faded the farther away he ran.

Parker led platoon sit-ups.

Womack's voice echoed in the dark morning mist. "Kelderman, tell Romberg to get the lead out and sound off!"

"I am a dumb-ass." Romberg rounded the far turn of the running track.

Soldiers in other PT formations were turning to look at Romberg and at Bravo Company Third Platoon.

Gerard sucked in a deep breath. "Louder, Romberg, and run faster!"

"Louder, Romberg, and run faster." Womack mocked Gerard like a little boy, rocking his head from side to side.

"I am a dumb-ass, I am a dumb-ass." The rifle sagged.

Womack rushed at Gerard and stopped with his mouth an inch from Gerard's ear. He spoke quietly and slowly. Gerard's neck hair stood up.

"Kelderman, would you like to join the Private Romberg PT program?"

"No, Drill Sergeant."

"Then motivate him!"

Gerard sprang two feet into the air. "Move it, Romberg! We can't hear you! Sound off! Louder! Yell! Get the lead out!"

Cooper chuckled. Womack whipped around and faced the formation.

"Private Parker, do we have a comedian in the platoon?"

"No Drill Sergeant!"

Cooper chuckled again.

"Private Parker, are you lying to me?"

"No, Drill Sergeant! I mean, yes Drill Sergeant," said Parker. "Shit. Cooper, shut the fuck up!"

"I am a dumb-ass, I am a dumb-ass."

"You better get control of this mob, Parker," said Womack.

"Drill Sergeant," said Snodgrass.

"What?"

"I thought *I* was supposed to be the platoon guide," said Snodgrass.

"Come on, Romberg, move it!" yelled Gerard.

"You are, Snodgrass," said Womack.

"Then how come Parker gets to lead platoon PT?" said Snodgrass.

"Oh, good God, Snodgrass," said Womack. "Because I told him to."

"I am a dumb-ass. I am a dumb-ass."

"The Titty Twister!" yelled Parker.

"The *what*?" said Womack.

"*THE TITTY TWISTER!*"

"But Drill Sergeant, doesn't the platoon guide get to—"

"Shut up, Snodgrass," said Womack. "Parker, who taught you that exercise?"

"Louder, Romberg," yelled Gerard.

"Kelderman, shut up!" Womack said.

Gerard turned toward Womack. "But you told me—"

"Okay, okay," Womack said. "Enough. Enough motivating."

Romberg rounded the last turn. His feet were dragging. "I am a dumb-ass."

"Parker, fall in," said Womack. "Romberg! Get over here. You're done. Kelderman, stay where you are. I'm not done with you."

"Yes, Drill Sergeant," Gerard said.

Womack faced Third Platoon. "Snodgrass, stand up straight. Libby, tuck your shirt in."

Womack turned around and faced Gerard and Romberg. Romberg's fatigues were soaked through. Sheets of sweat poured from under his helmet down the front of his face.

"You two have a new relationship now, don't you?" said Womack.

"Yes, Drill Sergeant," said Gerard and Romberg.

"Private Kelderman, do you understand the arrangement?" Womack said.

Gerard paused a moment. "Yes, Drill Sergeant."

"But you don't like it, do you?"

"No, Drill Sergeant."

"I know why you don't like it," said Womack. "Because it involves responsibility. It involves taking control. It involves being responsible for someone other than your own sorry self, isn't that right?"

"Romberg should be responsible for himself, Drill Sergeant," said Gerard. And he meant it. How would he be able to control Romberg, even for one minute? He wasn't a mental health professional. Gerard wanted badly to make a comment about Romberg's mental instability, about all the years he'd been in therapy, about the death of Romberg's mother when he was fifteen. But he couldn't. Romberg had trusted Gerard by telling him all that, and no one else in the platoon (with the exception of Fuller) knew anything about it. If Womack found out, Romberg would be kicked out of the army—Fraudulent Enlistment they would call it, according to Romberg.

"Deal with it Kelderman," said Womack. "You'd better figure out how you're going to control Romberg's little outbursts. Romberg!"

"Yes, Drill Sergeant," Romberg said.

"You've got a personal babysitter now," said Womack. "You need a babysitter, don't you?"

"No, Drill Sergeant," said Romberg.

"Yes you do, so now you've got one," Womack said. "How does that make you feel?"

"I don't know, Drill Sergeant," Romberg said.

"Private Yanni!"

"Yes, Drill Sergeant," said Cooper from the back row of the formation.

"Am I damaging Private Romberg's self-esteem by giving him a babysitter?"

"No, Drill Sergeant," said Cooper.

"Good," said Womack. "Romberg, you're a troubled individual. I don't know what all this raven crap is, but you wouldn't be hitting forty targets on the firing range if you didn't want to stay in the army. Is that right, Romberg?"

"Yes, Drill Sergeant."

"Good," said Womack. "Both of you, fall in."

Gerard sprinted to the back, and Romberg clattered behind him. Thin, white mist rose up from the soaked shoulders of the Third-Platoon soldiers; their gray PT shirts were sopping with sweat as they stood at attention.

"PT's over, men," said Womack. "Platoon—Right—Face!"

They spun to the right.

"Forward—March! Left, left, left-right-left."

Third Platoon tromped back to the company area, with Gerard marching at the front of Fourth Squad. How could he control Romberg when he didn't even understand him? Why didn't Womack just get it over with and have Romberg kicked out of the army? During the first few days of basic training it seemed that Womack thought Romberg was faking. A handful of soldiers from other platoons had left and gone home because they couldn't handle the pressure. Some of them simply couldn't stop crying, and one wet his bed every night. These sorts of details got around Bravo Company very quickly. Those people were now gone, sent home. There would be no official records of their enlistments; it would be as if they had never signed up at all. Fuller had told Gerard that there was a period of six months when a new recruit could simply decide to opt out of his enlistment under something called Failure to Adjust to Military something-or-other. In his moments of despair, that option appealed to Gerard, but he couldn't imagine facing the shame of his platoon mates. Worse, if he still did have a chance with Sylvia, there was no way he could go back to her having failed at his attempt to match Gilberto Cardenas's manliness. Sylvia, Sylvia. This would all be worth it when he was back in her arms.

# Seven

Mueller was the fireguard and turned off the lights. Another day of training was over. On this 30th day of basic training Bravo Company had completed a second round of the bayonet course, a relay race with lanes of rubber dummies for the soldiers to stab. When any drill sergeant asked Bravo Company the purpose of a bayonet, 224 soldiers thundered back *"TO KILL, KILL, KILL WITH COLD, BLUE STEEL!"* Private Libby had nearly done exactly that: he'd tripped and had almost fallen on his own bayonet twice. Gerard had wondered out loud if the drill sergeants had let Libby continue the course in the hope that he would hurt himself.

"No way," Fuller had said. "The brass blame the trainers if someone dies. Besides, no one would want to do all that paperwork and have to go through an investigation."

Gerard pulled the green wool blanket up to his chest. It had been ten days since Drill Sergeant Womack had put Gerard in charge of Romberg during the I-am-a-dumb-ass incident. Since his arrival at Fort Benning over a month ago, Gerard had lost probably fifteen pounds. His body was adapting to the heat and the physical abuse, Cooper had finally passed his rifle marksmanship qualification test (so had Libby), Romberg had seen no ravens and had done nothing to get himself or Gerard into trouble with Womack, and Parker hadn't called Gerard an asshole even once. Now it was Friday night, and Third Platoon was in bed at 10:00 p.m. Romberg was in bed too, snoozing away—Gerard had made sure of that before he'd tucked himself in.

When he was six years old Gerard would help his mom tuck baby Anna into bed after giving her a bottle of milk and reading to her. Gerard would be only halfway through *Goodnight Moon*, and Anna would lean against the couch pillow with her eyes closed and her mouth hanging open, the bottle dangling on her lower lip; the little kid never had any trouble falling asleep.

And here Gerard was, having slept only four hours a night for the past month, and he was lying awake in bed with his hands locked behind his head. 10 o'clock. At Monroe Hill College a Friday night wouldn't even get *started* until 10 o'clock at the earliest. St. Philip Fraternity threw parties that began at eleven. The night the Lambeth police had raided the house, most people had arrived at the house around 11:30. Gerard had told Sylvia about the party earlier that week, and she had said she'd be there, but after they'd had dinner at the Neighbor's Tavern on the Corner that night Sylvia had said she wanted to go home. She was tired.

Gerard now wondered if she'd really been tired or if she had planned a date with someone else. He did that often now—he played back scenes with Sylvia from their senior year at Monroe Hill and examined them all in a new light. She'd been unfaithful, though it was more comforting to Gerard to think of it as "screwing someone else." There was no word-mincing in that phrase; it got closer to what really was. And since they'd been engaged at the time of her activities, could he call what she did an affair? Was this what it felt like when your spouse has an affair, a real affair? When other people discovered cheating partners, did they feel hurt too, and did they sit around wondering what was wrong with them that would make their mates seek intimacy elsewhere?

Anyway, when Sylvia went home the night of that fraternity party—or wherever the hell she went—there was one thing Gerard knew she would *not* being doing, and that was reading her love letters from Gilberto Cardenas. Ha! Those letters, that very night, were tucked away in Gerard's dresser drawer upstairs (he would return them to her room the following day, just before dinner). Seventeen letters. Gilberto. Sylvia had set everything up perfectly for Gerard's fall that night—without her, none of it would have happened. If she had come to the party that night, she would have saved him from the fall—from getting high, from letting Rachel

Sheehan pile on solid layers of sexual tension, and from waking up with a headache and a desire to walk five miles to sort it all out. Because of Sylvia and Gilberto, and because Sylvia chose not to come to that party, Gerard had enlisted in the army and was now suffering in an environment where people forced him to stand in lines for hours and where he was tortured with exercises like the Titty Twister.

It was easy for Gerard to look back and blame everyone else for his entry into military service. He'd made a few bad choices of his own, but he couldn't have done it without all those other people. He imagined himself giving an acceptance speech in front of a huge crowd and humbly insisting that he couldn't have done it alone—that he had so many people to thank for their help along the way, especially Sylvia, Gilberto, and Rachel Sheehan.

Oh, Rachel. Sylvia couldn't make the party that night, but Rachel could, and she did.

"Gerard Kelderman smoking a *joint*?" Rachel had said. "Do I need glasses?"

Gerard lay sprawled across a musty sofa on the darkened, second floor of the St. Philip fraternity house. His friend Charles leaned on the arm rest at the other end of the couch. It was nearly 2 o'clock. Most people had left the party and gone to the Corner for Lambeth's most famous hamburger: the Statesman—a greasy tower of ground beef topped with fried eggs and bacon and available at any hour of the night. He looked across the room at Rachel, who slumped against the door frame on one leg with a bare foot perched against the side of her knee. The top buttons of her white shirt were undone. Gerard's eyes tracked from the brown beer bottle that dangled by her knee, up her long thigh to the fringe of her denim skirt. My God—those legs. The spring break Rachel had spent in Aruba had turned her legs a smooth hazelnut brown.

Gerard leaned back and blew smoke into the air. "Yeah, a joint." He giggled. "Tasty."

"What next, Gerard? Abandon your sweet little Sylvia?" Rachel chewed at the side of her lower lip and squinted at Gerard. Her voice was soft and raspy—probably from too much smoking and drinking Diet Coke.

Charles shook his head. "Naw, we got him to share some weed with us, but he'll never break off an engagement with the beautiful Miss Landon."

Gerard breathed deeply as he grinned at the ceiling. "Sylvia Landon. Sylvia Landon. The Oxford girl. And let's not forget Gilberto Cardenas."

"Who?" said Charles.

"Oh, nothing," Gerard said. "Never mind." How he wanted to tell Charles—tell everyone—about the seventeen letters and what was in them. Gilberto was a competent writer. Charles would have enjoyed the content. Gerard would need to sneak the letters back into Sylvia's bedroom soon, though it tickled him to consider having them published in an anthology of literary erotica.

He smiled, imagining Sylvia finding out he was smoking marijuana. What would she say that he couldn't answer? Nothing. Not a thing. "Really, Gerard, what are you doing?" she might say. And Gerard would answer, "Oh, I don't know, what were *you* doing at midnight on that park bench behind the North Lodge at Oxford with Gilberto?" He chuckled and snorted and then laughed out loud.

He'd never tried marijuana before. It was amazing. He placed the tip of the joint between his lips and drew a toke into his mouth—like sipping from a straw, nothing to it. His tongue tasted the white smoke; yes, it had *taste*, a sweetness, like fresh fennel or oregano. It felt warm against his cheeks and cool on his teeth. He pulled the smoke in against his throat and down his windpipe. It flowed smoothly like warm cognac. Why in God's name hadn't he done this sooner? When he was in the fifth grade he had taken one draft from a cigarette and sucked it in too quickly. The harsh sting in his lungs had made him dizzy and sweaty.

But this! Where had this been all his life? Gerard had Charles to thank for this marijuana. Charles was an underclassman fraternity brother whom Gerard had sponsored during rush, though Charles and Gerard were the same age. Because Charles was Mormon, he had spent two years in North Carolina doing missionary work before enrolling at Monroe Hill College. The only reason the brothers of St. Philip knew about Charles's past was because they had discovered his Mormon undergarment. The brothers had forced the rush-candidates to strip naked one evening, and Charles had removed his clothes to reveal a white, one-piece of underwear smattered with symbols—compasses and squares and the like. The brothers had guffawed and howled until Charles had explained it was part of his religion. All the laughing and joking had instantly stopped, and then came "sorry, dude" and "it's cool" and "okay, well, anyway..." Charles had quickly assured the group that he'd left the Mormon church, but a part of him couldn't let go of his undergarment; wearing it made him feel secure. No one had ever joked about Charles's undergarment again.

What a transformation Charles had undergone—first a devout Mormon and now scoring marijuana for a fellow fraternity brother. Gerard had politely refused earlier in the evening, but after a few cups of Sam Adams from the keg, he'd relented. What did he have to lose? Sure, his girlfriend had stomped all over him for an entire year, but he had other things: his cello playing, diamond cutting, and a long, hot summer at the Kasteel in Evans Glen. He knew he would have to find a job in the fall, but that would be easy. The only challenge would be deciding between diamonds and the cello—he had mastered both fully enough to be able to earn a living doing either. He wondered if Meredith would be in Evans Glen too. If she was, it would be another full summer of sex.

His chest billowed up with smoke and tasted the nutty, warm flavor. He never wanted to breathe out. His lungs were being gently toasted from the inside. He leaned his head back and flopped his arms. He released, and his chest cavity collapsed as if it would keep falling down into the beer-stained sofa, through the floorboards, and down to the foyer. He lifted his head to see Rachel straddling him, her short skirt hiking up as her knees caressed his ribs on both sides.

"Damn, Gerard, it's like you're having an orgasm." She tipped her bottle back and swigged.

The open buttons on Rachel's white shirt revealed the black lace edges of her bra. Her strong, full thighs squeezed against his sides. Damn. He drew another toke from his joint. Sylvia would never have straddled him like this, not in bed, not even as a joke (there had been one exception, but Gerard would later realize the reason Sylvia hadn't been herself that night). In general, sex with Sylvia was predictable: Gerard on top, Sylvia on the bottom. Every time. And sex with Sylvia Landon had to be scheduled; she always needed to plan ahead.

Oh, but not with Gilberto—no, no. Letter Three lucidly described plenty of spontaneous sex between Sylvia and Gilberto Cardenas. It was shocking enough to Gerard that Sylvia would administer oral sex when Gilberto was driving (Letter Eleven), but Sylvia had pulled Gilberto into the women's rest room at the *Gloucester Arms* (a pub, apparently) and hopped up onto the counter. Gilberto had wasted no time yanking her skirt up and—

"What do you say, Gerard?" Rachel pressed her palm against his chest and rubbed upward. "You're pretty relaxed for a change." Her full hips pushed downward onto him, forcefully nestling her pelvis against his. She massaged the side of his neck with her hand. "I've wanted this for years, Gerard."

Gerard was well aware of that—that for two years Rachel had wanted badly to take him to bed. Sylvia hated Rachel Sheehan. Rachel had never said so, but Gerard knew her challenge was to wrest him away from Sylvia Landon; it would be her triumph. Gerard giggled. So now Rachel was about to have her victory on the second floor of the St. Philip fraternity house. And why resist? Rachel felt good: her legs, her hips, her hand on his neck. She leaned forward and brought her warm mouth close to his ear.

"Charles is asleep, Gerard." She nipped his ear and sat back up.

Gerard looked over at Charles, who was loudly snoring and whose head was thrown so far back on the top cushion of the sofa that his Adam's apple pointed like a steeple toward the ceiling. Rachel leaned across the couch and took the joint from Charles's limp fingers. She sucked a long draw and blew smoke in Gerard's face. Gerard breathed in. Rachel disappeared for a moment behind

a smoke cloud that moments later broke apart to reveal her unbuttoning her shirt and then reaching behind her back to unfasten her
bra. The black lace cups fell forward. Gerard placed his hand on
her neck and rubbed. What was he doing? He couldn't. Yes he
could. No he couldn't. Oh hell—yes he could. He had never wanted
Sylvia this badly. In that moment, as doped up as he was, he had
never wanted anyone as badly as he wanted Rachel Sheehan.

Rachel grasped his wrist and guided his right hand lower, along
the front of her smooth neck and chest. She leaned forward so he
could touch every part of her soft skin. With his left hand he
sucked his joint. Was he high? Was this being high—this not being
able to speak or move or have any kind of palpable thought—and
not caring? Gerard was so loose, so free of tension, so tranquil, so
serene. His touch-hungry skin tingled and buzzed all over and
ached and his chest rose to meet Rachel's warm, firm, hand and
then her wet mouth and if his body could speak—oh, she *had* to
know what his body was saying—every cell and molecule would
sigh and wail and moan *yes, whatever you want, Rachel, I'm
yours, I will not resist, I will submit, take me, do it now, please do
all of it now—*

"Nobody move! Stay where you are!" There was yelling down in
the foyer and pounding footsteps on the wooden staircase.

Charles's eyes popped open and he jumped up. "Cops!"

Gerard's hand fell away from Rachel as she sprang from the
couch. His first consideration was that he hoped Sylvia wouldn't
find out about Rachel. He couldn't let go of that thought. Sylvia
had romped with Gilberto dozens and dozens of times, and still
Gerard was worried she would learn about this.

"Where's my joint?" Charles was patting the sofa. "Where the
hell's my joint?"

Rachel handed it to him. "Here it is. Take this one too."

Charles ran the joints into the hallway bathroom and slammed
the door. Two policeman appeared in the doorway.

"Stay put. No one move," said one of the cops.

Had they seen? Had they seen Rachel on top of him? Rachel had
buttoned up her shirt but Gerard couldn't tell if the cops had no-

ticed. The police herded the partyers into the library on the ground floor and then spent an hour searching the house. Instead of appreciating that Charles had skillfully disposed of his marijuana, Gerard spent that hour stewing in the worry that word of his fooling around with Rachel would get out.

Gerard tried to fluff his pancake of an army pillow. He lay on his back and stared upward. A faint red glow fanned out across the ceiling tiles from the light of the fire-exit sign. Cooper was in his bunk reading under the covers with a flashlight.

What if the cops hadn't arrived at that moment, or if they hadn't come at all? Gerard had no trouble imagining what would have happened between Rachel and him there on the couch, but the possible aftermath was a mystery to him. Rachel might have run to tell Sylvia that she'd finally done it and that Sylvia could stop being so sure of herself and confident about her fiancé's fidelity. Or maybe Gerard and Rachel would have been swept up in the current unleashed by the floodgate; maybe they would have devoured each other incessantly for the next few days or weeks, and Gerard would have lost Sylvia. Perhaps the intensity of sex with Rachel would have made it easy to let go of Sylvia. Now he'd never know.

Gerard flipped onto his side and sighed. Cooper stuck his head out from the blanket.

"Good night, Gerard." He smiled.

Gerard yawned. "Good night, Cooper."

# Eight

"Rise and shine, Bravo Company!"

It was day 41 of training. The company was on bivouac, sleeping in the field on Fort Benning sand in musty canvas tents. Each soldier, with his battle buddy, had snapped together his shelter-half to form a two-man tent. Under normal circumstances sleeping under Georgia pines in a tent would have been nice, but this was cramped and uncomfortable. Parker was a tent hog and kept rolling over, squeezing Gerard into a thin space while they slept. Because it was summer the soldiers were issued no sleeping bags. Instead Gerard had to make due on his foam sleeping mat and a balled-up shirt as a pillow, all the while hanging on to his NBC gas mask and M16, neither of which was very cuddly.

Even so, as Gerard now woke up, he was aware that his muscles felt hard and strong, and that he was instantly ready to hop up and get moving. He couldn't remember exactly when the change had happened, only that it was some time during the past three weeks of training, training that had included Rifle Bayonet Fighting Training—RBFT, land mines, the M240 machine gun, hand-to-hand combat, land navigation, hand grenades, the AT-4 anti-tank weapon, and plenty of marching, running, push-ups, and sit-ups. There was no scale available to the soldiers of Bravo Company, but Gerard guessed he had now lost about twenty pounds. He was actually starting to feel slim. Gerard sat up and stretched. On this fine, foggy Fort Benning morning, he was ready for anything.

"Come on, Bravo Company, up and at 'em!"

The company commander, Captain Fopp, was yelling as he walked among the bivouac tents. He was a short, whiny man. The drill sergeants tried to be judicious in laughing at him, but the soldiers of Bravo Company could tell how the drill sergeants felt about their commanding officer. Gerard sensed that the drill sergeants were aware that the recruits knew, but they didn't care. Captain Fopp had found a metal trash can and was banging it with a stick, just like in the movies.

All the recruits in Third Platoon (and throughout the company, Gerard assumed) were getting a healthy indoctrination into hatred of military officers. Sometimes Captain Fopp liked to pretend he was a drill sergeant. He showed himself around the company area every few days, perhaps to remind Bravo Company that he was the commander and that he was in charge. By now, though, everyone knew it was First Sergeant McFadden who ran the company, and Gerard smiled when he imagined Captain Fopp giving an order to First Sergeant McFadden. Rank insignia kept the first sergeant on good behavior; without it, McFadden would have eaten Captain Fopp.

The only company cadre member who could be seen less often than Captain Fopp was First Lieutenant Overman, the company Executive Officer—the XO. Lieutenant Overman was a buff West Point graduate who discreetly snorted whenever in the presence of Captain Fopp (Captain Fopp had received his commission through an ROTC program in Illinois, an apparent abomination to Lieutenant Overman). As far as Gerard could tell, there wasn't really anything for Lieutenant Overman to do. What exactly was an Executive Officer? Private Fuller had explained how the XO was second-in-command and the official assistant to the commander, but the explanation only furthered Gerard's perception of the worthlessness of the position.

Sometimes Captain Fopp got excited and drove his shabby Toyota pickup truck to the firing range during training. One day as the company lined up at the firing range for a safety briefing on the M240 machine gun, Captain Fopp had pulled in to the gravel parking lot, hopped out of his pickup, and run toward Third Platoon.

"You think I didn't *see* that, Private?" he said as he huffed toward Second Squad. "You, you in the middle there." He was pointing at Libby.

"Sir, yes Sir!" Libby said.

"Libby, it's only 'Yes, sir'," said Berkowicz.

"Shut up, Berkowicz," Womack said. Womack stepped back a little bit to give Captain Fopp more room, which was absurd, because Captain Fopp was skinny and about five-foot-four.

"You were scratching your nose in formation, weren't you, Private?" squeaked Captain Fopp.

Gerard noticed Drill Sergeant Hammer looking at Womack and smiling. Womack slowly shook his head, but Gerard couldn't figure out if he was doing that because of Libby or because of Captain Fopp.

"Sir, yes, Sir! I mean, yes, Sir!" Libby said.

"Drill Sergeant Womack," said Captain Fopp.

"Yes Sir," Womack said, walking over.

"Looks like we have a bit of a problem here." Captain Fopp stood with his hands on his hips and his mouth tightly pursed. "Yep, bit of a problem. You might say we've got a 'situation'."

Romberg chuckled. Parker slugged him hard with his elbow.

"Looks like this private doesn't understand the position of attention," said Captain Fopp. "What do you want, Private? Do you want *push-ups*? Because we can give you a *lot* of push-ups here in Bravo Company. Oh, yeah." His head nodded like a bobber doll. "Is *that* what you want, Private? Push-ups? Answer me!"

"No, Sir!" Libby said.

"Well, okay then," said Captain Fopp. "Okay then." And he slowed his speech way down. "Then you'd better watch yourself, I'd say." He was still nodding.

Libby's chin was tucked and his eyes were wide. Gerard thought Libby might urinate in his pants.

"Drill Sergeant Womack, he's all yours," said Captain Fopp. He turned and walked away.

Womack watched Captain Fopp walk toward the range tower (where he probably hoped to find a cup of coffee). Gerard and the rest of the platoon had braced for what they were sure would be a first-class smoking, but when Captain Fopp was out of sight, Womack had taken charge of the platoon and seated them in the bleachers for their safety briefing. Nothing! Not even a word. By doing nothing, Womack had clearly conveyed his attitude about Captain Fopp.

So now Bravo Company was in the field for five days, and Captain Fopp had decided to pay them another visit and continue the fantasy that he actually had anything to do with training soldiers.

"Let's go men, wake up. It's time to move," came Captain Fopp's shrill voice. He was earnestly clanging the stick onto the garbage can. "Come on, let's get moving. You there—you don't even have your socks on. Let's move it. You think we're playing games here?"

It was the second day of bivouac, or 'camping' as Cooper referred to it. That really angered the drill sergeants, the way Cooper called it camping. Never mind that no amount of physical suffering affected Cooper's mood; now he was changing the name of an event to make it sound like fun, and that was unacceptable. They'd smoke him until he'd relent and say bivouac, but there he'd be the next day talking excitedly about the upcoming camping trip.

Gerard and Parker were scuffling around in their cramped tent trying to get dressed. Gerard sat up and reached for his PT uniform.

"Hey man, that's my PT shirt," Parker said.

"No it isn't, it's mine," said Gerard. "I laid it out last night."

"Man, motherfucker, I swear to fucking God I'm gonna—oh, here's mine." Parker snatched his shirt from the ground and pulled it over his head. He and Gerard grabbed their rifles, pushed back the tent flap, and jogged toward the formation area.

"You'll be so goddamn close to your weapon in the field it's gonna want an engagement ring," Drill Sergeant Hammer had announced back at the company area before they'd loaded the cattle trucks.

Because the company was away from the arms room, each soldier had to keep his rifle with him at all times. PT was no exception. Stretches, warm-ups, and running—it was all done while holding the heavy M16A2 rifle. But in this sixth week of training it was easy. Gerard's body was strong. Push-ups were a breeze, he could twist titties with the best of them, and his two-mile-run time was under fifteen minutes. He was actually starting to enjoy running and the rush it gave him.

Drill Sergeants Womack and Hammer led Third Platoon in Rifle PT (the drill sergeants didn't have rifles. "Fuckers," Romberg had said). They spent thirty minutes doing exercises and then went on a formation run, during which Private Carroll had dropped his M16 on the asphalt and then tripped over it, knocking down an entire column of fourteen soldiers like dominoes. Womack's first reaction had been to scream at Libby; Drill Sergeant Hammer had to stop him and convince him it was Carroll.

Now the run was over, the sun was rising, and Captain Fopp had driven away in his pickup truck, probably to go back home and take a shower.

"Is this army getting too easy for you, Kelderman?" said Womack during cool-down stretches.

"No, Drill Sergeant," said Gerard.

"Yes it is," said Womack. "You've lost weight, haven't you?"

"Yes, Drill Sergeant," said Gerard.

Womack couldn't stand it, could he? Gerard was stronger and having an easier time now—sailing much more smoothly than Private Carroll. Carroll was nineteen years old, six feet tall, and had probably lost only about ten pounds since the start of training, which would put him now at about 240 pounds. For army fitness standards Carroll had to follow the table for 17 to 21-year-olds, and he still couldn't run two miles under the maximum allowed time of 15 minutes and 54 seconds. Gerard, for whatever reason, was shedding pounds and trimming half-minutes off his run time each week. Because Gerard was 22, he was allowed up to 16 minutes and 36 seconds to complete the two-mile run, though these days he was well under 15 minutes.

Gerard had worked so hard and improved himself so much that he thought he deserved a break from Womack's harassment. But clearly drill sergeants can sense when a soldier is having it too easy, and they adapt accordingly. Womack had a special sensor for Gerard. The jerk. Why did Womack always pick on him? Gerard knew this was a rhetorical question, because Womack had made it clear more than once that he had special ideas for Gerard. Womack could tell, he had told the platoon, when a recruit came into the service from a padded life. Somehow Womack had separated Gerard from the gaggle of eighteen-year-olds whom Womack called the Nintendo generation. Womack was harsh on the Nintendo generation but for some reason had gotten it into his head that Gerard had led a sheltered and luxurious life of his own before arriving at Fort Benning. It was Womack's mission to introduce Gerard to reality. Gerard had briefly considered telling Womack that he had never played Nintendo—that he had spent his time playing the cello—but he thought better of it and kept his mouth shut. The more information you gave a drill sergeant, the more material the drill sergeant had to use against you. Better to keep quiet.

Third Platoon changed out of PT clothes and into fatigues—BDUs. They shoveled through breakfast and then endured a sweltering day of advanced land navigation training. Gerard's BDUs stayed drenched all day; his sweat was so heavy that it soaked into his pistol belt and the straps of his shoulder harness. On some mornings his clothes and black combat boots were streaked with dry, white stripes of salt. The first time Romberg had seen white streaks on his own clothes, he hadn't believed it was salt until he'd licked his undershirt. "Saltier than a wrestler's armpit," he'd proclaimed.

That evening after a dinner of ham and rice on styrofoam plates, Womack called a platoon formation.

"Drill Sergeant Hammer and I have decided it's time for a change of leadership in this platoon."

"Thank God," muttered Gerard. He'd been squad leader for a month, since the first week of training, and he was tired of the whining and harassment of his Fourth Squad subjects, especially Parker.

"What are you mumblin' back there, Kelderman?" said Drill Sergeant Hammer.

"Nothing, Drill Sergeant," said Gerard.

"You ready to step down, ain't you?" Hammer said.

"Yes, Drill Sergeant."

"'Bout goddamn time," said Parker.

"Shut up, Hot Shit," Hammer said.

Gerard's eyes widened as another thought hit him: perhaps he'd be relieved of his Romberg-watching duty! Gerard had come to disdain that job as well. It was about time they spread the duties among soldiers who'd been sitting on their butts.

"Snodgrass, get back into your squad. You're not the platoon guide any more," said Womack.

Snodgrass couldn't conceal the grin on his face as he jogged around into formation.

"Fourth Squad, you got a new squad leader," said Hammer. "Private Hot Shit, you're on."

Parker took one step back and then walked to the right end of the formation. With his shoulder he shoved Gerard to the left. Gerard smiled, happy to be done with his squad leader duty. Following was easier than leading.

"Kelderman, are you sad that we've replaced you?" Womack said.

"No, Drill Sergeant."

"What?" said Hammer. "You don't want to lead? Bullshit. You miss it already, dontcha?"

"No, Drill Sergeant."

"Bullshit! You miss it. You like being a leader," Hammer said.

Gerard rolled his eyes. Why? Why couldn't they all crawl into their tents and go to bed? Why had he been singled out? Well, the quickest way to end it was to give him what he wanted.

"Yes, Drill Sergeant, I miss it already," said Gerard. "I can't begin to explain the emptiness in my soul." What was he doing? Why were these words coming out of his mouth? This was *not* the quickest way to end the ordeal.

"Outstanding!" said Drill Sergeant Womack. "Private Kelderman, you're the new platoon guide."

Gerard's stomach plummeted to his ankles.

"Get your ass up there," said Hammer.

Gerard jogged around front and faced the platoon. Berkowicz, Phillips, Romberg, Wiley, Carroll—they were all looking at him. And he knew that look because he himself had donned it many times during the past few weeks: *Thank God it's you and not me.*

Now it was him.

"Okay, Platoon Guide. Dismiss your platoon and get them ready for bed," said Womack.

"Dismissed," yelled Gerard.

"Get down, Kelderman!" screamed Womack.

Gerard dropped to push-up position.

"You don't dismiss a platoon without first calling it to attention. On your feet."

Gerard jumped up. "Platoon, atten—tion!"

The platoon clicked its heels and stood rigid.

"Dismissed," said Gerard.

♦     ♦     ♦

"You got enough room, *Platoon Guide?*" Parker lay on his back and was pulling his BDU shirt up to his shoulders like a blanket, shoving Gerard with his hip.

"Yeah, thanks," Gerard said. "I didn't ask to be the platoon guide."

Parker flipped onto his side, facing away from Gerard. "Just don't fuck it up."

Gerard folded his arms across his chest and stared at the top of the tent. High above the Bravo Company bivouac site, bugs and frogs hummed and chattered the soldiers to sleep. They were louder than locusts at dusk at Monroe Hill College.

It had been an autumn evening in the Pavilion gardens at Monroe Hill when Sylvia had announced to Gerard, over sandwiches from Neil's Deli on the Corner, that she was ready to have sex with him. She had gingerly placed her sandwich on her lap and dabbed her mouth with the edge of her napkin before making her proclamation.

"I don't mean right now, outdoors here in the gardens," she had clarified.

That had been during their second year at Monroe Hill, so Sylvia could have had no idea that one year later she *would* be having sex outdoors, in a garden, near the North Lodge at Oxford. Perhaps she'd been inspired by a sandwich there too.

But on that cool evening in the garden of Pavilion Six, on a white bench inside the brick serpentine wall, there would be no sex—only talk of sex. They had long ago discussed their own sexual histories: Gerard had experience, Sylvia had none. She had never pressed Gerard for details in the past, but on this night she demanded that Gerard provide a count of the number of people he'd slept with.

"And I mean intercourse, Gerard, not just sleeping."

So Gerard was honest and told her about the two people in his past. There had been Maya Ferguson, a girl he had dated during his freshman year when he'd lived in Kirsch Hall. Their relationship had entered its fourth month when Maya had abruptly dumped Gerard after getting wrapped up with the Campus Christian Fellowship. She'd announced one day that she was now born again and tried to force Gerard to join her in repenting for their sinful acts together. Maya was genuinely concerned for Gerard's soul and the torment he would suffer in the afterlife. Gerard had never thought of his relationship with Maya in terms of the *number* of sexual encounters, but Sylvia insisted he try to remember. He guessed the total to be about twenty or twenty-five. And as Gerard watched Sylvia's eyes widen when he said twenty-five, he knew Sylvia was in for a shocker when Gerard told her about Meredith, Gerard's neighbor and closest childhood friend from Evans Glen.

Beyond the carriage house at 330 West Dixon Road, behind the Kasteel's main house, was a vast expanse of trim grass and tall boxwood hedges. Meredith and her family lived around the corner from the Keldermans, at 14 Mitchell Park Road. The back edge of Meredith's yard shared a side with the Kasteel's property. Meredith and Gerard had known each other since they were five. In their early childhoods they'd played and biked and spent long days at the swimming pool. Many times they had jokingly held hands and pretended they were married, and when they were eight years old Gerard had kissed Meredith one day at the pool behind the snack machine. She'd been daring him all day to kiss her on the lips, and when he did they'd both exploded with giggles. As they matured together the kisses grew longer and the dares became bolder. Before long they were having sex, daily, at Meredith's house, at Gerard's house, in the carriage house, outdoors between the hedges—

"Okay, okay, okay," said Sylvia. "I don't need that much information."

"But you asked," said Gerard.

"Okay, okay. Enough."

One piece of information Sylvia did want to know, however, and which she would not let go of, was how old Gerard and Meredith had been when they'd first had sex.

"Fourteen?" Sylvia said. "You had sex with a fourteen-year-old girl?"

"I was fourteen too," Gerard reminded her.

"*Fourteen?*"

But Sylvia hadn't grown up in Evans Glen, Virginia, where there was never anything to do. She was from the exciting city of Atlanta, which Gerard imagined to be a fun and dynamic place. In Evans Glen teenagers would either hang around the Foxwood movie theater or sit on their car hoods in the McDonald's parking lot. That was the extent of excitement in Evans Glen, and when teenagers got bored they screwed themselves silly. It had been easy for Gerard and Meredith because of the proximity of their houses and because their parents had no clue (Gerard's parents were always working; Meredith's parents simply never paid attention). They'd agreed from the outset that sex would be purely recreational—that they would never call themselves boyfriend and girlfriend or use the word 'dating.' Dating was something they did with other people during middle and high school, even as they continued having sex with each other. Still, Meredith would joke about wanting to marry Gerard when they were old enough, just to get rid of her awful surname: Flanigan-Flambert.

It was her father's doing from the beginning. Patrick Flanigan had wanted to hyphenate with Lisa Flambert. He'd brought up the topic during their early days of dating, even before he'd proposed to her. Lisa would tell Rebecca Ward she sometimes felt Patrick was more interested in the cause than in being married.

"It's the only thing that's fair—you know, to the women," Patrick had said.

Never mind that Lisa had *wanted* to get rid of her name and become Lisa Flanigan. 'Flambert' may have had an elegant French pronunciation at some point, but the Flamberts had immigrated to the U.S. so long ago that the name couldn't have been more Americanized. "It's Flam-BURT," Meredith would often have to correct.

So Patrick Flanigan had triumphed and become Patrick Flanigan-Flambert. "A tribute to both our families," he'd said. He hadn't thought ahead to the effect the name would have on Meredith in the Cornwall County public school system. In the ninth grade Meredith had signed up for French I, and on the first day of class, Monsieur Calahan—prancing about the room with his clipboard— had pronounced her name with proud emphasis: "Flanigan-Flam*baire*." When Meredith had told him how the name was really pronounced, Monsieur Calahan had corrected her—about her own name!

"*Ah non, Mademoiselle*," he'd said, waving his index finger. "*C'est sans doute 'Flambaire.' Tout le monde, répétez: 'Flambaire'.*"

Gerard hadn't been there to see it, but the story had made its way around County High within the hour. Meredith had jumped up and flung her chair across the room with such force that it smashed through the window and scuffed across the asphalt smoking court outside.

"It's Flam-BURT!" she'd screamed. "Flam-BURT, Flam-BURT, goddammit!" And then she'd turned to her fellow students. "Any of you other assholes need to hear it again?"

Monsieur Calahan had slowly backed against the whiteboard with his palms facing outward, murmuring, "*Bon, bon. C'est bon.*" Meredith had earned a one-day suspension for the incident; it might have been three days, but Monsieur Calahan couldn't honestly claim that Meredith had directly called him an asshole. With Meredith slumped on the bench outside Mrs. Friedman's office, Monsieur Calahan had made the case to the principal that Meredith's meaning had been clear—she had referred to her peers as *other* assholes—but Mrs. Friedman had stuck to her decision.

Gerard never got in trouble in school. Meredith was the only friend of Gerard's who'd ever been suspended. Donald Meerschaum was the class clown who would try to shock his peers by *saying* vile and outrageous things, but he never did anything worth even an in-school suspension or a detention; he always knew where to stop without crossing the line. Meredith had a very different idea about Donald's crossing the line. Donald never stopped short enough for Meredith. His creative phrasing angered her, which surprised Gerard, given Meredith's own frequent use of colorful language. Crossing the line, in Meredith's view, involved mixing the images of food and bodily excretions. It wasn't enough for Donald Meerschaum to wave his hand behind his own backside and proclaim that his fart smelled bad; he had to take it a step further with an explanation that compared the stench to eggs and overcooked broccoli. That qualified as crossing the line.

"Fucking hell, Meerschaum," Meredith said (she always called him Meerschaum). "You see it, don't you? It's not like you don't know where the line is. You're standing right there in front of it—there's the line. You see the line and you march right across it. To hell with the people around you, right?"

Donald grinned and swung his head back and forth, emitting little grunts. "I can't help it."

"Does your dad put up with your shit?" Meredith said.

"My dad," Donald snorted. "My dad doesn't put up with anybody's shit."

That was true. The Meerschaums were neighbors with the Flanigan-Flamberts. Because Mr. Meerschaum was what Meredith called a landscape nazi (he was retired and had time to dote on his lawn), they had trouble getting along. Patrick and Lisa Flanigan-Flambert believed manicured lawns were evil, that all the energy and chemicals needed to maintain them were ultimately harmful to the earth. Mr. Meerschaum on the other hand spent two hours each morning preening his grass—spreading seed, fertilizing, cutting, raking, edging.

"The guy's obsessed with sharp edges," Patrick said one day, easing back the blinds with one hand and holding a mug of green tea in the other. "I don't get it. Gerard, do you get it?"

"I've heard him say edging protects the asphalt driveway," Gerard said.

"Asphalt," said Patrick after he sipped his tea. "The earth really needs more asphalt. Like it needs more American flags. Look at that. Another one!"

Meredith and Gerard came to the window and peered carefully out. Sure enough, Mr. Meerschaum had put up what was probably the sixth American flag on his property—this time on the mailbox.

"Do these people live in fear that they'll forget what country they live in?" Patrick said.

"Mr. Meerschaum!" yelled Meredith. "You missed a leaf on the lawn!"

"Meredith, quiet," Patrick said.

Meredith and Gerard laughed.

Mr. Meerschaum stood up from his edging and glanced around with the dazed look of someone who thought he might have heard something.

"Shit." Patrick Flanigan-Flambert ducked down below the window. "Get down, you two."

"Relax, Dad," Meredith said. "What's he going to do, attack us with his edger?"

But while Meredith enjoyed ridiculing others for reactions she considered silly, her complaint with Gerard was the opposite. She teased Gerard because she didn't think his reactions were ever pronounced enough.

"You're human, aren't you?" she had said one day in the back yard while helping Gerard groom Rebecca's two Great Pyrenees dogs. "I've never seen you get mad. Why is that?"

"I don't know," said Gerard. "I guess I'm even-tempered."

"My ass," Meredith said. "Come to think of it, I've never seen you get emotional about anything. Hell, you've never even said a bad word. Are you aware of that?"

"I guess," Gerard said.

"Say 'fuck'," said Meredith.

Gerard stopped combing and sat back on his knees. "No."

"Come on, say it. It's easy. 'Fuck'."

"I don't feel like it," said Gerard.

"Does it bother you when *I* swear?" Meredith said.

"Nope."

"You're one repressed dude," she said, stroking Alexander Hamilton's white hair with the wire grooming brush. (Because Rebecca Ward's father, George Randolph Ward, had been a navy captain, Rebecca named all her Great Pyrenees dogs after submarines in the U.S. fleet. Thomas Jefferson had died two months earlier and was buried in a metal cabinet behind the carriage house.)

Meredith handed Alexander Hamilton a biscuit which disappeared into his slobbery muzzle. "You never get mad, and you never swear," Meredith said. "And how long did it take me to convince you to have sex with me—when was it—two years ago? How long did I have to dare you?"

"Three weeks," Gerard said. He brushed Daniel Webster's head.

"Three weeks," said Meredith, clicking her tongue. She tucked her brown hair under the right side of her Boston Red Sox baseball cap. "You've got some crap stopped up in that body of yours, and it's going to kill you if you don't let go of it and let it out."

"Thanks for the lesson," said Gerard.

It wasn't the first time Meredith would bring up the theme. She'd talk about expression and how cathartic it was, and how Gerard should express more. But Meredith wasn't a musician, and she didn't understand what playing an instrument can do for a person. Gerard knew very well where most of his expression went—right through his hands and fingers into the cello. He had never confessed to Meredith that the cello rescued him from his own sadness; he assumed she wouldn't understand, so he'd never tried to convince her. Maybe if Gerard threw chairs she'd understand.

"Hey, Platoon Guide, you still awake?" Romberg's head was poking through the tent flap.

"God, Romberg, you startled me," said Gerard.

"Get your ass in bed, Romberg," grumbled Parker.

"Chill out, Parker," said Romberg. "I'm not here to settle a gang debt or anything."

"Man, that ain't funny," Parker said quietly, balled up on his side. He sighed.

"Sorry, man," Romberg said. "Hey, Platoon Guide, you're the platoon guide. That's cool. That's awesome."

Gerard flopped back down and pulled his BDU shirt up to his chin. "No, it isn't."

"It is," said Romberg. "You're in charge. You're like King Arthur." He thrust out his forearm and grinned at his Excalibur tattoo. "You're the man."

"I didn't ask to be 'the man'," Gerard said. "I want to get through this and be done with it." And to be home, and to be holding his Alberto Blanchi cello and his J.P. Bernard bow, and to be in Sylvia's arms, and to pretend he hadn't read the seventeen letters. He wished now that he'd never found out about Sylvia and Gilberto. If he thought about it long enough, and if he approached it from enough angles, he could convince himself that Sylvia's misadventure was a phase. She probably intended never to tell Gerard and to go ahead with the wedding next spring without mentioning it. That would have been fine with Gerard, if only he hadn't been nosy.

"Man, if I were you, I'd be savoring it," Romberg said. "I'd have the platoon doing push-ups 'til they puked. Oh, sorry. But hey, isn't it cool? I mean, you gotta admit, it's a cool experience. Where else would you get to do this?"

"You've got me there," Gerard said.

"It's exciting, man," said Romberg. "Kelderman, dude, it's like you're on valium or something."

"Third Platoon, I'm hearing things!" Drill Sergeant Womack's voice resonated through the forest.

"Shit," said Romberg. "Bye." He zipped away.

"Everybody should be asleep," Womack said. "You do not want me to tuck you in."

Gerard closed his eyes. Perhaps in Romberg's world everyone else seemed to be on valium when compared with his own constantly frantic disposition. It seemed to be a continuing theme in Gerard's life to have close associations with emotional people. His mother's passion manifested itself through her music and through her anger at Willem. She lambasted him for being forgetful or scattered or for not cleaning up after himself.

"You never learn, do you, Willem?" Rebecca had yelled at him one morning.

"It was late—I'm sorry. I'll just clean up now." Willem scurried around the coffee table, snatching up his diamond tools and holding them against his chest with one hand. "You're right. You're absolutely right."

"*Tweezers*, Willem," screamed Rebecca. "Of all things, the tweezers again? Like I need more fucking reminders?"

"Sh, sh," said Willem. "He's in the next room."

Gerard, eleven at the time of that argument, was finishing his breakfast in the dining room, and Willem knew he could probably hear them. As best as Gerard could remember now, that was the extent of the conversation; Willem's interruption had stopped it. Rebecca didn't need any reminders of what? Maybe she was referring to the famous diamond incident.

The story went that when Gerard was two years old he had ambled into the living room where Willem was finishing up a meeting with some associates. Gerard had grabbed a handful of small, cut diamonds and shoved them into his mouth before anyone could stop him, and gulped them down—all four of them. According to Willem the doctor at the emergency room had assured him they would pass right through, and that Willem needn't worry about any harm. But Willem wasn't worried about his baby boy; his mind was on the $900 worth of diamonds Gerard had swallowed! For the next two days, Willem had meticulously inspected every bowel movement with a spoon and a fork. He would shove Rebecca out of the way and volunteer to change Gerard's diaper. "No, no—I'll get this one," he'd say and shuffle Gerard off to the changing table. Willem claimed he found three of the diamonds, but that the fourth one—a ¾-carat marquise Margareta Van Leuven had brought from Australia—never showed up. From that time forward, Willem foretold that Gerard would become an expert in the field because he was part human, part diamond.

Expert in the field. And now he was actually *in* the field with Bravo Company 1/47th. Gerard opened his eyes and stared again at the top of the bivouac tent. He missed the mattress of his soft bunk back at Bravo Company and the red haze of the exit sign on the ceiling tiles. His foam sleeping mat on the ground was so hard, and his body was now so accustomed to four hours of sleep a night, that he couldn't fall asleep. Parker had no trouble; his breaths were long and deep. Gerard's chattering mind was once again keeping him awake. Never before had his thoughts taken on such a life of their own and whisked him so aggressively through scenes from his past. They were like clips from a film reel with no stop button. Gerard couldn't flip on the television or sit down at the polishing wheel or grab his cello bow and distract himself from his own memories.

No one else in Third Platoon shared Gerard's idea of the worst parts of basic training. Carroll loved all the down-time; he claimed to be able to grab little cat naps while standing up. Gerard hated waiting around. Standing in formation for hours was torture. The enormous expanses of silence and space were the most dreadful parts of basic. Gerard relished the frenzied parts of their day, like early morning in the bay, when fifty-six people had very suddenly to get dressed and dash downstairs for PT formation "in three goddamn minutes—and two of 'em are already gone." Those moments were a gift, because Gerard knew what he had to do and the choice to do something else didn't exist; there was no questioning, and no time for protest from his wandering mind.

Some nights when Drill Sergeant Hammer had Company Charge of Quarters duty and was feeling playful, he would rouse the platoon at some hour deep in the night and drag the soldiers outside for a PT session or a block of instruction in Drill and Ceremony review. Hammer delighted in the chorus of groans that rose up from the four long rows of bunks in the bay when he turned on the bright fluorescent lights and started yelling at Third Platoon to get up. Cooper didn't groan—Gerard had never heard Cooper groan—and neither did Gerard. Waking up had always been easy for Gerard, no matter how little sleep he had had, and no matter the hour.

He remembered being woken late one night at the Kasteel when he was eight years old. Rebecca, his mother, was gently rubbing his shoulder as he opened his eyes and squinted up at her from his warm bed.

"I need you downstairs, sweetie," she said.

He crawled out of bed and glanced at the digital clock on his way out the bedroom door. It was 12:30 a.m., and when he walked in to the music parlor, he could see from Rebecca's red face that she'd been drinking and crying.

"Sit down at the piano, Gerard," she said. "I'm going to sing the 'Pie Jesu'."

"Mom, no," Gerard said. "You shouldn't. It's not a good idea."

It had been one year since Anna had died. During her funeral service in St. Luke's Episcopal church on Wickham Street, a boy from the Washington Cathedral Choir of Boys had sung the "Pie Jesu" from Fauré's *Requiem*. It was the most beautiful sound Gerard had ever heard—the church pews resounded with sniffles and weeping by the middle of the third line.

The "Pie Jesu" is scored for soprano, but Dr. Beale's idea of hiring a young boy to sing the piece was perfect. Through his work with the Washington Cathedral Choir of Boys, he hired a boy named Stephen Winthrop. Young Stephen sang the piece with more passion than one would have thought possible from a ten-year-old: he masterfully commanded the crescendos, the rises and falls, and maintained intensity through the quietest pianos with smooth, sweet tones. Unlike the mourners in the church, Stephen Winthrop hadn't known Anna, so he wasn't distracted by the oak casket at the front of the church, or by the pictures of baby Anna that surrounded it, or by Rebecca's weeping, or by Gerard's sobbing into his father's shirt.

*Pie Jesu Domine, dona eis requiem, requiem sempiternam.*

Merciful Lord Jesus, grant them rest, rest everlasting.

They buried Anna in Unity Cemetery at the end of Wickham Street. Gerard had been crying during the entire ceremony, and he remembered exactly when he stopped: when her casket was lowered into the dark, narrow shaft in the earth. He and Willem stayed to watch, long after Rebecca had driven home and the other mourners had slowly peeled away from the grave site. Gerard dried his eyes and walked home with his dad; they plodded back down Wickham Street and then onto West Dixon Road, with not a word between them, and with not a single tear. Gerard hadn't cried since.

No one at the Kasteel had been able to listen to Fauré's *Requiem*—any part of it—for a year after Anna died. A few days after the funeral Rebecca had walked into the music parlor to find Willem scouring the shelves for every copy of Fauré's *Requiem*—vocal scores, orchestra reductions, and even the Cello I and Cello II parts. He was going to throw them all away. Rebecca grabbed his arms, and at first he tried to pull away, but he wrapped his arms around her and cried, dropping all the scores on the floor.

And now it was 12:30 a.m., a year later, and Rebecca was going to try to sing the "Pie Jesu" herself.

"Please, Gerard," his mother said.

"Mom—" Gerard interrupted himself with a yawn. He sat down at the piano; Rebecca had placed the score on the rack—it was a piano reduction of the full orchestra part. Gerard rubbed his eyes and yawned again.

Rebecca Ward took a sip of her wine and set it down on the end table next to the sofa. "Whenever you're ready, dear."

So Gerard played, sitting there at the piano in his pajamas. What else could he do, say no to his mother? For as long as he could remember he could never resist anything his mother asked him to do. It wasn't that she was authoritative; she was so sweet whenever she asked Gerard to do anything, and especially tonight Gerard felt such sympathy for her that he couldn't resist. He knew what was going to happen, but he played anyway, because it was what his mom wanted.

He squinted at the score—the parlor lamps were bright—and played the brief introduction to the fourth movement of the Fauré *Requiem*. God, he hadn't heard this music since the day of the funeral. His eyes moistened, but then he looked up from the piano and saw Rebecca's hands shaking as she held the vocal score. She wasn't going to last much longer, so Gerard would have to be the strong one. He choked his tears back down and concentrated on the music.

Rebecca sang. *"Pie Jesu Domine, dona eis req—"*

Her shoulders wilted and her head flopped down. Gerard jumped up from the piano—he wondered if she was fainting. Rebecca sobbed. Heavy tears dripped onto the music parlor's hardwood floor. Gerard gently clasped his mother's left wrist and elbow and led her to the red couch—the couch under the bay window all three of them knew so well—and sat her down. He dabbed her face with a tissue. He leaned her back on the pillow.

"It's okay, Mom," he said. "It's going to be okay."

"Oh Gerard, I miss her." Rebecca folded her arms across her chest and sobbed. "I miss my baby."

"Me too, Mom," Gerard said.

Rebecca lifted her hands to her face and quivered as she drew in a deep breath. Gerard sat down on the couch next to her. She reached up and stroked his hair.

"Remember the time she tried to play the piano?" said Rebecca.

Gerard nodded. He, his mom, and Anna had been eating popcorn in the living room on a Saturday afternoon and Anna had tottered across the front hallway into the music parlor with her diaper sagging and reached up to the piano keys. She'd wiggled her fingers along the white ivories while yelling "I play, I play, I play p'nano."

Gerard thought he was going to cry too—not for Anna, but for his mother. He didn't need his cello now to keep from crying; it was enough that he had to take care of his mom, that he had to be the strong one. He pulled a blue afghan up to her chin, kissed her forehead, turned off the parlor light, and climbed the stairs to his room.

It was curious that Gerard's grief affected him that way—that since age seven he hadn't cried. One hot Fort Benning morning on a cattle truck ride to the firing range, Romberg had explained his own grief as a child: his mother had died when he was sixteen years old, and he was still angry about it; he described the strange feeling he had that his mother had abandoned him—as if she had chosen to get stomach cancer and then die. But there was no fault-finding in Gerard's grief; Cooper had told Gerard what he already knew: that after fifteen years, it was Gerard's own doing. He consciously held his grief back because he didn't want to remember, even as he became more frustrated that he was unable to recall details about those summer months of his seventh year. He was convinced that if he let himself remember exactly how Anna had died, he'd be slammed and drowned by a hurricane of unhappy memories.

"We're supposed to like stay apart, Libby," Gerard heard Berkowicz say outside the tent. Berkowicz and Libby were on bivouac fireguard—a two-hour shift of silently walking among Third Platoon's tents in the dark while the other soldiers slept. As platoon guide Gerard would not be put on fireguard duty. A perk of leadership!

Gerard breathed in the smell of sand and dirt and musty shelter-half canvas. Outside, heavy wind was blowing the high pines and ruffling the sides of their tent. Until now the Fort Benning weather had been hot and very dry. Sand Hill, as the training area was called, had probably never been sandier. And now that Bravo Company was camping outside in bivouac tents, it was probably going to rain. Gerard lifted his head and rearranged the BDU shirt he was using as a pillow. He put his head back down and closed his eyes.

♦     ♦     ♦

"Get out of those tents, Third Platoon!" Drill Sergeant Womack yelled above the claps of thunder.

Gerard opened one eye and looked at his watch. Midnight. Water dripped onto his face from the saturated roof of the bivouac tent. The ground was wet and his clothes were soaked.

"Full gear, men, let's go."

Parker was already outside. Gerard pulled on his fatigues and boots, snatched his M16, and pulled on his poncho as he crawled out of the tent. Half the platoon was lined up.

"Let's go, Platoon Guide," yelled Hammer. "Your ass should be the first one out here."

Platoon guide—Gerard had forgotten. He slogged through the mud to the front of the formation. Stragglers emerged from their tents and shuffled into their squad positions. It was hard to see through the crashing sheets of rain. The drill sergeants had plastic covers stretched over their wide-brimmed hats. Why couldn't the army make those for tents?

"Okay men, it's time for a road march," said Womack. He shoved a plastic-coated map into Gerard's arms. "Private Kelderman, you're in charge. You've had land navigation training. I've marked our course with a grease pencil. There shouldn't be any excuses."

"Let's move out," said Hammer. "Clip on those flashlights. Libby, where's your fuckin' red filter? Hot Shit, Squad Leader, check your men."

Army maps were red-light readable. Gerard fumbled with his flashlight to try make out the details on the map. Drill Sergeant Womack marched the platoon to the road. First and Second Squad formed a single file along the left side of the road, Third and Fourth Squad on the right. In the dark, under the surging rain, Third Platoon walked silently in the dirt and gravel alongside the asphalt in two long rows, their red flashlights clipped to the front of their shoulder straps.

"Kelderman, get up front!" yelled Womack.

Gerard shuffled forward. He juggled the map and his weapon. He slung the M16 over his left shoulder. He unclipped the flashlight from his shoulder harness and pointed it down at the map. They were on a ridge, but where was it on the map? Drops of water pelted the plastic-coated map so vigorously that Gerard had trouble holding it up.

"Kelderman, you're in charge," screamed Womack over the rain. "Let's move."

Wonderful, thought Gerard—platoon guide, still in charge of Romberg, and now this. Rain, not enough sleep, and dinner had been a gray wedge of dry chicken meat, hard and rubbery. Wiley had called it superball chicken.

The two files of Third Platoon trudged down the road between tall pine forests on each side. Fifty-six faint, red circles of light bobbed along through the dark and the rain. The drill sergeants walked on the double yellow lines in the center of the asphalt.

Gerard dropped the map into a puddle. He reached down, picked it up, and wiped away the mud. There were Drill Sergeant Womack's grease pencil marks. Here was the ridge, Gerard thought, right near the bivouac site. The squiggly lines of the contour map had been confusing to him during their land navigation training, and that had been during daylight when the weather was dry. That had been a peaceful time, because when the soldiers were released to complete their exercises that day, no one had followed them. They'd been alone in the wilderness, wandering about, and all they'd had to do was find each point and record the number on their little cards.

"Just like mini-golf," Cooper had said.

There was silence now, too, not counting the thumping sizzle of rain on the trees and blacktop road. Neither Drill Sergeant Womack nor Drill Sergeant Hammer was yelling or speaking at all, and that made Gerard uneasy. Reacting to barked commands, he had come to learn, was beautifully simple; there was security in it. There was no questioning, no deliberation, no thinking, and no need for self-discipline. Yelling—jumping. Action—reaction.

Womack was doing it on purpose, Gerard decided. He was leaving Gerard in charge so the platoon would turn against him when it all went wrong, as had happened to Snodgrass back at the company area. One evening after Bravo Company had returned from the land mind range, Drill Sergeant Womack had left Snodgrass in charge of the platoon. Womack had punished Third Platoon with twenty minutes of flutter kicks simply because Snodgrass had forgotten to stand at the end of the chow line, the way the platoon guide is supposed to.

"I was hungry," Snodgrass had said. "I forgot."

At breakfast the next morning, Wiley, Hopson, and Berkowicz had grabbed all the food from Snodgrass's tray as he sat down, leaving poor Snodgrass to face a morning of Rifle Bayonet Fighting Training with no breakfast in his belly.

The platoon approached an intersection in the road. Gerard looked at the map. There, that had to be it. Four roads formed two separate intersections on the map, but only one of them was at the bottom of a ridge, which they had just descended. Drill Sergeant Womack's pen marks pointed left, so Gerard turned left. The platoon followed. Boots crunched the gravel of the shoulder and splashed through puddles. Gerard braced himself for the yelling. He could hear it now: *"Kelderman, what the fuck are you doing? We taught you how to read a goddamn map, and you're screwing up. Why are you turning left?"* But there were no voices. Only rain and thunder. Why weren't they yelling? Maybe it meant he was going the right way.

This rain made him think of baby Anna. Why was that? She'd never particularly liked rain; whenever they used to dash for the car from the front porch of the Kasteel with Gerard clutching Anna's hand, she'd squeal "Getting wet getting wet getting wet" all the way to the driveway.

It rained often in Belgium. Almost every time they traveled to Antwerp there had been rain. When Joske Vermeulen was late to meet Willem at Central Station, it had been raining. He hopped into the car on De Keyserlei one day, apologized for being half an hour late, and Willem floored the accelerator to make it to Westvleteren in time to get a case of Trappist beer that was made available to the public only twice a week. The Trappist monastery that made St. Sixtus beer didn't export it; you had to drive there and pick it up, and the batches were always limited. By the time they pulled in to the abbey, the monks informed them that all the beer was gone and they would have to come back Tuesday. Willem had missed getting some of the best beer in the world because Joske Vermeulen had been late. Joske was always late.

And Joske's lateness reminded Gerard of baby Anna too. Joske Vermeulen and rain. That was it! Gerard connected Anna and rain because it must have been raining on Anna's last visit to Antwerp when she'd died. The harder Gerard concentrated, the more sure he was—it had been raining the day of her death. But where exactly had they been? Gerard remembered Willem making a dash for cover from a patio and that there'd been someone with him, though it definitely wasn't Joske Vermeulen. Was it Margareta Van Leuven? It had been a woman, Gerard was now certain; Margareta was the most likely candidate. Yes, there'd been a downpour of rain, and they'd all made a dash for the inside. The inside of what? And where had Anna been? Gerard knew he had not been holding her as they all ran. She should have been with him. No one was holding Anna.

"Pay attention, Platoon Guide," said Drill Sergeant Hammer.

Gerard looked at the map again. According to the arrows he would have the platoon back at the bivouac site soon.

On they marched. Gerard lost track of time, but it had to have been at least an hour. Or was it an hour and a half? He had made several turns, one of them onto a dirt path. He wasn't entirely sure about that decision, but he was relying on Drill Sergeant Womack's pen marks. Walking was awkward now, because both rows of soldiers had to converge closely on the narrow path as they bumped rifles and ammo pouches and pulled their boots out of the wet, sucking mud with each step. Gerard emerged from a tangle of bushes onto another asphalt road. That wasn't right. He looked down at the map. Where was this hard-top road? He turned right and kept walking so the rest of the platoon could duck out of the brush. First and Second Squads tromped across the asphalt to the shoulder on the other side of the road.

Drill Sergeant Hammer walked in the middle of the street, between Gerard and the squad leader for First Squad, and Drill Sergeant Womack waited by the dirt path exit for the last soldier to emerge.

Gerard heard Womack yelling way toward the back, but he couldn't make out the words through the rain.

"Hold up," said Hammer to Gerard. "Stop."

The soldiers stopped. Drill Sergeant Womack walked down the middle of the road to the front of the lines.

"Okay, that's enough," yelled Womack. "Private Kelderman, care to tell us where we are?"

Gerard unfolded the map. "Uh, here, Drill Sergeant." He found his finger pointing to a road in the lower right corner.

"Wrong, Kelderman," said Womack. "F. That means you fail. But you've probably never gotten an F before, have you?"

"I—"

"Shut up, Kelderman" said Womack. He turned and walked back up the road, between the two lines of recruits. "Turn around and face the other direction, men. Let's move!"

Each recruit turned in place and walked. Gerard was now at the back of the line, with Drill Sergeant Hammer to his right.

"You fucked it up good, Kelderman," said Hammer quietly.

They tromped and trudged and after another hour reached the bivouac site. The lines noiselessly merged and amassed into a platoon formation at the center of a deep puddle. Gerard stood in front of the platoon, struggling to stand straight under the weight of his Kevlar helmet and water-logged gear.

Drill Sergeant Womack stood with his hands on his hips. "Well, Third Platoon, that was a nice little walk. Wasn't it a nice little walk, Yanni?"

"Yes, Drill Sergeant," said Cooper.

"I had a good plan, Third Platoon," said Womack. "It was supposed to be a one-hour road march. And how long did it last?"

"Three hours," said Phillips.

"Three hours," said Womack. "Your platoon guide screwed up."

In that moment, Gerard hated Drill Sergeant Womack like never before; he felt an urge to swing his rifle and pelt Womack on the side of the head. Man, that would have felt good. Maybe the rest of the platoon would join him in jumping on Womack and pummeling him into a trembling pile of contrition and remorsefulness. That'd teach him. But Gerard stood hunched over from exhaustion and embarrassment and faced his fellow trainees. The soldiers of Third Platoon were still, their ponchos soaked and dripping. They looked like dark ghosts with their boots submerged in water. Gerard felt like the accused in a trial, standing before the jury.

"Dismiss your platoon, Kelderman," said Womack. "We've got morning PT in two hours."

Gerard dismissed the platoon, and the dark ghosts turned slowly away. They lumbered toward the tents with their rifles sagging and their heads bowed over like executioners—grim reapers with scythes.

# Nine

The Third Platoon bay went dark. It was their first night back after bivouac and four days since Gerard's navigational error in the thunderstorm. Five days in the field had given Gerard a small taste of what life in the infantry would be like: being wet, feeling hungry, being attacked by ants and chiggers, eating tasteless food, feeling perpetually gritty and dirty, prying out hard and brittle field boogers, and—most challenging of all—having to dig a hole in the ground and then balance on two feet and one hand while trying to crap and avoid smearing his own fetid dung on his shirt and combat boots.

Gerard lay on his back appreciating an actual mattress and a white pillow. He stared through the dark at the ceiling tiles. Infantry. He wondered now if that had been the right choice. The recruiter back in Lambeth had tried to explain all the job options, but Gerard couldn't resist the images in those posters on the wall. He had recently learned of all the other jobs offered by the army: cook, truck driver, radio operator, computer network specialist, secretary, linguist; the list went on and on. There must have been hundreds of jobs—MOSs the army called them—Military Occupational Specialties. Gerard had heard he could have enlisted as a musician, perhaps even as a cello player. There was a specific MOS for piano players; he could have done that. Why did those army television commercials never show people working as mechanics or broadcast journalists or guitar players?

"Because the recruiters don't get as much credit for those enlistments," Private Fuller had told him during weapon cleaning one afternoon. "Their commanders get them all pumped up to enlist people into combat arms."

Private Fuller had an answer for everything. Gerard could never be sure if Fuller was right or if he was talking through his ass, as Romberg called it. Regardless, he always had army facts right at his fingertips.

"Besides," Fuller had added, "combat arms gives them all a bigger hard-on."

Gerard wondered if he would be able to change his MOS later. He doubted it. The army had its copies of the contracts with Gerard's signature on them. Army, four-year enlistment, infantry with airborne option. So after basic training and infantry school, he would undergo three weeks of airborne training. Could he still change his mind, at least about that? Could he really be forced to jump from airplanes if he decided he didn't want to?

Gerard flipped onto his side. He felt a blanket fall over his face. Another blanket covered his lower half, and both blankets tightened, holding him to the bed. Then came the blows. He felt punches, fists against his sides. One blow landed on his head, stinging his ear and making it ring. He heard whispering and jostling. Soldiers were filing by his bed, one by one, taking punches. He couldn't move. He knew from watching movies what was happening. Thankfully many of the punches were very weak. Probably every single person in the platoon was participating.

Slam—one to his stomach. Don't cry out, don't cry out. A slap on his head. There was pain on all sides of his body, his ribs throbbed, and he had pulsing knots in his thigh muscles. Then the punches stopped. The blankets loosened, and there was silence. He felt his bed rising, rising. It hovered for a moment. Gerard clenched his teeth and muscles. The bed dropped. Down Gerard went, ahead of his stomach. Crash. The metal bed smacked the floor, bounced once, and then lay still.

Gerard's body felt torn. He resisted the urge to cry. He balled his legs up to his chest and lay with the blankets still covering his head; he didn't want his platoon mates to see his head, and he didn't want to look at any of them. He thought of Cooper in the next bunk. For a moment, that was more unbearable than the physical pain—imagining that even Cooper had participated in the beating. He couldn't believe it.

Gerard whimpered to himself. He missed his mother. He missed Sylvia. He forgave her for everything. He was willing to forget Gilberto; he wanted Sylvia with him now. He craved the touch of her warm, slender fingers on his face and the way she would run them through his hair. At Monroe Hill, whenever Gerard stayed the night in Sylvia's room on the Lawn, she would stroke his face as he fell asleep in her bed.

Gerard breathed. His ribs hurt.

♦     ♦     ♦

Sunday morning. No PT. Since it was now the seventh week of training, there were no drill sergeants screaming at them to get out of bed. Private Fuller had set his alarm watch and flicked on the bay lights. As platoon guide, Gerard was supposed to rouse his fellow soldiers, but Fuller probably guessed that Gerard wouldn't be up for it this morning.

Gerard woke up with the blanket still covering his face. His body ached from the beating. He could hardly move. Don't be such a baby, he thought. He pushed the blanket away from his face and squinted in the glare of fluorescence and morning sun streaming through the tall, thin windows. No one looked at him. Cooper's bed was empty and made. Maybe he was in the bathroom.

Parker was making his bunk across the aisle, smoothing and tucking the sheets and green blanket. Gerard locked his gaze on Parker and watched every move. He looked at Parker's face, but Parker wouldn't look up. Gerard stared. Parker finished making his bunk and moved toward the bathroom. Parker's eyes glanced up for a second and caught Gerard's before looking away again. Aha—if we had been dogs, thought Gerard, I would have just won. But what was in Parker's eyes? Gerard didn't see fear. He had hoped to see fear. Was it more hatred, more violence? No, in that quick second, Parker's face said something like *this is the way it goes—deal with it. How else did you think it would be?* "How else did you think it would be, *asshole*" was more like it. Parker had disliked Gerard from day one; he had probably organized last night's beating.

What did Parker have against Gerard, anyway? Was it because Gerard was white? Was it because Gerard was an expert in diamonds—did Parker know that the diamond industry was built on the subjugation of black South Africans? No, Parker didn't know about that part of Gerard. Maybe Parker hated all white people, and Gerard was the scapegoat—the first white person Parker had ever known.

Gerard had known a black person once, during his first year at Monroe Hill College, in the men's glee club. Gerard had inherited his singing voice and his sight-reading skills from both his parents, so he joined the men's glee club as a freshman to keep his voice in shape. Lawrence Thaxton was a dark-skinned bass in the glee club, a third-year student when Gerard joined. Lawrence was from Sacramento, the only son of two lawyers. Gerard sang bass as well and sat next to Lawrence during rehearsals.

Lawrence Thaxton was a self-proclaimed *Ave Maria* aficionado—he could name every composer who had written a choral *Ave Maria*. During a dress rehearsal in Shepard Hall one Thursday evening, Gerard described to Lawrence the shelves in the music parlor at the Kasteel, packed with *Ave Maria* recordings and choral scores. Lawrence gasped and clapped his hands together. For the next hour, in whispers during pauses in the rehearsal, the two of them peppered each other with composer names and which parts of which *Ave Marias* were the best, and which composer had created the greatest *Ave Maria* of all time. The final contest came down to Biebl and Bruckner. Gerard lobbied for the Bruckner, but Lawrence quickly suggested that Gerard probably hadn't given the Biebl enough concentration to appreciate it. And Gerard countered that he had listened deeply to the Biebl and that there was too much *space* in it, and so few choirs could stay in tune given all that space, and that the final 'Amen' always came too soon; it sneaked up on Gerard and always left him unfulfilled. Lawrence's complaints about the Bruckner included how traditional it was, how predictable. So Gerard countered again that there was nothing wrong with a piece being predictable (for God's sake, how could anyone not be moved by those *mater dei* lines?), and wasn't it a sign of a great work that it could be so moving even as its ultimate direction was obvious?

Back and forth they went, and Lawrence's eyes sparkled more brightly as they argued in whispers, even after several stern glances from the conductor. Finally they agreed on one thing: the true nature of any choral *Ave Maria* could be unlocked and revealed only by a men's choir. This agreement, and Lawrence's realization that Gerard shared his penchant for port wine, was the clincher—according to Lawrence—that he had a chance with Gerard. Gerard had thought from the outset that Lawrence was simply being a nice guy and was focused on the details of their argument, but he'd figured out just in time where Lawrence was heading and had politely declined Lawrence's invitation to dinner at the Weeping Rhino and to Lawrence's place afterwards to look at his *Ave Maria* collection.

Gerard groaned and forced his battered body to sit slowly up. He pulled on his fatigues and laced up his boots. He made his bunk and walked out the bay and down the stairs. He walked slowly across the company area toward the Third Platoon formation. He was the last one down, and he didn't care. His body wouldn't have let him run anyway.

He took his place in front of the platoon and looked at all the faces. Not one looked back at him. The bastards. The cock-sucking sons of bitches. He glanced at Cooper. Cooper looked Gerard right in the eyes and smiled. Gerard hadn't expected that, and it almost made him cry. Cooper had a purple mark around his own eye. Had he been beaten too? Perhaps he had tripped while making his way past Gerard's bunk. But why was Cooper smiling at him? Surely Cooper should be avoiding his glances too, but there he was, Steven Cooper, giving Gerard that same honest, sincere look he always gave. Come to think of it, Cooper gave that look to everyone, no matter their behavior.

In the D-FAC the platoon coursed through the chow line in silence, grabbing their food at a pace that was unusually quick for a Sunday during the seventh week of basic training. Next week would be the end of basic training. Bravo Company would be granted a weekend pass, though Gerard didn't care about that right now—right now he wanted his bones and muscles to stop hurting. He hadn't looked at himself in the mirror, but his cheekbones and jaw felt swollen and hard. No one spoke in line—no jokes, no smiles. Nothing. There was only quiet movement, snatching up of trays, and noiseless side-stepping through the chow line. Gerard was silent, even though the platoon guide was expected to yell and keep the line moving swiftly. Drill Sergeant Womack had gone ahead through the chow line and was seated at the cadre table eating his breakfast. It was strange, being left alone by the drill sergeants. Gerard hadn't imagined this could ever happen during basic training.

As the last man in Fourth Squad stepped up to the serving line, Gerard fell in behind him and picked up a tray. The platoon guide eats last, always. Gerard was thankful they were in the D-FAC and not in the field, where food often ran out before the last man was served. When that happened the platoon guide went hungry. If the meat supply was depleted, he had to fill up on corn or potatoes. That was the sacrifice, the cost of leadership. So what? They were all going to the same place, eventually, and they'd all get there at the same time, more or less. What did a few minutes and a few bites of food mean, in the end? "The last shall be first," as Cooper would say.

Gerard picked up a plate with scrambled eggs and two strips of hard black bacon. He got his two pieces of toast, an apple (there were oranges, but Gerard didn't feel up to peeling), and seated himself at the end of a table. All heads were down. Gerard paused again and looked at his fellow soldiers. He wanted to scream, to dump his food on the floor and use the empty tray to smack all of them, especially Parker. Gerard wondered how Cooper would have handled this situation. Would Cooper have maintained his optimistic disposition, even if he had been beaten by fifty-five men?

Cooper professed to have genuine, unconditional love for all people. The idea wasn't new to Gerard—it was a common religious tenet—but the idea of putting it into practice was beyond his comprehension. Sure, he could easily love anyone, but there were always conditions—probably at the top of the list of conditions would be that the people he loved *not* beat him.

Then again, who could blame Parker and the rest of the platoon for being upset? Gerard had screwed up the navigation and kept fifty-five men out in the rain at two a.m. for three hours. Who wouldn't have wanted to beat the idiot responsible for such incompetence? This was a sensible analysis of the situation and of human behavior, but something much deeper than sense and logic made Gerard hate them all and want to commit unspeakable acts of gory violence.

"It's too goddamn quiet," said Romberg.

"Shut up, Romberg," said Berkowicz.

"Fuck you, man," Romberg said. "You're all acting like it's a fucking funeral or something." He lobbed his apple. It bounced off Berkowicz's forehead and into his eggs.

"Settle down, Romberg," said Carroll.

"William Tell!" yelled Romberg. "What we need is a food fight." He shoveled some eggs onto his spoon and flicked them forward, splattering the faces across the table. Bits of egg stuck to Gerard's cheek.

Gerard lifted his tray from the table and slammed it down. He stood up and shoved his chair back. It smacked into the chair of a soldier at the table behind him. He walked three seats over to Romberg, who had grabbed Phillips's toast and was cocking it back to throw it across the mess hall. Gerard grabbed Romberg's wrist and slammed it onto the table. The toast fell, jam side down, onto Parker's carton of milk. Parker looked up at Gerard and chewed his food.

"Kelderman, dude, let go." Romberg pushed Gerard's hand away.

Gerard jumped behind Romberg and slipped his arms under Romberg's arm pits. He clasped his hands together behind Romberg's thick neck and lifted him from the chair. He marched Romberg across the dining hall with Romberg kicking and squirming. At the end of the aisle, Gerard slammed Romberg into the tile wall. The clattering of stainless steel utensils stopped—what the platoon guide was doing was much more interesting than eating army food. Womack slowly stood up from the cadre table and walked toward Romberg and Gerard, but he said nothing. Romberg's face was pressed against the cool tile, pinned to the wall by Gerard.

"Bullshit, Romberg," said Gerard, through his red face and clenched teeth.

"Let go, Kelderman."

"Shut up. Shut the fuck up," said Gerard. "You need to control yourself. I'm tired of your shit."

And then Cooper was standing next to Gerard. "You know it's not his fault," Cooper said quietly.

"He can control himself if he wants to," said Gerard.

"He doesn't know how," said Cooper. "Not yet."

"Bullshit!" screamed Gerard. He shoved Romberg harder against the wall with each word. "Bull—Fucking—Shit."

"Nice language, Kelderman," said Snodgrass.

"Shut up, Snodgrass," said Libby.

"Can *you* control him?" said Cooper.

"I'm tired of trying," said Gerard.

He pulled Romberg back from the wall and pushed him to the floor. Romberg lay on his back. Gerard pounced down on top of him and grabbed Romberg's throat.

"If you don't stop it, all of it, I'm going to kill you," said Gerard. He tightened his grip on Romberg's throat. Romberg's face turned red.

"Kelderman, man. I can't breathe."

"Do you see ravens now, Romberg?" Gerard said.

"Gerard, let go," said Cooper.

Gerard loosed his grip.

Drill Sergeant Womack grabbed Gerard by the collar and pulled him up.

"Wild Man Kelderman," said Womack. "It's nice to see you coming out of your shell, Platoon Guide, but you're not leading by example."

Romberg stood up with his hands on his throat. "Fuck." He coughed.

Gerard pulled away from Womack. "You wanted me to be in charge of him, didn't you? So why'd you stop me? I think I was making some progress here."

"Shut up, Private Kelderman!" said Womack. "Romberg, sit down. Kelderman, finish eating. I want your platoon out of here in four minutes, and form up in the company area when you're done."

Romberg sat back down. Gerard stared at Womack.

Wiley tugged at Gerard's fatigue shirt. "It's cool, Kelderman. Sit down, man."

Gerard turned slowly and walked back between the tables. As he passed Parker, Parker looked up from his food and then back down again.

"What are you looking at?" said Gerard.

Parker stopped eating and stared at Gerard.

Gerard put his hands on the table and leaned in toward Parker. "You're a cock-sucker and a coward."

Hopson tried to push Gerard back. "Kelderman—"

"Let go," said Gerard. "Is this how it was for you, Parker, when you left your gang? Did they beat the shit out of you like they were supposed to?"

Parker stood up. "Shut up, motherfucker. Man, you got no idea—"

"Were there fifty-five of them beating you, Parker?" said Gerard. "You sack of shit."

Parker reached across the table, but Hopson shoved Gerard back out of his reach.

"Platoon Guide, sit down and eat," Womack yelled from the cadre table.

Parker sat back down. Gerard noticed Parker was shaking. Gerard dragged his chair back to the table and sat down. He straightened his tray and slowly buttered a piece of toast.

♦     ♦     ♦

The rest of that Sunday was casual. First Sergeant McFadden had scrawled 'Equipment Maintenance' on the chalkboard outside the door of the company office. It was his way of letting the soldiers of Bravo Company know they could take it easy but that they should be mindful not to make it *look* like they were taking it easy. Drill Sergeant Womack had indirectly taught Third Platoon this valuable skill by barking phrases like "You better move like you've got a purpose!" All the drill sergeants used that sentence with those exact words. Notice it doesn't say "Move with purpose" but instead takes a little extra time to get to the crux of an important Army Truth: "Move *like* you've got a purpose." Whether or not you actually have a purpose doesn't matter; it's the appearance, always the appearance.

On Sundays the platoon drill sergeants would disappear and leave the company drill sergeant on duty in charge of Bravo Company. Captain Fopp, the company commander, was nowhere to be seen; it was the weekend, and he was an officer. Same for the executive officer, First Lieutenant Overman. Gerard speculated again about what First Lieutenant Overman's actual job might be. He could often be seen hanging around the supply room. Was he in charge of the supply sergeant and the armorer, Specialist Sanchez? Sometimes he would show up for PT when there was a company run—an exercise in coordination where the entire company would have to run with their footsteps in sync with each other while singing and yelling in unison. It was Fuller's idea that Lieutenant Overman showed up for PT only when he anticipated that it might soon occur to Captain Fopp that Overman hadn't done PT with the company in a while. It made Gerard wonder what Lieutenant Overman's work ethic would be without Captain Fopp to keep an eye on him.

Third Platoon spent Sunday morning cleaning the barracks and doing laundry. As platoon guide Gerard was supposed to organize the cleaning and make sure everything was done properly, but he blew it off, and the platoon left him alone. Even though his body was broken and he nursed his anger and hatred over the beating, he felt powerful. He felt he could say or do anything he wanted to, and no one would care. As he moved through the day, faces avoided him, but it was because he was the one with the power. He had undergone physical abuse, but even beneath his suffering he felt a strangely deep satisfaction. Gerard was the only person in the platoon who was free of guilt: *he* had not taken part in the beating! He liked to imagine that the other soldiers in the platoon were suffering for what they had done to Gerard. How could they not be? Up until last night everyone seemed to get along with him and even like him. But Parker was probably so forceful with all of them that they decided three hours in the rain was reason enough for violence.

So as Gerard walked down the aisle between the bunks, he felt like Moses parting the Red Sea. It was like a choreographed Vegas show, or synchronized swimming. Gerard walked down the aisle, looking left and right, and faces peeled away as if on cue. There should have been music.

After lunch the soldiers of Bravo Company scattered about the company area, loosely grouped by platoon. Some were on the floor with their M16s disassembled, some were on the bleachers shining boots and writing letters. Wet, clean clothes were strewn around drying on walls and bleachers and chairs. Every washer and dryer in the laundry room whirred. Gerard sat by himself, cleaning the parts of his M16. "A clean rifle is a happy rifle." He scrubbed all the parts of the bolt assembly with the toothbrush in his cleaning kit. He lovingly applied oil to all the parts. If he couldn't play and clean his cello, then he'd lavish attention on his rifle—his trusty, solid, loyal M16A2. Today's rifle cleaning was bittersweet because Gerard knew they would have to turn their rifles in later that week when Bravo Company's basic training phase ended.

Advanced Individualized Training—AIT—was to start next week. This would begin the real phase of infantry training, the "gung-ho, supercool shit," Fuller had called it. Soldiers in non-combat-arms jobs ("support-pukes") spent seven weeks in basic training at one post and then traveled to another post for advanced training. But Gerard had volunteered for the infantry: One Station Unit Training—OSUT—thirteen straight weeks at the same post with the same drill sergeants. Next week Bravo Company would be issued M16A1 rifles for infantry school. Private Fuller had explained that the M16A1 was a much older rifle; it was likely these very rifles had been used in Vietnam. The M16A2 was more accurate and didn't have a switch for automatic firing; the story went that the army brass was alarmed by how much ammunition was wasted in Vietnam when young soldiers got scared, switched to automatic firing, and emptied an entire cartridge of rounds with one pull. So the next incarnation of the rifle was the M16A2, which, in addition to the *semi* setting, had a setting for a three-round burst. But even that setting was discouraged. All soldiers were indoctrinated: "One Shot, One Kill." Bravo Company had been forced to recite the phrase over and over during marksmanship training. It was a bullet-saving measure.

Gerard could hear the hushed conversations around him as he sat at the top of the bleachers in the company area, so that by the end of the day he had overheard enough pieces of the story to put together what had happened the previous night. Gerard was right: Parker had organized the move against him. After Bravo Company marched back from the bivouac site Saturday evening, Womack and Hammer had called Gerard into the company office to go over procedure for the next day. Parker had taken charge of the platoon while Gerard was away (never mind that the next-in-command was supposed to be the squad leader for First Squad) and explained to the platoon what would happen that night. He hadn't taken a poll to gauge the level of support; Parker had told Third Platoon what would happen and that every one of them would participate. Who would argue with Parker? Libby and Carroll had protested with pathetic squeaks that were drowned out by the mob rule of the platoon and by Parker's forcefulness. Anyone who chose not to participate would have to answer to Parker.

"You too, Cooper," Parker had said.

Cooper had looked back at Parker and simply shook his head.

"Yeah you will, Cooper." Parker had told him. "Yeah you will."

Thank God for Cooper! He hadn't helped; he had refused, which explained the bruise under his eye. Cooper had communicated his intention to abstain and then stayed firm to his conviction. True to his word, Parker had slugged Cooper for his decision. Gerard knew from eavesdropping on his platoon mates that Parker would have liked more help in doling out punishment to Cooper, but no one stepped up, and Parker had not pressed the issue. Apparently even a bullying leader knows his limits. So as Parker had passed by Gerard's bunk a second time (he had been at the front of the line, and then circled back for a second go), he had pelted Cooper on the face as Cooper lay on his bunk. And at various times later that Sunday, Cooper had encouraged Gerard to try to nurture feelings of compassion for all the soldiers who had beaten him—not for their benefit, but for his own. Gerard's response to that was simple: "Fuck that." And Cooper had answered with a silent smile.

Cooper, dear friend Cooper. Where were the Coopers of the world? Had Cooper refused for him, for Gerard? No, Cooper would have made the same decision for anyone in the platoon, even if the victim had been Parker. Gerard wondered if Cooper had "turned the other cheek" for Parker and stayed true to his commitment to love and serve his fellow humans, regardless of how they behaved.

In his pursuit of a minor in religion at Monroe Hill College, Gerard had learned about what Steuch, Leibniz, and Huxley called the perennial philosophy; Huston Smith's phrase for it was the primordial tradition. These were the tenets common to every major religion throughout history that existed regardless of insignificant differences like how exactly you're supposed to hold your hands during meditation, or precisely how many levels of heaven there are in the afterlife (if there's an afterlife at all), or what the word God means. Cooper's ideas were right out of the textbook on the perennial philosophy. He claimed distinctions and differences didn't matter.

"What does matter?" Gerard had asked Cooper.

"The experience you're gaining," Cooper had answered, and then he'd commenced a description of the Prodigal Son parable, but Gerard's mind had wandered off and he hadn't listened.

Gerard stopped cleaning his rifle for a moment and sighed. His fraternity brothers would never have done anything like this to him. There had been first-year rush for St. Philip Fraternity, but no one had beaten him. Probably the height of unpleasantness was the night he had been forced to run naked with his fellow rushers down Henry Park Avenue in Lambeth, smeared with the entrails of a dead cat someone had found on the side of the road. Gerard had nearly thrown up, but he had badly wanted to join St. Philip and had steeled himself ahead of time for any hazing the upperclassmen could throw at him.

Gerard's gaze stopped on Private Libby, who was reattaching the plastic hand guards on the bore of his rifle. His hands kept slipping, and the hand guards would bounce on the bleacher seat and crack to the floor. Libby looked up and met Gerard's eyes for a second. He grinned and then resumed his project. Gerard chuckled. It was hard to be mad at someone like Libby, especially when so many in the platoon stayed angry with him all the time. Every time Libby screwed something up he would apologize and promise he was going to do much better next time.

Gerard thought back to when Anna had entered her hitting phase, around age two. Gerard would be carrying her and she'd smack him on the face and laugh loudly. When Gerard rebuked her, she would say "I'm sorry" and gently stroke his cheek with her little hand. "You alright?" And then she would cup Gerard's face with both her hands and look him right in the eyes. "You gonna be okay?"

"It's chow time, Bravo Company." Drill Sergeant Ramirez stood in the middle of the company area. He had taken over Sunday CQ from Womack. "Platoon Guides, move your men into the D-FAC."

The company formed up for dinner and stepped cheerily to the mess hall. Drill Sergeant Ramirez sat alone at the cadre table and ignored the murmuring and whispering during the meal. The buzz of conversation centered around the upcoming weekend pass they'd be awarded for completing basic training. Gerard wished every day could be like Sunday.

Later as dusk approached, Third Platoon sat on the bleachers behind the company area, facing the big orange sun that hovered above the pines. It was boot-shining time. Gerard sat next to Cooper. He scratched his face and winced; he'd forgotten about the bruises.

"None of it lasts," said Cooper.

"Huh?" said Gerard.

"None of it lasts. Nothing," said Cooper. "It's all impermanent. Everything we have, everything we're experiencing."

Gerard dipped his cotton ball into the lid of his can of shoe polish, which he had filled with water. So often when Cooper spouted philosophy, it was either out of place or Gerard didn't understand it.

"Well then I'm glad this won't last," said Gerard.

Cooper nodded as he polished the heel of his boot. "It all passes. In fact, if you really think about it, it's not real. It's an illusion. Nothing belongs to us, we only think it does."

Gerard swirled his wet cotton ball into the black, creamy shoe polish. "I wish I believed that, but there are too many good things I would never let go of."

Damn, he missed Sylvia. He had resolved that day during weapons maintenance that he was going to tell Sylvia he knew about Gilberto Cardenas and that he forgave her. He would need to learn exactly what she'd been thinking at the time, and how she now felt about Gilberto, but then they could get beyond it and move forward together.

"Even the good things are impermanent," said Cooper. "Since nothing is really ours, everything is ours. We just have to release all things to realize that."

"Yeah, okay," said Gerard. "Now you're losing me."

It wasn't that Gerard didn't understand the words coming out of Cooper's mouth, it was that the concepts were so wacky that Gerard didn't feel like putting forward the effort required to understand them. It was as baffling as sitting in front of a piece of modern art. There was no sense in it.

Gerard remembered driving to Richmond during his undergrad days to see a piece of performance art. A drama teacher at Monroe Hill College had recommended it for extra credit. Sylvia had laughed at Gerard and refused to go (perhaps she had other plans), as if she knew what a waste of time it was going to be. So Gerard went alone, and for an hour he had sat and watched some hack do things that Gerard did not consider art, in any sense. The 'actor' had taken a nap on stage, had shaved and combed his hair in front of a mirror, had meditated (the fool had simply sat on a pillow for twenty minutes while the audience watched), and had wrapped up the performance with a rousing round of tooth brushing and flossing. After an hour of this nonsense, the audience had applauded.

Sometimes with Cooper, Gerard felt like a participant in a piece of performance art. Did Cooper understand his own words? On some level he had to, because goddamn if Cooper wasn't always calm and content—he was forever composed. It humbled Gerard, and he thought that if he could somehow bring himself to understand what Cooper said, maybe he too would feel some level of composure. But this was impossible with a drill sergeant like Womack and a squad mate like Parker.

Parker—the bastard. Gerard fantasized about punching Parker, but that was so unlikely and Parker was so strong that Gerard abandoned the thought and instead secretly wished that the Warlords from Detroit would find Parker here and kill him. Most Third Platoon soldiers knew Parker feared this, ever since he'd learned that Drill Sergeant Hammer was from Detroit and had been a member of the Warlords—the gang that had now issued a warrant for murdering Parker. Cooper had tried to counsel Parker too, giving him the lecture about fear being an illusion; Parker had brushed Cooper away with a comment about "crazy-ass shit."

Sometimes Gerard was glad he wasn't the only one annoyed by Cooper. There was too much going on. Gerard's brain was already too busy. If he wasn't figuring out how to set up a Claymore mine or memorizing the army phonetic alphabet (Foxtrot, Golf, Hotel, and so on), his humming mind was busy missing his previous life. Adding Cooper's discussion topics and the reflection required to grapple with them wasn't worth the effort. During times like boot-polishing, and especially on a Sunday, the kind of discourse Gerard longed for was the simple, the banal: Fuller nattering on about the 5.56-millimeter round of the M16, Romberg telling stories of the beach at Cape May and Stone Harbor, Wiley emphatically postulating that the Russians are still planning to take over the world. What Gerard least wanted was to have any discussion that required real thought.

Cooper clicked closed the lid on his can of shoe polish. "I'm just saying that we cause ourselves a lot of pain and suffering by holding on to things that were never really ours in the first place."

Gerard pinched a cotton ball and dipped it in the water he had dribbled into the lid of his polish can. He swiped up some black polish with the wet cotton ball and then rubbed it in small circles on the side of his boot. The water beaded and rolled off the sides, and the polish dried up, leaving a black shine.

"Mail call, men," yelled Drill Sergeant Ramirez.

Shoe polish canisters snapped shut and the soldiers of Third Platoon clanked off the bleachers to join the rest of Bravo Company in the company area.

"Mail on Sunday?" said Berkowicz.

"It means they've been holding it since yesterday," said Fuller.

They formed up in the platoon area and waited, with Gerard standing in front facing them. He hated being platoon guide.

"Phillips," said Ramirez as he flicked a letter into the air. It fluttered to the concrete floor.

Phillips ran to the front, dropped to the floor, and did ten push-ups—the cost of receiving a piece of mail.

"Cory, Walton, Libby." Ramirez flung each letter into the air, not even lifting his face from the stack he still held in his hand.

"Kelderman."

Gerard's heart skipped. The letter flitted through the air and landed in front of him. He dropped to the floor in push-up position looking at the letter below him. The front was facing up; it was from Sylvia. Ten times he pushed down and looked at the return address. Sylvia, Sylvia, Sylvia. He couldn't wait to read it. Ten— done; that was easy. He snatched the letter and stood up. He was smiling.

"Lemme smell that envelope, Kelderman," said Berkowicz. "That's not like from your mom, is it?"

"No, man, *I* got one from his mom," said Phillips, running his own letter under his nose and sniffing it.

Berkowicz and Phillips—Gerard suddenly loved both of them, and not only because he had received a letter from Sylvia, but because this was their way of apologizing, of reaching out and asking for forgiveness. Gerard smiled and pretended to ignore them—he knew they would interpret this as an acceptance of their apology. He held his envelope, fingered it, felt it, passed it slowly back and forth between his left and right hand.

Drill Sergeant Ramirez tossed out the last two letters. "Okay Bravo Company, up to your bays. Lights out in forty-five minutes." He walked away.

"Platoon, Atten—tion!" said Gerard. "Dismissed."

The soldiers of Third Platoon broke ranks and ambled toward the stairs. Gerard was the last one through the door of the bay. Some soldiers were opening their wall lockers, some were undressing, others were on their bunks ripping open their envelopes. Gerard walked straight to his own bunk and sat down.

Mail! This was his first letter. Finally. And from Sylvia! He raised the envelope to his face and sniffed it, which was silly, because Sylvia would never spray perfume on a letter. He thought of her scent—her own sweet fragrance mixed with the gardenia perfume she wore. Gerard always breathed in at the same place, on her warm neck, in that smooth notch next to her throat. Gerard inhaled. He tore the envelope open and pulled out the pages.

Atlanta, Saturday, July 6, 2002

Dear Gerard,

I find myself having a novel experience: I am at a loss for words. As you know, I'm generally quite deft with epistolary correspondence. Perhaps the most direct route will be the least painful.

I must end our relationship. I can't go on like this, especially considering that you'll be sent to God-knows-where for four years after your training is complete (I've spoken with my Uncle Michael; you remember him—the air force colonel. He tells me you can't be at all sure about Fort Carson). The past six weeks have been bad enough, but the thought of four more years of such an arrangement is unbearable to me. I don't want you to think I came to this decision lightly; I gave it long and careful thought.

A few days after you left for the army, I traveled to your home town of Evans Glen to visit your parents. I told them I wanted to see the house where you grew up and I hoped they didn't mind the intrusion. They didn't mind at all, and I must say, the house is magnificent. I felt like royalty walking onto that porch and standing in front of that majestic red door. You really are lucky.

Well, I stopped feeling like royalty when your mother showed me in and introduced me to your friend Meredith. They'd all been sitting in the kitchen together before I arrived, snacking on apples and baked brie. I felt like quite an outsider, walking into the kitchen, like I'd disturbed a family meal. And imagine how I felt when I became conscious of who this person was, this girl in shabby jeans and a T-shirt with her shoulders hunched over. Honestly, she was dressed like one of your fraternity brothers. Was this really the Meredith you told me about? I suppose I expected someone much prettier. She was very friendly, which surprised me. Surely she knows who I am, and she knows that I know who she is and that I know about her history with you. Yet she was sincere and kind. As I shook her hand I couldn't help imagining you and her sleeping together. I still don't know why you had to tell me all those details about the two of you; it really was unnecessary, and I wonder now if you did it to hurt me or to try to make me jealous.

Your mother gave me a tour of the house. The music parlor is as astounding as you said it was with that resplendent, dark cherry paneling along the walls. Very elegant. I even got to see your bedroom. It made me miss you, a little, but I couldn't help wondering if you and Meredith had intercourse there. Did you? Oh well, I suppose it's insignificant now.

Your mom even showed me your dead sister's room. Oh, it was heartbreaking. I knew before she opened the door what was in there, and I tried to stop her; I tried to tell her she didn't have to, but she was very forceful. She said she wanted to show me the room so I'd understand more about the family and about you. It was too much for me, after hearing you tell about Anna. Her empty room with that, well, I can only describe it as an altar, covered with Anna's personal effects. I had to nudge your mom out of the room. She just stood there quietly, smiling at the <u>Hop on Pop</u> book that was on the altar, open to the page where "That thing can sing!"

What else can I say? You seem to have become a very different person from whom I thought you were. Indeed, maybe you were this way all along and you hid it well. Oh, I don't know. For two weeks now I've done nothing but think about all this. I think back to our time at Monroe Hill and all the things we did together, and I'm unable to reconcile your sudden decision and the person I fell in love with those years ago. It doesn't fit. And while I'd originally decided to see this through and accept that difficulties always arise in a relationship, I finally realized that I can't trust you any more; if I'm going to commit myself to one person for the rest of my life, I need faith that I know who that person is and how he will act. You destroyed it all with one blow.

Really, were you thinking only of yourself? Were you trying to prove something? Did you give no thought to the consequences of what you were doing? You've caused pain. They're probably hiding it from you, but your parents are hurting; I could see it on their faces when I visited. As for me, I'm struggling, but I think I'll pull through. Please understand why I'm doing this. People who know us ask about you; what am I supposed to tell them? It's embarrassing and shameful. You can have no idea what it's like for me right now.

As difficult as this is, I know it is right. I have to get on with my life, now that I've made peace with the realization that it's unlikely you and I will ever get on with <u>our</u> lives together, as one.

I'm off for Denver in a few weeks to start graduate school. I will miss you. I mean that. I hope you'll let me know how everything is going, in a few years when all the dust has settled.

Fondly, Sylvia

Fondly? *Fondly?* That was a stinger. Sylvia had moved swiftly from love to fondness in six short weeks. She'd completely forgotten all the promises she'd made that night on the steps of the Rotunda. "I must end our relationship." Astonishing.

Gerard folded the letter and bowed his head, his elbows resting on his knees. Shit, shit, shit. He squeezed his eyes tight to keep them from swelling. He could feel tears against the insides of his eyelids, pushing to burst out. He clenched harder. He got up and walked to the bathroom. He bent over a sink and splattered water onto his face. He opened his eyes and splashed water into them. There: his eyes and face were wet from the water; he hadn't cried. He blew his nose into the sink. The snot was thin and loose and swirled down the drain with the cold water from the faucet. He snatched paper towels out of the stainless steel dispenser and walked back to his bed. He didn't look up because he wondered about the rest of the platoon and who might be watching. He thought of Parker and the other fuckheads who would probably laugh if they knew what had happened to him. He sat on his bunk and squeezed the letter between the fingers of his fist until his knuckles turned white. Private Mueller was standing at the end of Gerard's bunk, in his underwear, on his way to the bathroom.

"Shit, man," Mueller said.

Gerard looked up at him. Mueller's eyes were wide. He was holding a toothbrush in one hand and a brown towel in the other. His mouth was hanging open and he was nodding.

"You got a Dear-John, didn't you?" Mueller said.

Gerard leaped from his bunk and lunged at Mueller with both hands, his fingers extended like claws. Mueller zipped out of the way and scurried along to the bathroom. Gerard plopped back down on the green blanket and lay down on his back. He threw his feet up onto the bed.

He unfolded the letter and read it again. He reread the part where Sylvia had written she was "quite deft with epistolary correspondence." What the hell kind of language was that? Sylvia didn't speak that way, but she'd long had a habit of writing as if she had a broomstick up her ass. Her letters to him from Oxford had had a similar, affected formality about them, with just as many semicolons.

Gerard reclined on his bunk and read the letter four more times. Sylvia had grabbed two bricks, one in each hand, and slammed them like cymbals against the sides of Gerard's head. Last night's beating hadn't been as painful as this. Each time he read the letter, Sylvia became more and more foreign to him. Who was this person? It was hard to imagine her, sitting at home—a home where you could do what you wanted to *when* you wanted to, without being yelled at. Did Sylvia sleep in and get up at her leisure? What was that like? Was she real?

"You can have no idea what it's like for me right now." Gerard read that line again and again. The more he read it, the hazier Sylvia's face became in his memory. He couldn't even see her. She was right—he had no idea. What was it like *not* to be where he was at this moment? He couldn't conceive of it. The power supply to his imagination had been snipped.

He crumpled the letter again. Fuck Sylvia and her goddamned semicolons; good fucking riddance. Let Sylvia enlist in the army and go through what he was going through. Come to think of it, how could he possibly have a relationship with Sylvia now, after having become a soldier? He couldn't imagine they'd have anything to talk about. He pictured them having dinner at the Neighbor's Tavern on the Corner in Lambeth. "So Sylvia, the other day I was loading a thirty-round magazine into my M16A2, when, wouldn't you know it, Libby tripped over his own dick and sprained his ankle." Good. Good that she had done it. It was unavoidable.

No it wasn't. What was Sylvia doing? Surely she didn't mean it. They had planned to marry, after all. This was a phase. When Gerard finished training, his head would be sharp and unclouded. Everything would be back to normal. This was temporary. It would pass. It was exactly as Cooper had said! "It all passes." The clarity of Cooper's words struck Gerard—the phase Sylvia was going through was temporary. She would come to her senses; she would come around, and Gerard would be there for her. He had to be patient. He would wait.

# Ten

It was 9:00 in the evening, thirty minutes to lights-out. Bravo Company was in the middle of the final week of basic training. They had spent the last two days on the hot blacktop parking lots of 1/47th practicing Drill and Ceremony for the upcoming weekend when the soldiers would put on a show for visiting family before leaving Fort Benning for a two-day pass. "Marching up and down the square," Berkowicz had called it, in a continuing pattern of speech that betrayed his annoying affinity for Monty Python movies.

Gerard lay on his bunk with his hands behind his head, staring up at the ceiling. "I must end our relationship." Would Sylvia ever have said that to him in-person? Letter writing was cowardly; it was a chicken-shit way for her to hide. He couldn't picture her saying it to him, to his face. And if she had, what would he have answered? "No, Sylvia, that's not acceptable," or "You must have had a bad day Sylvia. Let's go to the Neighbor's Tavern and drink port. You'll feel better." He couldn't even answer her now. The date on the letter was July 6, and it was now July 17, so she must have held onto it for a few days before putting it in the mail. Had she hesitated? Was she changing her mind even now? Maybe Gerard still had a chance.

"Berkowicz, man, you got any shave cream?"

Gerard watched the can flip silently through the air. Wiley caught it with one hand and disappeared into the bathroom.

No. It was no good. He wouldn't want Sylvia back anyway, not after this letter. Didn't the letter reveal who she really was? Now that life was becoming more difficult than during their sheltered undergraduate days, Sylvia had provided more of a glimpse into her true personality. Gerard thought back to those windy days of autumn at Monroe Hill College. He thought of the Friday evenings when he and Sylvia would walk briskly along Waterford Road to be on time for her Patrick Henry Society meeting at 7:29 in Henry Hall. In those happy moments, holding her hand and watching her push away the wind-blown strands of blond hair from her face, he could never have even imagined that she'd be capable of writing such a letter. And certainly in those moments, if he'd been told that Sylvia had a tendency toward being unfaithful—to see how many times she and her lover could climax within a twenty-four period (eleven for Gilberto and nineteen for Sylvia)—he would have laughed. He would have nibbled her shoulder in the amphitheater in front of Kellogg Hall and said "Never!" He would have held her close with his back against a tree trunk on the Lawn, squeezing his arms tight around her gray Monroe Hill College sweatshirt, with the cool wind whipping yellow and orange leaves around their feet, and said "Impossible!" He would never have believed it; there had been only one route to learning who Sylvia was (if it was ever truly possible to know another person), and that had been experience. Experience was more authentic than words and promises. Sylvia had undergone a brief test given to her by experience, and she had failed. Thank God she had removed herself from Gerard before he had really committed to her.

Holy shit; he had nearly *married* Sylvia without learning who she was—without seeing her react to difficult situations. What if they had married and then he had later learned who she was? Was that why people went through divorce—when they realized that if they'd waited a bit longer and sought a little harder they could have done much, much better? What was it like to be struck with the revelation that you've made a big mistake and settled for less than you should have? Gerard felt a rush of gratitude for this lesson and that it had come early enough for him. Thank God. He'd been saved.

Gerard's thoughts turned to Rachel. If he'd found Sylvia out earlier, he could have had a relationship with Rachel. During his three years dating Sylvia at Monroe Hill, he'd had countless chances with Rachel; she'd made many offers to Gerard. Some of them were subtle, like the time she'd told Gerard she was thinking of taking up the cello, and would he be willing to give her lessons? Other times she was more explicit: she'd once asked Gerard if he enjoyed sex with Sylvia, if it was gratifying and *innovative*. She'd actually used that word, and Gerard kicked himself now to imagine what sorts of innovations she might have had in mind. If Gerard had known then what he knew now, he would have accepted her offers—again and again—even considering that Rachel's motivation for seducing Gerard was her hatred of Sylvia and everything Sylvia represented: privilege, conceit, self-righteousness. Gerard wouldn't have cared about that; he would have been there for Rachel!

But no, Gerard had been a good boy. He'd been so fucking good it made him sick to think about it. He'd been faithful to Sylva and had assumed she'd been faithful to him. He was committed not only to Sylvia but to making up for continuing to have sex with Meredith when they were both in high school and she was dating other people. He wanted to wash away the guilt he'd built up during those days, and Sylvia had been helping him do that. At the crux of his reformed attitude, though, was the assumption that Sylvia loved him and only him. Shit. Seventeen letters. In Letter Two, Gilberto mentioned Gerard by name and reminded Sylvia that sex with Gerard would never be as good as it had been with him, with Gilberto—Gerard had taken a long swallow of port after that sentence. He laughed now. Gilberto had probably been right; when Gerard and Sylvia had sex, the experience was planned, carefully choreographed, boring, and sterile. If Gerard had tried to write seventeen letters about his sexual experiences with Sylvia, and a panel of objective judges had compared them with Gilberto's letters, Gilberto would have won both for style and content.

Damn, he wished the police hadn't interrupted his foreplay with Rachel. Gerard felt a tingle in his loins as he thought back to the fraternity party and to Rachel straddling him, grinding herself down on him and whispering into his ear.

"Man, what crazy shit you talkin' about?" Parker grabbed his towel and headed for the bathroom.

"I'm not sure, it's just a feeling," said Cooper, getting up from Parker's bunk.

"Crazy-ass shit," Parker said.

Cooper walked to his wall locker and turned the dial on the lock.

"What's he talking about?" said Gerard.

Cooper shook his head. "I have a bad feeling, like Parker should be careful."

"Of what?"

"I'm not sure," Cooper said. "When this happens to me, I can't tell exactly what it is. But I'm always right."

"Did you tell Parker that?" Gerard said.

"Oh yes," Cooper said. "But you saw him. That's the other part of the problem. No one ever believes me until it's too late."

Gerard lay back down. Believing Cooper might be clairvoyant wasn't a stretch, and it was somehow made easier by his bizarre rhetoric. Gerard didn't understand a lot of it—like Cooper's belief that we're all clairvoyant, that everything is within everything—but Cooper was trustworthy. If Cooper said he was sure of something, Gerard believed him. Obviously Parker didn't.

Gerard looked at his watch. 9:28 p.m. He got up, opened his locker, found his toothbrush and toothpaste, and walked up the aisle to the latrine. He stared into the mirror as he brushed his teeth. He thought of Sylvia and of Rachel. They swirled together in his head. Where was Rachel right now? The last he'd heard was that she had an interview with a P.R. firm in Washington D.C. Maybe when he visited home after infantry training and airborne school he would try to find her.

"It's cool, Kelderman." Libby walked by and patted Gerard on the back. "It happened to me too, but you'll get over it. You'll forget her soon. You don't need her. We don't need any of 'em."

Gerard tossed warm water onto his face and head. He rubbed his towel all over his head, face, and neck. When he walked back into the bay, the lights were off. Through the red glow of the exit sign, he walked straight to his wall locker and put away his toiletries. He climbed into bed and pulled the sheet up to his chin and stared at the ceiling.

◆     ◆     ◆

Gerard woke hours later. Private Cory was on fireguard and had fallen asleep in his chair. The bay resounded with soft snoring and deep breathing.

Did something move? Gerard turned to the right. Five rows down, someone was walking between the bunks. Gerard strained his eyes. Who was up at this hour? He looked at the fireguard again; Cory was slumped over, soundly snoozing. The mystery figure tiptoed from bunk to bunk, peering into each face and then moving on to the next bunk. Was that Phillips? Who was that? Gerard lay still. He thought of sitting up, but that didn't feel right. The feeling he had was telling him he needed to stay still. The figure was now three rows away.

Gerard saw more clearly now. The person was dressed in street clothes. This was an outsider, a civilian, sneaking around in the barracks. The figure moved from bunk to bunk, closer to Gerard now. Gerard's body clenched. He should run. No, he should yell. He turned the other way and looked at Cooper. Cooper was asleep. He turned back toward the intruder, who was now one row away.

Shit, shit, shit. Gerard was shaking. He wanted to get away, but if he moved, it would see him. Maybe it would pass him by as it had the others. The figure reached Gerard's row and moved silently to Parker's bunk. The intruder leaned over Parker's face and paused. It stood up straight and paused again. Gerard saw the intruder reach into its jacket.

Gerard pushed the sheets away and slipped onto the floor. He glided across the aisle in his stocking feet. He tucked his shoulder and rammed into the man, aiming square at his middle. The tall figure slammed against the window shades.

"Help!" yelled Gerard. He pushed hard. The man's hands grabbed Gerard's ribcage. Gerard yanked him away from the window and wrapped his arms around the man's waist and pulled back toward the aisle. They both fell to the floor, and Gerard was pinned.

"Parker, get up!" yelled Gerard. He rolled over on top of the intruder and punched. He punched again and again into the man's kidneys and back.

The lights came on. Parker stood up. Sleepy-eyed soldiers gathered around in their underwear.

"Let me help," said Carroll. He walked forward and plopped down on the man's back.

Gerard stopped punching and sat up on the intruder's rump. He was sweating and breathing hard.

"Kick ass," said Romberg.

The intruder spoke. "Get off me."

Beneath Gerard and Carroll was a black man with his cheek pinned to the white linoleum floor.

"Cory, get the CQ," yelled Gerard.

Private Cory ran out the door.

"So who the fuck are you, huh?" said Romberg. "Some fucker from Second Platoon?"

"He's not a soldier, Romberg," said Cooper.

"Let's beat his ass anyway," Romberg said.

"Third Platoon, what the crap's going on here?" Drill Sergeant Gundacker, the company CQ for the night, ran down the aisle toward them.

"An intruder, Drill Sergeant," said Snodgrass. "A civilian."

"The MPs are on their way," Gundacker said. "You, what's your name, Private?"

"Private Carroll, Drill Sergeant."

"You stay right where you are until the MPs get here, Private Carroll."

"Yes, Drill Sergeant."

So Gerard and Carroll sat on the poor man for about three more minutes, until two MPs stormed into the barracks. They grabbed the man, slapped silver handcuffs onto his wrists, and shoved him out door.

"Okay Third Platoon," said Drill Sergeant Gundacker on his way to the exit door. "Excitement's over. Back to bed."

# Eleven

It was now Friday afternoon. Bravo Company was getting ready for a short ceremony before being released for their weekend pass. They had spent all day Thursday practicing more Drill and Ceremony—D&C. Gerard wouldn't have thought it possible that so much time would be needed to teach a group of people to walk in a straight line without looking like a herd of drunken buffalo (a "cluster-fuck" in army phraseology). Third Platoon had practiced longer than the rest of the company; invariably, Libby would step off using the wrong foot, or take a wrong turn, and the entire platoon would have to repeat the exercise—again and again. In the end, Womack had to admit that Third Platoon looked sharp, and that even Libby had made progress toward learning the difference between left and right.

But Parker kept making mistakes. Twice his rifle had slipped from his right hand during parade rest, a command requiring a vigorous thrust forward of the fist gripped around the muzzle. He'd turned right on a half-left command and had tripped during about-face.

There'd been intense whispering in the bay Wednesday night after the MPs had left and Drill Sergeant Gundacker had turned the lights off. Parker had wanted to be left alone, but the masses were too demanding: they wanted to know who the intruder was, even though any of them could have guessed. Parker was forced to explain that the man was a Warlord gang member and had come to Fort Benning to kill Parker. The platoon learned the next day that the MPs had found a knife in the guy's pocket, and that he had told the MPs—and later the civilian police—that he had planned to rob some of the soldiers.

Parker had assured Third Platoon that night that this wasn't the end; the attackers would keep coming until he was dead. Parker was scared and angry, but at the same time Gerard could tell Parker was genuinely concerned for his platoon mates. He had cautioned them to stay out of it and not to say anything to anybody. In formation the next morning, Parker had quietly told Gerard to watch himself—that the Warlords might now come after him if the intruder had successfully identified Gerard and was able to communicate Gerard's identity to the gang members back in Detroit. Parker also vowed to help protect Gerard.

But Gerard wanted to tell Parker to fuck off. If they came after Parker again, Gerard would let them kill him. It was good that Gerard hadn't had time to think when the intruder entered the bay, because he might not have taken the action he did. Gerard knew that if, at the time, he'd recognized the intruder as a Warlord, he would have let Parker die.

Who was he kidding? He would still have defended Parker; he wouldn't have been able to help it—a very good and *Cooper*ish way to react, but it was annoying to Gerard. And then after Parker had given Gerard the warning there in the back row of the platoon formation, he'd done something curious. He'd held out a fist toward Gerard, down low at waist level. He hadn't done anything with it—Gerard half expected Parker to hit him—he'd just held it there and looked at Gerard. Clearly he expected Gerard to do something, but Gerard had stared stupidly at the fist until Parker retracted it and snorted. Gerard noticed a grin beneath Parker's snort.

Fuller had later told Gerard that this was Parker's way of offering a friendly gesture, that it was a kind of black handshake. What Gerard should have done, it turns out, was to make a fist himself and bump the top of Parker's fist with his own. Parker would then bump the top of Gerard's fist, and then they were supposed to sort of punch their fists together at the knuckles to finish it. How was Gerard supposed to know that? How could he possibly have known about this street version of one-potato-two-potato? He wished Parker would do it again so he could show Parker he knew what to do—that he was now 'hip' to the ritual.

Gerard's body had healed from the beating a week ago. Over the past few days he had come to a new perspective of the whole incident: everyone was now even. He, as platoon guide, had screwed up and caused the platoon to suffer. The platoon, in turn, had caused him to suffer. It was a primitive interpretation, but it was simple, and above all, right now, Gerard yearned for simplicity. He had spent days blaming others for his pain, but he had now accepted that in the army-basic-training-platoon-level-informal-code-of-conduct his pain had been his own responsibility; he blamed himself.

Gerard had learned about blame early in his childhood. He was sure that his mother's tendency to find fault with Willem had its foundation in the death of his sister; she never stopped blaming him. If Willem had been more careful, Rebecca claimed, Anna would still be alive.

"And why do you suppose I had to take the kids with me to Belgium, anyway?" Willem had said. "It's because you were so busy traveling around singing that you didn't have time for them."

"Don't pull that old shit, Willem," Rebecca had answered. "You fucked up, and I lost my only daughter."

"Does that mean you have to expose our only son to your obscene language?"

"Would you rather I use *Flemish* swear words?" Rebecca had said. "Would you prefer that?"

And on the argument went, back and forth; Gerard couldn't remember the details. He did now remember one incident in particular that highlighted Willem's dejection and Rebecca's ferocity. It was spring, Gerard remembered. He was ten years old. On a Saturday morning he and his parents were eating breakfast in the kitchen.

"Look at Daniel, staring at the back door," said Willem, looking out the window into the back yard. "He's sitting so proper, isn't he?"

Daniel Webster was perched upright in the middle of the lawn, motionless, staring at the back door of the house. The white fur of his paws and chest were muddy; he'd been digging.

Rebecca turned to the window. "He only sits like that when he thinks it's supper time," she said. "You did give the dogs their dinner last night, didn't you?"

"*I* didn't feed them," said Willem.

"Well neither did I. I didn't get home until after midnight last night," Rebecca said. "When I came into the house, I thought you would have already fed them."

"Why did you think that?" Willem said.

"What do you mean 'why did I think that'?"

"You make that mistake all the time, don't you?" said Willem.

"What mistake?" said Rebecca.

"The mistake where you assume something, instead of checking to make—"

"Jesus Christ, here we go," Rebecca said. "Okay, who was home last night when the dogs *usually* eat dinner?"

"Yes, yes, I know," Willem said. "I forgot to feed the dogs. I admit it. But that doesn't mean you should have assumed I fed them, does it?"

"I can't believe this. I can't believe you're being such a bastard."

"Rebecca—"

"No, don't 'Rebecca' me," she said. "You really are being a bastard. I'm talking about one incident—last night—that specifically has to do with feeding the dogs—that's all. But you have to take it farther. You have to generalize about how I'm 'always this' and 'always that.' It's annoying Willem, and it doesn't do any good."

"But there's a pattern, isn't there?" Willem said.

"Well, I don't know, Willem," said Rebecca. "Why don't you tell me, since you're such an expert. Since you seem to know me better than I know myself. Is there a pattern?"

"Yep." Willem shoveled in a big bite of scrambled eggs.

Rebecca clenched her teeth and looked sideways at Gerard as she considered what to say next. She was shaking her head, as if to say to Gerard, who was only ten years old, "Can you believe this? Can you believe what I put up with?"

"Well goddammit, Willem, you're right," she said.

"There really isn't any need for—"

"Maybe I do assume things," said Rebecca. "And you're right, I should stop assuming things, especially when it comes to you."

Willem put his fork down and put his face in his hands. Gerard recognized the gesture; it was Willem's way of escaping. If he was stuck, if he couldn't run for the basement and refuge of his diamonds, he would hide his face in his hands. And Gerard remembered now that any time Willem did that, he would stop talking. For Willem the argument had ended and he wasn't going to play any more.

"No, no, I shouldn't have assumed that you would feed Daniel and Alexander," said Rebecca. "I mean, shit, you probably had your dinner, so who cares? Did you feed Gerard?"

Willem sighed, his face in his hands. He was an ostrich.

"Gerard, did you get dinner last night?" said Rebecca.

"Yes, Mom," said Gerard. Willem was a very good cook. He'd roasted a leg of lamb.

"Well, good." She turned back to Willem. "What else shouldn't have I assumed, Willem, huh? Can you remember?"

Gerard tried now to race ahead a little in his memory to get a glimpse how the argument had ended, but he couldn't do it. His memory was now unfolding at exactly the same rate as the original conversation. All he could do was watch and listen.

"What did I assume when you took our children to Antwerp four years ago?" She pushed her long, black hair out of her face. "I assumed they would be safe, didn't I? I assumed you would take care of them. My mistake. Sorry. I assumed you were perfectly capable of taking care of a two-year-old and keeping her from getting hurt."

Willem stood up from the kitchen table and walked toward the door.

"I assumed my only daughter wouldn't *die* because *you* had your head in your ass."

Willem was down the hallway now. He'd reached the basement door.

"Come to think of it I made some assumptions about our marriage vows, too." Rebecca was still seated at the kitchen table, screaming through the open door down the hall. The basement door clicked softly closed.

"Silly me," said Rebecca quietly, resting her elbows on the table.

And there it was, another full transcript from Gerard's childhood that he was only now remembering. It was bizarre that not only had he completely forgotten the exchange, but now, many years later, he recalled the entire dialogue. He remembered all the details: the lines in Rebecca's facial expressions, the sun on the lime-green cabinets of the kitchen that morning (God—the kitchen really was painted lime-green), and even that Willem had splashed his scrambled eggs with red hot sauce when he'd first sat down at the table.

If his parents had mounted a coordinated effort to shield from Gerard the details of Anna's death, it was now clear to him that there'd been plenty of slip-ups. This most recent exchange that had jumped into Gerard's consciousness gave him no new information about how she had died, but Gerard doubted that his parents had agreed it was okay for Gerard to know, at so early an age, the harsh anger Rebecca felt toward Willem—that she placed all blame on Willem for the accident. And as the weeks of OSUT infantry training crept along, Gerard realized how frequently the darts of anger had flown out of Rebecca at Willem, with Gerard sitting right in front of them. How many arguments had he missed? Maybe his parents really had been careful to protect Gerard, and the truly bitter arguments and accusations had happened when he was away. He had lived at home only until he was fourteen, when he'd moved to Vermont to attend Belden Academy.

Gerard wondered now if Rebecca and Willem had sent him away to protect him. He couldn't remember whose idea it was that he would attend a boarding school 500 miles from home—he only remembered being shocked at having gained admission. His mother had told him Belden Academy was intensely competitive, so the acceptance letter in the mail had surprised him. He'd barely passed English each year since the sixth grade. Gerard had always struggled with grammar, reading, and writing. God, how he hated to write; Mr. Hicks, his eighth-grade English teacher, had told Gerard's parents that perhaps Gerard should consider enrolling in the vocational/technical school when he reached the ninth grade. Maybe it was then that the idea of boarding school had occurred to Rebecca. It had been Rebecca's idea, Gerard would discover only a year later.

During morning assembly one day at Belden Academy Gerard had glanced over at the wall and figured out why he'd been admitted to the academy. Lining the walls of the assembly hall were paintings—portraits of stern-looking, important white men who had had influence on the academy in some way or other. And then Gerard saw the name at the bottom of one of the portraits: George Randolph Ward. "Grandpa!" Gerard remembered thinking. That was him—it was definitely him, and if Grandpa Ward had been involved enough in Belden Academy to have a portrait in the assembly hall, he was probably important enough that Gerard's application had been rubber-stamped.

"Berkowicz, what time is it?" said Wiley.

"Three-thirty."

"Awesome." Wiley flopped back on his bunk.

Bravo Company had thirty more minutes before the formation for the ceremony. Gerard stretched; he pressed his feet—caressed in the cool sheer of black army dress socks—against the gray metal railing at the foot of the bed. His hands touched the wall locker behind him. He sighed. He felt relaxed; it had been a long time since he'd felt relaxed. Romberg was asleep—drooling on his pillow, Parker was ironing the collars of his green Class B shirt, and Cooper was reading a novel called *Whores of Lost Atlantis*.

Leaving his home and his friends at age fourteen to attend a boarding school in Vermont had been difficult. He did fly back to Evans Glen for holidays like Thanksgiving and Christmas, and he also had a week-long spring break and the entire summer off between school years. He'd gotten to spend time with Meredith and

Donald Meerschaum, but it hadn't been the same. When he came back home on holiday he would have to spend time catching up with his friends before they could really relax with each other. Because of the extended separation, they were all completely ignorant of each others' day-to-day existence. Back when they were in the same middle school, meeting with friends had been casual: walking into Meredith's bedroom and crashing onto the bed, then lying there with her while they listened to R.E.M.'s "Losing My Religion" and planned what to do for the rest of the lazy afternoon. At Donald Meerschaum's house they would head straight to the attic, without a word between them, to play with the electric trains for hours and hours. No talk, just play.

But when Gerard returned from Belden for holidays, simply being with his old friends felt like hard work; he no longer knew them as he used to. Meredith was on the varsity soccer team at Cornwall County High and would probably get a college scholarship. She was also dating the captain of the basketball team, a lanky senior named Alden Fields. Donald Meerschaum had become a blazingly good electric guitar player, and he and some friends had started a band called *Steep the Fat Tick*, a name Meredith had characterized as "Textbook Meerschaum." (Donald had the good sense not to tell Meredith that the runner-up name for the band had been *Hostile Mucus*.)

Even going to Meredith's house became awkward. When Meredith and Gerard were growing up, Gerard would walk into the Flanigan-Flamberts' house without knocking. That had taken him some time to get used to, but Patrick Flanigan-Flambert had insisted on it; he'd also insisted that Gerard call him and Lisa by their first names. That had been very easy, since Gerard felt silly just saying the name Flanigan-Flambert. So Meredith's parents were 'Lisa' and 'Patrick' (Patrick had wanted Meredith to call her own parents by their first names; Lisa vetoed). But every time Gerard flew back from Belden to Evans Glen, he never felt as comfortable at the Flanigan-Flamberts' house. Meredith's parents were still Patrick and Lisa, but from age fourteen onward Gerard used the doorbell at the Flanigan-Flamberts' house.

"And here's the Beldenian!" Patrick Flanigan-Flambert would say, flinging open the front door. "What's with the doorbell?" Ever since Gerard was accepted to Belden Academy, Patrick would refer to him as the Beldenian. Patrick Flanigan-Flambert had attended the Hayden School in Massachusetts as a boy, and he was trying to cultivate a chummy school rivalry with Gerard. It never clicked for Gerard, especially since he felt like a fraud for being at Belden.

Meredith, however, had no trouble maintaining the casual familiarity she and Gerard had enjoyed during their entire childhood. She still wore baseball caps and tattered sweatshirts, and when Gerard walked into her bedroom the first Thanksgiving of his freshman year at Belden, she cheerfully threw her arms around his neck and wrestled him onto her bed.

"God, I've missed you," said Meredith. "So how is it? How's Vermont? Tell me about Belden."

And as Gerard talked about Belden Academy—about his classes and his roommate and the town of Belden—Meredith began energetically tugging his shirt and unbuttoning his pants. For her, it was as if Gerard had never left!

"Meredith, you have a boyfriend now," said Gerard. "I heard about Alden Fields."

"Lighten up, Gerard. Have you forgotten our agreement? I'm not your girlfriend—you're supposed to think of me as one of the guys, remember?"

That would be the pattern for the next four years while Gerard attended Belden. He would return to Evans Glen and do everything he had done growing up: play the cello, polish diamonds, (Donald Meerschaum was too busy rehearsing with *Steep the Fat Tick* to play with trains), and hang out with Meredith. And since hanging out with Meredith led to sex from time to time—well, all the time—that was how they continued, even as Meredith had boyfriends at Cornwall County High. Meredith had been spirited and forceful that first day back during Thanksgiving break, and Gerard had ultimately given in, but he'd had to work to convince himself it was okay to carry on this way.

For example, Gerard had dated a few girls at Belden Academy. Each year toward the end of the spring term, he would plan ahead for the coming summer by either breaking up with his girlfriend or becoming so distant that *she* would break it off, so he could face Meredith without any attachments. For those four years Gerard had managed to fool himself into believing that this plan made his relationship with Meredith ethical, even as Meredith maintained relationships with steady boyfriends ('steady' was Meredith's word) throughout the summers.

But these were little games of the mind for Gerard. The real pleasure of his sexual relationship with Meredith was that it eased the awkwardness of leaving Evans Glen and then returning. He felt a pull at his chest when he thought of his childhood—chasing soccer balls on the field next to the school board annex, roaring down Old Windsor Road at dusk on his bike as gnats smacked into his eyes and teeth, lifting up baby Anna in the front yard of the Kasteel so she could splash the water in the fountain. All that was over. Anna was gone. Gerard could relive those happy parts of his childhood only through the arduous work of imagination and thought. Meredith, at least, was a solid connection to his past that stayed with him; he could still touch her and kiss her and hold on to her. His physical relationship with Meredith made returning to Evans Glen easy for Gerard—to know that that part of his childhood was still alive and well.

But how did Sylvia justify cheating on him with Gilberto Cardenas? During their senior year at Monroe Hill College—the year after Sylvia's Oxford stint—did Sylvia miss her relationship with Gilberto? She couldn't have willed herself to forget, not with the seventeen letters that trickled in to her mailbox from August to March during that year. And Gerard knew Sylvia was writing Gilberto back, because Gilberto referred to her letters when he wrote. In Letter Three, Gilberto wrote that he had gone to the library and found James Joyce's letters to his wife, Nora—as Sylvia had instructed him to—but that he couldn't emulate Joyce and bring himself to call her his 'whorish Sylvia.' It was bizarre enough to imagine Sylvia even using the word 'whorish,' let alone asking someone else—a lover—to call her whorish. Prim, elegant, *whorish* Sylvia! Perhaps Sylvia's technique in grappling with her conscience was to face her demons head on: to try to get someone to say out loud that she *was* being whorish.

How Gerard wished he could see the letters Sylvia wrote to Gilberto. The way Sylvia was drawn to 'epistolary correspondence,' there were likely more than seventeen. Gerard would have tried to search Sylvia's laptop computer in the days after he'd found the letters, but in Letter One Gilberto had made reference to Sylvia's instructions that they were not to send each other e-mails; e-mail messages, Sylvia believed, could be more easily intercepted than snail-mail letters. She'd really thought it through! It nauseated Gerard to think that Gilberto might not have been Sylvia's first (or last) escapade.

So of course Sylvia didn't want Gerard to visit her in Oxford. Gerard had been disappointed by Sylvia's excuses, but he'd believed them: Sylvia had a paper due, or a research project, or an exam to write. For the Christmas break Sylvia flew home to Atlanta, and Gerard drove twelve hours from Evans Glen to see her. He stayed in the Landon's guest room for three days, during which time he and Sylvia shopped for Christmas gifts; she must have dragged Gerard to five malls in three hours one day. Everything was normal. Looking back on that holiday break, Gerard couldn't remember anything that would have clued him in to the fact that Sylvia was, by then, deeply involved with Gilberto (they had met in September, and on October Third, Gilberto had spent the night in Sylvia's Oxford dorm room—Letter Two). Sylvia had coordinated with her Pembroke College roommate, someone named Karen Shlaudecker, who had spent the night at a cousin's house in Wolvercote so Sylvia could have the room to herself. October Third— that was when Sylvia Landon and Gilberto Cardenas had sex for the first time.

But on that winter holiday during his junior year at Monroe Hill College, when he visited Sylvia in Atlanta and was a guest of the Landons, he had no clue that Sylvia had surrendered her lithe body to manly, tawny Gilberto, and that Gilberto had so passionately stimulated Sylvia that her appetite for sex soared far above her typical tolerance of occasional, superficial intercourse. No, in Atlanta, Sylvia had hidden it well. She'd carried herself with the same rigid elegance she always had. It wasn't until two weeks later, the day after New Year's, that Sylvia had given Gerard the strongest clue. At the time he had no idea it was a clue. He'd been blind and stupid.

Gerard had returned to Evans Glen to spend time with his parents for the remaining two weeks of the winter holiday. He had finished dinner with his parents and was sitting on the couch in the music parlor at the Kasteel, thumbing through albums of photographs of the Great Pyrenees puppy litters Rebecca had raised over the years. The fireplace roared hot. Benjamin Britten's *Rejoice in the Lamb* played softly on the stereo. Sylvia telephoned from Atlanta.

"I have to see you," said Sylvia.

"Uh, okay," said Gerard. "Is everything alright?"

"Yes, yes, everything's fine. But I have to see you. Soon."

"Okay," said Gerard. "You want to fly to Evans Glen?"

"I've checked online. Everything's booked."

"Well, it's a twelve-hour drive," Gerard said.

"Let's meet halfway," said Sylvia. "I've booked a hotel room in North Carolina, in Chapel Hill. I'm leaving in fifteen minutes."

"Uh, alright," said Gerard. "You sure everything's okay?"

Sylvia assured him again that nothing was wrong, so Gerard told his parents he was driving to North Carolina and that he wasn't sure when he'd be back. Five hours later he was waiting for Sylvia in a room at the Siena Hotel on Franklin Street in Chapel Hill. What was it? Had he done something wrong, and was Sylvia going to break up with him? As Gerard sat upright on the edge of the bed in room 304, he tried to imagine what had gone wrong with their relationship (maybe he had been too sexually forceful), and if Sylvia was going to dump him, why she hadn't done it over the phone.

But when Gerard answered the knock at the hotel room door, Sylvia stormed into the room and pinned him to the closet door with a deep kiss. She dropped her bag, kicked off her shoes, closed the door with her heel, fumbled with Gerard's belt buckle, and wrestled him to the bed—all with her mouth securely clamped onto his. For the next five hours she blasted Gerard with sex that was unfettered, uninhibited, and very un*Sylvia*. He should have been aware at the time, but he'd been a fool. He should have known that no one changes habits overnight; he should have been more skeptical; he should have wondered about Sylvia's sudden stamina and the effortless contortions of her body. But this was all hindsight; what twenty-year-old would take the time to ask questions in the face of such sexual energy? Sylvia was an acrobat, scrambling up and down all sides of Gerard and grinding her heels into his rear end to push him more deeply into her. She grabbed the headboard for support and lowered herself onto Gerard at least three different ways. At one point, with Gerard on top of her, she had her legs pulled so far back that her knees were in her own armpits. She moaned and shrieked and growled through gritted teeth, "Don't you dare fucking stop."

If Gerard had thought of those scenes in the Siena Hotel only five days earlier—before Sylvia had sent her Dear-John letter to Fort Benning—he would probably have become angry and bitter as he realized, for the first time, that Sylvia's gymnastics that night in room 304 probably had more to do with Gilberto Cardenas than with Gerard. But now that Gerard had been flung aside by his fiancée and severely beaten by his platoon mates, it was easy. This was nothing! After what he'd been through he could now look back *fondly* on those five hours with Sylvia, especially considering that the night at the Siena Hotel was when they became engaged.

"Marry me," Sylvia said, straddling Gerard and pounding up and down on him like a piston, her hair matted with sweat against her cheeks and forehead. "Tell me you'll marry me, or I'll stop. I swear to fucking God I'll climb off right now."

Good Lord; in those seconds before Gerard's climax, Sylvia had to know that the last thing he wanted on earth was for her to *climb off*. This was pure coercion. If Sylvia had proposed to him under calmer and saner circumstances—maybe over glasses of Syrah and across a white tablecloth—Gerard couldn't honestly say he knew what his answer would have been. But in the grip of a sexual tornado on the floor of room 304, he had said 'yes.' Had Gilberto taught Sylvia how to exploit a man's vulnerability in the moments leading up to orgasm? Gerard wondered what Sylvia might have squeezed out of Gilberto during such times.

So from that moment on, Gerard and Sylvia were officially engaged, though Sylvia never admitted to anyone that she had asked Gerard to marry her, much less where they'd been and what they'd been doing. She had trouble enough facing her parents because Gerard hadn't asked her father for permission before popping the question. Her parents would have been shocked to know how their dignified daughter, their little debutante, had carried on in the Siena Hotel with Gerard that night. It really was a spectacular event—Sylvia's adventurousness and creativity had been on par with Meredith's—and Gerard had benefited. Gerard should have felt thankful to Gilberto for schooling Sylvia in the more innovative side of sexual intercourse. Cooper would have been proud of Gerard's mindfulness that night, of his being in the present moment. When it came to sex, Gerard had no trouble being in the present moment.

"Check it out! I did it!" Private Mueller stood in the doorway of the latrine with his arms stretched out and his palms facing the ceiling. The two ends of a dog tag chain dangled down below his chin.

"Dude, that's disgusting," said Romberg.

When Gerard looked more closely at Mueller, he saw that one end of the chain was hanging out of Mueller's mouth, and the other swung from the cavern of his right nostril.

"Cool," said Wiley, looking up from his letter. "How'd you do it?"

"Took me a while," said Mueller. "I had to start in my nose, sorta shove it up in there." He was holding up both ends of the chain between the thumb and forefinger of each hand. "Gagged a couple times, too." Mueller gagged on the chain as he said the word 'gagged.'

Berkowicz was buttoning the short-sleeved green shirt of his Class B uniform. "Hey, let's grab both ends of it and do like a shoe shine."

"Cool!" Wiley said, putting aside his letter and standing up.

"Oh, no way, man," Mueller said. "No way." He backed into the latrine and closed the door.

Berkowicz and Wiley ran to the latrine door tried to push their way in, but Mueller was holding the other side. Mueller let go of the door, Berkowicz and Wiley fell over each other into the bathroom, and Mueller zipped out the other entrance into the second aisle of the bay.

"Get him!" Berkowicz yelled.

"Fuckin' shoe shine," Wiley said. "Awesome."

But Mueller managed to extract dog tag chain even as he jumped from bunk to bunk with Berkowicz and Wiley in pursuit.

"Oh man," said Berkowicz. "Shit."

"Crazy fuckers," Mueller said. He fell backwards onto his bunk.

"Who's the crazy fucker who stuck a chain up his nose?" Wiley said. "Huh, huh?" He was offering Berkowicz a high five.

Berkowicz swung his arm up and smacked Wiley's hand. "Ha, *ha!*"

Gerard looked at his watch. 15:40. They were due in formation at 16:00, to be ready for the 16:30 ceremony. Most of Third Platoon was half-dressed, including Gerard.

"Ten minutes 'til we form up, Third Platoon," Gerard announced.

"Yeah, yeah," someone said from the other side of the middle row of wall lockers.

Gerard started to get up from his bunk to pull on his green slacks, until he realized he had an erection; it would have been instantly noticed through the thin fabric of his brown boxer shorts. Thoughts of Sylvia and her whorish antics at the Siena Hotel had aroused him! Shit. He sat on his bed with his back against the wall locker, drawing up his knees for concealment—cover and concealment as it was called in the infantry. This was the first erection he'd had in seven weeks, the first since he'd enlisted in the army.

How was he supposed to let go of Sylvia if she could still arouse him? Gerard tried to think angry thoughts about Sylvia—her Dear-John letter, her affair with Gilberto Cardenas, her criticism of his weight problem. None of it worked. His erection stood as tall and proud as a Fort Benning infantryman. He couldn't muster any anger for Sylvia.

His erection led to thoughts of Meredith, who had been the cause of countless hard-ons in Gerard's adolescence. Simply walking into her house would get Gerard excited—the sound of zither music on the stereo or the smell of Lisa Flanigan-Flambert's patchouli incense; the woman burned so much incense that the furniture and drapes reeked of it even when it wasn't lit. Of all the sex Gerard and Meredith had, most of it happened in the many rooms of the Flanigan-Flamberts' house.

Damn. In eight minutes Gerard would have to get dressed for the ceremony, and none of these thoughts were helping him shrink what felt like an M203 grenade launcher in his trousers. Now it was Meredith. Meredith and sex. Sex and Meredith.

Sex between Gerard and Meredith matured as they matured— well, it changed, anyway. It gradually took over as their primary means of communicating with each other, at all times and in all places. Every event, every conversation—any situation at all—led to sex, regardless of the circumstances. For instance, when Gerard and Meredith were juniors in high school and Gerard was home from Belden Academy for spring break, Meredith showed Gerard a diamond ring that her then-boyfriend, Terry Shiflett, had given her. She and Gerard were sitting in the living room at the Flanigan-Flamberts' house, on the couch in front of a gaudy floral wall mural Lisa had painted there.

"Your boyfriend gave you a diamond?" Gerard said. "That's serious. How long have you been dating?"

"Six months," Meredith said. She pulled a necklace out of her shirt and showed it to Gerard. The rock was huge. "Take a look. Give me your expert opinion."

How many girls have the advantage of a close friend who's the son of a Flemish master diamond cutter? Unfortunately Gerard did give her his expert opinion. Willem had shown Gerard many examples of cubic zirconium and moissanite; one of the giveaways is that unlike diamonds they're both double-refracting. The copy of *Mother Jones* magazine on the coffee table was open to an ad page. Gerard placed the stone on a straight, single black line on the magazine page and could see *two* lines refracted up when he squinted through the alleged diamond. The stone was moissanite: a recent invention and more difficult to spot than cubic zirconium, but still a fake. Shit. If he had considered keeping the truth to himself, it was too late now. He and Meredith had spent enough time together that she probably sensed what he had discovered. Gerard tried to stall.

"So what did Terry tell you about this stone?" Gerard sat up straight on the couch. He held the gem between his thumb and index finger and turned it, pretending to examine closely.

"He went to D.C. for it," said Meredith. "He made a special trip, just for me!"

"Mm hm," Gerard said. Damn, that came out wrong.

"Oh shit," Meredith said. "You're going to tell me there's something wrong with it, aren't you?"

"Well—"

"Dammit, Gerard. Is it a fake? Is that what you're going to tell me?"

"I wasn't going to—"

"You're jealous, aren't you?" Meredith said.

Good grief. "No, I'm not jealous."

"Terry and I have sex," said Meredith. "All the time."

"Well, good," Gerard said.

"See, you are jealous," Meredith said. "Admit it."

"I'm not."

"What if I tell you the things Terry and I do. Would that make you jealous?"

"I'm really not interested," said Gerard.

"What if I tell you what Terry does with his mouth?" Meredith said.

"What about our agreement?" Gerard said. "We're not supposed to talk about this."

"Aha! Jealousy—I can see it."

"Drop it Meredith. I'm not jealous."

"Fucking hell, Gerard. Do you get jealous? Or mad? Or anything?"

"What's that supposed to—"

And Meredith kissed him. She had dropped the hint earlier that day that her parents wouldn't be home until dinner, so there they were again, stampeding toward sex on the couch of Meredith's living room. Why? In those moments when Meredith made her move, what was she thinking? She loved sex (she claimed it was the place in her life where she could be most expressive), but Gerard wondered now if Meredith's habit of changing the subject was part of her campaign to reform Gerard—to help him get over what she perceived as his inability to be passionate. Maybe that day on the couch, Meredith had resorted to sex because Gerard had refused to show any signs of jealousy about Terry Shiflett. But even after sex, Meredith would give Gerard a hard time because she was always the instigator.

"Why do *I* always have to jump *you?*" Meredith would ask.

But Gerard never had a chance to jump Meredith! She always beat him to it. If they got into an argument of any kind, Meredith would jump him. If they were having a particularly long, meaningful discussion, Meredith would jump him. Gerard wondered now what they would have uncovered about their relationship to each other, and about themselves as individuals, if sex hadn't always been there to distract them. It's possible Meredith suspected that if she didn't jump Gerard all the time she would have ultimately figured out she didn't like spending time with him. He had never discussed these questions with Meredith. "Lighten up, Gerard," he imagined her saying. "It's just sex." These thoughts hadn't even occurred to him until now—now that his mind sat idle during the long army minutes and hours of sitting and waiting.

It was toward the end of high school that Gerard's relationship with Meredith went through its biggest change. In the spring of

1998, Gerard was a senior at Belden Academy and had received his acceptance letter to Monroe Hill College. Meredith would be moving away to go to Yale, as Patrick Flanigan-Flambert had thirty-two years earlier, and somehow Gerard knew that he and Meredith were about to mature—that they were facing a void where they would outgrow their sexual adventures. Gerard imagined that having sex as an adult would be very different—less playful and more somber.

And he'd been right. The last time he and Meredith had had sex was after her senior prom. Joe Zadwick, her boyfriend, had broken up with her five days before the prom, and Gerard had caught a flight out of Rutland, Vermont to be her date at the last minute. They'd had dinner, danced in the Cornwall County High gymnasium to the sounds of Donald Meerschaum and *Steep the Fat Tick* (Donald used the prom to introduce his latest opus: *P.T.A. Mama in an S.U.V.*, a clear knock-off of Mellencamp's *R-O-C-K in the U.S.A.*) and then they'd camped out in Paxton Park outside the north end of town. Gerard knew it would be their last fling.

Gerard stretched and checked his watch again. 15:50. His erection had withered, thank God; he imagined the comments Romberg would have made, about how Gerard now had his own Excalibur to thrust proudly outward. Bravo Company 1/47th was only a few hours away from its first weekend pass. Freedom! He sat up and reached for his black dress shoes; their hard plastic uppers felt foreign to him after seven weeks in worn leather combat boots.

He wished Drill Sergeant Womack would come and tell them it was time to form up, but Gerard knew Womack would expect him to take care of that. Gerard was sure Womack had picked him to be the platoon guide because somehow Womack knew Gerard would hate it more than anyone else would. That kind of intuition was second-nature to drill sergeants.

"Let's go, Third Platoon," said Gerard. "Formation time."

Soldiers groaned and slowly lifted themselves from their naps. Magazines closed, shoes slipped on, and wall lockers opened.

"Rock and roll," said Romberg. "Tonight we hit the town."

"Yeah," said Carroll. "I can't wait."

"For what, the all-you-can eat buffet at Pizza Inn?" said Wiley.

"Oh yeah," said Carroll, rubbing his belly. "Oh yeah."

The mood in the platoon was bubbly; there was cheer and vigor as the soldiers chattered and ambled out the doors of the bay into the stairwell. Only Parker was quiet and sullen. Gerard thought he was the last one out of the bay, but when he turned the lights off and looked down the white linoleum aisle, he saw Parker sitting on the side of his bunk, sulking. This was awkward. Should he go back and ask if everything was okay? Parker saved him.

"It's alright, man," Parker said. "Go ahead on."

So Gerard walked through the doors, determined that if Parker was going to be dour and fearful, Gerard would have to be the chipper one, the one to hold it all together. Everything would be fine. The Warlords wouldn't dare attack them again.

# Twelve

The ceremony went quickly. Gerard remembered some marching and some standing around and a long-winded speech by Lieutenant Colonel Pinkerton, but for most of the half-hour he stared straight ahead and daydreamed about being set free for an entire weekend. Many of the soldiers of Third Platoon would spend the weekend with mothers, fathers, girlfriends, wives, and friends who had come to Columbus for the occasion. Gerard hadn't seen civilian people in nearly two months; they looked strange to him, alien, freakish—their varying body shapes and their colorful clothes and hats and the diversity of their posture for God's sake. These people had no discipline; Gerard was repulsed. What did the civilians see and think when they looked at the soldiers? Did they think of those TV commercials? They had no idea what it meant to be a soldier of Bravo Company 1st Battalion, 47th Infantry Regiment.

But no one came to visit Gerard, Romberg, Parker, Carroll, or Cooper, so they banded together and made plans for the weekend. They caught a cab from Fort Benning up I-185 into the town of Columbus, with Romberg changing out of his "goddamn un-fucking comfortable" clothes right there in the back seat. At a Denny's restaurant they ordered so much food the waitress couldn't fit all the plates on their table. Gerard ate two grand-slam breakfast platters on his own. The food was so good!

"Fuck, Kelderman," said Romberg. "You're a goddamn vacuum cleaner."

But Gerard couldn't slow down, even with no screaming drill sergeants anywhere in sight. He ate and shoveled as if the food might be taken away from him any second. Even here at Denny's, he could feel Womack over his shoulder telling him to hurry up and get Third Platoon back into formation.

After packing their stomachs like muskets, the five men from Third Platoon ambled across the street with their bags and booked two rooms at the La Quinta Inn. They showered and watched TV (Cooper found a cable channel with Brady Bunch reruns) and lounged and horsed around with pillows and took turns on the phone with family and girlfriends. Gerard called the Kasteel, but no one answered, so he left a message with the phone number of the hotel and the extension in their room. He knew no one would call back; Willem rarely returned phone calls, and Rebecca was likely out of town singing.

"Let's go, man," said Romberg. "I'm ready."

"Boogie woogie," said Carroll.

"Parker, you gonna teach me to dance?" said Romberg.

"Why you think I can dance?" said Parker as he put on a pink button-down shirt.

Everyone looked at Parker. Oh good, he was smiling. He was smiling a smile that said, "You sorry fuckers are terrified to talk about race, aren't you?"

"Duh," said Romberg. "'Cause you're black."

"Yeah," said Parker. "Yeah, I'll teach you how to dance."

"I'm the one who needs teaching," said Carroll.

"I'm not dancing," said Gerard. "I'll drink and watch."

"You'll dance," said Cooper.

"I'm just kidding, Parker," said Romberg. "Not about the black part, I mean about dancing. I can dance my ass off. Really."

So off they walked down Macon Road to the Chickasaw Club at exit 5.

By eleven o'clock that Friday night they were in full swing on the dance floor. Gerard had never liked dancing at all—pop music made him want to vomit—but Cooper was persistent in convincing Gerard that he needed to dance *because* he didn't like dancing and was terrible at it. So Gerard self-consciously stepped around in time with the music, which wasn't all that difficult, but he couldn't decide what to do with his hands. He tried letting them hang at his sides, but that made him feel like an ape. Waving them in the air anywhere above his shoulders was out of the question—it would have been too obvious, Gerard was sure, that he was trying too hard. At last he settled for holding his elbows against the sides of his torso with clenched fists and making downward punching movements to the beat of the music. This felt like a good compromise: subtle but earnest. It made him feel less awkward about participating simultaneously in two events that were entirely foreign to him—dancing and listening to pop music.

Gerard was the last person to judge the dancing skills of others, but Romberg did seem shockingly good, and with a tight-fitting blue t-shirt that accentuated the rolls of muscles on his torso and biceps and left his glorious Excalibur tattoo in full view, he soon had young women swirling around him. Parker was a natural, just as Romberg had guessed, and Carroll did his best, jouncing and jiggling and not caring.

Then there was Cooper. Cooper flailed around like an ungainly stork, like an entranced sufi who'd been kicked out of whirling-dervish school for being too enthusiastic. From what Gerard could tell, the convulsions Cooper was making didn't correspond at all to anything going on in the music or to the flashing lights in the floor. And, as usual, Cooper was having the time of his life. His smile couldn't have been any broader, and he couldn't have been any more energetic—likewise, the space given to him on the floor by the other dancers couldn't have been wider.

They must have spent three or four hours at the Chickasaw, and since they intended to sleep in the next morning—something none of them had done in two months—no one gave a rip what time it was. As the evening went on Gerard established a comfortable routine for himself: he would dance for a few tunes and then go sit down and drink beer. Cooper would come to the table and sip along with him. Gerard thought it strange that someone with Cooper's experience—having studied with mystical gurus in India and then having spent five years with the brothers of Taizé—would be interested in drinking alcohol. But there he was, relishing each cold bottle as much as he had enjoyed thrashing himself around on the dance floor.

Then again, Willem Kelderman loved Belgian beer, especially Trappist beer, because it was brewed by monks. He'd rejoiced when it was announced that the La Trappe brewery, the only Trappist brewery in the Netherlands, was to lose its Trappist distinction because a commercial outfit was taking over the operation. A beer couldn't technically be called Trappist if monks weren't doing the actual brewing.

"This means that the only true Trappist breweries in the world are in Belgium," Willem had said. "It's down to six now, and they're all in the motherland!" He'd raised a goblet of Westmalle Dubbel and sucked down half the glass like a camel at an oasis.

Parker became zealously attentive to the beverage needs of Carroll and Romberg (Carroll was only eighteen and Romberg nineteen; they couldn't buy beer themselves). They'd all be sitting around the table amid cigarette smoke and thumping music, and Parker would eye Romberg's bottle to check the level of beer. "You good?" he would say, and Romberg would raise his bottle with a guttural grunt. But if Romberg or Carroll weren't good—if there was less than, say, three ounces at the bottom of their bottles— Parker would jump up from the table and come bouncing back with another round. After about twenty minutes Parker was having such a great time being the beer boy that he fetched drinks for all the revelers, including Gerard and Cooper, who could legally get it themselves. All night Parker made sure everyone was 'good.'

So this was being a soldier. Just one week before, Parker had orchestrated a mass beating of Gerard, and now he was cheerfully bringing Gerard beer as if it had never happened. Bygones, that was all. The beer had nicely loosened Gerard's limbs and his inhibitions, so accepting the bygones was very easy. Like the farmer in the parable, he was going to keep his eye on the plow in front of him without looking back, just as Cooper had suggested.

"Ha, ha!" Cooper raised his bottle and smiled at Gerard.

He *is* reading my mind, the fucker, thought Gerard.

"Ha!" Gerard answered back, and they clinked bottles. This was being a soldier—a manly soldier. Fuck you, Gilberto Cardenas.

Sometime after midnight, Parker, Cooper, Romberg, Carroll, and Gerard were good and full of beer, hopping on the dance floor amid the flashing lights and gyrating, full-breasted women. Through his peripheral vision Gerard saw what looked like Parker feverishly dancing with another person. But when Gerard turned and looked, he saw that Parker was in a tussle with another man; they were wrestling and struggling. The Chickasaw bouncers rushed over to throw them both out. The stranger then pushed himself away from Parker, pulled out a short knife, and slashed at Parker, slitting the muscle in his forearm and spritzing the dance floor with blood.

At the same moment, someone grabbed Gerard from behind and spoke in his ear.

"You too, white boy," the voice said. "You wanna be a he-ro, you got it. We're comin' after you." Gerard felt a jab in his side. "FTX gonna be judgment day for you. You got that, He-ro? Judgment day."

He shoved Gerard away and disappeared through the throng of dancers. The bouncers threw out the man with the knife. The person who had grabbed Gerard had vanished. The music and dancing at the Chickasaw hadn't stopped or slowed for an instant. Parker took his shirt off and wrapped it around his arm. Romberg rounded up the group and got them into a cab to Martin Army Hospital, where Parker received nine stitches. During the cab ride back into town to the hotel, Parker leaned against the back window of the cab, murmuring "shit, shit, shit" and apologizing to Gerard for involving him in a past he couldn't escape. Romberg tried to reassure Parker that he wouldn't let anything happen to either of them. Romberg hoped the gangsters would "bring it on" and he would handle the whole situation.

"We're soldiers, man," Romberg said. "You fuck with one soldier, you're fucking with all soldiers."

"Yeah," said Carroll, "and can't that guy get arrested for damaging government property or something? Shouldn't we ask Fuller? We're government property now, right?"

And Parker looked ready to deliver his speech about how this was his fight and his past, and how he was the only one who could right the situation, but his head flopped over and he fell asleep against the window.

At four o'clock in the morning they were back at the hotel, snoozing in their soft beds. Gerard couldn't sleep. He lay awake with his hands locked behind the back of his head, reviewing the night's events. He had saved Parker from the intruder in the barracks, and the Warlords were now after Gerard; he was officially marked. The gang members had announced their plan to strike during FTX, the field training exercise—a fatiguing week-long stay in the woods, the crowning event of infantry school. Some of the more gung-ho soldiers in Third Platoon, including Romberg, were looking forward to the FTX. Romberg had decided the experience would be just like the commercials on television.

In a detached way, Gerard was fascinated by what had happened at the Chickasaw, and that he was now directly involved in a gang situation. He had never experienced anything like this before; Cooper would approve of this attitude, though if Gerard aspired to be truly Cooperish in this case, he'd need to face the challenge with no fear and with complete love and compassion for Parker and the Warlords and anyone else involved. Then there was the business of divine will, of submitting to a Divine Will and being ready and open to serve the Divine Plan. No, Gerard wasn't quite up to Cooper's standards.

And surely judgment day meant that the Warlords would try to kill Gerard, to murder him. Gerard was decidedly not fascinated by that, but he didn't see any way out of it. He also knew that Parker wouldn't tell the drill sergeants what was going on (he had told the staff at Martin Army Hospital that he'd been mugged in the parking lot of the Chickasaw). Parker was still sure that Drill Sergeant Hammer maintained loyalty to the Warlord gang, even if he was no longer an active member. Romberg and Cooper had no luck convincing Parker this wasn't so; they knew nothing about gangs, Parker said. Now Gerard had to decide if he was going to tell anyone about these new threats—anyone official, that is. There was no doubt the whole platoon would soon know about the Chickasaw knifing incident.

When Gerard next opened his eyes, it was bright—12:30 in the afternoon, with sunlight streaming through the motel room window. Carroll snored loudly in the other double bed, and the pullout bed where Cooper had slept was empty; it was more neatly made than when they'd checked in the night before.

Romberg walked through the door from the adjoining room. "Damn," he said, looking at Cooper's tidy bed. "What has the army done to this guy?"

Gerard stretched and then walked to the bathroom. "I think he was like that before he got here."

The outside door of the room flung open. Cooper stepped over the threshold into the room with a big smile on his face. "Let's eat," he said.

"Yeah, man," Romberg said. "I want a Big Mac. Let's go."

So after dragging Carroll out of bed and waiting for him to get dressed, they took a cab north on I-185 to Manchester Expressway and Peachtree Mall where they could scarf and barf at the food court. They then wasted the entire afternoon at the mall, wandering around and enjoying their general lack of purpose. Parker set off on his own to "find something for my lady." Romberg and Carroll slouched in the food court ogling young girls in short shorts while munching on Little Debbie snack cakes. For a moment Gerard considered telling them about the evils of hydrogenated oils in processed food, but then he remembered where he was. (Meredith would have been proud of him for thinking of it! He had continued to eat Twinkies for years, even after her lectures.) Gerard and Cooper moseyed aimlessly through the bustling mall crowd.

Gerard sucked in a deep breath. Ahead of him stretched an entire day of glorious nothing—an expanse of time that belonged to him and to no one else. He could do what he pleased. Outside

Diamond Jim's arcade he saw a pay phone; his heart skipped as he considered calling Sylvia, but then he reminded himself there was no point, that probably neither of them would be interested in reviving the relationship. What he really wanted to do was pick up the phone and tell Sylvia what he had found out. He wanted to call and tell her he knew all about their little sex games—about how Gilberto Cardenas had introduced Sylvia to oral sex with ice in his mouth. Big fucking deal: Meredith had thought of that when she and Gerard were seventeen. He wanted Sylvia to know that her secret wasn't a secret any more, that her letter to him was laughable because he wouldn't have wanted to marry her now anyway. If he did marry Sylvia, he'd be forever wondering if she missed fucking Gilberto.

"You okay?" said Cooper.

Gerard now realized he was staring at the pay phone and crushing his soda can with his right hand. "Yeah, I'm fine," he said.

"You're bleeding," Cooper said.

The can had cut into his hand. He released his grip. Cooper gave him a napkin.

"You probably know what I'm going to tell you," Cooper said.

"Yeah, yeah, I know," Gerard said. "Let go, right?"

"Yup," said Cooper.

"Okay, there," said Gerard, dropping the can into the trash in front of Mrs. Fields' Cookies.

"Holding on isn't worth the pain, is it?" Cooper said.

"I guess not," said Gerard.

"I want a drink, man!" Romberg walked up with Carroll and Parker behind him. Parker was holding a small, white paper bag.

"What'd you buy, Parker?" said Cooper.

"Little something for my lady," Parker said.

"He's gonna ask her to marry him, isn't that awesome?" Romberg said.

"Let's see it," said Carroll.

Parker produced a small box and tilted the lid open. He pulled out a gold ring with a sparkling gem on the crown and held it between his thumb and forefinger.

"Check it out, man," said Parker.

"A diamond," said Romberg. "Awesome."

"How many carats?" said Carroll.

"One," said Parker. "That's what I could afford. I got a deal, though."

"Here, let me see," Gerard said, reaching for the diamond. Parker snatched it away. "See it with your eyes, motherfucker."

"Oh, lighten up and let me look," said Gerard.

Parker slowly handed the ring to Gerard. Gerard held it against the light and squinted. Shit. Goddammit, not again. He turned the stone a few times as he tried to decide what to say. If only he didn't know—if only, like an average person, he couldn't tell the difference between a real diamond and a fake, then he'd be happier; then he could stop causing such sorrow.

"I hate to tell you this."

"Tell me what?" said Parker.

"Where'd you buy this?" said Gerard.

"Right down there," said Parker, pointing. "At Schliemann's."

Gerard had never heard of Schliemann's. "What did they tell you this was?"

"Man what the fuck you mean, 'what did they tell me'?" Parker said. "It's a fucking diamond, man. It's for my girl."

"Parker, it isn't real."

"Man, *fuck* you," said Parker. He snatched the ring back. "Fuck's wrong with you?"

"You want me to help you or not?" Gerard said. "Or will that get me beaten up too?"

"You had it comin', man," Parker said. "That's over now."

Gerard stared at Parker and searched his eyes. He wasn't sure what he was looking for, but what he saw in Parker's rigid stare was defensiveness; there was no defiance. That was enough for Gerard. He didn't want to push.

"Let's go," said Gerard, walking away.

"Where?" said Parker.

"To get your money back."

They all walked into Schliemann's Jewelers in a closely-huddled group. The two salesmen in that establishment couldn't have been happier; here came a satisfied customer bringing along four more of his buddies. Shaved-headed recruits on weekend passes made all Columbus, Georgia shopkeepers salivate. One of the grinning salesmen stepped forward.

"Yes, gentlemen, how may we help you today?" His slick, black hair caught a shine from the track lighting above the jewelry case. He reminded Gerard of the piano salesman from the Flintstones.

"Gimme the rock," said Gerard, holding his hand out. Parker snapped to attention and handed him the bag.

Gerard pulled out the ring and placed it on the glass counter. "Where's the Diamond Grading Report for this?"

"The what?" said the salesman.

Gerard rolled his eyes. "The certificate."

The salesman looked down at the ring. "Well, sir, this ring was on special, so it doesn't have a certificate."

"Is this a diamond?" said Gerard.

"Heh— Of course it is, sir."

Gerard looked around the store. Sitting on a far counter was a paperweight made of gray rock, probably granite. He grabbed it, bent over and placed the ring on the floor, and startled his friends and the salespeople by smashing the ring with the granite. The stone pulverized and left a splatter of shards and white bits on the floor.

Gerard stood up straight and slapped the paperweight down onto the glass counter. "Bullshit. Would a diamond do that?" A diamond would have suffered damage from such a blow, but it wouldn't have shattered so dramatically.

"I'll call security," said another man behind the counter.

"No, Larry, no. I'll handle this." The salesman nodded toward Parker. He was trembling. "Of course, if the gentleman isn't pleased with his purchase, if he isn't one hundred percent satisfied, I'd be happy to offer a discount on his next—"

"Here's what's going to happen," Gerard said. "I'm going to pick a nice diamond out of this case for my friend, and you're going to set it in a gold ring the same size as the other one. Then we'll call it even."

"Excellent, sir," said the salesman. He looked like he might cry.

Gerard tapped his finger on the glass. "This one. We want this one." He was pointing to a glimmering cushion-cut diamond that looked to be about two carats.

"Oh sir, that's a very expensive—"

"No it isn't," said Gerard. "We've already paid."

"Yeah, motherfucker," said Romberg. "We already paid." Carroll bumped Romberg with his elbow.

"Sir, we can't possibly—"

"Do you think I don't know what cubic zirconium looks like, you sack of shit?" said Gerard. "Do you want your little store closed down?"

The salesman snatched up a huge ring of keys. His hands shook. "Okay, okay. Yes, yes. Okay." The keys quivered and jingled as he tried to open the case. "Okay. Yes."

"We'll be out front, if you'll bring it out when it's done," said Gerard. He turned and walked out, and his friends followed.

"Motherfucker was about to piss his pants!" Romberg said. "Fucking awesome."

"How'd you know, Kelderman?" said Carroll.

Parker was shaking his head and smiling. "Yeah man, how you know about diamonds?"

"My dad cuts them for a living," said Gerard. And trades them on the black market, and knows a lot of people in Antwerp and Johannesburg, Gerard could have added, but he was used to delivering the short version when describing what his parents did for a living: Dad cuts diamonds and Mom sings; he liked to keep it simple whenever he could. Besides, right now, Gerard was having too much fun to want to talk; he enjoyed being reminded of the deep pleasure of knowing something well, of being one of the few people in the world to have mastered a skill so completely. And such appreciation from his friends! His dad was always supportive, and Meredith told him his skills were pretty cool (when she wasn't calling him a pompous know-it-all or a smart-ass). But here, in the middle of Peachtree Mall, his new friends were laughing and slapping his back. It was exhilarating. Not even at St. Philip Fraternity had Gerard ever done anything that made someone say "fucking awesome." It *was* fucking awesome. Even more fun was watching Parker's reaction to the whole scene. Tough, stoic Parker was smiling and shaking his head.

"That's alright," Parker kept saying. "That's alright."

And this time when Parker offered Gerard a fist, Gerard proudly bumped the top of it with his own. He resisted the urge to give Parker a big hug. Gerard would have to settle for a hearty fist-bumping. For Parker, this was a gushing of emotion.

The rest of Saturday was like a dream. Gerard was so giddy about the diamond incident that his memory of the rest of the evening was smeared and hazy. There'd been eating and drinking and a strip bar, and they'd ended up at a quiet waterfront park in the historic part of town on the Chattahoochee River.

◆     ◆     ◆

There were many possible reasons for Gerard's vibrant dream that night—the alcohol, the second-hand smoke inhalation, the excess of sleep—when they returned to the La Quinta Inn at 3 a.m. There was sharp contrast in the dream, vivid imagery, bright sound. Gerard didn't wake up to remember that he had had a dream; he was aware as it was happening, as if he were in the dream now, in real time.

*Hundreds of black diamond mine workers are piled on each other in a huge mound, all wearing those miner hats with the little flashlights on the front. There are so many of them that they're crushing under their own weight. They moan and wail, even as they're suffocating.*

*And weaving with the sounds of yelling is Fauré, again Fauré—the Offertorium from the Requiem:* Domine Jesu Christe, Rex gloriae, libera animas defunctorum de poenis inferni, et de profundo lacu. *Lord Jesus Christ, King of glory, deliver the souls* of the dead from punishment in the inferno, and from the infernal lake.

And right there on top of the heap, on that wailing mass of sweating, black South Africans, is Sylvia. She's on all fours and naked, except for the skimpy shreds of a black graduation gown. Gilberto Cardenas is there too, also naked and on his knees. He has mounted Sylvia from behind and is drilling into her with such force that the miners below can feel each thrust. They roar like the crowd in a soccer stadium every time Gilberto rams. Sylvia is silent, but her mouth and eyes open wide with each lurch.

Libera eas de ore leonis, ne absorbeat eas tartarus, ne cadant in obscurum. *Deliver them from the mouth of the lion, lest the abyss swallow them up, lest they fall into the darkness.*

*Gilberto pushes and plunges. His hands pull Sylvia's hips toward him with the strong, smooth motions of a rower. His strokes are powerful—long and even. Sylvia hangs her head down. The edges of her blond hair dangle on the sleek, shiny backs of the miners below her. Back and forth her hair sways as Gilberto strokes and strokes.*

*And then Sylvia looks up and sees Gerard watching. Pearls of sweat drip from her nose and chin, and as they fall they change to polished diamonds, and the diamonds bounce down onto the backs of the miners—the vanquished and enslaved. She looks him in the eye. "Whose fault is it, Gerard? Couldn't you see? Weren't you paying attention? Why weren't you watching more closely? Don't you see that it was all your fault?"*

Gerard sat up in bed. The miners disappeared. The diamonds were gone. Sylvia and Gilberto, though—they were still wedged in his consciousness. In one instant Gerard could picture all the escapades described in the seventeen letters; their sexual life passed before his eyes!

It was early Sunday morning, before dawn. The hiss of wet car tires on Macon Road outside the La Quinta Inn mixed with the happy snoring of Carroll in the next bed.

Gerard rubbed his face with his hands. He sighed deeply to slow his heart rate. Since Gerard had consciously resolved to stop obsessing about Sylvia and Gilberto, he wondered if his subconscious was revolting and taking over the task. Cooper would have told Gerard that this dream was the product of Gerard's own thoughts—thoughts that had form and substance and, from the moment he projected them, had his name attached to them and would necessarily return to him at some point. "And it's a gift when they return in this lifetime," Cooper had said.

Gerard didn't want any more gifts. He flopped back down in his bed. The cool sheets and the pillow were so soft. He didn't want to go back to Fort Benning and to Bravo Company 1/47th—to hard bunks and scarce sleep and Romberg's psychosis and Parker's control issues and Womack's harassment and two pieces of bread and heat and sweat with no comfort and no escape. He wanted to stay in this bed forever.

# Thirteen

Bravo Company's weekend on the town was over. Nearly everyone had checked back in to the company area by 4 p.m. that Sunday afternoon; the exception was Libby.

"Looks like Libby's case of the dumb-ass runs in the family,"
Private Fuller had said after Libby's father had gotten lost driving
around Fort Benning with no one but his son to help navigate.

"But the battalion buildings all look the same," Private Libby
had whined to Drill Sergeant Weston, the CQ. That was true; the
brick 'starships' were all identical. Still, it was a statistical amaze-
ment that out of 224 soldiers only Libby had failed to return on
time. Drill Sergeant Weston put Libby on morning KP duty with a
platoon from Echo Company.

On Monday morning Bravo Company would begin Advanced
Individualized Training—AIT; at Fort Benning that was the infantry school. Basic training was over, even for Libby. Since all four
platoons of Bravo Company were now being left alone and putting
up with only minimal harassment from the drill sergeants, the
company area felt like a resort—people wandering about leisurely,
talking on pay phones, reading newspapers. Their only restriction
was to stay in the company area; they could wander only as far as
the boot-shining bleachers outside the far wall of the battalion
building.

Drill Sergeant Weston had handed out mail after evening chow.
There was a letter for Gerard from Rebecca Ward, his mother! He
sat now on the floor of the company area and nestled his back
against the brick wall outside the arms room. Cooper sat cross-

legged beside him, reading Thomas Merton's *Thoughts In Solitude.*

A letter. There was nothing better during basic training than receiving a letter (not counting a letter from a promiscuous fiancée, breaking off the engagement). But this was a letter from home—from his mom! Gerard opened the envelope and unfolded the pages.

July 17, 2002
Dear Gerard,

I'm sorry it's taken so long for me to write. I've had six major singing engagements in the past five weeks alone, and I'm exhausted. I didn't know how it was in the army, whether they would let you read a letter from me, but your dad was sure it would get to you.

Everything is quiet around the Kasteel and Evans Glen. I hate that. We miss you and your cello playing. Meredith and Donald have asked about you. I gave them your address. Have they written? Donald is going to be an officer in the navy reserve. He's getting ready to head to Tulane for medical school, though I don't think he really wants to be a doctor. He's doing it for his father. Meredith is off to Houston for two months to get ready for something called Teach for America. Afterwards she has to spend two years somewhere in Louisiana as a teacher. Her parents are very proud of her.

Right now your dad and I are sitting in the living room. He says hello. You know how he hates writing. He hates it even more than you do. He says to tell you the scaife (I'm not sure if I spelled that right) is dusted and ready for when you come back. And when will you come back, Gerard? Will it be late August as you said in your letter to us last month? You wrote that after you finish your training you would spend three more weeks in airborne school (isn't that what you called it?), and then you'd get to come home for a time, right? And then what happens? Is it really true that your four-year contract with the army doesn't begin counting until <u>after</u>

your training is done? It hurts me to imagine that you'll be stuck in the military for four years. Is there no way out? Can't we make some arrangements or something? Your cello playing is going to suffer badly. It's not right. It's depressing. I'm sitting here stretched out on the sofa with a chilled glass of Petulama Riesling in this huge, gorgeous mansion, and it's so empty. It makes <u>me</u> feel empty. It's too quiet. There's no noise, no music, no kids running up and down the stairs.

God, I miss the days when you were young and your sister was still alive. Those were the best two years of my life. You used to play hide and seek with Anna in the music parlor. Do you remember that? She would scurry around behind the furniture, giggling and cackling, and then when she'd had enough, she would demand that you "play the pinano, play pretty music." Music hasn't been the same for me since you left for Belden Academy eight years ago. My God, it really has been eight years. Come home, Gerard. I feel like I've lost my only other baby.

You'll be happy to know that I don't spend as much time in Anna's room any more. I try to make time to go in there and light the candles every day, but it's getting harder and harder to remember to do it and to make time for it. I feel very guilty, because I don't want to forget Anna. I'm worried if I don't spend time in her room I'll forget.

Your dad is sitting in that hideous Louis Philippe needlepoint armchair across the room, staring through his lens at a pear-looking diamond. We haven't sat together on the couch for years, Gerard (that isn't the only thing we haven't done together in years, but I know this isn't something you want to hear about your parents). Then again, maybe you should hear it. I mean, you parents are human, too. Christ, your father is <u>very</u> human. Now you're wondering what I mean by that. Well, I agreed never to discuss it with anyone, but to hell with it. Your dad is sitting not fifteen feet from me, and he has no idea what I'm writing! I'm about to tell you a secret, and he doesn't know I'm going to do it. It feels like I'm cheating on him, and I admit I'm enjoying it. I owe him one, goddammit, as you'll see in a minute.

You probably think your dad and I are perfect, don't you? I remember thinking that about my own parents. I'm just a singer trying to make a living (I know I don't need to, as Willem likes to remind me), and your dad is a diamond cutter and a businessman. But we're people, Gerard. We're people with problems like everyone else. I hope you can read my handwriting. I think the wine is going to my head and making me ramble. I hope you don't mind.

Well, we've had problems over the years, but as I look back I see that it could have all been much worse. You remember Patrick and Lisa Flanigan-Flambert, Meredith's parents. Well, they had the nerve one evening to hint that they'd be interested in some sort of spouse-swapping arrangement. Can you imagine! Of course the idea came from Patrick. He's always made me uncomfortable. They were over at the house for dinner one night, and he brought up a practice he called Responsible Non-Monogamy. He explained how, for some couples, it's a true sign of enlightenment not to be attached to one person, not to hold too tightly and be possessive, and to want to share love and beauty with more than one (or two or three) people. Willem smiled that stupid smile of his as he sat at the end of the dining room table. He had no idea what Patrick was really talking about. Me, I snorted a mouthful of Shiraz through my nose because I knew exactly what he was talking about. I've always had a funny feeling about the Flanigan-Flamberts. Anyway, he said he was only discussing the theory, you know, like it was all just an intellectual exploration, but the whole time he was eyeing me like it was happy hour at the singles bar. I jumped up and began clearing dishes from the table. Lisa wouldn't look up from her plate. It was the end of the discussion.

Willem didn't believe me later when I told him what Patrick had been hinting at. Like your father is such a goody-goody! The bastard. He isn't. Goodness, I've rambled haven't I? Okay, here's what I started to say earlier. Years ago your father had an affair. I can't believe I'm writing this. Right now your dad is looking over and smiling at me, one of his passing, chummy smiles, not like the way he used to smile at me.

So anyway, your dad's affair. You're getting a real intimate look at your father, aren't you? I'm envious. My own dad is still alive, but I don't know him very well, even to this day. Okay, back to the subject. When you were eight years old, I accidentally opened a letter that was addressed to Willem. I remember because it was late summer, and the leaves on that dogwood outside the front door, next to the porch, were bright green. There was warm wind blowing along the front lawn and it rolled across the porch, rippling my skirt as I looked through the day's mail. Well, the letter I opened was written in Flemish, so you'd think I wouldn't know anything. But do you know who it was from? It was from that Margareta. You may not remember her. I know a few words in Flemish, Gerard, and I knew from the length of the letter that something was going on. It made sense to me, too, because Margareta is so tall and gorgeous. Yes, I admit it, she's beautiful, and ever since finding that letter I've watched your dad like a hawk, especially when there are females around. I had no idea he was interested in that sort of thing. Another thing that was in the letter was all sorts of cute little smiley faces and exclamation points with hollow dots. It made me sick.

You know what I did when Willem got home the next day? I threw the letter onto kitchen table and forced him to translate it, the whole thing, word for word. Oh Gerard, you should have seen him squirm! I was right. They'd been having an affair for seven months. After we spent a long night of screaming and crying and throwing things (you were asleep, thank God), Willem promised to break it off and never see her again. I really had to push him to agree to that, if you can believe it, because he admitted he felt no guilt about the whole thing. No guilt! To this day, I don't understand that. Eventually he did apologize and admit it was wrong, but that wasn't until months later. Can you believe that? He wondered why he should feel guilty. He had the love of two wonderful women, he said, and what could be wrong with that? Your dad had become a disciple of Patrick Flanigan-Flambert! I threw my grandmother's porcelain vase at him when he said that (the one with the Mayflower on it), but he ducked and it smashed against the dining room wall.

Over the next few days, I asked him a lot of questions. I had to. There were things I had to know. He admitted from the first moment that he was in love with her (a desperate love he called it), but I wanted details. He resisted, but I played hardball, Gerard, and I told him that if he didn't tell me what I wanted to know that I'd walk right out the goddamn door and take my little boy with me. I was so mean, Gerard. I told him that a Virginia judge wouldn't look kindly on a husband who screwed around, especially a foreign husband. Mean, yes, but I was mad. Goddamn I was mad.

Turns out foreign had a lot to do with it. Willem said he got tired of me criticizing him all the time and of making fun of his home country and the language he spoke. Margareta, he said, was more Flemish than he could have wished for. Their affair was a Flemish one. Margareta was Flemish, Willem said over and over as he pointed fingers at me that night. She was so Flemish it turned him on, especially when they drank Belgian beer together. Your dad cried that night, too. He screamed and yelled as much as I did. He told me he went to Margareta for all the things I wasn't giving him, and he capped it all off by reminding me these were things I would never be able to give him, ever. Margareta understood him. Margareta completed him. Margareta made him want to become a better person. He was so mean to me, Gerard. I felt like I'd been ripped apart.

Now I'm crying. I'm trying to keep the tears from dripping all over this letter. Your dad just now looked up from his diamond and asked me what's wrong. I told him it was the same thing as always, and he looked right back down at his work, the way he looks away when he thinks I'm about to criticize him. He thought I meant Anna. It's just as well.

Please, Gerard, come home. Everyone in my life has left. Your sister died. I've never gotten over that. Ever since his extracurricular activities, as I call them, your dad has never been as intimate or sincere with me as he used to be. And now you've gone away too, into the army. None of this is what I expected, not even a bit of it. What happened to my life, Gerard? Why didn't things turn out the way I wanted them to?

I love you, Gerard. I miss you badly. I want everything to be as it was before. I'm tired of hurting. I want to know where the comfort is. I want my family whole again.

Please write back, Gerard, if the army people will let you.

Love, Mom

Gerard put the pages of the letter down onto his lap. So Willem Kelderman and Margareta Van Leuven had had an affair. Gerard chuckled out loud. Cooper continued silently reading his book. Gerard wanted to read the letter again, but it was four pages long, and his brain needed to review all this new information.

The vase—his great-grandmother's porcelain vase that used to sit on the antique sideboard in the dining room at the Kasteel. Yes, Gerard remembered the vase. "...but he ducked, and it smashed against the dining room wall." As Gerard's eyes rolled across that sentence, he remembered. The night Willem and Rebecca had argued and she had thrown the vase, the crash had woken Gerard. He was eight years old at the time. He remembered sitting up in bed, scared. He crawled out from under the sheets and padded down the dark hallway in his socks toward the top of the stairs, but he stopped when he heard the yelling.

"You son of a bitch!" Rebecca screamed. "Not guilty? That's good, Willem. That's really fucking good. You're some kind of—"

"What do you want me to say?" Willem said. "Do you want me to fall down on my knees and beg for forgiveness? No, that's right, I don't feel guilty. I'm glad Margareta came into my life. She was there at the perfect moment."

"I can't believe this," said Rebecca. "Oh my God—so last February when she was here with you, and you were sipping that Corsendonk crap or whatever it was in the living room, you two were doing it, weren't you? You'd started screwing by then, hadn't you?"

"Yes," Willem said.

"Unbelievable. I can't believe any of this," Rebecca said. "Oh my God—did you ever do it here, in our bed?"

"No," said Willem. "Never."

"Jesus Christ," Rebecca said, more softly. "I can't get over this. How could I have been so stupid? I should have known. She's a knockout."

"Rebecca—"

"No, I should have seen it," Rebecca said. "It was all right in front of me, and I wasn't paying attention. God, I'll never make that mistake again."

And then Rebecca had walked toward the bottom of the grand stairway in the main hall, so little Gerard had run back to his room. He'd clicked the door gently closed and scrambled back into bed.

All these years he had blocked out the entire memory until this moment. He rolled his head back and forth against the brick wall behind him. Some soldiers from First Platoon were throwing a baseball in the company area. Margareta Van Leuven. She *was* a beautiful woman—very carefree and cheerful. Gerard had always had a crush on Margareta when he was little, and she was always so sweet to him. To think of his father having an affair with Margareta Van Leuven made Gerard feel jealous. If he had been older, would Margareta have been interested in him? She'd be much older now, but Gerard could only remember her from his very young years. He remembered her long, light brown hair and how she would wear long skirts and dressy leather boots that squeaked when she walked. It now made sense to Gerard why she had suddenly disappeared from their lives—why he'd never seen her again since he was eight.

Well if Willem was going to have an affair, Gerard was glad it had been with Margareta Van Leuven. In a strange way, that made it easier to handle. Margareta had been a close family friend, even to Rebecca, which made Gerard wonder why Margareta did it. Who knows what had been in her head. Perhaps she'd been nursing her own emotional wounds, or maybe she'd always been attracted to Willem and had simply been waiting for the right moment for Willem to be ready.

And the Flanigan-Flamberts—that was hilarious! Thank God his parents hadn't accepted the offer. The thought of his parents swinging with the Flanigan-Flamberts was absurd. Patrick Flanigan-Flambert was such a ridiculous person that Gerard couldn't imagine him having sex with anyone—even with his own wife. Did Meredith know about her parents and their practice of Responsible Non-Monogamy?

Goddamn, Gerard missed Meredith. He should have tried to call her before their weekend pass so she could come down and visit. No, there wouldn't have been time—he'd read Sylvia's letter Sunday night and then Bravo Company had been released for the pass the following weekend. Meredith couldn't have made it to Fort Benning on such short notice. Anyway, she was in Houston. What about Rachel? Gerard could try to call Rachel before AIT ended and see her after he graduated from infantry school. Wouldn't Rachel love to know that Sylvia had engaged in *Ir*responsible Non-Monogamy and had dumped Gerard, and that he was now available. Then again, if Rachel knew he was single she might lose interest in taking him to bed. (Not that Rachel required a bed. Word around the fraternity house suggested she was much more daring and creative than to need a proper bed.) Maybe Gerard would no longer appeal to Rachel as a conquest now that he was single.

Gerard read Rebecca Ward's letter again, and then a third time. Each time, the experience became more bizarre; it was as if he were reading a story about other people—people he didn't know. At the same time, the more he read, the more he recalled disjointed shards from his childhood that now snapped into place: Margareta's hand on Willem's knee when they rode the Antwerp city bus, Willem whispering into giggling Margareta's ear at the Café De Fenix, Margareta's silver barrette on the hotel end table. That was careless of her. Gerard had woken up one morning in their room at the Hotel Firean in Antwerp and seen Margareta's barrette next to the bed. Margareta had been out to dinner with Gerard and Willem, but she hadn't come up to their hotel room afterwards. Gerard remembered earlier that evening coming back from the bathroom at the Minerva restaurant and seeing Willem and Margareta pull their hands away from each other across the table. Later that same night as Willem and Gerard checked in to the Hotel Firean, Willem turned and spoke to Margareta before they parted. Gerard remembered the entire Flemish sentence.

*"Kom dan terug tegen elf uur of zo. Hij zal aan 't slapen zijn."*

On that day, in the lobby of that hotel, it was March of 1988 (Gerard had just turned eight). He hadn't been listening to the Grote Van Kloten tapes long enough to understand at the time what Willem had said, but his mind had recorded each word and was playing it back now. Here at Fort Benning, of all places, that Flemish sentence flowed gently through his brain as if he had understood it then: "Come back around eleven o'clock," Willem had told Margareta. "He'll be sleeping by then." Now it was Gerard who felt betrayed; Willem was perfectly aware at the time that Gerard didn't yet know enough Flemish to understand what was going on. What other clandestine utterances had Gerard missed during the seven months of their affair? The 'he' was Gerard— Margareta and Willem must have carried on right there in the hotel room where Gerard was sleeping in the next bed. That was creepy. Margareta had forgotten to take her silver barrette with her when she'd slipped out of the room in the middle of the night.

"Son of a bitch," Gerard said.

"What?" Romberg sat down against the brick wall and wiped his forehead with his BDU cap.

"My dad had an affair when I was kid," said Gerard.

"No shit," Romberg said.

Cooper stopped reading and looked up.

"Incredible," said Gerard.

"Who told you, your mom?" said Romberg.

"Yep," said Gerard, giving the letter a little wave in the air.

"Dude, I miss my mom," said Romberg. "I'd kill to get a letter from her now."

"What'd you do when she died?" Cooper said.

"I was sixteen," Romberg said. "I'll never forget. I started lifting weights and seeing the ravens. Fucking ravens, man, they won't go away."

"What are they trying to tell you?" said Cooper.

"Fuck if I know," Romberg said. "They're a pain in my ass."

"What makes them go away?" Gerard said.

"When I help other people."

"No shit?" Gerard said.

"Yeah," Romberg said, nodding. "I worked as a lifeguard in Cape May when I was eighteen. That was awesome. I didn't see ravens for a whole year. Then I came here and wouldn't you know it—fucking ravens again."

"So who are you supposed to be helping now?" said Cooper.

"You and your fucking questions," Romberg said. "Fucking Yanni, man. You're like the fucking guru on the mountain, only there's no mountain. I'm just kidding, man. I think you're cool. Meditating is awesome. I should meditate too."

Gerard agreed that Cooper was cool. He wondered how Cooper would have handled a letter like this—a letter where you mom tells you that when you were little, your dad had sex with another woman. Gerard considered asking Cooper his opinion about the letter, but what was there to say? Besides, after two months of being with Cooper every day, Gerard knew exactly what Cooper would say about the letter and about Gerard's parents.

He'd probably start with a shrug—not a dismissing shrug, but the kind of shrug that says it's really not a big deal. Cooper would then have explored the likely viewpoints of both Willem and Rebecca. He'd point out that anyone who was not them was not qualified to judge them. Each of them, Cooper would explain, was hurting and had made the best choices they could. And since those choices had caused pain to others, Cooper would say that Willem and Rebecca were making decisions from an impure source. The ego—with its needs and fears and insecurities—was still the driving force behind their choices and decisions.

"We're all actors, playing out our own dramas," Cooper had said a few weeks back, after Berkowicz and Wiley had finished brawling in the laundry room. He'd gone on to explain that the outer part of ourselves, the part motivated by ego and the illusion of needs, isn't who we really are. The outer shell is simply an icon, he'd said, and the goal of our multiple incarnations is to chip away and eventually shatter the icon to get at our true selves. This was why Cooper believed that salvation-based religions were off the mark, because shattering the icon—hard work that involved years of deep self-examination—was impossible to accomplish in only one lifetime.

"In the end, we judge ourselves," Cooper had said. Parker had then accurately captured the sentiment of most of the soldiers of Third Platoon when he'd characterized Cooper's ideas as crazy-ass shit. Still, people liked Cooper because he never judged anyone.

And as the training cycle went on, Gerard was beginning to realize more and more how forcefully judgment had swirled around the Kasteel throughout his childhood. During the night of that big argument, the theme had dominated.

"So now you're going to judge me for my sin, is that it?" Willem had said. Gerard could hear them even after he went back into his room.

"Fuck sin, Willem," Rebecca had said. "I never used that word. I'll leave the idea of sin to you and your fucking Catholicism."

"How dare—"

"Shut up!" screamed Rebecca. "Shut up. You've said enough. You've done enough, don't you think? Because of you, my daughter died, Willem. You're so fucking careless about leaving your shit scattered all over the place that someone actually died. Doesn't that bother you? I don't know how you live with yourself, Willem, I really don't know how you do it. And now. Now you've had seven months gushing your seed into another woman—into someone who's *not your wife*—and you tell me you're not feeling guilty about it? What the *fuck!*"

"My God, Rebecca." Willem's voice was soft; Gerard could barely make out the words. There was a long silence, and Gerard remembered feeling bad—naughty—for overhearing what was going on downstairs. He felt guilty for eavesdropping, even though he couldn't help it.

"So what kind of idiot wife would stay with you, after all this?" said Rebecca.

Gerard couldn't tell if Willem was saying something, or if there was just silence. It lasted a while.

"No, I'm not leaving," said Rebecca, a little more loudly. "I'm staying—not for you, but for Gerard. You remember that."

And then Rebecca had walked up the stairs. Gerard had heard a door opening, and he knew it was Anna's bedroom. Rebecca had closed the door to Anna's room, but Gerard could hear her weeping. He could picture exactly what she was doing, because it was what she always did: she kneeled in the middle of the room, facing the shrine with the pink gingham shorts and the Dr. Seuss book and the blue pacifier, and sobbed with her face in her hands.

Gerard stood up and put his BDU cap on.

"Where you going?" said Romberg.

"I don't know, upstairs, to shine boots, to get some laundry," said Gerard. "To do something. I have to do something. I'm tired of sitting around." He hopped up the stairs to the Third Platoon bay.

# Fourteen

"And y'all already know about the fuckin' woodpeckers, so I'm not even gonna go into that." The range sergeant stood with one foot up on the bleachers, his elbow resting on his knee. His belly lopped over the pistol belt that was too tightly attached.

Bravo Company was four days into Advanced Individualized Training—AIT—infantry school. They were seated in the bleachers listening to the range sergeant twang a safety briefing for the second day of Advanced Rifle Marksmanship. Gerard felt he had spent half his time at Fort Benning sitting in metal bleachers. He wondered what the army's recruitment statistics would look like if they ran commercials that showed soldiers sitting in bleachers listening to safety briefings, or side-stepping through the chow line in the mess hall, or standing in formation waiting for the drill sergeants to emerge through the door of the company office. You'd never see a Private Carroll in one of those commercials, or a Libby struggling to tie his own shoes. No, the ads were electrifying and flashy with fit, young, camouflaged men firing fancy weaponry. There was running and jumping, energy and excitement, movement and action.

"Goddamn fuckin' woodpeckers," drawled the range sergeant. He spat beside the bleachers into the pine needles. "You know they actually got civilians that come out here enforcing that shit?"

Ever since the first day of rifle marksmanship the soldiers of Bravo Company 1/47th were admonished not to shoot anywhere near pine trees with white rings painted on the trunks. For some reason the red-cockaded woodpeckers that resided there were protected. Shoot machine guns to kill Iraqis, drive your bayonet through Ivan's guts, but the woodpeckers are off-limits. Romberg had admitted to shooting at those white-banded trees during BRM practice; either the drill sergeants hadn't noticed, or they didn't care.

The range sergeant tipped his hat back and looked up at the sky. "Well then, I guess we better get started. First Sergeant, if you'll line 'em up by platoon, we'll get firin'."

Since Fourth Platoon was duty platoon this week, they would go first, making Third Platoon last on the firing line. More sitting. More waiting. More sweating on hot bleachers.

"You ready, Parker?" said Drill Sergeant Hammer.

"Yes, Drill Sergeant."

"You wish you had a Glock, don't you Parker?" said Hammer.

"No, Drill Sergeant." Parker's face clenched up, the way it always did when Hammer harassed him. Gerard knew that Parker was still convinced Hammer, as a former Warlord, was going to settle the gang debt and kill him. Hammer seemed to have sensed this from the beginning and took great delight in toying with Parker to see how he reacted.

"Yeah you do," said Hammer. "What're you doin' here, Hot Shit?"

Parker paused. Romberg turned toward Parker, his eyes wide.

"I'm startin' over, Drill Sergeant," Parker finally said.

"They beat you down?" said Hammer.

"Nope."

"Then you ain't done yet," said Hammer.

Parker stared straight ahead of him. The cracking and popping of Fourth Platoon's rifles resonated across the firing range.

"Can you hit a moving target, Parker?" said Hammer.

"Yes, Drill Sergeant."

"Yeah, I'll bet," said Hammer. "Me too. Man, can't *nobody* move fast enough to dodge *my* fire." He turned and walked away, toward the chow shelter where the other drill sergeants had congregated.

"He's just messing with you, dude," said Romberg.

"Fuck it," said Parker. "I don't care what he's doin'. Just fuck it."

Parker had taken to saying that often—fuck it—ever since the incident at the Chickasaw dance club. "What else I'm gonna do," he'd said, "sit around waiting?" Romberg continued to vow that he would protect Parker, that he would be Parker's bodyguard and that if anyone came near him Romberg would personally rip his fucking throat out. The comment had made Parker smile; he seemed touched by Romberg's enthusiasm.

For the next hour while Third Platoon rotted on the metal bleachers in the Georgia heat, Private Fuller talked and talked about the army, and about what all of them could expect not only today and next week, but after training was done and they were assigned to their permanent duty stations. For today he reminded the platoon that they'd each be given two thirty-round magazines for practice-qualification on the range, that they had to pass advanced rifle marksmanship to graduate from AIT, and that the infantry school used to let its recruits fire AK-47s during this portion of training.

"No shit!" Romberg said. "Goddamn, that would be awesome."

Fuller went on to describe how the AK-47 was a much more durable weapon than the M16; its 7.62 millimeter round made it more versatile, and therefore a favorite around the world. He talked about the introduction in 1974 of the AK-74, the new Kalashnikov, with a caliber of 5.45 mm, but that hard-core soldiers in Russia and other Eastern countries still prefer the original AK-47.

"Drop an AK-47 into a mud puddle, pick it up, and the sumbitch'll fire just as good," Fuller explained. He almost provoked a fight with Wiley, who couldn't believe Fuller would say anything positive about a weapon that had been the choice of commies.

"Form up, Third Platoon!" Drill Sergeant Womack stood on the gravel with his arms crossed.

"Rock and roll, man," said Romberg. "This is it."

The soldiers shuffled toward the entrance to the range and snapped into four neat rows.

"One shot, one kill," said Berkowicz.

"Depends on which lane you're shooting at," Phillips said.

"Fuck you, Phillips," said Libby.

"No, no, fuck *you*, man," Phillips said. "How about shooting your own fucking targets this time, assfuck?"

"Don't worry, Phillips," said Private Wiley. "Get Cooper to help. He can do like a meditation or a ritual or something to make Libby shoot better. Oh, but you need incense for worshipping the devil, don't you, Yanni?"

Romberg reached forward and grabbed the back of Wiley's shoulder harness. "You leave Cooper the fuck alone, you backwards, stupid country fuck. I'll fuck you up good."

Wiley tried to shake loose, but Romberg held fast.

"Let go, man," Wiley said.

"Mess with Cooper again and I'll ram your bayonet up your ass," said Romberg. He shoved Wiley forward, and Wiley stumbled out onto the open gravel.

"Private Wiley, why are you out of formation?" said Womack.

"I fell, Drill Sergeant."

"Well then fall back in," Womack said.

Wiley backed into his space.

"Okay Third Platoon, listen up," said Womack. "This is your last chance to practice with live-fire before you qualify tomorrow. I want to see some targets falling."

"*HOO-AH!*" thundered the platoon.

"Move out," Womack said.

The platoon filed past wooden crates crammed with loaded thirty-round magazines.

"Two each, men, let's go," said Womack. "Let's move."

Gerard grabbed his two magazines and headed toward the right end of the firing line, where the foxholes were perched high on mounds like Aztec ziggurats. He climbed the stairs to the top and stood behind his foxhole. Cooper was on his left, Carroll was on his right. Gerard wanted to go ahead and load a magazine into the well of his rifle, but that was a no-no: every instruction would come from the range tower—every part of the flow, every movement. Back at the barracks one evening, Berkowicz had stood in the bathroom, mimicking the voice of a range sergeant, delivering detailed directions to those seated on the toilets.

"Reach to your left and secure one square of toilet tissue," he'd announced, cupping his hands around his mouth. "Is there anyone down range? Is there anyone down range? Rotate your hand behind you, and wipe—your ass." It reminded Gerard of Donald Meerschaum, who delighted in hovering over the changing table as Anna's diaper was removed. "Looks like we've got curried cottage cheese, ladies and gentlemen," he'd say, as Willem, himself gagging, shoved Donald back while holding Anna's bare heels away from the soupy mess.

The range sergeant's voice boomed from the P.A. system atop the high range tower. "Rotate your selector from *safe* to *semi*, and watch—your lane."

Targets popped up and the M16s cracked. Gerard was hitting nearly everything, even the 175-meter moving target. The trick was figuring out how far to lead the target, much the way a football quarterback leads his wide receiver.

"It's a good goddamn thing we don't have those guns in the house anymore, or I swear to God I'd shoot your Flemish balls off," Gerard suddenly remembered Rebecca saying to Willem. "You'd be pretty useless to Margareta then, wouldn't you?" she'd said.

Gerard had learned later that his parents used to hide two handguns by their bedside and would attend training sessions, both for firing and cleaning guns. They'd gotten rid of the guns when Gerard was born. Gerard smiled to imagine Willem Kelderman with a handgun. If they'd kept the guns, his careless dad would probably have left it on a coffee table when the kids were in the house.

But it wasn't a gun that had killed Anna, it was a pair of Willem's diamond tweezers. "Of all things, the tweezers again?" Rebecca had said to Willem. "Like I need more reminders?" And if the patio tables at Monroe Hill College hadn't solidified Gerard's doubt about the story of Anna's death involving a swerving driver and a sidewalk, he now had the reminder that tweezers were somehow involved. Belgium and tweezers—those were the two most recent clues.

"Holy mother fuck," yelled Drill Sergeant Hammer. "Not again. Drop it, Private! Put it down!"

"I can do it," screamed Romberg. "I'll shoot the fuckers, and that'll be the end of it."

Romberg had jumped out of his foxhole and was hiding behind a bush, firing his rifle out onto the range. Gerard didn't have to wonder what was happening; Romberg saw ravens and was trying to shoot them.

"Get down, everybody get down!" Womack was crouched over, walking toward Romberg.

"I told you, I told you," Hammer said to Womack. "He ain't right, and he's got to *go.*"

Womack stood up straight. "Put down your weapon, Romberg. That's an order."

Romberg ran out into the firing range and dove behind a rock. His head popped up. He scanned left and right, looking for his prey. His eyes stopped and fixed on a pine tree with a white ring around the trunk. He leaned over the rock and fired. Soldiers on the firing line and in the bleachers dove for the dirt.

Gerard stepped out of his foxhole. "I've got to stop him."

"Forget it, Kelderman," said Carroll. "Don't be a nut case. He's not your responsibility."

"He's going to hurt someone," said Gerard. And as he looked out over the range at Romberg, stooped behind the rock, Romberg looked like a kid playing with a toy gun and taking out his frustration on the bad guys. The image shattered as a 5.56 millimeter round whizzed past Gerard's head and lodged into a tree trunk.

"Kelderman, get down!" Womack was on his belly, high-crawling toward Gerard.

Gerard looked at Cooper. "What do I do?" Gerard asked him. Why was he asking Cooper what to do? Why wasn't he taking cover like the others? Surely Romberg would calm down soon on his own. He always did.

"Go with your instinct," said Cooper, "and don't be afraid."

"Don't be afraid?" said Gerard. "Why don't *you* go out and get him?"

"No, you go ahead," said Cooper. "You'll be safe." And then he smiled that smile of his—that know-it-all smile, not cocky but honest and genuine. In that moment, Gerard believed Cooper. He turned and walked out onto the range, with its jagged boulders and African-plain-like grasses. He didn't duck, he didn't run, and he didn't even try to stay out of Romberg's line of fire. It was as if he was in a trance. As he walked, he looked behind him, and Cooper was at the top of the ziggurat, standing tall.

"Cooper, get down!" Womack yelled.

Womack's voice sounded faint, as if traveling from miles away through morning fog. Romberg was still firing, and every other soldier (including each drill sergeant) was lying flat on the ground or hiding behind cover. But Cooper stood straight; he looked like a god or a wizard. Gerard half expected Cooper to raise his arms up and part the waters. And still the rounds flew past Gerard toward the trees, where Romberg had perhaps seen ravens perched at the top. Gerard turned toward Romberg and walked on.

"I've got to do it," Gerard was mumbling to himself. "If something happens, it'll be my fault. I've got to help."

In the next moment Gerard was standing over Romberg, who had stopped shooting and was staring at Gerard.

"There aren't any ravens," said Gerard. "You've got to let go, Romberg. Your mom's gone, and you can't get her back."

Romberg let his rifle fall and sat down on the dusty ground. He put his face into his hands and cried. He sobbed and shook and then bawled like a baby, with tears and snot running down his face. Gerard sat next to him and patted his shoulder.

"Come on, let's go." An MP grabbed Gerard by the arm.

"Not him," said Hammer. "The other one."

"Right," said the MP. "Come on, let's go." And he led Romberg away to a white pickup truck topped with flashing blue lights.

"Alright, Platoon Guide, get back over there with your men." Hammer walked away back toward the range tower.

Cooper had picked up Gerard's M16 and was holding it for him in the parking lot, where the drill sergeants had assembled the soldiers into a company formation. As Gerard approached, a cheer erupted from the mob, and then applause. There was yelling and whistling and thunderous clapping.

"Shut up!" yelled Womack. "Shut up, all of you. I said shut up."

The noise died down, but the smiles on the faces of over 200 men remained.

"Kelderman, what was that?" said Womack. "What's wrong with you?"

Gerard squinted one eye at Womack. Was he kidding? What was Gerard supposed to say? Gerard was tired of trying to figuring out what was expected of him, so he simply stood and glared at Womack.

"You had the safety briefing this morning, Kelderman, so I want to know why you decided it was okay to disregard range protocol," said Womack.

This was incredible. Fuck the safety briefing. And fuck Womack.

"Range protocol?" said Gerard. "You're kidding, right?"

"Do I sound like I'm kidding, Private Kelderman?"

"You sound like you always do, Drill Sergeant, so how am I supposed to tell?" Gerard was yelling as loudly as Womack was. The eyes of the Bravo Company soldiers opened wider as Gerard fought back, and their heads wagged left, then right, like spectators at a tennis match.

"You walked out onto the firing range, straight toward a soldier with a loaded weapon," said Womack.

"Well I didn't see anyone else—"

"Shut up, Kelderman, I'm not finished," said Womack. "You put yourself at risk, Private Kelderman. You wanted to be a hero, didn't you? I could give you an Article Fifteen right now for endangering yourself. You're the property of Uncle Sam, Kelderman, so when you pull a stunt like you just did, you're putting government property at risk."

"I didn't see anyone else taking action," said Gerard. "Who was taking charge, Drill Sergeant? Who was in charge? It wasn't you, was it? You were hiding behind a rock. Aren't you supposed to be our leader?"

What were these words coming out of Gerard's mouth? He thought Womack might reach out and punch him to shut him up. Bravo Company was silent; even the other Drill Sergeants held their breath.

"Private Kelderman, you don't know anything about leading," said Womack. He paused for a moment and breathed a deep sigh. "Not the first thing, do you understand me?"

Holy shit, Gerard was winning: Womack's pause and then his feeble response were the clear signal. When an authority figure used a phrase like "do you understand me," it was usually the first sign of defeat—like a bad public school teacher in a verbal spar with a student who knows the teacher is hopelessly stupid. And if someone who demanded "do you understand me" was pushed farther into their corner, "because I said so" was soon to follow. Even through his fury and his heavy panting, Gerard knew he had to go easy on Womack, especially since they were both performing for a company of soldiers.

"Drill Sergeant, you told me I was responsible for Romberg," said Gerard. "I was taking care of him." Gerard stood a little taller, not at attention—that would have been too blatant—but he held his shoulders back a bit and straightened his spine.

"You screwed up, Kelderman," Womack said. "You were dangerous and careless. Drop and give me twenty. And I'll speak to you back at the company area."

That was it, then. Womack had accepted Gerard's offer. Womack was able to save face and put an end to it. Gerard dropped to the dirt and started his push-ups. He resisted the urge to do them quickly. This late in training, twenty push-ups was a joke and Womack knew it. Gerard felt like racing through his push-ups; it would have felt like talking back, or having the last word, like screaming out loud what the entire membership of Bravo Company already knew: that in this moment Gerard held the upper hand, and Womack had conceded it. He wanted to shout at Womack, to tell him he was a fucking coward. He wanted to ask

Womack why it took a recruit to save Romberg—where were the cadre? He wanted to make fun of Womack for being a drill sergeant; weren't the real infantry soldiers assigned to what they called line units—units where authentic combat training happened? What kind of a person became a drill sergeant, Gerard wanted to ask Womack. Gerard did his push-ups slowly and smoothly. What he really felt like doing was leaping up and grabbing Womack by the fucking neck.

The range closed down for the day, and the company loaded back onto the two cattle trucks that had arrived to return them to $1/47^{th}$ and to the Bravo Company area. In the cattle truck the other soldiers jostled Gerard and made jokes about how *he* was the crazy one, to walk right into live fire. Gerard could tell Parker was impressed, even though Parker had told Gerard that he wouldn't last one day in the hood, pulling shit like that. Parker had never seen such luck, he said, even as Cooper told them both that luck was an illusion.

Later in the evening after chow and boot-shining, when Third Platoon was lounging inside the bay, Cooper continued his philosophizing. He told Gerard that Womack had berated him on purpose to draw him out and that Womack wasn't truly upset with Gerard. What did bother Womack, Cooper claimed, was that Gerard was slow to express his emotions. Gerard laughed out loud at that one—at the idea that a drill sergeant might be concerned about emotions. Cooper shrugged. He rarely tried to convince anyone of anything. He talked about what he believed, and then he shut up. He had told Gerard that it's not a good idea to try to convince anyone of anything, ever—that people would come around to their own beliefs based on their current levels of awareness and their own consciences. Cooper often claimed he was adept at figuring out what other people were ready to hear and stopping short of sharing too much. Too much truth, he claimed, would do damage to those who weren't ready to hear it. Parker, for one, was never in a mood to listen to any of Cooper's crazy-ass shit ideas.

"Uh, *huh.*" Parker sat on his bunk and had pulled the diamond ring out of its box and was turning it over. Gerard flipped onto his belly and hugged his pillow under his chest as he watched Parker admire the diamond. This was Parker's way of initiating a dialogue with Gerard, he was sure. His 'uh, *huh*' had been deliberately loud enough for Gerard to hear; Parker would never have said something like "Hey, what you did for me on pass that day at the jewelry store was really cool. Thanks." Gerard couldn't imagine Parker saying thank you for anything; a direct thank-you would have made Gerard feel funny, so he lounged on his bunk and appreciated Parker's round-about way of communicating and showing his feelings.

"What'd you say this was?" said Parker.

"It's a cushion-cut," Gerard said. "I'd say it's about two carats."

"Man, that is *nice*," said Parker. "My lady's gonna love this."

What's your lady's name? How long have you been seeing each other? Gerard wanted to know. But Gerard had learned that Parker didn't like direct questions. Maybe direct questions led too quickly to intimacy. Direct questions were too forward, too aggressive, in the way that staring at your opponent could be interpreted as a provocation. So instead of coming at Parker head-on, Gerard tried to be casual about shooting the shit. He babbled.

"Oh, she's got to love it," said Gerard. "The cushion cut was very popular during the nineteenth century." Gerard hopped off his bunk and plopped down next to Parker. "See these ridges here? Beautiful, aren't they? They're very difficult to cut, which is why they're so expensive. Well, normally they're expensive."

Parker leaned away a bit from Gerard, but Gerard pushed forward. He grabbed the diamond from Parker and held it up, turning it to show all the sides.

"I think this may be an antique diamond. You don't see many cushion cuts any more, because they don't shine as brightly under electric lights."

"Pretty damn shiny to me," Parker said.

"Oh sure, it's shiny," said Gerard. "But wait 'til you see this baby in candle light. See how deep this diamond is? You can see *into* it. That's the beauty of a cushion cut. You'll see it best in candle light."

Gerard handed the stone back to Parker. Before he continued, Gerard quickly assessed Parker. Parker was being cautious, but Gerard could tell he was interested in learning more about the diamond. The whole conversation (more of a monologue, really) was a success because Parker wasn't telling Gerard to shut the fuck up or get out of his fucking face or kiss his black ass, the way he used to when Gerard would try to initiate a conversation (before the beating, that is; Gerard was willing to let go of the whole unpleasant incident—after all, hadn't Parker reacted the only way he knew how? In Parker's experience, what else could he have done? Surely Gerard couldn't have expected Parker to talk to Gerard about his feelings. "You know, Kelderman, we're all really upset that, because of your mistake, we were out in the rain for three hours when we could have been sleeping. We're very angry, and we want you to understand how we feel"). Gerard was riding a wave with serious momentum, and he wasn't going to stop.

"Yep, cushion cuts were all the rage when people used candles for light," Gerard said. "Then along came electric lighting, and we discovered we could get a brighter look with the brilliant cut, because the brilliant cut has so many more facets."

"We?" Parker said.

"Oh sure," Gerard said. "I'm a master diamond cutter. Well, my dad is a master diamond cutter. I don't have any official certification. He taught me everything he knows. I can cut or polish any fucking diamond in the world. In fact, when we get out of here, if you ever need any diamonds polished, or if you need diamond advice, you know, like you did back at Schliemann's, you let me know. Man, that son-of-a-bitch jeweler about crapped his fucking pants, didn't he?"

Damn. Now Gerard was overdoing it. He had impressed Parker many times over during the past week, but he couldn't resist throwing in some extra swear words to show that he was cool, that all was forgiven, that there really wasn't all that much difference between him and Parker. And now Parker did his little chuckle. Shit. Gerard recognized the Parker-chuckle. It was the same chuckle Parker had delivered when Gerard said he knew something about black people because of his association with Lawrence Thaxton in the Monroe Hill College Glee Club. Parker had chuckled then and told Gerard that Lawrence Thaxton—because of his background—didn't count as a real black person. Oh well, fuck it. He was having a good time anyway.

"Yeah he did," said Parker, still smiling. "'Bout crapped his pants."

Okay, Gerard hadn't completely blown it. He got up from Parker's bunk and walked to the bathroom. This was a good time to go away, before Gerard said something else stupid. Parker had responded, and Gerard wanted to leave it at that.

"Bullcrap," Wiley said as Gerard stepped into the bathroom. "He's a nut case. They'll kick him out."

"Nope," said Fuller, who was shaving over the sink. "Romberg's uncle is a three-star general at the Pentagon."

"Hammer knows he's a nut," said Wiley. "Hammer wants him out. I've seen Womack and Hammer argue about it."

Fuller patted his face with a towel. "Womack's the head drill sergeant, and he knows about Romberg's uncle. Why do you think Romberg has lasted this long? I'm tellin' you—he's staying in."

"What do you think, Kelderman?" said Wiley. "Is Romberg a nut case or what? They're gonna kick him out of the army, right? We can't keep a nut case in the army, can we?"

Gerard splashed cold water over his head and face. "I don't know."

"I mean, would you trust Romberg to watch your back?" said Wiley.

"I would," said Fuller. "I'd trust him a lot more than Libby."

"Hey, I'm sitting right here," said Libby, from one of the toilet stalls.

"So what?" Fuller said. "It's true. You're a fuck-up, Libby. You and me better not get assigned to the same unit."

Libby was silent.

Gerard looked into his own eyes in the mirror. "Yeah, I would too," he said. "Romberg's loyal."

"This is bullcrap!" Wiley stood half-shaved, in PT shorts and a brown army towel over his shoulder. "He's a wacko. He better not come back."

"He'll be back," said Fuller.

Gerard patted his face with his own towel and walked out of the bathroom. He slid his boots off and lay down on his bunk as the fireguard flipped off the lights. Gerard had no doubt Fuller was right that Romberg would rejoin Third Platoon; Fuller had assured everyone that the old-boy network was alive and well in the army, and since Romberg's uncle was a lieutenant general on active duty, there was simply no discussion. Romberg would actually have to kill someone to be kicked out of the army. Only Private Wiley doubted that Romberg would be back.

Gerard remembered having to assure baby Anna her dad would be back whenever Willem Kelderman left the room even for a moment. Anna was very fond of her father, so much so that if Rebecca was holding her and Willem walked by, Anna would dive out of Rebecca's arms toward Willem even if Willem wasn't watching. She never imagined for a moment that her father might not catch her. It was unnerving to Willem, who always had to be on the lookout for diving Anna. If she wasn't diving for him, she'd be hugging his calves saying, "hold you, Daddy," or "up please."

"He'll be back," Gerard had told Anna on United Airlines flight 950 between Dulles and Brussels (how could Gerard remember an obscure flight number and not recall how his sister had died?). Willem had gone to the bathroom, and Anna had asked to go with him. Gerard had assured her that Willem would be back soon. As Willem walked away down the aisle, Anna stood up in her seat and announced to the other passengers in the first class cabin that her daddy "had a poopie" and needed to "go get a fresh diaper." When he disappeared into the lavatory, she plopped back down and resumed organizing the pretzel sticks on her tray, meticulously ordering them from right to left in ascending order by height. Anna had turned two the previous month; that would put the trip right in July of 1987.

Gerard lay on his army bunk, staring again at the red glow of the exit sign on the ceiling. Rebecca hadn't been on that trip. Willem was always harried on the trips where he had to mind both kids (Rebecca insisted it was impossible for her when she had a singing engagement—especially if it was out-of-town). But Willem Kelderman never minded juggling both kids, which didn't explain why Gerard could remember his father later referring to Rebecca's excursions as "your goddamn singing trips." Then again, Willem only spoke that way in answer to Rebecca's own foul language. Each was resentful of the other's travel schedule, but Willem always had the kids, and after Anna had died, he always had Gerard.

"Don't touch that," Gerard remembered telling Anna on the plane. She had stood up on her chair and was reaching for the attendant call button. They'd been on the flight for an hour, during which time she'd pressed the button twice. The haggard flight attendant had forced a smile the first time, but the second time (after checking to see Willem wasn't looking) had scowled so forcefully at the children that her front teeth jutted out like a vampire's. It only made Gerard wish they'd flown Lufthansa or British Airways, both of which flew directly between Dulles and Brussels. Flight attendants on foreign airlines were much more kind and patient.

"No, Anna," Gerard said, pulling her down. "Don't ever touch that. No."

"I wanna push it," Anna said.

"No," said Gerard. "You're going to make the lady mad."

Anna's eyes widened. She clearly did not want to make the lady mad. She sat down in her seat.

"No mean lady," said Anna.

Gerard smiled and pulled out the tattered copy of *The Paper Bag Princess*. He read the book to Anna over and over for the next half hour. She cackled when he read the part of Prince Ronald in a Scottish accent. "Again," she'd say after each time. "Again."

How long ago was that plane trip—fifteen years? And the memory now seemed a day old to Gerard. He could remember that flight to Brussels and then the train ride to Antwerp with such clarity—the sound of the P.A. on the train platform in Brussels, the clack-clack of the train ride, the feeling of sleeping Anna's warm head against his arm; the memory of his sister filled him like never before.

Gerard remembered standing in Unity Cemetery in Evans Glen, with his parents, visiting Anna's grave. They didn't do it very often—it was too much for Rebecca, who couldn't control her crying for hours afterwards. He pictured the tiny granite grave stone and that inscription: *Anna Kelderman. Our Sweet Baby. We Will Never Hold You Again. June 5, 1985 - July 19, 1987.* July, 1987. The same month as the plane trip! It *was* July of 1987, because Anna had turned two years old and could no longer fly for free. Willem had had to buy her a first-class ticket, round-trip, from Dulles to Brussels. And then Gerard's brain flashed to the return plane trip—he could picture his dad, slumped on the chair, sleeping. Gerard himself sat rigid for the entire trip back, with his arms folded across his chest. Anna was not with them.

Holy shit. That was it. Somehow she had died during that trip to Antwerp with Willem and Gerard. And the more Gerard turned it over in his head, the more convinced he was that he'd been there when she'd died. God, he didn't want to think about it. He didn't want to remember. He wanted to stay protected.

So he should take Cooper's advice and avoid looking behind him at the past. He needed to focus on what was in front of him, on all the upcoming infantry school training: ARM qualification, training on the M249 Squad Automatic Weapon, Military Operations in Urban Terrain—MOUT, training in advanced anti-tank weaponry, more hand-to-hand combat training, more land navigation, more ten-mile road marches, more PT, more formation runs, and more time in the field. All that would help him forget.

# Fifteen

"Come on, Kelderman, get up." Parker nudged Gerard through his blanket in the bivouac tent. "It's time."

"Oh, I don't want to," Gerard whined. "I want to sleep."

"We got to do this now," Parker said. "Second Platoon got it coming."

Yes, Second Platoon had it coming—time for revenge. It had all started with Romberg's anger about getting a bread heel at chow that counted as one of his two pieces. Since then the pranks had been flying back and forth all during basic training and AIT. Most recently Second Platoon had invaded the Third Platoon bay at 2 a.m. with water balloons. They had hog-tied Libby, who was on fireguard at the door, and then had run silently down the aisles pelting the sleeping soldiers of Third Platoon with large water balloons. They'd come and gone within twenty seconds, and Gerard had scrambled to get his platoon mates to clean up the place before the drill sergeants arrived for PT. Even so, Drill Sergeant Hammer had found pieces of balloon on the floor and had put the platoon through forty-five minutes of the Titty Twister when no one would explain how the bits had gotten there.

Now it was Third Platoon's turn for retaliation. Now Second Platoon would suffer as Third Platoon had suffered. Gone were the days when only Romberg was fixated on Second Fucking Platoon. It was full platoon warfare. This time Romberg would be in charge; he was the leader of tonight's commando raid.

As Fuller had predicted, Romberg was back among the members of Third Platoon the day after the raven incident on the Advanced Rifle Marksmanship range two weeks earlier. He said

Womack had told him this was his last chance—one more raven incident, and Womack was going to have Romberg removed from the army.

"Yeah right," Wiley had said. "You think Womack doesn't know that your uncle's a three-star general?"

"Yeah, he knows," Romberg had admitted. "But I want to stay in. I can do it, man."

Cooper agreed that Romberg could do it. When Romberg had returned to the company area after the incident, Cooper had assured Romberg that he wouldn't be seeing any more ravens.

"I know, dude!" Romberg had said. "I've got 'em licked. Somehow I know it."

Romberg had enthusiastically agreed with Cooper but hadn't asked Cooper how he knew—how Cooper could possibly know that about another person.

"I can see by looking at him," Cooper had explained when Gerard asked. "It's like this big cloud of crud has been lifted from him. You can tell a lot about a person by looking, by really focusing and paying attention."

And now it was the third day of Squad Tactical Training—STT— a five-day bivouac (still Cooper called it camping) that included instruction in squad and team movement.

After slipping his boots on and grabbing his M16, Gerard zipped out of his tent and into the nearby woods, where about twenty Third-Platoon soldiers were gathered to plan their attack on Second Platoon. Romberg was organizing the troops, proudly putting to use knowledge they had gained during the day's STT session.

"Okay men, it's just like we rehearsed it this afternoon," said Romberg, as if today's infantry training had been practice for the real night raid! "Traveling overwatch. Fuller, you're the fire team leader. Cory, you're the trail fire team leader."

"Man, *I* wanted to be trail fire team leader," Libby said.

"Yeah, my ass," said Wiley. "Like we'd trust you to be in charge of anything."

"Shut up," whispered Romberg. The soldiers huddled around him, dressed only in their underwear and combat boots. It reminded Gerard of the night he and his St. Philip Fraternity brothers had streaked the Lawn at Monroe Hill.

"We get into position here and here," Romberg said. He drew in the sand with a stick. "On Fuller's signal, we move. We sweep across here, right into Second Platoon's bivouac area, when their fireguard is on the far side of the clearing. We pull up as many tent stakes as we can grab, and we make off with their fucking tents."

"They're gonna kick our asses," Carroll said.

"Shut up, sissy," said Berkowicz.

"We'll be too fast, Carroll," said Romberg. "Don't worry."

"Well then Hammer's gonna kick our asses," said Carroll.

"Oh, mother of fucking goddamn Christ, Carroll," said Cory.

"Hey," said Wiley. "Language."

"Are you kidding?" said Gerard.

"No, I'm not," said Wiley. "There's limits, you know."

"Shut your cunt, Wiley," said Cory. "Get over it."

Cooper laughed. Wiley shook his head.

"Carroll, Hammer's not gonna find out," said Berkowicz.

"He's going to find out if we keep standing here talking," Cory said.

"Okay men, let's move," whispered Romberg.

The troupe of soldiers padded silently on the pine needles through the dark of the trees and settled into position along the woodline outside the clearing of Second Platoon's bivouac area. Fuller led his A-team into position. Cory was right behind with the B-team. It was silly, really, because there was no need for tactical squad movement or team maneuvers at all. Fuller and Cory solemnly organized their fire teams, but Gerard—like all the other men in the platoon—was standing in his underwear with his arms folded and his M16 slung over his back, waiting to dash out among the tents and pull up stakes. Everyone was playing along with Romberg's need to pretend that organization was necessary. It was much more interesting this way and would make a better story when they were done with basic training; when they were home on leave, they'd be able to convince their friends and family that the operation had been a success *because* of their advanced infantry training. Fuller held a fist up in the air. He pulled it down, the way children try to get truckers to honk their horns. Romberg whispered "Rock and roll" as twenty bodies silently emerged from the darkness between the trees. They darted quietly among the tents. Cory sprinted out into the lead and headed for the far end of the clearing. Gerard stooped down and grabbed a tent stake. He pulled and yanked; it didn't budge. He looked around and saw his platoon mates having the same problem. All across the tent village, soldiers were hunched over, bobbing up and down as they pulled at the tent stakes. Every single one of them had been on bivouac before, but no one had thought ahead to how securely the stakes were driven into the hard, dry Fort Benning clay. Shit. And no one else in the platoon was working on the same tent where Gerard was, so even if he did get this stake out, he'd have several more to unearth before he could drag away a whole tent. Instead of organizing a squad traveling overwatch, they should have arranged themselves into groups—each one assigned to work on one tent. It was too late now. The only one having any success was Private Cory, who was handily yanking up stakes like candles from a birthday cake.

"Ow, fuck," said Libby.

Gerard turned around. "What's wrong?"

"I cut my fucking hand." Libby was holding one hand in the other. He had managed to slice the flesh of his palm on the edge of one of the metal tent stakes.

"Well shit," whispered Gerard. "You'd better get back to your tent and get a towel or something."

"God, man, this sucks," Libby said as he stood up and walked slowly away, his head turned down. He had lost all urgency. Gerard wondered for a brief moment what it was like to be Libby. Did Libby get tired of screwing up all the time? Did he really believe he was going to get better? Or was he, the way many stupid people are, completely unaware of his own idiocy? It couldn't be that—there were too many drill sergeants and fellow recruits to remind him, all the time.

Carroll jerked at the ground, grunting.

"Need help?" said Gerard.

"Yeah," Carroll said. He was sweating.

Gerard dropped to his knees and pulled.

"Hey, what the fuck?" The Second Platoon soldier on fireguard became suddenly aware that something was happening. Romberg had correctly guessed that the fireguard would be slow to notice the event, simply because no one ever expected anything to happen on fireguard watch. In that same moment, another soldier from Second Platoon poked his head out of his tent.

"Fuck! Where's the fucking fireguard? Wake up, Second, wake up!"

But he was whispering, even as frantic as he was, and even as he sounded the alarm to rouse his comrades. It was understood during all these pranks that the drill sergeants were never to be involved; this Second Platoon soldier was respectfully honoring that unspoken agreement by not screaming and causing more commotion. That would have been tattling.

"We've got it!" whispered Carroll. He had pulled up the last stake. He whipped away the tent and ran for the woods. Gerard followed.

And finally, at the same moment, two then three then four tents came up. The sleeping soldiers inside blinked their eyes; they were like ants and beetles under rotting tree bark, suddenly exposed to daylight. The fireguard ran among the tents, whispering and flapping his arms. A sea of dark bodies scurried across the clearing with canvas tents waving and fluttering behind them.

"Rock and roll."

"Motherfuckers."

"Shit."

"It's fucking Third."

"Fucking assholes."

"Fuck you."

"Fuck *you*."

"Gimme that."

"Suck on it, fuckwad."

"Next time we'll bring fucking water balloons."

"Let go—Ouch."

"Airborne!"

"Dick."

Carroll crashed into the brush holding a tent that dragged behind him like a bridal train. There was no exit strategy for the operation. As Gerard remembered it, the last part of Romberg's plan had been to make off with their fucking tents. That was it. Well, now they were making off with Second Platoon's fucking tents, and no one had any idea what to do next. When Gerard reached the edge of the clearing, Cory was there guiding the soldiers out.

"Let's go, go, go." Cory was whispering and waving, trying frantically to get Third Platoon, somehow, to safety (wherever that was).

Gerard stopped too, at the edge of the clearing, and turned around to help Cory. It was obvious Cory didn't need help, but Gerard was the platoon guide, so he felt he should at least put in an effort at being a leader. Romberg was nowhere to be seen (wasn't he in charge of this mission?), so it was Cory and Gerard, shepherding people from the clearing into the woods. The last one to come sprinting from among the tents was Berkowicz. Close behind Berkowicz were two soldiers from Second Platoon, reaching for him and grabbing at the tent in his hands. Berkowicz barely made it through the woodline, and as he zipped past, Cory spread open one of the tents he was holding. He stood holding the edges of the tent, with his arms outstretched, and when the two Second Platoon soldiers got close enough, Cory cloaked them with one sweep and wrapped the tent around them. In the same motion, he pulled them to the ground and rolled them up like a burrito.

"Go, go!" Cory yelled at Gerard.

Gerard turned and ran into the woods. Cory was right behind him an instant later. They tripped over tents that the other Third Platoon members had dropped as they ran (there'd been no plan for the booty, either), and in a few short seconds, they were back in the Third Platoon tent area; each man ducked into his own tent.

Parker was hiding under his BDU shirt when Gerard stumbled in.

"Man, that was close," said Gerard.

Parker was loudly laughing. "Did you hear that motherfucker: 'Where's the fucking fireguard?' He 'bout wet his drawers."

Gerard collapsed onto his sleeping mat and giggled. "Cory was awesome. He saved us from two of those goons. They almost got Berkowicz."

"That's one tough motherfucker," said Parker.

"Yep," said Gerard. He breathed deeply and then tried to listen. He heard nothing. Probably most of Second Platoon had realized by now what had happened, and they were likely looking for their tents. But there would be no squealing and, if the pattern continued the way it had, there would be no retaliation that night. This prank was over. It would be up to Second Platoon to plan the next attack. Not a single drill sergeant had woken up.

# Sixteen

"Chow time, men," said Parker.

"Yes sir, Mr. Platoon Guide," said Romberg.

Parker smiled. An hour earlier, before Bravo Company had boarded the cattle trucks to return to the company area from the Squad Tactical Training bivouac site, Drill Sergeant Womack had appointed new squad leaders and a new platoon guide. Finally Parker got to stand in front of the formation and tell people what to do.

"Move 'em out, Platoon Guides." Drill Sergeant Cifuentes had CQ duty and was the only drill sergeant around. It was Friday night and the end of five days in the field. After chow they'd get to turn on the television in the barracks. Life was good.

Parker marched Third platoon around the corner of the building and lined them up at the door of the D-FAC.

"Man, I'm one hungry motherfucker," said Romberg.

"Yeah, I never thought I'd be looking forward to the mess hall," said Wiley. "Field chow sucks."

And then a horrible rumor rippled through the ranks: the D-FAC had run out of bread. No bread! Gerard couldn't conceive of a meal without his two pieces of white, gummy army bread. The soldiers had all come to expect that bread, even to love it. It was one of the consistent pleasures of basic training, even if you did get the heel. You might get dirty during the day, the drill sergeants might smoke you and bring you to your knees, but it all melted away when the sun went down. At the end of the day when dusk settled on Fort Benning, you'd line up at the mess hall, side-step through the line, and get your two pieces of bread with dinner. Even if the main course was another unidentifiable, gelatinous meat product, there was always bread. Gerard hoped the rumor was false.

"No way, man," Fuller said. "They better give us more of everything else."

"You don't *fuck* with a soldier's *bread!*" screamed Romberg.

"Hey, settle down," Carroll said. "Let's wait and see."

So they did wait and see. Sure enough there was no bread. Gerard hoped that whoever was on KP duty would compensate by upping the portion sizes, but his hopes were dashed as the line wound around the corner and he saw who had KP: Second Platoon.

"Goddamn fuck," said Romberg. "Second Fucking Platoon. We're fucked."

And fucked they were. The Second Platoon KP soldiers grinned as they spooned out Third Platoon's tiny portions. And the main course this evening *was* an unidentifiable, gelatinous meat product.

"God, this meat sucks," Carroll said, after they had sat down.

"It's fucking rubber," said Romberg, who had seven pieces of the meat piled on his tray. Romberg had worked himself into such a frenzy that when he'd reached the serving line, he had lunged over the aluminum counter and plunged both hands into the tray of meat and gravy. He'd slopped the treasure—a quivering mound of meat slabs, shimmering with gravy—onto his plastic tray. "Tell Cifuentes and I'll strangle you, you fucks," he'd whispered to the Second Platoon soldiers behind the serving line as he wiped gravy onto his BDU trousers.

"Here, have some," Romberg now said, cheerfully picking up individual pieces of meat with his hands and slapping them down onto the trays of the soldiers around him.

Carroll's eyes lit up. "Thanks, man!"

Gerard looked down at the two pieces of meat on his tray. The gravy jiggled and glistened. He smiled to imagine that he would never have touched anything like this back at Monroe Hill. Whenever possible, he and his first-year roommate had avoided meals in O'Connell Cafeteria by ordering pizza from the Corner.

But here he was now, centered and focused on this meal—this plastic tray arrayed with mismatched textures and unnatural colors—and Gerard was awash with gratitude. It was food, it was hot, and he had a double portion of meat-like product. He jabbed it with his fork and ripped off large mouthfuls of the substance. The soldiers had been conditioned to eat quickly, though Drill Sergeant Cifuentes clearly didn't give a rat's ass how slowly they ate. Cifuentes had been stuck with company CQ duty on a Friday night, and he wasn't going to make it hard on himself by paying even a bit of attention to his 224 charges.

So the pace of dinner was leisurely. Gerard tugged at his two pieces of meat product and then washed it all down with two cartons of chocolate milk. That was another rule—if you wanted milk, you were only supposed to take one. But on this casual Friday night, everyone was taking chances and grabbing armloads of whatever food they could reach. The mess hall had probably run out of bread because Third Platoon was last through the chow line for Bravo Company. Gerard imagined that the soldiers before them had grabbed bread slices by the handful. That made it a little easier; Third Platoon would have behaved the same way, given the chance.

"Let's go, Third Platoon. It's TV time!" said Romberg, standing up from his tray, his mouth and chin still dripping with brown gravy.

"Hoo-ah!" said Wiley. "Man, I can't even remember what's on TV on Friday nights."

And when they got back to the barracks, they found out exactly what was on TV on Friday nights in Columbus, Georgia: crap. It was the middle of summer, so everything was a rerun, and apparently the army didn't have much of a line-item in its budget for television, because there was no cable connection. Every platoon of Bravo Company was at the mercy of local programming. There were about six channels to choose from, and after heated arguments about what they would watch, they all settled on the Friday night movie: *Gone With The Wind*.

"Awesome," said Romberg, as he flopped onto Berkowicz's bunk and tucked a pillow under his chest.

"No, no, please," Berkowicz said. "Make yourself comfortable."

"You heard the man," Fuller said, and he pounced onto Berkowicz's bed next to Romberg, jouncing the bed and jostling Romberg.

"*Gone With The Wind?*" said Wiley. "We're watching *Gone With The Wind?*"

"Sit down and shut up," said Parker, who had pulled up a chair backwards and sat down. "You got somewhere to be?"

Parker seemed excited about the movie; he said he'd never seen it before. His enthusiasm dulled, however, when the scenes behind the opening credits showed slaves hoeing in the field and picking cotton.

"Oh, fuck," Parker said.

"What?" said Wiley.

"*What?*" Parker said. "You kidding me? Look at that shit."

"What shit?" Wiley said.

Fuller and Hopson laughed. Parker shook his head.

So Third Platoon settled in to watch *Gone With The Wind* with the TV volume turned as high as it would go. During the next hour, Private Fuller provided running commentary about every military aspect of the film: the Confederate uniforms, the guns, the cannons.

"Fuller, how do you keep all this shit in your head?" said Hopson.

"You should be on Jeopardy," said Romberg.

To a man, the soldiers broke into song—the Jeopardy song—even though no one quite agreed on the syllable. Some sang "Ya da da da, Ya da daaaaa...," others used "Na na na..." What they all did agree on, and what they timed perfectly in unison, was the "boomboom" at the end.

Parker couldn't sit still during any scenes with slaves. He couldn't stop making comments containing the words 'bullshit' and 'racist.'

"Come on, Parker," Wiley said. "That's the way it used to be for you people."

"'You people?'" Parker said. "Man, what the fuck you know about my people?"

"Plenty," said Wiley. "I've seen this movie before. I saw *Roots* too."

"Wiley, you fucked in the head," said Hopson.

Parker jumped up from his chair and ran down the aisle between the bunks, holding his cheeks in his hands and quoting Miss Prissy: "Lawdsy, we got to have a doctor! I don't know nothin' 'bout birthin' babies!"

Fuller and Hopson laughed and punched fists with each other. It was hilarious, seeing Parker carry on like that, but Gerard sensed this would not be an appropriate time for a white person to laugh.

"Did you hear that?" said Wiley. "I heard a bang."

"Well, duh," said Carroll, "Sherman's shelling the dog-shit out of Atlanta."

"No, no," said Wiley. "Back there, in the latrine." He rushed to the back of the bay and pushed into the bathroom. He crashed right back out.

"Call 911!" Wiley yelled. "Get the CQ. Cory shot himself." He ran back into the bathroom and emerged again, holding Cory's arm over his shoulder and walking him to the door. Blood poured from Cory's socks and left a bright trail of shining red on the white tile down the middle of the aisle. Wiley dragged Cory out the door and down the stairs.

"What the fuck?" said Berkowicz.

"Cory shot himself?" Gerard said. "Cory?"

"Dude," said Romberg, slowly sitting down on his bunk.

"Why were his feet bleeding?" Hopson said. "What was he trying to do?"

Drill Sergeant Cifuentes banged through the front bay door. "Somebody tell me what happened here."

"Is he okay, Drill Sergeant?" said Wiley.

"Yeah, he's gonna be fine," said Cifuentes. "Battalion CQ's taking him to the hospital. What happened?"

"We don't know," Romberg said. "We were watching TV, and he shot himself in the bathroom."

"In the feet," Libby said.

"Well, shit," said Cifuentes. "I'm gonna have some paperwork for this one." He took off his wide-brim hat and scratched his head. "Son of a bitch."

"Where'd he get the gun, Drill Sergeant?" said Libby.

"I don't know, I don't know." Cifuentes shook his head. "Let's get this floor cleaned up, men. Lights out in thirty minutes."

And so movie night at Bravo Company 1/47th came to an end. Half an hour later all the bays went dark. Gerard lay staring at the ceiling. First, Second, and Fourth Platoons were probably wondering what had happened, and were likely formulating their own opinions and rumors. Cory. Unbelievable.

"It just happens," said Cooper, as they lay awake in their bunks.

"But Cory?" said Gerard.

"Why not Cory?" said Cooper.

"Because he's Cory," Gerard said. "The guy's perfect. Who wouldn't want to be like Cory?"

And Gerard remembered that Rebecca Ward, his mother, had tried and tried to become more like Margareta Van Leuven after she'd learned of Willem's affair. Rebecca had taken up studying Flemish when Gerard was nine years old.

He remembered the time well, because during the same month a new electrical system was installed at the Kasteel. All the outlets, Willem Kelderman had explained emphatically, would now have ground fault circuit interrupters. Gerard never knew why (the old outlets worked fine)—he only remembered that men in overalls occupied the Kasteel for two days, pulling out the wall outlets and replacing them with new ones. They had arrived early one morning while Gerard and his mother were still eating breakfast. Rebecca was hunched over her toast, studying a *You Can Speak Dutch* book. (Rebecca had also stopped referring to Flemish and Dutch as "the same goddamned thing." For language study, the only materials available were Dutch.) Her anti-Flemish rhetoric had flared up briefly after she'd made the discovery about Willem and Margareta Van Leuven, but over time she softened and made a sincere effort to learn about Flemish language and culture. Rebecca had even asked Gerard for some of his Grote Van Kloten tapes and then needed explanations her Dutch dictionary couldn't provide.

"So what's a *rookworst* again?" said Rebecca at the breakfast table as she paged through her Dutch dictionary.

"Smoked sausage," Gerard said.

"Oh right, so the song is an anti-meat song, right?"

"Yeah," said Gerard. He shoveled in a spoonful of *Life* cereal.

Gerard loved the song about the *rookworst*. At age nine, he didn't care about animal-rights politics, he just thought Grote Van Kloten was pretty cool for writing a song about killing rich people and sending them through the meat grinder to make smoked sausage.

"Okay, now tell me about that song where the singer shoves a beer bottle down his pants to impress women," said Rebecca. "What's the name of that song?"

But this was all too strange! His mom wasn't supposed to be involved in anything Flemish. Flemish was strictly for Gerard and his dad. For instance, when ordering pizza for delivery, Willem and Gerard would make up names that included Flemish obscenities. The trick was to be creative but also to come up with likely-sounding surnames. Van de Lul ("from the cock") was Willem's favorite. It was especially gratifying if the pizza delivery man would *say* the name at the door.

"Yeah, pizza for Van de Lul?" And the puzzled pizza guy would watch while Gerard and his dad stomped and hooted.

Gerard could tell that Rebecca felt shut out in those moments, even before she had intercepted Margareta Van Leuven's letter. And now that Gerard knew exactly when his mother had discovered the affair, he understood why—for a time—anything vaguely Flemish would send her through the roof. When the family went out for dinner at the Lion's Broach Inn, Willem couldn't even stack his mussel shells together at the end of the meal without causing a scene. Stacking mussel shells was too Flemish. But then Rebecca started studying Flemish herself, trying to force an unnatural fit. When his mom had begun her Flemish kick, Gerard had been immersed in Flemish for over a year, and all of Willem's diamond associates told him his accent was perfect and his vocabulary was very good. Margareta Van Leuven had been especially encouraging and helpful, until Rebecca banned Willem from having any further contact with her. In light of his mother's recent letter to him, Gerard now understood why Rebecca wanted to learn Flemish, and why that summer was the last time Gerard ever saw Margareta Van Leuven.

"It's *Nonkel Flesbroek*, Mom," said Gerard. "The name of that song is *Nonkel Flesbroek*" (Uncle Bottlepants). He put his cereal bowl in the sink and headed out the kitchen door. "Gotta catch the bus." He pushed his way past the electrical workers in the dining room and walked out the front door to the bus stop one street over on Mitchell Park Road.

So after this one letter from his mom, many pieces from his past clicked into place. He realized, lying there in the Bravo Company 1/47th barracks staring at the ceiling, that he'd been aware of all these events when he was a kid, but he'd had no reason at the time to try to figure out why they were happening. What kid cares why his parents do what they do? To kids, adults are oafish trolls who lumber around sulking and being serious. He'd given them no more thought than trying to remember how his sister had died.

Guilt was the first feeling Gerard had when Wiley had dragged Cory and his bleeding feet across the floor of the bay. Why Gerard should feel guilty about Cory shooting himself he had no idea, but that's what he'd felt—that he somehow should have been able to keep Cory from shooting himself. Some part of Gerard wondered if there was something he could have said to Cory earlier that day, or earlier during training, that would have made Cory not want to shoot himself. Then again, maybe Cory's wounds had been an accident; perhaps Cory was playing around in the bathroom, curious about the gun, and had somehow managed to shoot both feet with one round.

"I don't think any of us could have prevented it," said Cooper, through the dark from the next bunk.

Gerard jumped. "Cooper, don't do that."

"Sorry."

"How did you know what I was thinking about?" said Gerard.

"I figured it was probably what we're all thinking about," said Cooper.

Damn, he was probably right. But there had been many times when Cooper had cut right into Gerard's thoughts with some comment that indicated he knew exactly what Gerard had been thinking, with no obvious point of reference like Cory's shooting. Sometimes it frustrated Gerard, but most of the time it felt natural. If Cooper could read minds, he was never invasive; he was always respectful about it.

"Maybe it was an accident," said Gerard.

"I don't think so," said Cooper. "I think Cory had a lot of problems he never told anyone about. Ever notice what he looked like after reading his letters?"

"No," said Gerard. It was true that Cory received shitloads of letters—more than anyone else. It was part of the reason everyone wished they were in his place.

"Yeah," said Cooper. "There was something going on there. Letters can do that."

And Gerard had an urge to say something like "Yeah, no shit," or "You got *that* right," but he caught himself. He was determined to resist, as long as possible, the effect of the speech patterns of his fellow soldiers. Formulaic little phrases had been sneaking into his speech for weeks now, and he'd had to shove them all back—"Ain't it the *truth*" and "*Yeah* it is" were as persistent as army-specific phrases like "Hoo-ah" and "Roger that."

"But it's not our fault," said Cooper. "Cory chose his own path, and no one was going to stop him. Each of us chooses his own path—from adults all the way down to little kids."

Gerard wanted to cry. Scenes of his baby sister's short life reeled through his mind: Anna eating yogurt at the kitchen table, Anna grabbing the long, white fur on Alexander Hamilton's neck, hugging him as he trotted with her still in tow, Anna patting a large woman—a stranger—on the stomach.

Gerard giggled. He'd forgotten about that one. He and his family had been sitting in the front room of the Flaming Griddle restaurant in Evans Glen, waiting for a table. Anna had recently learned about pregnancy from Aunt Jackie. Aunt Jackie was pregnant with her first child, and when Aunt Jackie and Uncle Lloyd had last stayed at the Kasteel, Aunt Jackie had explained to Anna why her tummy was so big. It had taken Anna a few minutes truly to understand what Aunt Jackie was saying, but once she got it, she was astounded. A baby—actually inside someone! For the next few weeks, whenever Anna spied a pregnant person, she would loudly point it out.

So it was inevitable, what had happened next, there in the lobby of the Flaming Griddle. Anna was sitting on Rebecca's lap, leaning back against her mother and casually kicking one leg forward and back. She perked up when she saw a mountain of a woman standing in front of the hostess podium. Anna hopped down from her mother's lap, toddled right over, and patted the woman's protruding abdomen.

"It have a baby in it!" she proudly proclaimed.

Neither Rebecca nor Willem had been quick enough to guess what Anna had seen and where she was headed, but their reactions suggested that the corpulent woman's belly did *not* "have a baby in it." Rebecca scooped up her child and rushed out the front door. Willem dragged Gerard by the arm and followed his wife.

"But we haven't even eaten yet," Gerard said.

"Keep walking," said Willem.

Gerard laughed loudly, having forgotten he was lying in an army bunk and that it was past lights-out. His eyes were moist, but it was dark and no one could see him. Besides, he was laughing—that was always a good excuse when your eyes watered.

"What's so funny?" said Cooper.

"What, you don't know?" said Gerard, giggling and wiping his eyes.

"Huh?"

"Oh, never mind," said Gerard. "I had a funny thought. I was remembering something."

"Oh," said Cooper.

And when they'd reached the car in the parking lot, Rebecca and Willem had catapulted into an argument about whose fault it was that Anna had done what she did.

"Why didn't you stop her, Willem?" Rebecca said.

"She was on *your* lap, wasn't she?" said Willem.

"Oh, so that makes it my fault?"

"I didn't say that," said Willem.

"Well then what *are* you saying?"

And so on, in the same pattern. Had there been a time when his parents didn't carry on this way, when they weren't bickering and blaming each other? And Anna was still alive, during that argument in the parking lot of the Flaming Griddle. For years Gerard had been holding on to a mistaken notion that the blaming had blossomed only after Anna's death—that her death was the reason his parents had developed their habit of accusing each other when they got frustrated.

Perhaps Gerard had inherited the blame gene from his parents and that was why he was blaming himself for Cory's accident. Even if Cooper was right and there was nothing anyone could have done about the path Cory chose for himself, Gerard wondered how the evening would have ended if he, Gerard, had needed to use the bathroom at the same moment. Probably Cory would have put the gun away or tried to hide it. Surely Cooper didn't believe people were that isolated—that it was impossible to influence the actions of others. And Cooper had said the same about little kids. Bullshit. Bull fucking shit. Had Anna chosen her own path when she'd died? Maybe she wouldn't have died at all if Gerard had been watching her more closely; but the more he tried to explore that, the more tired he became. And Cooper, sage-on-the-mountain Cooper, had the answer for that too: he claimed that your brain puts you to sleep when it senses you're about to delve into thoughts and feelings that will be too painful. "It's a protection mechanism," Cooper had said.

Bullshit again. Gerard knew it wasn't his thoughts that were making him sleepy; it was the red glow on the ceiling tile that was dragging him down into slumber. In the Third Platoon bay the red exit sign was his night light. It was always there. It relaxed and soothed him and slowed his breathing and made him yawn and close his eyes.

# Seventeen

Gerard dug. For half an hour now he'd developed a nice digging rhythm, scraping his entrenching tool into the dry, hard Georgia dirt; it was like scooping granite with a soup spoon. His BDU cap and brown undershirt were soaked with sweat. Fort Benning was gritty, hot, and dusty. Parker dug beside him. They had carved out about half of their foxhole. Snodgrass and Carroll were toting the dirt back behind the foxhole into the assembly area and filling sandbags; soon it would be their turn to dig. Gerard glanced at Parker between throws. Parker was digging vigorously and grunting. Gerard wanted to ask him, "Aren't you scared?" The Warlord gang members at the Chickasaw dance club had warned them that FTX would be judgment day. Parker was nervous about Drill Sergeant Hammer—the whole platoon could tell that—but he hadn't admitted to being worried about the threats at the Chickasaw. Gerard knew Parker was worried; he could see the way Parker's eyes shifted around, even when there was nothing in view to be concerned about. He could hear Parker's deep sighs after lights out when Third Platoon lay in darkness. But ever since that night five weeks ago Gerard had stayed true to his sense that Parker didn't want to be asked about it, or to talk about it at all.

And here they were on FTX—the Field Training Exercise—the final event of the infantry school curriculum. Early that morning Bravo Company had been trucked into the field and dropped in the woods for five days. They set up a perimeter and began digging foxholes in a wide circle that stretched about a quarter mile at its diameter. At the center was the assembly area, the communications tent, and the cadre tents. The mortarmen—the Charlies—were building their sandbag pit within the perimeter. Gerard hadn't thought much about being scared until now. His life had been threatened for the first time ever. Maybe his training as an infantryman would help him, or maybe it was unlikely a group of civilians would dare try to attack on a military post; Romberg had vowed to help kick their fucking asses if they did. His enthusiasm was reassuring. Yes, Gerard admitted he was scared, but he hadn't taken the time to face his fear until actually arriving in the field for FTX. Especially for the past few days, Gerard had been so focused on preparing his equipment and being ready for what Bravo Company would have to do on FTX that he hadn't given the threats much thought. Now that he considered it, remembering the threat on the dance floor gave him the shivers, even as the temperature in the shade of the pine trees was a sticky ninety-eight degrees. Parker and Gerard were going to be killed some time during FTX. Killed. Death. What a bizarre thought. Gerard had spent three months being programmed as a professional killer for the U.S. government, and here he was realizing how abstract and odd death and murder seemed to him. Someone was going to try to murder him. Really? It didn't feel real to him even when he considered that voice again, in his ear, telling him FTX would be judgment day.

*You got that He-ro? Judgment day.*

Romberg, Cooper, Wiley, and Berkowicz were in the foxhole—the two-man fighting-position—to Gerard's left. In the foxhole to the right were Hopson, Libby, Phillips, and Fuller. They were all close enough to each other that they could carry on conversations outside hearing range of the drill sergeants. Romberg and his team had angered Drill Sergeant Womack earlier that morning because their foxhole was too wide; the Jacuzzi syndrome, Womack called it. A fighting position was supposed to be only two Kevlar helmets wide and two M16s deep.

"But if we're going to have to live in the fucking thing for five days, we might as well make it comfortable," Romberg had said.

Now it was 11:30 in the morning, almost lunch time. If someone could have risen above the Fort Benning pines, Bravo Company would have appeared like a hive of ants, all digging and zipping among a neat circle of 120 foxholes.

Gerard sighed and stopped digging. He stood up straight and squeezed sweat from his cap onto the red clay beneath his boots at the bottom of the hole. He uncapped his canteen and gulped warm water.

"Man, there's no way those gang fuckers would attack an entire platoon of infantry soldiers," said Romberg, flinging dirt behind his foxhole.

"You don't know," Parker said. "They some crazy-ass mother fuckers."

"And we don't have any real ammo," said Wiley, from the next foxhole over.

"Makes you like miss Cory, doesn't it?" said Berkowicz. "He'd have real ammo!"

"Man, that's not cool," said Romberg.

The day after the shooting eleven days earlier, Third Platoon had learned some of the details of the Private Cory incident. The evening they had returned from the STT bivouac, Cory had helped Specialist Sanchez in the arms room for weapons check-in and had slipped an M9 handgun into the cargo pocket of his BDU trousers. Bravo Company hadn't received any training with the M9, and when Cory was in the bathroom figuring out how to see if he had successfully chambered a round, the gun had fired. Because of the way Cory's ankles were crossed and because he wore only socks, the bullet had ripped through the middle of both his feet. No one would believe that he was thinking about killing himself, and they would never know—Cory never returned to Third Platoon; he'd probably left the army from the hospital.

"I'm sure he's fine," said Berkowicz. "It isn't like he actually killed himself."

"Yeah, like Phillips with that razor blade," said Libby, pausing to swig from his canteen.

"When are you gonna let that shit go, fuckass?" Phillips said. "I made a mistake, okay?"

"It's cool man," Libby said. "I'm just fuckin' with you."

"Well stop fucking," said Phillips. He flung a shovel-full of dirt behind the foxhole.

◆          ◆          ◆

The rain fell hard from the dark sky in driving showers, pelting the mud and the puddles inside the Bravo Company foxhole perimeter.

"Where's Private Romberg?" said Womack.

"Here I am, Drill Sergeant." Romberg splashed through the mud and jumped into formation.

Womack yelled through the roar of the rain. "Gentlemen, you've got four hours until it's your turn in the foxholes. Get some rest."

Gerard and Parker crawled into their tent and took off their boots. It was now the fourth soggy night of FTX. Two soldiers in each group had to be in the foxhole at all times, watching their lane with their M16s pointed outward, guarding the perimeter. The drill sergeants patrolled the circle, constantly smacking soldiers' Kevlar helmets to wake them up. Captain Fopp had warned Bravo Company many times that "that sorry piece-of-crap company" from 2nd of the 49th" would probably try to pull something on FTX. Furthermore, Captain Fopp told the company, he didn't want to be embarrassed by a defeat. All soldiers on FTX wore MILES gear—Multiple Integrated Laser Engagement Simulation—an elaborate system for war games used by the army for training. Third Platoon learned all it needed to, and more, about MILES from Private Fuller. The system had first proved itself years earlier in the Royal Netherlands Marine Corps. MILES gear included a harness with laser sensors, a band that wrapped around the Kevlar helmet, and a laser box on the muzzle of the M16 rifle that activated when blank rounds were fired. If someone fired a laser beam that hit your harness or your headband, it was recorded with your player ID code. The MILES system recorded all hits and injuries, and once you were dead, the Small Arms Transmitter attached to your muzzle would disable itself.

"Like a fuckin' video game!" Romberg had said.

Snodgrass and Carroll were now watching their lanes in the foxhole the four of them had dug together; each man had done his share—Gerard was thankful for that. The poor group in the foxhole to the right had been stuck with Libby, and during the digging, Libby continually scraped into the walls of the foxhole, creating huge pocks in them.

"You gotta admit it's kind of cool," Libby had said. "Look, we can put stuff in the holes."

And even Fuller approved, because after about an hour of gouging earth out of the side of the foxhole, they had a storage shelf. Gerard appreciated it too. In the foxhole Gerard felt safe, like being in a bunker. Stretched across the top of the foxhole were metal posts, and stacked on top of the posts were sandbags and concealment material: brush, leaves, branches. It was every boy's dream: building the ultimate fort, and inside the fort were spaces to hide stuff—safe and cozy. Oh, and in this fort, you got to have real guns and wear camouflage clothing and face paint and everything. It was goofy and childish, but ultimately it was cool—just like in the commercials.

Back on the first day of FTX, Gerard's group had taken five hours to dig all the way down and complete their foxhole. Then they had laid sandbags along the metal beams that stretched across the span of the hole. But now, four days into FTX, two straight days of rain had filled the bottoms of the foxholes with water. Even the grenade sumps—the little trenches at the edges of the foxhole floor—couldn't absorb the rainwater quickly enough, so the soldiers in the foxhole had wet feet.

But in this moment, Gerard was inside his tent and would have four hours to sleep before he had to drag his ass out again and go stand in the foxhole. He felt like a little boy camping out with his friends in his own back yard.

"Rock and roll, man, someone's out there!" Romberg was splashing around outside.

"Romberg, get in your tent," yelled Womack.

"Look, Drill Sergeant," said Romberg.

Gerard heard machine-gun fire in the distance. Echo Company.

"That ain't our SAW," Parker said.

Of course it was *their* SAW. It had to be. Echo Company wouldn't bring their SAW with them. The Squad Automatic Weapon was the only automatic gun on the FTX site. Mueller and Cortes were manning it in the pit.

"I'm tellin' you—that ain't ours." Parker was pulling on his boots. "This is it man, they're here."

"It could be Echo Company," said Gerard. "Their perimeter's only a mile away."

"Rock and roll, I wanna get in the foxhole," Gerard heard Romberg screaming outside.

Parker pulled out his bayonet and affixed it to the end of his rifle.

"What are you doing?" Gerard said.

"You best do it too, man. This is it," Parker said. "They found us, and they got Uzis." Parker zipped out of the tent.

"Shit," said Gerard. He grabbed his rifle and his ammo belt, but he left his bayonet in its sheath.

Gerard pushed out of the tent. A shower of warm rain thrashed his face. Romberg was on the ground in the middle of the assembly area, rolling around in the mud puddles. It was nothing new—Gerard had seen him do this before. "Better camouflage," Romberg had told him. He looked like a bird taking a bath, fluttering and flopping—except that birds don't yell "rock and roll" when they bathe.

"Romberg, we're under attack," Womack screamed. "Get up out of that puddle and get to your post."

Romberg jumped up. "I'm ready to kick some ass!"

"Let's go," Parker said.

"Where?" said Gerard. He heard more gunfire.

Snodgrass appeared through the trees. "Drill Sergeant, they're real. I mean, they're not soldiers."

"Private Snodgrass, why are you out of your foxhole?" Womack said. "What are you talking about?"

"They're running from foxhole to foxhole, shining flashlights into our faces. They're civilians, Drill Sergeant." Snodgrass wiped mud from his face. "I think they're looking for someone."

Parker grabbed Gerard's arm and yanked him towards the trees. "Come on," he said. "We got to stop this."

Parker and Gerard ducked into the thick of the trees.

"Where are we going?" said Gerard. "What's the plan?" He squinted ahead of him to try to see Parker, but the rain was whipping straight into his eyes.

"We got to surprise them," said Parker.

Gerard heard a grunt ahead of him, and then snapping branches and more grunting.

"Parker, what was that?"

"Go, Kelderman, go," Parker said. "They got me."

Two arms reached out of the darkness and wrapped around Gerard's shoulders. They squeezed tighter and tried to pull him down. Gerard's body reacted without waiting for his brain: he pushed backwards as hard as he could, digging his heels through the pine needles into the wet sod. He shoved with his upper back, all the time bracing for a thud he knew would come amid all these trees, and forced himself backward until he was almost running. Smack—a tree. Gerard's assailant slammed into the tree trunk and his arms loosened. Gerard pushed off and ran forward, then turned a sharp right into the underbrush. He sprinted through the trees and showering rain and dove behind a fallen log. He waited. He tried to listen over the rain and his own hard breathing. Shit. What next? Should he go back and face those two people? One of them had grabbed Parker. Had Parker broken free too? Gerard heard yelling in the distance, in the direction of the assembly area. He got up and sneaked toward the voice.

"Come on out, He-ro!"

Fuck, fuck, fuck. Even though he'd faced these gang thugs in the Chickasaw, none of it had felt real to Gerard until this moment. Now he was scared. His platoon mates had been mockingly calling him He-ro for weeks now, but Gerard knew that the person yelling was not a soldier; he was probably someone who had taken a long road trip from Detroit to settle a score that now included Gerard.

Gerard high-crawled through the mud and between the trees until he reached the edge of the clearing. All the soldiers of Bravo Company were lying on the ground, on their stomachs, with their hands behind their heads. Three men—or boys, or whatever they were—wearing wet blue jeans and black t-shirts, were standing over the soldiers. Each of them had a small two-handled machine gun supported by a shoulder strap. Gerard had never seen an Uzi, but he guessed the guns were Uzis. So these were Warlords. Even through the rain, he could see that the Warlords were young, maybe teenagers.

Teenagers or not, they had control. They were holding Uzis and had an entire company of U.S. Army infantry soldiers lying face-down in the mud. One of the Warlords was clutching Parker by the shirt and pointing the muzzle of a handgun against his neck. The second Warlord slowly stepped among the Bravo Company bodies—watching, harassing, and poking anyone who moved.

The last Warlord, Warlord Three, was walking the perimeter of the assembly area, yelling for Gerard. "Come on out, He-ro. Here He-ro, He-ro, He-ro."

Why should Gerard come out? They already had the entire company, so what good would it do for Gerard to put himself in their hands? No way. No fucking way was Gerard going to walk into that clearing.

"You don't come out, we gonna cap *Private* Parker," said Warlord Three.

Warlord One, still holding Parker, laughed. "You a big shot, now, ain't you, Private?" he said to Parker, ramming the handgun into Parker's neck. "Too big shot for us in Detroit, I guess."

Parker said nothing.

"That what you want, He-ro?" said Warlord Three. "You want him dead? You want that on your hands?"

Shit. Gerard took a deep breath. The entire front side of his body was now soaked; cool water pooled around his body as the rain pounded his back. What was he supposed to do now? If he went out, wouldn't they kill both Gerard and Parker? Were they planning to massacre the entire company? Shit.

"Come on, He-ro," said Warlord Three, who was now approaching the edge of the clearing just ten feet from where Gerard was plastered flat to the wet earth. "You know what 'cap' means, right? White people know that word, right?" He was screaming over the rain. He turned his head back to the center of the assembly area. "Motherfucker might be right here on the ground with the others."

"Naw, I checked all the names," said Warlord Two.

"Best check 'em again," said Warlord One.

"Man, fuck," said Warlord Two. "That's bullshit, man." He faced the sprawl of bodies in front of him. "All y'all sorry-ass *soldiers*, flip over on your back."

As one man, Bravo Company rolled over in the mud and rain; they lay with their faces to the sky.

"I don't wanna die!" said Wiley.

"Shut up, Wiley," said Romberg.

"Both y'all shut the fuck up," said Warlord Two.

"He started it," Romberg said.

"Romberg, shut up," yelled Phillips.

"All y'all shut the fuck up!" said Warlord Two.

Warlord Three still had his back to Gerard and stood even closer now to the edge of the clearing. Gerard put his rifle down, reached to his ammo belt, and snapped his bayonet out of the sheath. He leaped into the clearing and pounced onto Warlord Three's back. In one movement he spun Warlord Three around and grabbed the Uzi.

Warlord Two charged toward Gerard with his Uzi muzzle raised. "Motherfucker!"

Gerard flung Warlord Three's Uzi into the woods. He grabbed Warlord Three's shoulders and pulled them downward; at the same time, he drove his knee upward and slammed it into Warlord Three's solar plexus. Even through the roaring sheets of rain, Gerard heard the crack. With one hand he held Warlord Three in a half-nelson, and with the other hand he held the edge of his bayonet against Warlord Three's jugular vein.

"Stop!" Gerard screamed. "Put it down!"

Warlord Two jerked to a stop.

"You come closer and I'll slit his throat," Gerard said. He pressed the blade more firmly into Warlord Three's neck, and when he looked down, he saw a thin line of blood trickling down from the blade. Parker had been right to tell Gerard to sharpen his bayonet before FTX. He remembered one of the instructors during STT teaching Third Platoon how to kill someone by cutting his neck. The images from movies where killers pulled people's heads backward was nonsense; to cut effectively, you were supposed to shove your victim's head *forward*, pressing his neck into the blade as you sliced. Gerard was ready.

He had them—all three Warlords—at least for the moment. Gerard had a strong hold on Warlord Three, a child of fourteen or fifteen years whose upper body strength was no match for a 6'4" soldier so close to the end of infantry training. Warlord Two was frozen in the middle of the assembly area with his Uzi pointed at Gerard, his arm trembling. Warlord One was inching Parker, bit by bit, across the clearing, closer to Gerard.

"You let him go," Warlord One said as he dragged Parker. "You hurt my kid brother, I'll kill you."

Gerard held tight to Warlord Three. In the middle of the sea of prostrate bodies, Gerard saw something move in his peripheral vision. Gerard turned his head. Warlord Two saw Gerard looking and turned his head to look too. Shit—it was Libby. Libby was high-crawling right toward Gerard. Drill Sergeant Womack stood up and lurched in Libby's direction.

"Libby, stay down!" Womack screamed.

Warlord Two raised his Uzi and pulled the trigger. A spray of bullets ripped through Womack's midriff, and he buckled over.

Romberg stood up and threw his rifle into the woods. "My weapon, my weapon!" he yelled. He dove headfirst into a mud puddle and began flopping around.

Womack writhed on the ground with his hands on his stomach. Warlord Two turned toward Romberg and then back to Gerard. He turned again to face Romberg. Warlord One had stopped scooting toward Gerard and stood with his gun pressing forcefully into the side of Parker's neck. Warlord Two looked back and forth between Gerard and the mud puddle where Romberg fluttered and splashed.

"Drill Sergeant, are you hurt?" said Libby.

"Shut up!" said Warlord One.

Warlord Two walked cautiously toward the mud puddle. He stood at the edge of the water, pointing his Uzi down into it. "Get out, bitch. Get outta there," he said to Romberg.

Warlord Two turned around to Warlord One. Romberg's arm emerged from the mud puddle and grabbed the muzzle of Warlord Two's Uzi. It was like a cartoon. Romberg yanked, and in the next moment Warlord Two was in the water with Romberg, flopping and splashing, fighting to keep water out of his lungs. The Uzi flew out of the mud puddle, as if on its own, and Romberg leaped up holding a bayonet. He jumped down onto Warlord Two. Gerard feared there would be more blood, but when Romberg landed, like Hulk Hogan in a wrestling match, he slammed the handle-end of the bayonet onto Warlord Two's skull, knocking him unconscious. Romberg grabbed Warlord Two by the shirt and flung him out of the puddle and into the mud.

Romberg rose from the mud puddle, holding his bayonet high above him in a ridiculously ceremonious way. He walked out of the water, clutching the bayonet with two hands, wielding it like a sword. He strode among the bodies of Bravo Company toward Warlord One. Water poured from the sky and streaked the mud on Romberg's face. During brief flashes of lightning Gerard thought he saw Romberg grinning.

Warlord One's eyes were wide. "Tell him to stop, He-ro," he said. "Tell him to stop or Parker gets it."

"Fuck you, man," Parker said. "Kelderman, tell him to fuck off."

"Shut up, *Private*," said Warlord One, shoving the pistol into Parker's neck.

"You ain't gonna shoot me," said Parker.

"Shut up," said Warlord One. "Do it, He-ro. Tell him to stop, and let my brother go."

Gerard paused a moment.

"No," said Gerard.

"Mother fucker," said Warlord One, shaking his head.

"He said no, shithead," Romberg said, coming closer.

"Man, fuck you," said Warlord One.

"Fuck *you*," Gerard said.

"Fuckin' white-ass piece of mother fuckin'—"

Warlord Three broke free of Gerard's hold and ran away. He headed for the woods where Warlord Two's Uzi had flown.

"And that is it, boys and girls," said Warlord One, shoving Parker to the ground. "Game over." He pointed the gun at Parker's head.

Someone rose up behind Warlord One and tackled his shoulders. It was Drill Sergeant Hammer. He yanked Warlord One into the mud and grabbed his Uzi. Hammer rolled onto the top of Warlord One and punched his face repeatedly.

"Stay down, Bravo Company!" Drill Sergeant Cifuentes yelled from across the assembly area. "There's still one more."

"He's gone, Drill Sergeant," said Wiley, standing up.

"Get down," said Carroll, yanking Wiley back into the mud.

"Drill Sergeant Womack, are you okay?" said Libby. He was looking into Womack's face.

That's right—Womack had been shot. Gerard squinted to try to see through the streaming rain as he walked toward Womack.

Drill Sergeant Hammer pointed at some of the soldiers. "You three, get over here and tie this one up so he can't get away. You and you, get the other one out of the mud and tie him up too."

Hammer lifted Warlord One's Uzi from the mud and wiped it off. He turned it over and examined the side.

Parker stood next to him. "You got to slide the safety off, on the right side of the receiver."

"Man, Private, I know," Hammer said, turning the Uzi over.

"It's right there," Parker said.

"Where?" said Hammer.

"It's an Uzi," Parker said. "Right there on the back of the grip."

"Shit," said Hammer.

"Time to die!" Warlord Three emerged from the woods. He had found Warlord Two's Uzi. He walked toward Gerard, Parker, and Hammer.

"Got it," said Hammer. He held up the Uzi and pointed it at Warlord Three, who came closer.

Warlord Three pointed his gun at Gerard; Hammer pointed his gun at Warlord Three.

"Motherfucker cut me," said Warlord Three.

"I didn't mean to," Gerard said.

"Shut up!"

"No, you shut up," said Hammer. "You come closer and I'll shoot your ass."

But Warlord Three kept walking toward Gerard. Had he forgotten about Parker? Wasn't this whole thing supposed to be about Parker?

"You ain't gonna shoot my ass," said Warlord Three. "You ain't gonna shoot a brother."

Cooper stepped in front of Gerard and faced Warlord Three. Where had he come from?

"Move!" said Warlord Three. "Or I'm gonna shoot two white boys."

"Man, it ain't firing," said Hammer, yanking the trigger to shoot Warlord Three.

"Gimme that," said Parker. He yanked the Uzi away from Hammer and fiddled with the safety switch.

"Bye bye," said Warlord Three. He pointed his gun at Cooper, who was still protecting Gerard by standing in front of him. Warlord Three pulled the trigger, but *his* trigger didn't work either!

"Ha!" said Romberg. "It doesn't work! We get to kick your *ass*!"

Warlord Three turned from Cooper and pointed his Uzi at Romberg.

"No!" said Gerard. "Romberg, get down." He scrambled past Cooper as Warlord Three fired the Uzi at Romberg. Gerard shoved Romberg down. Bullets sprayed the tree trunks.

Romberg dove into the mud. "What the fuck? I thought his gun didn't work."

And then there was another burst of fire, and bullets plinked into Warlord Three's back, tore through his torso, and sprayed out the front of his body. He buckled and dropped. Parker had figured out how to fire the Uzi. The rest of Bravo Company still lay in the mud.

Hammer stood up. "Alright, everybody up," he said. "You got those other two tied up?"

"Yes, Drill Sergeant," said a First Platoon soldier.

"Good. Keep 'em down," Hammer said.

"Womack needs a medic," Phillips said.

"Drill Sergeant Cifuentes, radio the medivac," Hammer said. "We need MPs too."

"Drill Sergeant, can the medics bring Womack back?" said Libby.

"Back from what?" said Womack, who was still doubled over, clutching his stomach.

"Ahhhh!" said Libby. "I didn't know you were, um—"

"Alive?" Womack said. "Good God, Libby, give me a chance."

But Womack was bleeding badly. He didn't see the blood that had pooled into the water and mud surrounding him. He was probably numb enough from shock that he didn't feel anything. At least two bullets had ripped through his stomach.

"There's more coming!" said Berkowicz. "I see them through the trees."

"Fuck," Hammer said. "Everybody get back down and high crawl for the trees."

"Mother fuckers," said Libby. He unsheathed his bayonet and stood up. "I'm not letting them kill anyone else!"

"Libby, I'm not dead," Womack said.

"It's Echo Company," said Carroll.

"Oh fuck," Hammer said, standing up. "Fucking Echo Company."

Gerard faced Libby and grabbed his shoulders. "Libby, settle down. It's over. Give me that bayonet."

"Move, Kelderman!" Libby said. "I'm kicking some ass."

"Libby, it's Echo Company, you dumbfuck," said Berkowicz.

"Gimme that," said Gerard, reaching for Libby's bayonet. But as he reached for Libby, Libby tripped and fell; and as Libby fell he grabbed hold of Gerard's ammo belt to try to steady himself, so Gerard went down too. Libby hit the ground, still clutching his bayonet, which pointed straight upward. Gerard fell sideways, directly onto the bayonet. The blade sliced through his right side and penetrated deep into his torso.

It burned; the metal slid further into his flesh and felt instantly hot. Then came the pain: it crawled from the tip of the bayonet deep inside him outward toward his skin. Gerard rolled onto his back and tried to breathe, but his lungs felt stuck—snagged on the bayonet blade. He tried to draw in air, but the sharp heat in his side stopped each breath.

"Kelderman," said Libby.

Gerard opened his eyes. He didn't remember closing them.

"Kelderman, don't move," Libby said.

Libby was leaned over Gerard, peering into his face, looking as stupid as ever. It made Gerard giggle, which was painful but allowed him to draw in a few short breaths of air.

"Move away, Libby," said Hammer.

There was gun fire close by, through the pines.

"Somebody tell Echo Company to stop!" said Hammer.

"We can take 'em!" Gerard heard Romberg saying. "We've got real weapons now, with real bullets." Romberg was waving the Uzi that Warlord Three had dropped in the mud. "Let's go."

"Romberg, don't do it," said Wiley.

And Gerard giggled again.

"I'm kidding, fuckface," said Romberg.

"Womack's hurt, and you're still fucking around!" screamed Wiley. "Not to mention the dead body on the ground right in front of you."

"Yeah, but he's a bad-guy," Romberg said.

"You're going to be okay, Kelderman," Libby was leaning over Gerard, breathing into Gerard's face and talking too loudly. Gerard's eyelids were lazy and heavy. He blinked slowly. Sleep would feel so good right now.

"I'm just gonna take a nap," Gerard said.

"Snap out of it Kelderman!" said Hammer. He grabbed Gerard's jaw and shook it back and forth.

"Okay, okay," said Gerard.

"You stay awake, Kelderman, you hear me?" Hammer said.

Yes, yes, Gerard heard him.

"You hear me, Kelderman?" said Hammer.

Yeah, yeah.

"Kelderman!"

"Yes," Gerard said.

"Chopper's on the way," Hammer said. "You hang on."

"Hi!" Cooper's face came into view.

"Get back, Cooper," said Hammer. "Unless you're gonna heal him."

"No," Cooper said. "He'll be fine."

Ha! Gerard was going to be fine. Hammer propped Gerard's head on a wadded-up poncho. The rain had stopped. Gerard's eyesight suddenly sharpened. He could clearly see heavy drops of water dripping from tree limbs and pine cones. He could see little bits of stubble on Hammer's black face and white steam rising from Libby's shoulders.

Drill sergeants from other platoons shoved the soldiers away from Womack. Two drill sergeants hunched over him, holding dressings against his wounds and muttering; Gerard couldn't hear. First Sergeant McFadden herded the soldiers into a company formation at the other end of the assembly area. Gerard saw rows and rows of red lights through the dark; the flashlights were on. Drill sergeants were taking attendance.

With every breath Gerard felt heat and pain. He was glad he had heard Cooper speak, because otherwise he would have wondered if he was about to die. Had Anna felt pain when she died? Her death was sudden, Gerard now remembered—very sudden.

"No, no!"

Gerard turned slowly to the right and saw Parker hunched over the dead body of Warlord Three. Parker's face was in his hands, and he was sobbing. Warlord Three's wilted corpse was twisted with its arms splayed in the mud high above its head.

"I shot him," Parker said. "I killed him. He's just a kid." Parker cried into the palms of his hands.

"Take it easy, Kelderman," Hammer said. "You got a bayonet in you, but you're gonna be fine."

Breath—pain, breath—pain. Gerard felt dizzy, and as he looked at Parker, Parker transformed into Willem Kelderman, sobbing over a dead body. Anna. The body was Anna. Gerard remembered. She had just died. Gerard closed his eyes and pictured the scene. Anna was on a brick floor, outside. Gerard was watching the patio from inside. It was the patio of a café—the Café De Fenix on the outskirts Antwerp.

"It's okay, man." Romberg squatted next to Parker and put a hand on his shoulder. "It's not your fault. You saved us. You had to."

Gerard watched Parker crying and felt the familiar dance deep in his abdomen. The bayonet had pierced into the center of his stomach, but the dancing pushed up past the pain, up his esophagus and bumped at the back of his throat. He remembered the comment made by his four-year-old cousin, Elizabeth, when told the news of Anna's death. "But I want to play with her. When will she be done being dead?"

Gerard felt his eyes moisten. He was too tired to fight. He was in too much pain, and he knew there was blood flowing out of his body onto the ground. He wouldn't have to fight it now, would he, because he'd been stabbed through the torso with a bayonet. It was okay to cry about that; his fellow soldiers wouldn't know the difference.

Tears rolled off the edge of his lower eyelids, and then the flood rushed out. Gerard cried softly. He tried to steady his blubbering lips. His shoulders and chest shook. Warm tears coursed down his cheeks.

♦     ♦     ♦

The hour Anna died, the rain had just stopped. It was late in the afternoon. July. July 19, 1987. *We Will Never Hold You Again.* Gerard was seven years old. Willem was stooped over her limp body on the wet patio, starting C.P.R.

*"Kom binnen, Jongen. Wij zullen wat snoep vinden."*

A well-meaning café guest stood in the way to keep Gerard from seeing his sister and nudged him into the bar with the promise of candy. It was as if, from the first minutes after Anna's death, there was an unspoken conspiracy—that included complete strangers as well as his family—to shield him from his sister's death. And as Gerard remembered the kind lady leading him away to go find some candy, his brain rapidly rewound to hours before that moment when Willem, Gerard, and Anna—cuddly, sweet baby Anna— were on their way to the café.

Willem was driving Gerard and Anna west out of Antwerp on the *Expressweg* to the Café De Fenix. He pulled the car into the De Fenix parking lot between the abbey and the café. Gerard couldn't form a complete picture of the place, but he remembered a tall brick wall and green elm trees. Willem was to meet Margareta Van Leuven and Joske Vermeulen at the café adjoining the abbey— diamond business, no doubt. Gerard considered that maybe Willem was on his way to have a tryst with Margareta, but then he remembered from Rebecca's letter that his dad's affair hadn't started until later that year, in December.

Willem was personal friends with the proprietors of the Café De Fenix, so he was greeted with the warm welcome that followed him everywhere around the globe. Inneke and Rutgeer Coelbrant were a husband and wife team who ran the café. Their own house was adjacent to the café, like a parish rectory. Gerard remembered that

Willem had brought him to this café on their previous trip to Antwerp. Willem's favorite beer in all the world—until that day—was the De Fenix Dubbel Trappist in a wide, glass goblet. Gerard had heard that the beer tap in the café was connected directly via underground pipes to the casks across the street at the abbey where monks brewed the beer. Willem stocked the cellar at the Kasteel with bottles of De Fenix Dubbel, though he preferred to have it fresh from the vats.

Gerard realized now that Willem had never gone back to the Café De Fenix since that day, or drunk any De Fenix beer. And later that summer when they had returned to Evans Glen and after Anna was buried, Willem had ransacked the cedar cabinet in the living room at the Kasteel where he kept all his beer glasses. Every chalice with the De Fenix logo was thrown out—Willem tossed them all into a cardboard box and dumped them into the garbage bin outside. Gerard guessed that Rebecca had not forced him to do this; it was probably Willem's own doing—a ritual to help him cope with his grief. For Gerard there had never been any rituals, because he'd never been allowed to mourn; his anguish had been tidily packed away—first by the De Fenix candy-lady, then by his parents, and later by his own subconscious mind. For years everyone else was allowed to cry; even Meredith would cry whenever she and Gerard walked to Unity cemetery to see Anna's grave. Willem cried as he emptied the cellar of all bottles of De Fenix Dubbel. Gerard remembered thinking, as a seven-year-old, that if parting with all his yummy beer was so upsetting to Willem, he should stop throwing it out! Only now did Gerard understand: Anna had died at the Café De Fenix and Willem didn't want any reminders.

When the Keldermans arrived at the café that afternoon, Margareta was there, sitting at a table on the wide patio. She was hunched over a small, hand-held mirror, dabbing her mouth with lipstick. Her legs were crossed, and the backs of her smooth, white calves peeked out through the slit in her black skirt. Willem and Gerard walked out to meet her. Anna was flopped in Willem's arms with her head on his shoulder, slowly kicking one leg; she'd missed her nap that day.

Margareta snapped her mirror closed and stood up. *"Dag, Wim."* She was the only one who ever called Willem 'Wim.'

*"Engels, Margareta, Engels,"* said Willem. *"De kinderen spreken nog geen Vlaams."*

How interesting that Willem had told Margareta the children didn't *yet* speak Flemish, as if Willem had always had a secret plan to teach Flemish to Anna and Gerard behind Rebecca's back. And even though Gerard didn't yet speak Flemish at the time, his seven-year-old brain had accurately recorded these Flemish sentences. Margareta and Willem switched to English, out of courtesy to Gerard and Anna. (Gerard smiled; the idea—showing courtesy to kids. Willem had always been adamant about that.) Margareta and Willem hugged lightly and exchanged three cheek kisses, alternating one cheek after the other. Not a big deal, Gerard thought now; this was a common custom in Belgium among close friends. Gerard wouldn't notice the more intimate embraces until months later.

"What time is it?" said Willem.

"Exactly two o'clock," said Margareta, sitting back down.

Willem pulled out a chair. "Where's Joske?"

Margareta snorted. "Oh, you can't be serious. We told him two o'clock, so when do you think he'll actually get here?"

Rutgeer Coelbrant strode onto the patio—laughing and wiping his hands on his green apron—and gave Willem and Margareta each a hearty hug. The talk was too quick for Gerard to follow; Rutgeer spoke only Flemish. When they were done Rutgeer led Gerard and Anna through the café to his house and his backyard where they would get to play. Gerard remembered their yard well with its trim lawn circled by a hard-packed, sand pathway. When they walked through his house and onto the back lawn, Anna perked up. She couldn't have remembered the place from the last time they'd visited—she'd been nine months old—but she saw the yard and the toys. There was a tricycle, a plastic car with pedals, a basket of balls, and a sandbox. Rutgeer's own children had grown up and moved out, but he and Inneke kept toys in the yard for just such occasions. Gerard looked at his watch: two-ten. They had almost two hours ahead of them to play in that glorious yard. "Four o'clock, Gerard," Willem had said back on the patio. "You and your sister should return here at exactly four o'clock so we can head back into the city."

Gerard set the alarm on his digital watch for three-fifty. That would give him ten minutes to convince Anna that they really would have to leave; he knew that by then she'd be having so much fun it would be difficult to pull her away.

Out on the café patio, Willem and Margareta were probably sipping from glass goblets of De Fenix Dubbel. Sometimes Willem ordered bread and cheese—*Trappistenkaas*, another specialty of the abbey. The waiter would probably be bringing them large pieces of fresh, brown bread, a small crock of butter, and a long, thick slice of *Trappistenkaas*. Gerard now wondered how long the affair between Willem and Margareta had been brewing. Maybe it was Joske Vermeulen's fault, and all the times he was late provided Margareta and Willem time to build intimacy. Did the romance develop over time, or did Anna's death and Rebecca's unending criticism of Willem cause it to erupt? Maybe Margareta had been waiting for years and when Willem was finally ready, when the time was ripe, she was there to help Willem work through his pain. And what did Margareta want? What void in her own life did she need to fill? Gerard couldn't remember if Margareta Van Leuven was married, or even what kind of person she really was. She could have been hoping to entice Willem away from Rebecca and then live with Willem in the United States. Or perhaps Margareta wanted to lure Willem back to Belgium, to team up and open a family diamond business—a mom and pop store in Antwerp close to Central Station, or a wholesale outlet near the port. Or maybe, like Sylvia with Gilberto, Margareta had wanted boisterous sex with no strings and no commitments.

"The chopper's comin', Kelderman. You hang on." Drill Sergeant Hammer pressed a balled-up shirt against Gerard's right side, above his hip. Gerard had a vague memory he'd been injured—stuck with a bayonet, that was it, because of clumsy Libby.

Even in the dark of night he could see clearly: two drill sergeants were hunched over him, Hammer and Gundacker. Fuzzy sounds faded in and out, as if someone were tuning a radio (the Titty Twister!) and couldn't quite find the station. He heard the distant *fwap fwap fwap* of a helicopter and was aware that Drill Sergeants Hammer and Gundacker were talking; their voices sounded canned, as if crackling through a transistor radio. *'Loosen his clothing,' 'Don't push too tight on that wound—the bayonet's still in him.'*

"Shouldn't we pull the bayonet out of there?" Libby's eager face popped into view over Hammer's shoulder.

"You want him to bleed to death?" Hammer said.

"Get into that formation, Private," said Drill Sergeant Gundacker.

"How's Drill Sergeant Womack?" Gerard said.

"Fine, fine," said Hammer. "He's good." Hammer's eyes met Gundacker's for a brief moment and then turned to Gerard. "You concentrate on you right now. Chopper's here."

The *fwap fwap fwap* was louder now, and the assembly area flooded with light from the descending helicopter. *There* was a jagged pain, right where the bayonet was. *Pulse*—more pain. Gerard felt his eyes roll up into his head, and there was Anna again, giggling in that back yard.

Gerard and Anna played and played. Anna sat on the tricycle while Gerard pushed her around the packed sand path. A few times she tried to pedal herself (*"I* do it. I do it by my*self."*), but her chubby little legs weren't strong enough to pull the tricycle along the sand. And they played in the sandbox too. Anna loved sandboxes. Her favorite game was to scoop sand with a plastic shovel and fling it out of the box, cackling the whole time. When Gerard tried to tell her to stop she pointed the shovel at him.

"No. No throwing sand. That's very bad," she said, punctuating each word by jabbing the shovel in the air. Now *she* was doing the scolding; she loved role-reversal. And then she happily continued scooping and flinging.

"Wake up, Kelderman!" said Drill Sergeant Hammer. "We're almost there."

Gerard was on a stretcher in the helicopter. He was slipping in and out of consciousness and felt like he had a high fever.

God, he missed his sister. How many years had it been? Something like fifteen? If she'd lived, she'd be finishing her junior year of high school right now. But to Gerard she would always be a baby—a happy little baby who loved to dance in circles and yell 'hooray' at the ends of songs and suck mouthfuls of warm, dirty bathwater from washcloths. Gerard's tears had dried now, but it was too late—he'd cried before the chopper had lifted off, and now he was remembering. He'd destroyed what Cooper called the wall of oblivion—the divine mercy that had caused him to forget. Were it not for divine mercy, Cooper had said, we would remember every detail of all our past lives and go insane; the brain could never handle such overload. But where was divine mercy now, in this life? Only in this moment did Gerard finally agree with what his subconscious had long held: it was better for him not to remember how his sister had died. The scenes from the Café De Fenix were now streaming through him. He couldn't stop them. Gerard's defenses were rapidly thawing, he couldn't run to his cello, and his mind wasn't strong enough to create its own distractions. He was too weak to stop himself from remembering. Even amid the pounding of the helicopter blades and Drill Sergeant Hammer's yelling, Gerard's consciousness faded out again.

It was during his baby sister's sand flinging that Gerard's watch alarm sounded.

"Time to go, Anna," Gerard said. "We have to go back to Daddy."

"No!" Anna said, pointing the shovel at Gerard. She had chocolate smeared around her lips and on her cheeks. Sand clung to the chocolate, making Anna's face look like a piece of Shake-and-Bake chicken.

"Get your shoes and socks, Anna," said Gerard. But Anna ignored him ('norging' she called it) and continued playing. Gerard dug around in the sandbox and found the socks and shoes. Anna had them stuffed into the bottom of a green, plastic bucket and then filled the bucket with sand.

"We'll put your shoes on later," Gerard said. "Come on, sweetie, let's go." He reached under her arms and lifted her up.

"I don't want to," she said, resting her head on his shoulder.

Gerard walked out the gate and back toward the café. "Are you tired, Anna? Do you need a nap?"

"No," she said, grinding the back of her grubby wrist into her eye.

When Gerard stepped onto the patio with Anna at two minutes before four o'clock, Willem and Margareta were slouched in their chairs, sipping beer and giggling. The table was littered with crumbs and bits of cheese, uncut diamonds, a pair of tweezers, and a magnifying glass. Where was Joske Vermeulen? Gerard knew Joske wasn't punctual, but he was now two hours late.

"Gerard!" said Willem. "You're right on time, as always."

"I wanna get down," Anna said. She slid out of Gerard's arms and stood on the floor.

"Unfortunately, our Joske Vermeulen is not on time, so you two can go play some more," Willem said.

Gerard sighed. He'd had enough play time; he was tired and ready to leave. A snap of thunder from the overcast sky rattled the patio furniture.

"We should go inside," Margareta said, leaning back in her chair and staring upward. "It's going to rain."

"Dad, you said we would leave at four," said Gerard.

"Well I didn't imagine that Joske would be this late," Willem said. "We have to wait for him. I can't leave Antwerp until I've seen him."

Gerard sighed and looked at the table. "Hey, can I have some cheese?"

"Sure," said Margareta. She reached for the plate.

Gerard took two chunks of cheese. "Anna, you want some cheese? Anna?" Gerard looked behind him and then at Willem. "Dad, where's Anna?"

Willem was looking at the table. "I can't find my tweezers."

The thunder cracked again. Water splashed down from the sky. The patrons on the patio grabbed their coats and purses and rushed for the inside of the café.

"Come on, let's get inside," Margareta said as she gathered the diamonds from the table.

"Where are the tweezers?" said Willem. He picked up the magnifying glass and his black leather pouch and pulled his jacket over his head.

Where was Anna? They all rushed inside, but Anna wasn't there either. She was gone. None of them knew they had seen her alive for the last time. She'd slipped out of sight for ten seconds, but that was all she needed. They didn't see her when she'd reached up to the table and grabbed Willem's tweezers. None of them saw her toddle away, around the patio corner. And none of them could possibly have known that when she'd turned the corner she had found an electrical socket on the outside wall, which was a perfect fit for the metal tweezers. It wasn't until after the storm passed and all the café patrons surged back outside to help look for Anna that a waiter found her—long after CPR would have done any good. She was lying on her side on the patio floor in a puddle of water. Gerard remembered seeing the soft bottoms of her small, bare feet, before the portly lady jumped in front of him and nudged him back inside with the promise of candy.

But Gerard had seen her. He remembered. He had tried to get over to have a closer look, but the candy-lady had assured Gerard that his sister was going to be fine. He had managed one more glance as the woman shoved him through the patio doors. The tweezers lay on the floor next to her open hand. Anna would have said they were 'benext' to her.

# Eighteen

Drill Sergeant Hammer clicked his heels together. "Platoon, atten—tion!"

Third Platoon stood rigid. Gerard smiled.

"Congratulations, men," said Hammer. "Dismissed!"

And there was instant mumbling and smiling and laughing.

"Fuck yes. *Fuck* yes!" Romberg danced and stomped. "Rock and motherfucking goddamn roll."

"We did it, man," said Fuller.

Berkowicz and Wiley slapped a high five.

"Yeah, buddy."

"Infantry blue."

"I am *outta* here."

"Gimme a cigarette, man."

The infantry school graduation ceremony had just ended; three companies had "turned blue" and entered the ranks of the infantry on the clipped lawn of the sunny parade field. It was 11:30 on a hot Saturday morning. The soldiers of Third Platoon milled around, pumping fists and whacking backs. They hooah-ed and bumped chests and yelled with open throats and wide smiles. They had survived infantry training and would never have to go through it again.

"Yes!" Libby slapped Gerard on the side.

"Ow, careful," said Gerard.

"Oh, sorry. Forgot."

Gerard still ached from the bayonet and from the three hours of surgery he'd undergone to stop the internal bleeding. He'd spent four days in the hospital and then had returned to Bravo Company in time for the graduation ceremony. His platoon mates had given him a nice homecoming. There were balloons tied to his bunk and a card on his pillow, signed by all the soldiers of Third Platoon. He'd smiled and cried again.

"You're a fucking Hallmark commercial, Kelderman," Romberg had said.

Now that graduation was over, everyone would be moving on. Parker, Romberg, and Cooper would start airborne school in two days (Gerard's airborne school assignment was now delayed a month while his wound healed). Final duty assignments varied. Parker had orders to go to the 82nd Airborne Division at Fort Bragg in North Carolina. Romberg would stay at Fort Benning and be assigned to the Third Ranger Battalion, and Gerard and Cooper were shipping out to Korea. Korea! No one had ever told Gerard about Korea as an option for an infantryman. It was only after he had received his orders a few days ago that he'd learned about the Korea assignment: one long year helping South Korea guard the demilitarized zone against the North Koreans. Gerard couldn't have cared less about the fucking Koreans, North or South. Let them defend their own goddamned border.

"That kicks ass, man," Wiley had said. "You might get to fight some commies. Real commies." Wiley would go to the 82nd with Parker.

Cooper had smiled and said it would be a good experience for both of them.

"Have you ever been to Korea?" Gerard had asked Cooper.

"No."

"Then how do you know it's going to be a good experience?" Gerard had said. "What if it sucks?"

"I've decided that it won't," Cooper had said.

Then Gerard had smiled. Cooper. Maybe some day Gerard would learn how to control his feelings, how to make thought the master and sentiment the slave. At the moment he was a little depressed because all his friends were going to start airborne school without him; his injury had fouled up the schedule. For a month he'd stay assigned to Bravo 1/47th and then start airborne school when he was fully healed.

"You get to work for the first sergeant," Berkowicz had said. "That's scary."

Even the drill sergeants feared First Sergeant McFadden, the way he would stand quietly in a dark corner of the company area and watch drill exercises with his arms folded. But the first sergeant had visited Gerard in his hospital room after surgery, and he was actually a nice guy! He was jovial and smiling and told Gerard that since Bravo Company was now between training cycles there wouldn't be much to do, so Gerard would get to take it easy for a month before starting airborne school. Gerard hadn't told Berkowicz any of this; it was more fun letting Berkowicz believe that Gerard would have to suffer a harsh month with the first sergeant.

During his hospital visit, McFadden had told Gerard some details about Drill Sergeant Womack, who was recovering down the hall on the same hospital ward. Three bullets had torn through his body, one of which lodged in his spine and took the surgeons seven hours to remove. He would need many months of physical therapy before he'd be able to walk properly again. The first sergeant suspected Womack would be given a medical discharge from the army.

"Womack's gonna get to go teach math sooner than he thought," said Fuller. He pulled out two cigarettes, one for him and the other for Hopson.

"Teach math?" Gerard said.

"Yeah," said Fuller. "He was gonna take a twenty-year retirement in four years and then teach high school math in Atlanta. He's been taking correspondence courses for his teaching license."

Gerard shook his head. "How the hell do you know— Oh, never mind."

"Cool," said Hopson. He lit his cigarette.

It was weird watching Hopson and Fuller stand there casually smoking, with Drill Sergeants so close by. But it was finished. The big game was over. Graduation was done, putting an end to the mind games of the relationship between trainee and drill sergeant.

The soldiers were literally smoking and joking in the Georgia sun. A throng of civilian spectators descended on Bravo Company from the grandstand like an army of ants.

There was hugging and smiling and kissing and picture-taking and "this is my Mom" and Romberg's nineteen-year-old sister was a shapely Barbie-doll knockout and a few dads were in military uniforms themselves, even one bald fellow in a Coast Guard outfit who looked like Captain Stubing.

"Gerard!" Rebecca Ward tossed her arms around Gerard's neck and kissed him on one cheek and then the other. "Jesus, how much weight have you lost?"

"About thirty-five pounds," said Gerard. When he last weighed himself he was 215.

"There's our conscript!" said Willem, vigorously shaking Gerard's hand even as Rebecca still clung to him.

"Ow, ow, ow," said Gerard.

"Oh, sorry," said Rebecca. "Which side is it?"

"This one," said Gerard, patting his right side. "It punctured my stomach, but I'm okay."

"You poor baby," said Rebecca.

The sight of his mother and the feel of her arms filled Gerard's eyes with warm tears. Since last week he'd cried several times a day over the simplest things: Cooper's smiles, Romberg's silliness, Parker's friendliness. They'd all visited him in the hospital; he'd awoken to find them crowded around his bed and had cried upon seeing them.

"Hi Mom," said Gerard, sniffling.

"I've missed you, Gerard," said Rebecca.

Gerard cried harder. It made his side hurt. He didn't care that his platoon mates could see and hear everything. In fact, they all started shuffling away. Gerard wasn't the only one crying in the arms of a mother or girlfriend or wife. It was okay. It was cool.

"I remember, Mom," said Gerard. "I remember about Anna. I remember all of it, every detail."

Rebecca Ward pulled back from the hug, and she must have seen in Gerard's face that he really did know and he really did remember. Now Willem started sniffling too. Gerard's mom hugged him again.

"I'm so sorry, Gerard. I'm sorry, I'm sorry. We didn't know what else to do."

"It was my fault, Mom," said Gerard. "I could have saved her. I only looked away for a second, just a second, and then it rained and—"

"Gerard, it's okay," said Willem. He wiped his eyes with a handkerchief. "Don't do that. Don't think like that. I've been doing that for fifteen years, and don't you start."

"But Dad, it's tr—"

"No, Gerard," said his mom. She held him tighter and rocked him. "It's okay. It's okay." She pressed her hand against the back of his head.

"I want her back," said Gerard. "I want to go back and do it over, and this time I would be more careful. This time I—"

"You can't go back," said Willem. He put his arms around Gerard and Rebecca.

"She's gone, Gerard," said Rebecca. "It took me a long time to realize that she's really gone. I cleaned out her room, finally. It's a guest room now."

Gerard was amazed that his mom had let go of Anna's bedroom, but Rebecca's advantage was the fifteen years she'd had to work through her grief and arrive at a sense of closure. Gerard, with his fresh knowledge and memory of the accident, was only now taking the very first steps of a long journey through grief and anger and confusion and who knows what else. He'd had four days in the hospital to think and think and think. Fifteen years of suppressed memories now at the surface of his awareness had made his brain spend those hospital days sifting through everything and trying to make sense of it. Cooper would have agreed with Willem that there's no going back, but Gerard knew that he had to go back, in his mind, to get through it all and come out the other side of all the anguish and pain.

No matter how hard he tried, Gerard arrived at the same conclusion every time: his sister's death had been *his* fault. He was guilty. He was responsible. He was the last one to put her down, the last one to have held her and touched her and felt her warmth and talked to her and to be hugged back by her. Why had his attention left Anna? Because he wanted a piece of cheese. No wonder Sylvia's unending disapproval of his eating habits had always made him feel so bad about himself. His subconscious mind knew all along that because he was a glutton, his kid sister had died.

Gerard had tried to come at the issue from many angles to try to bat away the fast-pitch of guilt. That fucking Joske Vermeulen, for example, always late. It was Joske forever fouling up other people's plans because of his inability to be organized. If the group was in a rush and had to be somewhere, it was Joske who would slow everything down. "Can we just stop at a cash machine? I won't be but a minute." If Joske had arrived at the Café De Fenix at the appointed time, Anna would not have died.

Or the tweezers. If only Anna hadn't grabbed the tweezers from the table. Gerard had tried a few times to convince himself that the whole tragedy really was Willem's fault, as Rebecca had always charged, because of the tweezers. Willem should have been more careful; Willem should have been more mindful about his tools. He should have realized that the table was low enough that Anna could see everything on it and reach whatever she chose.

Then there was the European electricity angle. Electrical wall sockets in Belgium were 220 volts strong—more than enough current to kill a two-year old under the right conditions, which that day at the De Fenix were perfect. *That* wasn't Gerard's fault. If the voltage had been 115 or 120, Anna might have survived. Or if the café had been outfitted with ground fault circuit interrupters, the circuit wouldn't have been completed long enough and there would have been no current even to cause Anna much harm. And the damned holes in the outlet were round—a perfect fit for the tweezers she had grabbed. Anna had been used to being told "No" when she approached electrical outlets back in Virginia, but the sockets in Belgium were different; no one had ever told her about those, that they were off-limits. Sharp-pronged tweezers and a small, round hole in the wall; she had done her duty as a two-year-old and found a snug fit.

Finally there was the rain—the drenching surge of Belgian rain. The clouds had opened so suddenly and the water had fallen so quickly that the surface of the patio turned instantly into a glassy pond of water, just in time for Anna—in her bare feet—to become a conduit for the surge of voltage from the outlet. The logical side of Gerard's brain knew that he had no control over the weather.

But all these excuses, as sensible as they were, didn't relieve Gerard's burden. Pointing at all the other reasons for Anna's death was a cop-out, like a misguided avoidance of the guilt he'd been carrying around all these years. It was almost too much for him, and he wished his guilt had come to the surface of his consciousness much earlier, when he'd had a support network more familiar to him: the cello, the music parlor, and Meredith. But here it was, and he had to start the work now of sifting through these feelings. Then from another angle, it wasn't at all sensible that he should feel guilty. He was seven years old! Willem's guilt was more justified: he was the parent. Who would believe that a seven-year-old could bear full responsibility for the safety of a two-year-old toddler? No one, though Gerard suspected it would now take many years before he'd finally come to believe it and to feel it.

Rebecca and Willem released Gerard. They dabbed and sniffled and smiled. Gerard laughed. Rebecca puffed her cheeks and blew out air. Willem held her hand. Rebecca squeezed back and smiled.

"Okay, then," said Gerard. "So now I'm an infantryman."

"On his way to defend the free world against communism!" said Willem.

"Unbelievable." Gerard shook his head. "Korea. I don't want to go."

"You'll be fine," said Rebecca. "Can you take your cello along?"

Gerard laughed. A cello in the demilitarized zone. "I don't know," he said.

It had been three months since Gerard had played the cello—the longest he'd ever gone without even touching the instrument. And now he was reminded how much he missed it. (Would he now cry about that too?) He imagined gripping the neck and bow and sitting beneath the shelves in the music parlor. The piece before him was the Rachmaninoff *Cello and Piano Sonata, op. 19.* Which part, which part? Gerard could see himself there in the parlor, playing, as if he were standing outside himself watching. The first two movements of that Rachmaninoff were very difficult, but no, those weren't the movements. He was playing the third movement—the matchless Andante. Good God, he did want to cry.

And then he saw himself floating outside the Kasteel and over the snow-covered back yards in Evans Glen to Unity Cemetery and Anna's grave. The family was warm in front of the fireplace inside the Kasteel, and Anna was out there in the cold, under the ground, where she would now be forever. He stood before her gravestone and he heard the Fauré *Requiem*—the last movement. *In paradisum deducant angeli.* May the angels lead you into paradise. *Aeternam habeas requiem.* May you have eternal rest.

Goddamn Fauré. Now Gerard was crying again. Rebecca grabbed his upper arm and squeezed it. He was weary of being sad. Okay, okay, he understood his grief, and he was ready to be done with it, to be liberated. Now it was the sixth movement: *Libera Me Domine.* Deliver me O Lord. Would Gerard ever be free of his burdensome grief?

"Stop it, man." Parker slapped Romberg's hand away as Romberg tried to hold bunny-ear fingers behind Parker's head. "This picture's for my girl."

Mueller held the camera. "You guys ready? One, two—"

"No, wait, we ain't ready," said Parker. "Romberg, stop."

Cooper crowded into the picture and squatted down in front of Parker, smiling and extending one arm forward with his fingers spread wide, as if performing a Broadway finale.

"Hey, take our picture too," said Wiley as he muscled in.

"Yeah," said Berkowicz. "Move over, Parker."

"Man," said Parker.

Libby stood next to Parker. He had removed his right shoe and was hamming for the camera by holding the shoe to his nose and sniffing the inside.

Mueller squinted through the camera. "Okay. One,—"

Parker stood tall and crossed his arms. Romberg stuck out his tongue and kept the bunny ears over Parker's head. Wiley and Berkowicz put their arms around each other's shoulders. Cooper wiggled his extended hand. Libby sniffed his shoe and crossed his eyes.

"—two, three." Mueller clicked the shutter. "Good one."

Parker dropped his arms. "Bunch of fuckin' clowns, man."

Libby bounced over to Gerard. "Hey Kelderman, you got Korea?"

"Yeah."

"Me too!" said Libby.

"Great."

"And me," said Cooper.

"Awesome," said Libby.

"Korea," said Fuller. "DMZ. Way to go. Hopson's going to Germany, and Carroll's gettin' shipped to fucking Alaska."

"I heard Berkowicz got School of the Julios here at Benning because he speaks Spanish," said Libby.

"What's that?" said Gerard.

"School of the Americas," said Romberg. "But it has a new name."

"School of the Julios, man," said Libby. "That's what it's called, right Fuller?"

"Yeah, but technically it's Defense Institute for Hemispheric Security Cooperation."

"Fuck that," said Libby. "It's the School of the Julios."

"Where'd you get assigned, Fuller?" said Gerard.

"Fourth ID," said Fuller. "Fort Carson."

How about that. Fuller would be near Sylvia in Denver. At least Gerard wasn't going to Fort Carson. Maybe Korea wouldn't be so bad after all; at least he'd be half a world away from Sylvia.

Standing here amid soldiers Gerard felt that far away from Sylvia even now. He felt half a world away from everything and everyone he knew before. Sylvia was like a foggy dream or a childhood memory. His mom and dad were the only connection to his former life because they were standing right here—touching him, hugging him, smiling at him. At this moment, Gerard's parents were his only reminder that he'd even had a life before becoming a soldier.

"Alright, man, I'm outta here," said Romberg. He walked away with his father and sister. "See you Sunday night, Cooper."

"Yep," said Cooper.

Soldiers slated for parachute training had to check in at the airborne school on the other side of Fort Benning on Sunday night. Week One of airborne school would begin Monday morning. The non-airborne soldiers were done with training and received a week of leave before shipping out to their permanent duty stations.

The crowd thinned as soldiers and their families ambled toward the parking lot.

"Well then," said Willem. "Shall we go have some lunch?"

"That'd be great," said Gerard. "Cooper, where's your family?"

"It's just me." Cooper smiled and shrugged.

"You want to come eat with us?" said Gerard.

"Sure!" said Cooper. "Thanks."

Gerard turned to his parents. "Mom, Dad, this is Coop— uh, Steven."

"Hi."

"Hello."

"Parker, you want to have lunch with us?" said Gerard.

"Naw, it's cool man," said Parker. "I'm gonna eat with Hopson."

"I'll come," said Libby. "I'm hungry."

"Alright," said Gerard.

Willem leaned down and peered at Libby's name plate. "Libby," he said. "Oh, you're the one with the bayonet."

"Yeah." Libby looked down at the ground. "Kelderman, I'm so sorry, man. I didn't mean to hurt you."

"It's okay," said Gerard. He jostled Libby's shoulder. "It was an accident."

"Well son, at least you didn't lose any parts!" said Willem, waving his left hand and showing the space where his ring finger used to be so many years ago.

The soldiers chuckled timidly; Gerard could tell from their faces that no one was going to ask about Willem's finger.

"Anyway," said Rebecca.

"Yeah, let's eat," said Gerard.

They turned and walked from the parade field into the gravel parking lot. Gerard looked behind him over the empty grass field where soldiers from a detail company—probably in its third or fourth week of basic training—wore orange road-guard vests and picked up trash on the field and under the bleachers. Gerard shuddered and then smiled when he realized he was done. No more basic training! No more being treated like garbage! He turned back around to the front just in time to see Willem's arm slip around Rebecca's waist. Rebecca leaned her shoulder into Willem's side and nuzzled his cheek with her head.

To Gerard's left, Libby tripped over some gravel and then steadied himself. He looked at Gerard. "Kelderman, do you really forgive me? I mean, shit, that was a bad cut."

Gerard could still feel the cut when he thought about it. If his mind focused on the right side of his body, just below his ribs, he could feel pain every time he stepped. In the hospital he had tried concentrating on the wound using visualization techniques to help it heal, but that never worked as well as just forgetting about it. It was as if his body was trying to tell him that it would heal itself if he would only be kind enough to get the hell out of the way. The pain dissipated when he didn't dwell on it, when he thought of other things.

He turned his attention from his right side back to the left where Libby was ambling beside him with big, round eyes—eyes that clearly needed yet another assurance that Gerard wasn't angry about the accident.

"Libby, forget it," said Gerard. "It really is okay."

"You forgive me?" said Libby.

Jesus, enough. Gerard wanted to tell Libby that forgiveness wasn't needed, because Gerard sincerely felt it was an accident and that Libby, in the end, was just being Libby and couldn't really be faulted for something he didn't seem able to change. But obviously Libby needed to hear that Gerard forgave him.

"Yes, I forgive you," said Gerard. He put his left hand on Libby's shoulder and rubbed it a little. "You can let it go. Really."

And now Gerard was determined to leave Libby to himself, because he simply couldn't think of any more ways to say it. Gerard dropped his hand and turned to the front. In this moment, nothing could bother him. He had a sudden shockwave of gratitude when he understood that for the first time in many months, he was the master of what mattered; he felt powerful enough to decide what would or wouldn't affect him. The high, hot sun baked his black beret and steamed his sweaty head, but he didn't care. What was a little heat for a few more minutes? The gravel crunched under his shiny black shoes, powdering them with fine grit and a gray dust that might have been troubling to the drill sergeants, but it didn't matter.

As Gerard now approached the edge of the present moment—a moment that would soon become part of his past—and prepared to step off into the next one, he realized how lonely he felt and that no one would tell him what was there. It was both thrilling and terrifying.

# Bibliography

De Belder, Alfons. *Antwerpen in Beeld*. Antwerp: Antwerpen Kunstuit-geverij, circa 1970.

Epstein, Edward Jay. *The Rise and Fall of Diamonds: The Shattering of a Brilliant Illusion*. New York: Simon & Schuster, 1982.

Suvorov, Viktor. *Spetsnaz: The Inside Story of the Soviet Special Forces*. New York: W.W. Norton & Company, 1988.

Vleeschdrager, Eddy. *Diamonds: Reality and Passion*. Alleur: Perron, 1997.

## Web Sources

Abarder, Gasant. "Crowd pays tribute to slain girls." *Independent Online* [Cape Town, South Africa] 26 July 1999. February 2001 <http://www.int.iol.co.za/index.php?set_id=1&click_id=13&art_id=ct19 990726012236501C431807>.

The Boat Race Company. "The Oxford and Cambrige Boat Race." Copyright 2006. February 2001 <http://www.theboatrace.org>.

Bonsor, Kevin. "How Diamonds Work." *HowStuffWorks, Inc.* Copyright 1998-2007. February 2001 <http://science.howstuffworks.com/ diamond.htm>.

Boyd, Robert S. "SPETSNAZ: Soviet Innovation in Special Forces." *Air University Review* November-December 1986. January 2001 <http://www.airpower.maxwell.af.mil/airchronicles/aureview/1986/nov-dec/boyd.html>.

Brobst Violin Shop. "Brobst Violin Shop." Copyright 1999-2007. April 2001 <http://www.brobstviolins.com>.

Cuellar, Fred. "Ask The Diamond Guy." *Diamond Cutters International (DCI)*. Copyright 1996-2002. February 2001 <http://www.diamondcuttersintl.com/diamond_education/ask/ add.asp>.

Epstein, Edward Jay. *The Diamond Invention*. February 2001 <http://www.edwardjayepstein.com/diamond/prologue.htm>.

Harrison, Karl. "Virtual Tour of Oxford." University of Oxford. Copyright 2000-2005. February 2001 <http://www.chem.ox.ac.uk/oxfordtour/ default.html>.

Kamaldien, Yazeed. "Video puts Pagad boss at Staggie killing." *Independent Online* [Cape Town, South Africa] 20 January 2000. February 2001 <http://www.int.iol.co.za/index.php?set_id=1&click_id=15&art_id=ct20000120215215352A132228>.

La Rocque, Matthew. "In the Spotlight: People Against Gangsterism and Drugs (PAGAD)." *Center for Defense Information* 14 November 2005. 22 February 2007 <http://www.cdi.org/program/document.cfm?documentid=3211&programID=39>.

Roberts, Janine. "Diamonds Are For Shame." *The Web Inquirer*. Copyright 1996, Janine Roberts. February 2001 <http://inquirer.gn.apc.org/afrodia.html>.

Roberts, Janine. "Working Conditions in De Beers Coastal Diamond Mines in South Africa." *The Clean Diamond Web Site*. Copyright 2002, Janine Roberts. October 2004 <http://www.sparkle.plus.com/kleinzee-A.html>.

"Row after De Beers sends workers' wives to jail." *Mail & Guardian* [South Africa] 24 November 1995. February 2001 <http://www.mg.co.za/articledirect.aspx?articleid=187787>.

Smith, Ashley. "Courts poised to wipe out gangsterism." *Independent Online* [Cape Town, South Africa] 5 February 2005. 22 February 2007 <http://www.int.iol.co.za/index.php?set_id=1&click_id=15&art_id=vn20050205101713547C630887>.

Thackara, W.T.S. "The Perennial Philosophy." From *Sunrise* magazine, April/May 1984. Copyright 1984 by Theosophical University Press. March 2001 <http://www.theosophy-nw.org/theosnw/world/general/ge-wtst.htm>.

Town of Leesburg, Virginia. "Civil War—Leesburg, Virginia." The Town of Leesburg. Copyright 2004. April 2001 <http://www.leesburgva.gov/about/CivilWar>.

Town of Leesburg, Virginia. "History—Leesburg, Virginia." The Town of Leesburg. Copyright 2004. April 2001 <http://www.leesburgva.gov/about/History>.

Unsworth, Andrew. "Smoking Round the Rim." *Sunday Times* [Johannesburg, South Africa] 11 October 1998. April 2001 <http://www.sundaytimes.co.za/1998/10/11/lifestyle/life05.htm>.

Vander Nat, Arnold. "Translation of Fauré's *Requiem*." Loyola University Chicago. Copyright 2003, A. vander Nat. April 2001 <http://orion.it.luc.edu/~avande1/requiem.htm>.